THE SIEGE OF EARTH

THE STARSEA CYCLE BOOK EIGHT

KYLE WEST

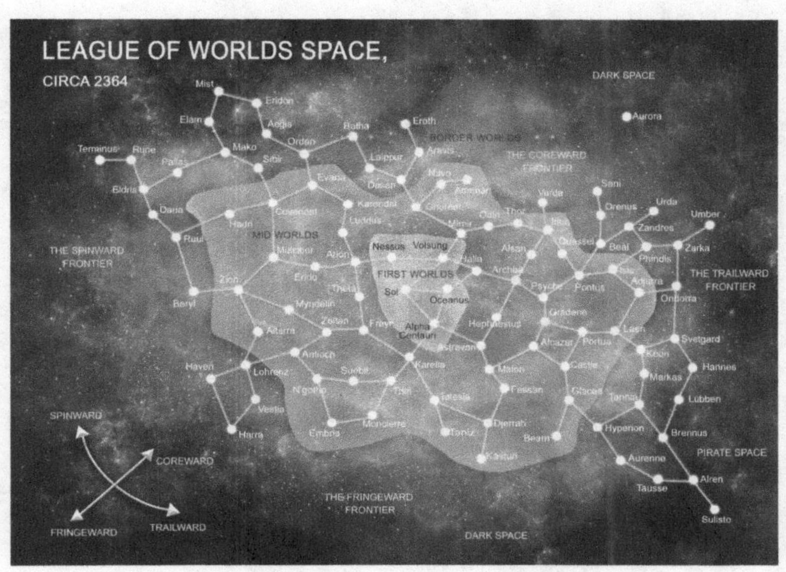

LEAGUE OF WORLDS SPACE,
CIRCA 2364
DARK SPACE
BORDER WORLDS
THE COREWARD FRONTIER
THE SPINWARD FRONTIER
THE TRAILWARD FRONTIER
MID WORLDS
FIRST WORLDS
PIRATE SPACE
THE FRINGEWARD FRONTIER
DARK SPACE
SPINWARD
COREWARD
FRINGEWARD
TRAILWARD
Mist
Eridon
Elam
Aegis
Botha
Eroth
Aurora
Terminus
Rune
Mako
Orden
Laippur
Aravis
Pallas
Sibir
Navo
Sani
Eldria
Evora
Dasan
Ammar
Varda
Orenus
Urda
Dane
Karandri
Thor
Zandres
Umber
Covenant
Lyddus
Odin
Zarka
Haun
Mirar
Beal
Ruul
Muratar
Nessus
Volsung
Alsan
Quassel
Phindis
THE SPINWARD
Ahon
Halia
Archia
Isis
Zion
Eridu
FIRST WORLDS
Adhara
Onboria
Beryl
Theta
Sol
Psyche
Pontus
Myndelin
Oceanus
Gradena
Lash
Altarra
Zeitan
Heph aestus
Alcazar
Portua
Svetgard
Haven
Fren
Alpha Centauri
Astrevon
Castle
Kbon
Hannes
Lohrenz
Antioch
Suebe
Karelia
Maion
Markas
N'gofio
Tressan
Glacea
Tanna
Lubben
Vestia
Thei
Tatesia
Djerrah
Hypenon
Brennus
Harra
Embra
Monderre
Taniz
Beam
Aurenne
Alren
Karitun
Tausse
Sulisto

SERAH FLOATED in the blackness of space, her lashes frozen and blue eyes eternally open.

Though her eyes were unfocused and undoubtedly dead, Lucian couldn't help but feel they were staring at him accusingly. And why *wouldn't* they be? He had allowed this to happen. He had failed to protect her.

Emma's form floated next to her, slumped and still. His mother was spiraling somewhere in the distance, impossible to pick out in the void.

Lucian wrapped Serah and Emma in a Space-Time aura, attempting to reverse the death that had taken them. Though their bodies regressed in time, it didn't resurrect them.

Why wasn't this working? Could not even the Eight Orbs of Starsea reverse death? It had saved Serah back on Mako. But then, Serah had never died. Perhaps even the Orbs couldn't change that.

Lucian raged, trying to make it work. Magic burned through him in a torrent, but it made no difference. Some things even magic couldn't do.

There was no point in going on. No point in fighting. There was nothing left to fight *for*. No one left to fight for. Let the Worlds fall. Let the *Alkasen* prevail.

Lucian did what made sense. He let go of the Binding aura surrounding him.

Instantly, the air ripped from his lungs and mouth. He went blind as the void dislodged his retinas. Frostbite immediately inflicted his skin. He uttered a silent scream, knowing he deserved this pain for leading them on this failed attack. Though he had seen the vision of Commander Carthen and Captain Warwick overseeing the destruction of Psyche, the knowledge hadn't been enough to stop them. He had missed a critical piece of the puzzle.

If there was one condolence for the people of Psyche, the instant death of the tachyon lances would be a mercy compared to the Swarmers.

Seconds before Lucian lost consciousness, a dark, familiar voice whispered in his mind.

And now we've reached the end. I warned you. You may hold my Orbs, but without me, you are nothing. As always, your friends were your weakness. And to think you would have challenged me directly. Pitiful fool! I am the Ancient One, and the Aspects of Magic are mine!

Lucian couldn't resist anymore. He closed his eyes.

THE VISION DISAPPEARED as the power of the Orbs of Psionics and Space-Time faded. Lucian couldn't control his breaths, even though he knew the horrific images were a prophecy of a potential future, not his reality.

Control. Focus.

Slowly, he regained mastery of his thoughts. His Focus

permeated his entire being, allaying his fears. Now more settled, he could focus on the vision and its meaning.

First, he knew in his bones that the visions were genuine. They just hadn't happened yet. If he kept going, they would become a reality. They were a potential future, and through the magic of the Orb of Space-Time, it was just one of many.

Lucian recalled his original vision, that of Commander Carthen ordering the destruction of Psyche. He had wanted to know what would happen if they directly attacked Warden Prime to prevent this. The Orbs of Space-Time and Psionics allowed him to explore that possibility.

And it had shown him death.

He couldn't think clearly after the emotional shock. But he had to do it. He had to prevent Serah's death, along with the deaths of his mother and Emma. He had to keep that future from becoming a reality.

Lucian rose from the stone floor of the small chamber he had requisitioned for meditation. He knew he had to stop this Commander Carthen from ever giving the order to enact Operation Tabula Rasa, and he had to do it without others dying.

There was only one answer. Lucian had to delve the future, even if he didn't want to.

He sat back down and closed his eyes, entering the Ether again.

Combining the Orbs of Space-Time and Psionics, he delved. He sat like that for untold hours, playing out possibility after possibility. He would not rise until he found a future where his friends survived *and* the Wardens did not destroy Psyche.

The surrounding Ether roared in response to his need. He felt like he was at the center of an exploding sun. Holding all Eight Orbs, Lucian had the keys to reality itself. A mere thought could shape that reality. Whatever he willed, if it were within the realm of possibility, it would be done, and the universe would turn itself inside out to make it happen.

And there lay the danger. *Anything* might be ripped apart by the rampant currents of the Manifold. Lucian was the only check on that power. But Lucian had absolute control of the stream. The more possibilities he explored, the more intense the requirement for ether. Lucian *had* to know the correct option. He burned through so much ether that he practically extinguished it for kilometers, a sphere of emptiness in the Light Realm. It was becoming difficult to sustain these prophecies as each one branched into others ad infinitum.

The City of Malia was burning. He saw his friends dead in many futures. He saw the *Alkasen* attacking Psyche, the blue light of the Wardens' lances pulverizing the moon's surface. The lives of tens of thousands were in his hands. The lives of *all* the Worlds.

At last, after hours, he found the correct possibility of thousands he had explored.

He opened his eyes and knew what he must do. It was time.

He warped above the City of Malia, floating over the seaside city. Peering down on its eastern half, he saw the beginning of a great fire, as he had witnessed in his prophecies. Within hours, that fire would become an inferno burning the entire city.

He shot south, across the Sea of Eros, gathering ether. His Orbs sang as they stored potential energy. Once he had enough, he bent his will toward warming the surrounding water and air. For hours he worked until he gathered a great storm cloud brimming with energy and moisture.

Then, he ushered that gale north. He flew with the storm, becoming one with it. The waves leaped tens of meters high. Lightning slashed around and even *through* him, but he merely redirected the energy, using it to power his flight. Despite the horror of his prophecies, commanding the weather was a thrill beyond description. The southern shore of the Golden Vale was fast approaching, along with the city.

The fires raged on the city's eastern half beyond the Golden River. In his prophecy, thousands of people died, but Lucian would stop it before it reached that point. It was all the proof he needed that what he saw was real. And more than that, the future could change if he performed the right actions.

The storm fell like a hammer on the shoreline. Wave after wave crashed against the southern cliffs as lightning forked across the sky. The wind gusted down ruined streets, sweeping around broken towers and bridges, forcing the airships to the ground. It would only be a few minutes before the torrent doused the fires.

Lucian looked down upon the city like a god surveying his domain. Stopping the fire was only the first part of his plan, and he knew there wasn't much time left to enact the rest. The Wardens were perilously close to wiping the entire moon of all life, and he only had a few hours to stop it.

Lucian warped to the entry hall of the Summer Palace, where he had left everyone, including the Mage-Lords and Ladies of Ansaldra's court. The hall was one of the few places in the city that had remained intact and relatively unspoiled, though water leaked from the high, vaulted ceiling, and puddles had accumulated on the stone floor. Rain fell upon the outer courtyard through the open entryway, where small streams gathered and rushed down the streets toward the river.

At his appearance, the lords and ladies let out a collective, startled breath. His friends had seen this before, so they didn't have as much of a reaction.

Serah seemed more impressed with the storm, peering through the open archway. "Damn. That's a lot of water."

Her observation went unanswered as every face looked at

Lucian, noticing the severity of his expression. Selene, Emma, Serah, Fergus, Jagar, and Mira were all there. All were safe, and none knew the terrible future that awaited them if events were allowed to progress normally. His eyes lingered on Serah a moment longer than the rest. She smiled, starkly contrasting to the pale mask of death in his vision. A small part of him *still* felt like he had lost her, even if she was standing there.

The Mage-Lords and Ladies of the late Queen Ansaldra's court also watched him, but unlike his friends, their faces were demanding and entitled. At their fore stood Mage-Lord Cantos, a mustachioed man with gray hair, probably in his mid to late sixties. He was the ringleader, as the other lords and ladies seemed to defer to him. His face was stern, as if he were ready to criticize Lucian for failing to pick up the pieces of the battle's aftermath. But once he met Lucian's steely gaze, Cantos deflated a little.

It was enough of an opening for Lucian to get a word in before the Mage-Lord could. "The battle may be over, but the war is about to begin."

Cantos found his voice. "War? I can speak for all when I say Psyche desires peace."

Several of the nobles muttered their assent, but it was half-hearted. They saw Lucian's power and didn't want to go against him. They were trying to size him up. Despite his power, perhaps they could use him. Lucian couldn't help but smile at that quaint thought. Such was the province of these aristocratic jackals.

His prophecies had instructed him on how to deal with them. And so he would.

"War is coming, whether you want it or not, Mage-Lord. Listen and listen well. If you don't, it will mean your death."

Cantos looked more than a bit miffed, but Lucian didn't care. He took in the crowd, all of whom watched him expectantly.

"There's some business we need to address," Lucian said. "The Sorceress-Queen is dead, and she has no successor. She intended to live forever, constantly switching bodies while growing in power. I ended that dream of hers. We need a new leader now. A storm is coming, and that storm is called the *Alkasen*. Only one person is powerful enough to save humanity: the Chosen of the Manifold."

"I very much agree, Mage-Lord Lucian," Cantos said.

"Mage-Lord?" Lucian asked. He almost wanted to pin this blowhard to the wall. "I will accept nothing less than Sorcerer-King of Psyche from you, Cantos. Though Chosen will also suffice."

The face of every lord and lady, about two dozen, went white. Even his friends seemed shocked at the suggestion.

Lucian went on relentlessly. "Psyche needs a king, and I'm the only one who can do it. I brought justice to Ansaldra. I defeated Xara Mallis. I hold all Eight Orbs of Starsea. I am the Chosen of the Manifold and the Sorcerer-Ascendant of Magekind." He gave a small smile. "I think the Sorcerer-King of Psyche would be the most minor of my titles, especially since I don't intend to stop here."

"What is the point of this?" Cantos asked, feigning boredom. "You want to play at king? Well, your kingdom is a burned husk! You are the king of ash and ruins!"

Lucian couldn't help but pity him a bit. He was like a child, believing himself wiser than he actually was. And from the helplessness in Cantos's eyes, he realized it.

"The point is *your life*, Mage-Lord. Your life, and the life of every person on this moon."

Lucian floated above the floor stones, and the lords and ladies, even Mage-Lord Cantos, recoiled at this sudden move. After this, Lucian knew there would be no going back. But it was the only viable path to save this world and his friends. That was all that mattered.

"I am the Sorcerer-King of Psyche, the rightful successor of Queen Ansaldra. I will require oaths of allegiance from everyone here except those already on my Council, who have already sworn it." He nodded to his friends, letting them know they weren't required to swear the oath. He could trust them, but he couldn't trust these nobles further than he could throw them in Jupiter's gravity.

"You can't be serious," Mage-Lord Cantos said.

"I am serious, Cantos. Kneel. All of you."

2

THERE WAS a beat of silence that seemed to last an eternity. Lucian stared, waiting for them to break. If he wanted to save lives, he needed to be king. Otherwise, the nobles wouldn't listen and would do what they thought was best.

And if they did what they thought was best, tens of thousands would die.

Some lords and ladies had understood this and quickly dropped to one knee in supplication. The older ones had seen enough of politics and intrigue in their lives that they knew what Lucian had said wasn't a threat. What happened next was up to them.

Cantos looked left and right, shocked that the others had been so quickly cowed. Now, Lucian stared at him, waiting for the inevitable.

Muttering a curse, he sank to the ground on one knee and lowered his head, his body seeming to resist the motion. Whatever Cantos had planned with the other nobles to curb Lucian's authority, the Mage-Lord could see it wasn't going to work. He sighed and lowered his head in defeat.

Are you sure about this? Serah asked, her voice entering his mind.

Yes, Lucian said, communicating the reluctance he felt.

Serah said nothing more, but he could feel her frustration ring through his connection with her. She knew what he was doing and agreed with it in theory, but she didn't like its drastic nature.

He felt the same way. He knew this action would ultimately result in more lives saved. Not just on Psyche, but in all the Worlds. But it would require him to become this world's master. His rule here would require him to become someone different. Someone harder. He had to ignore that thought and rule as well as he could.

He took a deep breath and squared his shoulders.

"Repeat after me," he said.

He said the following words, and the nobles repeated them.

"I swear my undying loyalty to the Sorcerer-King of Psyche, Lucian Abrantes, the Chosen of the Manifold and the Sorcerer-Ascendant of Magekind. I swear to follow his commands, to rule with honor in his name, to withhold no tax or liability owed to his person, and to follow him into war, along with the full resources of my house, retinue, and armies. I swear this by the Manifold itself."

Once they finished repeating the oath, Lucian nodded. "Rise."

Everyone rose, blinking as if they had come out of a dream. While they had been giving the oath, Lucian had been branding every one of them. Not to control them outright, though it was possible if it came to that. It was more to keep himself and his friends safe in case these nobles ever tried anything.

"I thank you for your loyalty," Lucian said, knowing full

well he couldn't count on it. Better to let them think he did, even if it was all an act.

They all watched him, wondering what came next. They knew who was in charge. If he gave an order, they would follow it. Not happily, but they would because they feared him.

"Now," Lucian said, "everyone will die unless they follow my orders to the letter. We are in a crisis Psyche has never experienced. I have had a prophecy. Even now, the League Wardens are moving their defense platforms into position. Within hours, the entire surface of Psyche will be glassed by tachyon lances."

At this news, everyone began speaking all at once. Lucian raised a hand to get everyone's attention back. They went silent.

"In my prophecy, I witnessed two men discussing this. Their names were Commander Carthen and Captain Warwick. Carthen is in charge of all the defense platforms orbiting Psyche. He will order the destruction of this world within hours."

Mage-Lord Cantos cleared his throat self-importantly. "Err . . . Sorcerer-King. If I may be so bold?"

Lucian gave him a hardened stare, letting him know not to push his luck too far. "Speak."

"My King, if the Wardens are moving their orbital platforms into position, I fear there is nothing we can do. I had the ear of Ansaldra Dara herself. You might say I was deep in her counsels, and of course, I offer my advice to you, the rightful monarch of Psyche whose authority is not to be questioned in the least." Lucian knew Cantos had said that to cover himself, and he couldn't help but notice the irony in his voice. "She told me that if the League decides to wipe Psyche from the face of the Worlds, there is no chance of escaping their tachyon lances. They have about two hundred platforms designed to obliterate Psyche's surface with deadly efficiency. Within hours."

Lucian watched him dangerously. "So, what do you suggest? That we give up? Or is there something else you wish to propose? Because I would very much like to hear it."

Cantos' cheeks flushed. "If we wish to survive the coming destruction, we had better get underground and posthaste! If we hurry, we can save many lives. But as for stopping them? It's an impossible task. We cannot stop what is already in motion."

"Nothing is impossible, Mage-Lord. I am the Chosen of the Manifold. There has never been a mage as powerful as me. Not even the Second Immortal could match me. I hold all Eight Orbs of Starsea and know how to use them."

"How can you be so sure?"

"I have seen the future, but I don't have time to explain that future. If everyone listens and does what I say, we can save Psyche."

"Sorcerer-King," Cantos continued, "of course, we witnessed your great power. You battled Xara Mallis in the sky, laying waste to the city below. Even Queen Ansaldra could not resist you, and you handled her like she was a child! The most powerful sorceress this moon has ever seen, aside from Xara Mallis herself. But yet even you, Sorcerer-King, must see that this is hopeless. If you direct your powers instead toward saving the people, perhaps creating these *warps* to get a chosen few off-world, that might be a better use of time."

Lucian frowned. He saw precisely where the Mage-Lord was going. He wanted to save Psyche's aristocracy, leaving the rest to burn.

Even as Lucian's eyes bored into the Mage-Lord's, Cantos sputtered on, clearly not getting the hint. "I mean, if you *prophesied* that the orbital platforms are moving into position, why even bother rescuing the moon? Let us use this opportunity to plan our escape and our revenge if that is what you desire."

"The prophecy is not set in stone. I have a plan."

"My king, if that is so, then surely I am not the only one who wants to hear your plan?"

The other mages of the old Queen's court murmured their agreement.

"Yeah, seriously," Serah said. "I know I'm supposed to agree with you on everything, Lucian, but this is *my home*. I know people here. I have family. If you can save Psyche, tell us how!"

Lucian watched as everyone looked at him for guidance. He had them exactly where he wanted them: afraid for their lives. If they needed him, Lucian could control them. He knew the aristocracy would take advantage of him if he showed weakness.

"Here's how this will work," Lucian said. "Everyone will do as I say, and I don't owe anyone an explanation about anything. Otherwise, everyone dies. Is that understood?"

There was a moment of hesitation on the part of the court, and then heads nodded all around.

"Here's the plan," Lucian said. "Fergus, I need you to come with me. Selene and Jagar, too."

"Come with you where?" Selene asked.

Lucian nodded upward in the general direction of space. "There. We're going to take over the Warden fleet."

The lords and ladies gasped as if Lucian had announced they would dive across the event horizon of a black hole. Taking over an entire fleet with four people seemed like suicide, but they didn't know what Lucian knew.

Four was the perfect number to accomplish his goals, though they couldn't understand it. He had to trust the prophecy.

"That's four of us," Jagar said. "Against an entire fleet of hundreds of ships and thousands of soldiers."

"And what about the rest of us?" Mira asked.

His mother, Serah, and Emma were all standing shoulder to shoulder. That reminded him of the prophecy. He could still see their dead faces staring at him accusingly. That only firmed his decision to stick to his guns.

"Under no circumstances will the three of you come with me. Your job is to stay safe and get as many people underground as possible."

"*What?*" Emma asked. "You *can't* expect us to stay here doing something these nobles can easily do! If you have a plan, we want to be a part of it."

Lucian locked eyes with her. "I mean it. You guys have about an hour to organize the people and save who you can in case things go wrong up there." Lucian knew things *wouldn't* go wrong if everything went according to plan, but they didn't need to know that. "There are extensive catacombs beneath this palace. Get as many people down there as you can. Save as many as possible, then get underground yourself."

"Hey, wait a second," Serah said, putting her hands on her hips. "Emma is right. If you've got a plan, I want in on it, too! You'll need us. Besides, this world was mine long before it was yours! I have every reason to go with you to save it."

Lucian hardened his heart. "No. You're staying here, and that's final."

"What is this about, Lucian?" she asked. "Is it because we're women or something? Are we unable to handle ourselves? I don't care if you're the rotting king of the galaxy. No one tells *me* what to do!"

Lucian opened a link to her. *Listen. You don't have to call me king, but these people will stab me in the back if you don't act like I'm in charge.*

She stared at him in disbelief, but thankfully, she didn't

challenge him. He knew there would be hell to pay later. More than hell, but it was worth it to save her life.

"So, when are we leaving?" Selene asked. "Of course, Sorcerer-King, you have my loyalty to the ends of the galaxy."

Serah's eyes smoldered at that. "Yeah? Well, he's probably just going to use you as cannon fodder." She turned back to Lucian. "All I know is there's something you're not telling us, and I want to know what it is."

"He's a sorcerer," Selene explained. "The most powerful sorcerer that has ever existed. Even Ansaldra had prophecies of the future, which came to pass. I trust the Chosen's judgment, who's even more powerful than her."

Lucian was getting impatient. They had limited time, and he couldn't just be explaining his decisions every second of the day.

His mother was next to speak. "Lucian, you can't attack the Wardens with four people. Do you realize how many ships they have? Thousands of League sailors and marines man Psyche's orbital defense system. Fifty thousand, if memory serves, and as many as a thousand ships. It is one of the largest bases in the entire League. The four of you and *Blood Wyvern* against that is madness! I don't care if you're the Chosen of the Manifold. That's suicide, and I won't allow you to go."

Though she was his mother, Lucian knew her words were empty. "I don't have a choice. Everything must happen according to the will of the Manifold. If it doesn't, everyone dies. Do you think I'm following *my* ideas? I can see the Manifold's plans, and I must follow them perfectly. If I don't . . ."

Again, the image of Serah dying, her eyes glazed and lashes frozen, hit him full force. All he had to do was remember that would be her fate if he allowed them to have their way.

"This . . . makes no sense," Serah said. "You're acting crazy!"

"He's the Bringer of the Storm," Mage-Lord Cantos said. "The Ruler of Starsea. The Chosen of the Manifold!"

Serah rolled her eyes. "Okay, calm down, buddy. I thought you hated him."

Lucian had to resist the urge to roll his eyes. Cantos seemed like a bully. A bully who became the attack dog of whoever had subdued him. That could have its uses, but it was damn annoying.

"All right," Lucian said. "It's time."

Without waiting for a response, he opened a portal to the wardroom of *Wayfinder*, Vera and Xara's old ship.

"Whoa," Fergus said. "That's not *Blood Wyvern*."

Lucian was already stepping through. Fergus rushed to keep up, awkwardly turning back toward the others. "Err . . . I guess I'll catch up with you guys later?"

"Wait," Mira said. "How do you expect to pilot that thing without me?"

"We'll be fine," Lucian said. "Remember what I said." Before his mother could say anything else, he looked at Selene and Jagar. "The both of you ready?"

"Of course," Selene said.

She slipped through the portal gracefully, as if she'd been doing it her whole life. Jagar followed shortly after, shaking his head disapprovingly as he entered.

Lucian met Serah's gaze. It was hard to leave her behind when her expression seemed hurt and betrayed.

It was the will of the Manifold. He had to tell himself that. To get everyone to follow him, he had to overstep boundaries. He hated it, becoming someone he wasn't to ensure the best outcome for everyone. But there was no choice if humanity was to be saved. He had to hold his ground. The stakes were too high.

A coldness spread through him when he realized that was

the thinking that had led Vera and Xara to do evil things. And yet, he wouldn't allow Serah to die, nor his mother or Emma, so long as it was within his power. If he had to be a bully to get his way, that was what he would do.

"Hide somewhere under the palace. We'll be back soon."

Nothing more was said, and the portal closed behind him.

3

LUCIAN, Fergus, Jagar, and Selene stood in *Wayfinder's* wardroom. The ship was cold and silent, JUST as Lucian remembered it. A sense of foreboding loomed in the metallic air as if Vera and Xara's presence had left an indelible mark.

Jagar frowned, blinking a few times. Lucian didn't think he would ever get used to going through portals.

"So . . ." Fergus said, breaking the silence. "Care to explain what's going on?"

Before Lucian could answer, a robotic voice emanated from the direction of the bridge. "Master?"

Alistair, Vera's old pilot droid, appeared in the doorway, its eerie red eye pieces regarding Lucian with what seemed like suspicion.

"*You're* not my master."

Lucian raised his right hand. "I'm about to be."

A stream of green magic surrounded the droid's head. Lucian bent the droid to his will using the Orb of Radiance. The droid's encryption was nothing against the Orb's power, especially considering Vera and Xara had neglected to register its ownership token to any data network. Vera probably hadn't wanted it to be searchable. It would make the conversion process a lot simpler.

Lucian wiped Alistair's memory, making it forget everything except its name and programmed capabilities.

And that *Lucian* was now its master.

Lucian cut off the stream, and the droid stood stiffly for a moment. "Master . . .?"

"Call me Lucian. Take this ship into orbit. And be quick about it."

"That would be impossible. I . . . don't believe you own this ship, Master Lucian."

Lucian sighed. "Hold on."

Lucian walked to the pilot's terminal, placing his hands on it. Once again, he opened himself to Radiance and hacked into the network. Lucian willed two things; that the ship recognized that both Vera and Xara were dead, and that he was their rightful heir. He accomplished this in less than ten seconds.

He nodded to Alistair. "We should be good now. Take us into orbit."

The droid gave a mechanical nod. "Yes, it seems the security protocols have been . . . recalibrated. Most curious."

"Impressive," Selene said, taking a seat behind the pilot's chair. "There's not a Radiant in all the Worlds who could have pulled that off."

"There's one other," Lucian said, thinking of Emma. "Let's strap in. There's no time to waste."

They all took their seats behind the droid, with Lucian in the copilot's seat. Alistair began his preparations for liftoff.

"All right," Fergus said. "Why aren't we using *Blood Wyvern*? I don't enjoy being in the dark."

Lucian strapped himself in. "*Wayfinder* is closer to Warden Prime. That's the orbital platform we need to go to, with

Commander Carthen on it. If we take *Blood Wyvern*, we won't make it in time. Not only that, but we'd also have to fly through the entire orbital defense network because of the approach vector. That would almost certainly lead to our deaths."

"I see," Fergus said. "I suppose you saw this in your visions, too?"

Lucian nodded, but didn't want to elaborate.

"One other question," Fergus said. "How do we know these visions are even real?"

Lucian understood where Fergus was coming from, but he did not doubt his prophecies' veracity. "They're real. I used Psionics and Space-Time to delve the Manifold. Psionics alone will give prophecies, but prophecies take on additional dimensions when combined with Space-Time. The sheer number of futures I saw goes beyond anything you can imagine. What we're doing now is the best possibility with the best outcomes. All we have to do is play our parts. Avoid the pitfalls and do the things the Manifold showed me."

"I think I understand," Fergus said. "If you had only explained as much down there, Mira and the rest would have understood."

"Maybe," Lucian said. "But maybe not. As long as they stay on Psyche, they're safe."

As soon as the fusion engine began its steady thrum, the ship lifted off, and Alistair pointed it toward the violet sky. Lucian saw they were close to the City of Dara as the ground fell away. The high mountains in the west cast their long shadows over the city and the Golden Vale beyond. Aside from the leveled palace, everything else was still in order. The war hadn't touched the city. But if they failed in their mission, it would be blasted from this moon's surface.

"This is what you need to know," Lucian said to the others.

"There are two Wardens, Commander Carthen and Captain Warwick."

"Yes, you mentioned that," Jagar said.

"I didn't bring the others because they died in almost every future I delved. That might happen to us, too. But if we do nothing, everyone on Psyche will die. That's something we have the power to stop."

"I understand that," Jagar said. "But what's this business about you being king? What kind of game are you playing?"

"The game of saving humanity and not dying."

Jagar stared at him. "I don't like secrets."

"I'm not keeping secrets."

Jagar didn't look convinced, and Lucian didn't blame him. Jagar was his friend. Had even saved his life. But Lucian found it necessary to keep the details to himself. If the others knew too much, it might cause deviations from the overall plan.

Within a couple of minutes, they were locked into orbit above Psyche. Lucian created a Radiant shield around the ship to deflect any potential LADAR sweeps. He felt limited by this vessel, by the others. It would have been easier for him to go it alone, but his prophecies were clear. If he attempted to do that, it led to bad outcomes in every situation.

He remembered what the Ancient One had said during his prophecy: *As always, your weakness was your friends.*

"No," Lucian said in response to the memory.

Selene looked over. "What's that?"

Before Lucian could respond, red warning lights flashed as Alistair swerved the ship upward. "Incoming ripsaw fighters!"

"I thought you were shielding the ship," Fergus said.

"I was. They must have picked us up on the surface before I set the shield."

This, too, was part of the plan, though Lucian didn't know the exact reason. He knew the basic beats of the mission, not every minutia that led to ultimate victory. There were still plenty of chances for this to go wrong.

"What do we do, Master Lucian?" the droid asked.

The droid seemed to be uncomfortable to be on a first-name basis. It probably had something to do with its programming.

"Fly straight into them."

"Master Lucian, if we do that, they will destroy us!"

"Do it. You have your orders."

"Master, such a wanton risk goes against my programming. I cannot allow you to come to harm."

"That's an order, Alistair. Do it, or I'll force you."

Alistair seemed to be caught in some moral dilemma. "I . . . will do as you say."

The pilot droid righted the ship as it advanced toward the oncoming vessels, which were still out of visual range. On the LADAR screen, there were twelve bogeys, with more appearing on their scopes. It seemed eight of them were ripsaw fighters, backed up by four larger javelin-class corvettes. Those were especially dangerous. Each carried a payload of twelve torpedoes besides their railguns. One direct hit would blast away whatever hull *Wayfinder* had.

"Incoming torpedoes," Alistair said. "They have a lock on us!"

"Keep flying," Lucian said. "All is well."

"Master, we have six seconds before impact!"

Lucian judged enough time had passed. He streamed a Space-Time aura around the ship and warped it into the distance, bypassing the torpedoes and oncoming ships. A space station was fast approaching.

"Warden Prime," Lucian said.

"Incredible!" Selene said.

"Empty," Fergus said. "Where are all the ships?"

"That's why we're approaching from this direction," Lucian said. "And that was the purpose of being caught. It drew our enemies away from our true target."

Jagar didn't answer, looking a little unsettled at all this action, while Selene stared out of the viewscreen with widened eyes. This was her first time seeing Lucian's powers on display, not to mention her first time in space. She was also staring down at the violet world beneath her, the world that had been her lifelong home.

"That . . . is Psyche?"

"It is," Fergus confirmed. "Just one small world in an incomprehensibly large universe."

Lucian checked the LADAR. "Picking up a lot of ships, but they're on the opposite side of the station. And moving away from us. We should have no trouble docking."

"Strange that they're moving that way," Fergus said. "But I'm not complaining."

"There will be Warden soldiers in the hangar we're about to enter, so don't get complacent." Lucian turned to the droid. "Slow down and dock, Alistair."

"They'll never let us in," Fergus said.

"No," Lucian said. "Launch Bay 3 is open."

"How do you know that?" Jagar asked.

"Prophecy," Selene said. "Believe!"

The dash lit with an incoming hail request.

"Ignore it," Lucian said, remembering this complication. "It's a trap."

"I've . . . located Launch Bay 3," the droid said. "I've accessed Warden Prime's schematics from my data stores. The source of the data is unknown."

"Vera or Xara installed it," Lucian said.

"Vera or Xara?" the droid asked.

Lucian had forgotten the droid wouldn't remember them.

"Never mind that. Proceed to the launch bay. Your data is accurate."

Lucian *was* surprised at the lack of resistance. Things were almost going too smoothly. From his previous delving, he knew that the launch bay was already filling up with Wardens, who were planting gun batteries to blast the exterior of *Wayfinder* as soon as it pulled in. The ship would be torn to shreds unless they came in guns blazing.

"Prepare the railgun turrets," Lucian said. "As soon as we're within sight of the doors, start blasting. Expect heavy resistance."

"Of course, Master."

"I want off this ride," Fergus said.

They drew level with the hangar. As Lucian predicted, dozens of armed Wardens in gray EVA suits stood waiting. They didn't stand a chance as *Wayfinder's* railguns blasted into their ranks. Lucian watched the destruction, saddened at the loss of life, but also knowing there was no avoiding it. It was this, or failing to stop the lances from firing.

"That's enough," Lucian said after half a minute. "Pull in."

"The hangar is depressurized now," Alistair said. "How do you expect to get inside the station?"

"A minor detail like that won't stop me."

"If you insist. But there's a good chance this ship will be destroyed if you leave me here."

"That's why you won't be staying here. As soon as we're off the ship, go to Malia and await further orders. Don't show yourself. Just wait. Avoid all Warden vessels and stations. They're going to be busy with something else."

"I'm . . . not entirely sure that's possible."

"It's possible. Just see it done." Lucian nodded, turning toward the others. "All right, here's the plan. I need the three of you to create a distraction. Draw as many guards as you can from me. Carthen will try to escape when he realizes what's happening."

"And what do you plan on doing with him?" Fergus asked.

"Stopping him from ever giving the order. We have about fifteen minutes left." Lucian walked up to the blast door, and the others followed. He nodded toward the operations room. "Suit up."

Within the minute, all had changed and were out the door. Lucian neglected to put on his suit, instead surrounding himself with a Binding aura, within which he refreshed the air with an Atomic ward.

They followed him across the blasted hangar littered with fallen bodies. It was a gruesome scene, but Lucian felt no remorse within the numbing shelter of his Focus.

They approached the blast door leading into the station. Lucian hacked the terminal with Radiance, forcing it open. Once everyone was through the airlock, he closed it off. The corridor was empty on the other side, running left and right.

Lucian nodded toward the right. "Head that way. Our eventual goal is to take over this station and its soldiers, not just to stop the lances. So avoid killing when possible. Just mess things up inside, draw attention to yourselves, but don't stray too far from the hangar. I'll be back soon."

"Easy enough," Jagar said.

"One other thing. The fraying is over. You can push yourselves much harder than you did before. Your only limit is your Focus. You can keep streaming until it becomes exhausted."

No one had time to marvel at this. Lucian only told them because they needed the reminder. The path ahead wouldn't be easy. They couldn't hold anything back.

"What about you?" Fergus asked.

"Don't worry about me. What matters is saving Psyche."

"Right," Fergus said, drawing his shockspear and extending it. "Let's go cause a distraction, then."

Jagar extended his spear while Selene just watched Lucian.

"Be careful," she said. "You might be the Chosen, but you can still get yourself killed."

"I'll be fine. I'll find you guys later."

"Let's move," Jagar said. Then, with a nod to Lucian: "Give them hell, lad."

They headed off to the right while Lucian took the path to his left. He floated down the corridor with a tether since it was faster.

Two Wardens rounded the corner ahead, bearing impact rifles and regaled in gray power armor. Rather than kill them outright, Lucian reached for their minds, instantly bending them to his will. He set the possession streams with brands so he wouldn't have to maintain them actively.

They fell in by his side, becoming his bodyguards.

As they ran across more soldiers, Lucian did the same thing. Soon, he had a small army at his back.

By the time he had several dozen Wardens marching up the main corridor with him, he had them fan out into separate passages, blocking every access point to the command center.

Now alone, he flew forward, summoning Lightspear in his hand. He shone with white brilliance. He was just moments from entering the main viewing deck, where Commander Carthen and Captain Warwick were located even now. Within minutes, Carthen would give the order to enact Operation Tabula Rasa.

As Lucian approached the metal door, he combined Radiance and Space-Time to phase through the metal door ahead. A moment later, his body reverted to physicality as he landed lightly on the deck, Lightspear still in hand.

Before Lucian was the scene from his prophecy. Warwick

and Carthen stood before the viewport, the violet light of Psyche's atmosphere silhouetting their forms. Their heads were bowed as if in meditation. Warwick was tall, with short gray hair, his uniform perfectly pressed. Carthen stared out of the viewport, his hands clasped behind his back, his uniform tight around the waist. Such had been the silence of Lucian's entrance that they didn't even know he was there.

Lucian was about to complete mind control streams to take control of both men when Serah's voice entered his mind.

Lucian?

Lucian stopped what he was doing, a thrill of fear coursing through his body. If she had communicated with him so easily, there was only one plausible explanation.

She was close.

Serah, where are you?

That's the thing. We're . . . in a bit of trouble right now.

What trouble? Tell me where you are.

Um . . . we're in orbit above Psyche.

What? I told you to stay on the surface!

With horror, Lucian realized she could die along with the rest. They might only have seconds left. This was why it had been so easy to enter the station.

All the ships had been sent after *them*.

Ahead of him, the two men continued their conversation, utterly oblivious to his presence.

Rotting hell, there's so many of them! Serah said.

Serah, turn that ship back toward the surface. If you don't, then—

At that moment, the connection was severed.

Serah? Serah!

Mouthing a silent curse, Lucian warped to the main deck of *Blood Wyvern*.

4

THE DECK of *Blood Wyvern* looked as it should have, much to Lucian's relief. He had not foreseen this contingency. Even with the power of prophecy, the Manifold only showed him what he needed to know. He would not have done things this way if he had known their lives would be in danger.

That meant they could still die if he didn't play this right. He had to save them before his prophecy of their deaths could manifest.

He sprinted to the bridge, bursting through the open doorway. Serah, Emma, and his mother were safe and sound, to his extreme relief. Outside the viewscreen was Warden Prime, along with dozens of ripsaws and javelin-class corvettes converging on their position.

Lucian drew as much ether as he could to warp the ship. A hail of concentrated railgun fire shot from the ripsaws, followed by dozens of torpedoes from the corvettes. As the women screamed, Lucian warped the vessel a couple of kilometers to escape immediate danger.

The scene shifted. Outside the viewport, Warden Prime was

a fair bit smaller than it had been before, while the size of Psyche remained the same. Only now did the three turn to find him standing there, expressions of shock on their faces. As he drew ether to warp the ship farther away, his entire body glowed with ethereal light.

"Lucian!" Serah sputtered.

Even though Mira had engaged the cloaking screen, they weren't far enough to conceal their ship. It bought Lucian half a minute to complete the warp. He continued to work, even as the Wardens picked up their new position and moved to engage.

Once he'd gathered the requisite ether, the viewport lit up with black Space-Time Magic, and Psyche and Warden Prime disappeared from view. The ship reappeared at the edge of Kandi's orbit a second later. The icy moon seemed still and silent, a far cry from the battle above Psyche.

Lucian regarded the three women watching him for the first time, his look demanding an explanation.

"It was my idea, son," Mira said. "Don't be mad at them."

"Well, we went along with it," Emma said.

Lucian looked at Serah, who held back a smile. Did she not know that, without him, they would be dead right now? "And what's your excuse?"

She sighed. "I didn't want your mom to think I was lame."

Lucian shook his head. "As long as all of you are safe. I'm thinking it was *supposed* to happen this way."

"What do you mean?" Emma asked.

"This was the Manifold's plan. If you hadn't caused this distraction, there would have been too many ships around Warden Prime for the rest of us to dock."

"You docked?" Mira asked. "Where are the others?"

"Still there. Fighting. I'd love to chat, but I need to get back. Stay here and stay out of trouble. I'll return when I can."

Explaining nothing further, he warped back to the command center of Warden Prime.

About a dozen soldiers in power armor surrounded him. He immediately raised a Psionic shield just as a barrage of impact pulses slammed into him. He strengthened the defense to match, and such was the shield's power that he didn't even feel the impact of the blasts. This amount of pulses would almost certainly overwhelm even the most accomplished mages, but Lucian held the shield with barely any effort.

While holding the shield, he reached out to each soldier's mind and branded them with Psionics. The onslaught ceased as their eyes glowed violet behind their faceplates. Looking around, he saw that Commander Carthen and Captain Warwick were not among them. The surface of the moon outside the viewports was serene. There might still be time.

Lucian approached the closest Warden, a young man with the insignia of a lieutenant commander impressed on each shoulder. From the expression of utmost loyalty and dedication on his youthful face, it was like he hadn't been attacking Lucian just a second before.

"Where's Commander Carthen?" Lucian demanded.

"Gone, sir."

"Gone where?"

"To Hangar One. That's where *Barbarossa* is."

From a quick scan of the soldier's mind, Lucian learned *Barbarossa* was the largest ship in the Warden fleet, a heavy cruiser that served as the commander's flagship.

"Did he order the lances to fire?"

"Not that I'm aware of, sir."

"How many soldiers are stationed on Warden Prime?"

"About a thousand, sir. And four thousand in other stations, including the defense platforms."

"Only five thousand in all? Where are the rest? I thought there was supposed to be fifty thousand here."

"Most left weeks ago. Recalled to the League Fleet to aid in the general defense. Admiral Lowell took them. That's why Wren is in charge."

"I see." Lucian would have to figure out the rest later. So, Lucian used Psionic Magic to read the man's mind and find pertinent information. He discovered his name was Henson, though that information was also on the lapel of his uniform.

"These are your orders, Lieutenant Henson. Hold the control room to the last man. I'm going after the commander. Don't let anyone pass those doors."

The lieutenant stood stiffly to attention and gave a sharp salute.

From Henson's mind, Lucian knew the exact layout of the station. He warped out of the command center and back to the hallway outside Hangar Three. He flew down the empty hallway toward Hangar One.

But just as he reached the door, the blasts of impact rifles emanated from a nearby mess hall. Lucian entered to find Jagar, Fergus, and Selene sheltering behind a Psionic shield of Jagar's conjuring. The shield was eating a barrage of impact pulses from about two dozen soldiers. From the strain on Jagar's face, it was clear the shield wouldn't last much longer.

Lucian gathered enough ether to brand every Warden. He didn't want to kill them if he didn't have to. That would make things more complicated when he needed their loyalty. Lucian set the brands individually and willed them to be loyal to him.

Slowly, the stream of pulses slowed to a trickle, and then nothing.

Lucian stepped forward to address them. He almost sent them to the command center to back up Henson until he realized Henson would have no way of knowing whether they were friendly.

"Disperse to your quarters and remain there until you receive further orders. Move!"

They rushed to obey. Lucian floated forward toward his friends, all staring at him in shock.

"Come on," Lucian said. "We don't have much time. The commander is about to get away."

Slightly dazed, they followed Lucian to Hangar One. But when they entered the airlock, a red light flashing above signified that the space on the opposite end was a vacuum. The ship had already left.

Lucian surrounded the four of them in a Binding aura that would hold in their air. Lucian felt Selene streaming an Atomic ward set to refresh the air within the bubble. The action wasn't essential, but he appreciated the effort.

"My magic feels . . . *clean*," she said. "I've never been able to stream like this!"

"Even so," Fergus said, "we were almost overwhelmed back there."

"Should've just killed them," Jagar said.

"We can't kill too many," Lucian said. "This will jeopardize their loyalty once we take over the station."

"This is something you've foreseen?" Fergus asked.

"Yes."

Fergus sighed. "I suppose I have to trust you."

Jagar tapped on the door ahead with the butt of his spear. "Don't tell me we're going out there."

"Yep," Lucian said.

Lucian reached for Radiance, placing his hands on the terminal and hacking it. The doors rolled back, and air blasted out of the airlock. Lucian kept everyone firmly planted with a gravity ward. A large ship, an Orion-class heavy cruiser, had just escaped the hangar, its thrusters blasting it into the distance.

Lucian realized the others couldn't follow him. He redirected his magic, warping them back to the corridor. They would have to hold on for as long as it took him to finish the job.

Lucian tethered the ship and shot forward, his Binding aura protecting him from space. As he neared the cruiser, he combined Radiance and Space-Time, phasing through the ship's outer hull above the engine. With his temporary mass reduction, he instantly snapped into position on the cruiser's main deck.

Lucian found himself in the ship's central hub, amid several soldiers decked out in gray Warden EVA suits. They had a moment to register surprise before Lucian snatched their rifles with a flurry of tethers. He then used reverse Dynamism to plant them on the walls magnetically. They wouldn't be coming down until he decided they could.

He floated down the corridor, passing rows of empty rooms. He turned a corner and saw two Wardens—one male, one female—standing within a compartment filled with rows of bunks. They aimed impact rifles at him but didn't have time to fire. He branded both with Psionic Magic, instructing them to remain still for the next two hours.

These brands were barely any effort for him to maintain. He was a sorcerer with practically unlimited power. The only constraint was the speed he could draw ether. A limit, to be sure, but it was only a limit when streaming the most potent magic.

With no obstacles left, Lucian shot onto the bridge, where Commander Carthen and Captain Warwick were waiting.

5

THE CAPTAIN and the commander were a trifle for Lucian to handle. He grappled both of their handguns with tethers and pocketed them. Weaponless, they raised their hands in surrender.

Lucian wasted no time, reaching out to Carthen's mind and sifting through his thoughts. He quickly discovered the commander had yet to give the order for the operation. Lucian held back a sigh of relief. He hadn't been too late.

"Hand over your slates," Lucian ordered.

The men reached into their pockets and handed him their slates.

Lucian took both machines and pocketed them inside his robe. Now, Carthen had no access to the tachyon platform codes. Lucian had already determined that Carthen didn't have the cybernetic implants sometimes allowed to League officers, an implant which could enable him to give the order without a slate.

Psyche was safe. For now.

"Please," Commander Carthen began, his voice oddly calm and in control, given the situation. "There is no need for violence."

Lucian held back a laugh. "That's rich, coming from the man who planned to wipe out an entire moon."

The two men's eyes widened in surprise. In their minds, there was no way Lucian could have known that.

"You can't lie to me, Commander Carthen," Lucian went on. "I can see into your mind. There is no way for you to wiggle out of this one."

"You're frayed," Captain Warwick said, finally finding his voice. "That is madness speaking!"

"No, I haven't frayed. I've *stopped* the fraying. And I will spare both of your lives, but only if you agree to help me with the Swarmers."

"The Swarmers?" Carthen asked with a laugh. "What do *they* have to do with it?"

Now, this had been the most crucial part of Lucian's visions. It hadn't been just about protecting Psyche from the Wardens. Psyche was about to be under assault by the Swarmers, and he needed the Wardens to defend it.

"They have everything to do with it. They will be here soon. If we are to survive, then we must work together."

Carthen guffawed. "You may have taken us hostage, Lucian Abrantes, but I have already sent out a wide-band emergency broadcast. Within hours, the entire League will descend upon Psyche and end this pathetic insurrection." He gave a victorious smile. "Your days are numbered, terrorist."

Lucian could only marvel at how Carthen could be so bold —and stupid. "Commander Carthen, I'm going to be blunt. The Swarmers are falling on the League like a hammer. They'll be here on Psyche even sooner. The Believers are also mobilizing for an attack on the League. The League can't spare a single ripsaw to save you, much more an entire fleet."

Warwick looked at Carthen for direction. Lucian noted a flicker of doubt on the commander's face.

"What is your point, Abrantes?" Carthen asked.

"I must decide something in the next minute or two."

"And that is?"

"Whether I can use you."

Both men's faces turned pale as they realized the true precariousness of their positions.

"This is ridiculous," Commander Carthen blustered. "I will *never* work with you!"

"I'm allowing you to do it of your own will. I'd rather have your loyalty than use you as a puppet. But if you'd rather be a puppet, I can arrange that."

Captain Warwick cleared his throat nervously. "Commander, it would seem the reports of the traitors were . . . accurate."

Carthen looked at Lucian dangerously. "You mind-controlled my men?"

Lucian nodded. "I did it to spare as many lives as possible because I don't plan to destroy the Wardens. I plan to *save* them."

"Save the Wardens?" Warwick asked. "How?"

Carthen shot him a vicious glare that told him to stay in line.

"Yes," Lucian confirmed. "The Swarmers are descending on this system. We have hours left. Maybe even less. We need to stop shooting at each other and work together."

"We detected some Swarmer vessels passing through the Gradene Gate several days ago," Warwick said. "They should be quite distant, though."

"Warwick," Commander Carthen said dangerously. "If you

give the enemy classified intel again, I will have you court-martialed."

Warwick went silent, but from the reddening of his face, he almost had enough of his commander. As a captain, he wouldn't have been much less in rank than him, and for all Lucian knew, he might outrank the commander outside Warden Prime. Commanders tended to be in charge of static orbital installations, while captains controlled individual vessels. Either way, there seemed to be some friction there. Friction Lucian could use to play them off each other.

Carthen gave Lucian a superior smirk. Lucian didn't have to read his thoughts to know that asking for his loyalty was useless. Carthen would never work with him. At least not willingly.

"What do you suggest, then?" Carthen asked. "That I fall on my sword?"

"No, Commander. I want you to take up that sword and point it at the real enemy that matters. The one that will kill every human in the Worlds if we don't stop them." Lucian retrieved the commander's slate from inside his robes. "I want you to send a message to every Warden ship, station, and platform. Every sailor under your command."

Carthen looked at Lucian mistrustfully. "What message?"

"You are to announce the Wardens' unconditional surrender to the Sorcerer-King of Psyche."

"*Sorcerer-King*?" Carthen spat. "And I suppose that's you? What's happened to Ansaldra?"

"Ansaldra is dead, Commander. By my hand."

Carthen's face blanched.

Lucian proffered the slate again. "Surrender."

Even as Carthen eyed the device, Lucian kept a psychic stream open to both the commander's and captain's minds. He knew what the commander planned: to fall on his sword. As soon as Carthen had access to the machine, he would order the tachyon platforms to fire on the moon, even if it meant his sure death. Such was his hatred for the mages that he considered a worthy sacrifice.

Warwick, however, could be brought to see reason. He disagreed with the commander's order to wipe out Psyche's surface in the first place and only followed it because of the chain of command.

"I know what you plan to do, Carthen," Lucian said. "I already said you can't hide your thoughts from me."

Carthen held out his hand. "Give me the device."

"Don't believe me?"

"You're raving mad. If you're going to kill me, just be done with it!"

"Give the order."

Lucian reached for Radiance, breaking the encryption on the commander's slate. All Lucian had to do was tap the screen, and a closed channel would open that would reach every Warden in the fleet.

"This is your last chance. My mages are safe underground. The lances won't hit them. All you'd be doing is killing tens of thousands of innocent civilians who don't have a drop of magic in them."

Doubt flickered on the commander's features. Lucian could tell Warwick was one hundred percent committed to surrender now, even if Carthen wasn't.

"I don't believe you," Carthen said.

"The Swarmers are in this system. That is a fact. And it's also a fact that the League can't save you. Even Admiral Lowell saw the writing on the wall. Why do you think he took ninety percent of the Wardens with him?"

Lucian could tell that Carthen hadn't wanted him to figure that out. It was the last card he had.

"So why fall on your sword?" Lucian went on. "The sacrifice would be pointless."

Carthen smiled. "My lack of men is the only reason you were successful in this minor rebellion. The soldiers here are the worst of the lot, it's true. That bastard Lowell took the best men, the best ships. I had to grovel and beg to get *Barbarossa*, and she's in dire need of repairs. But make no mistake. The Wardens are committed to protecting the Worlds from psycho filth like you. You will *never* have the Wardens' loyalty, especially when you're mad from the fraying."

"I would have their loyalty if you told them the fraying is no longer any danger. Wouldn't it be better to work with me than die to the Swarmers? How long will your men remain loyal to you once they find out you did nothing to protect them? Maybe you're willing to walk into the grave for no reason. But are your men?"

Carthen seemed to be unsure about that. He glared at Lucian with pure, powerless hatred.

Lucian continued. "Believe it or not, Carthen, I want to stop the Swarmers. I want to help the League, even though they want to kill me. I can save the Wardens. Every word I've said is true. The mages are no longer a threat. I've cured the fraying, have repaired magic itself. No mage will go mad and die. Not anymore. And since this is true, it removes the Wardens' original purpose. If you still want to kill us, you're blind with hatred."

"Lies!" Carthen spat. "Cured the fraying? You expect me to believe that?"

"Commander," Captain Warwick said, licking his lips nervously. "Perhaps there might be something to this. Could we not at least hail Grand Admiral Thorin or even the Hegemon?"

"Whose side are you on, Warwick? I'll have you stripped of your command!"

"You don't have the authority to do that," Warwick said. "The Swarmers *are* coming, and it would make sense to work together, at least for now. If Admiral Lowell were here, he'd see that."

Carthen was fuming. "Admiral Lowell? The same Admiral Lowell who took ninety percent of the Wardens to Archea, allowing this madman to take over?" He gave a crazed laugh. "*I'm* in charge of the Wardens now, and you are out of line!"

Warwick straightened his back. "I was ready to follow through on your orders, Commander, but that was before all this. If the fraying has ended, we'd be killing tens of thousands of people for no reason. I won't allow that to happen!"

"Strange how you've grown such a backbone while I'm staring down the barrel of a gun," Carthen spat. "I have never seen such treachery."

"I should've stood up to you before. But everything Lucian has said is right. The Swarmers are coming, and we can't stop his magic even if we try. Hell, Commander. He can read our thoughts if he wants to! He can *force* us to do what he wants."

"Surrender then, faithless captain," Carthen said. "But as long as I'm alive, the Wardens will not fail their charge."

Lucian knew it would be easy to bend the commander to his will, but there were also drawbacks. Total mind domination was great when giving simple orders, but it also removed agency. The greater the control exerted, the less agency. Psionic mind control worked best when there was willingness behind it. He wanted Carthen to keep some of his agency so he could still be of use. If Lucian could get a toehold, a little softening of his stubborn mindset, he could nudge Carthen in the right direction.

But sadly, it seemed that wasn't going to happen. The man was stubborn beyond belief.

Just as Lucian was preparing to set a powerful Psionic brand that would force him to surrender, emergency klaxons blared while red light bathed the bridge.

By instinct, Warwick turned to the LADAR screen. Dozens of new ships were registered, along with several massive ovoid carriers. All were inbound to Psyche.

"Swarmers!" Warwick said. "Decelerating for battle."

6

COMMANDER CARTHEN JOINED Warwick at the LADAR screen, seeming to forget Lucian for the moment. "Impossible! I thought you said we had a week left."

Lucian shook his head. He had told the commander not minutes before that the Swarmers would be here sooner. Warwick wisely elected not to point that out.

"Blast it all. How long until they're here?" Carthen asked.

"LADAR predicts they'll be in firing range in thirty minutes."

Carthen closed his eyes as if in great duress. He then opened them and looked at Lucian with pure loathing, as if he had engineered this diversion.

"Hand me my slate, Lucian. The surface of Psyche is safe. For now."

"So, what?" Lucian asked. "You're working with me now?"

"Unfortunately, my hand has been forced. I had hoped there would be more time, but now we have a new priority. My role is clear. I must save whoever I can by whatever means necessary. If that means working with you . . . then that's what I must do."

Lucian read his thoughts and saw that he was telling the truth. He no longer intended to exterminate the mages. He wanted to *use* them. Carthen's old plan was to destroy Psyche and order what few Wardens remained to evacuate the system. The Swarmers had put a pause on that plan. He finally saw that he needed Lucian if anyone was to survive.

"Sir," Warwick said, "from the number of inbound vessels, we don't stand a chance. Three Swarmer carriers hold over fifteen hundred interceptors. As you know, we have less than two hundred ships in our entire fleet. Most of them fighters, corvettes, and destroyers, at that."

"That's it?" Lucian asked in disbelief.

"Yes," Warwick said. "Not counting the assault transports, many of which were left behind. They have no fighting capability."

"That shouldn't matter," Lucian said. "With me on your side, victory is assured."

"How?" Carthen asked.

"Who do you think defeated the Swarmer fleet in the Hephaestus System? It wasn't Admiral Yang."

Warwick looked at Carthen. "Yang's fleet *was* outnumbered terribly, yet they survived."

Carthen watched Lucian dangerously. "What are you proposing?"

"I need your guarantee that you won't enact Operation Tabula Rasa. Otherwise, I have no reason to help."

"How do you know that name?" Carthen asked.

"He can read minds, remember?" Warwick looked imploringly at the commander. "Lucian Abrantes is right. We need to work together."

"Didn't I say as much?" Carthen asked. "This terrorist has

already told us our fate if we resist. As soon as he takes care of the Swarmers, what then? He'll destroy us, too!"

"No, I won't," Lucian said with forced patience. "The Warden Fleet will join forces with Psyche."

"I don't consent to that."

"Your consent is not part of the equation." Lucian drew himself up and floated slightly above the deck to remind Carthen of his power. The commander saw this as an attack and lunged for him, but Lucian raised him off the deck with Gravitonics, binding his hands behind his body. Carthen writhed against his invisible restraints as his face went pumice.

"You think . . . this will . . . convince me?"

Lucian looked at the commander's eyes, read his thoughts, and saw that he would *never* surrender. Carthen would betray him at the first opportunity, and he could do nothing about that. From Lucian's previous scans of his mind, Lucian learned that Carthen's father had indoctrinated him to hate mages.

But he could neutralize that hate with a Psionic brand that allowed the commander very little of his original thoughts. Lucian knew that many would have crushed this man by now. Carthen *would* have destroyed Psyche's surface and killed tens of thousands of innocent people, all to stop him.

But Lucian couldn't bring himself to kill him in cold blood. Carthen still hadn't done anything wrong. He merely *would* have done something wrong. Was it right to punish someone who had yet to commit a crime? Carthen might have been guilty of attempted genocide, but Lucian was the only witness unless he could count on Warwick turning against his commander.

And it was at this point that Lucian recognized the impossibility of this task. He could not turn his back on Carthen for one moment, yet he couldn't kill him for something he hadn't done yet. Ansaldra would have, and Xara *certainly* would have.

Yet he could not.

As imperfect as it was, he had a solution. He could not count on the Wardens following him by conventional means.

He had to use his magic.

"I'm going to let you live," Lucian said, finally lowering the commander and himself to the deck. Carthen took a deep intake of breath. "But I need guarantees."

"There's no time for that!"

"We have twenty minutes left before the Swarmers are here. It would help everyone, not just me, if you told your soldiers to stand down. Surrender now."

"Then force me."

Lucian had given him more than a chance. Lucian reached out with his Focus and set up the Psionic brand. In a few seconds, it was over.

Carthen's eyes gave a subtle violet glow as he kneeled and lowered his head. Warwick's eyes widened at the sudden about-face, and hastily, he followed his superior's example. Lucian realized he had to brand him, too. If Warwick told the other Wardens what Lucian had done, it could undermine his authority.

Lucian set both men's brands with every Aspect at his disposal. They would not be undone except by Lucian's will or his death.

Lucian streamed Psionics to inspire loyalty in both men. He let go of the stream.

"My king," Commander Carthen said. "What are your orders?"

"Get up."

Carthen did so, as did Warwick. Each man's eyes no longer shone violet.

Lucian continued. "Call off the tachyon platforms and get your fleet into position to face the Swarmer attack."

Carthen nodded. "At once, my king." He raised his slate to his mouth while Captain Warwick watched. "This is Commander Carthen speaking. Psyche has a new Sorcerer-King. Whatever differences we have, we must set them aside." At a stern gaze from Lucian, Carthen swallowed. "I . . . have turned over the Wardens' ships and soldiers to the Sorcerer-King. I will deal with anyone who questions this transition most brutally. This partnership is for our mutual survival. According to sensor data, a Swarmer fleet is inbound to Psyche. It will be impossible for the Wardens to survive it alone. We must join forces with Psyche and fight back against the invaders."

"Tell them to point the lances away from Psyche," Lucian reminded him.

Carthen nodded. "I am ordering every tachyon crew surrounding Psyche to disengage from standby mode and face your turrets along the Swarmers' attack vector. You'll find that data on the Warden network. If any Swarmer vessel crosses your path, fire at will. Combining forces with Psyche and the Sorcerer-King is our only shot at surviving. We have less than fifteen minutes to prepare. By order of the Sorcerer-King, all ships must get into attack formation at Point Beta. Further orders forthcoming."

Commander Carthen lowered his slate and nodded at Lucian. "It's done."

"Thank you, Commander. You did well."

Carthen stood straighter at the praise.

Lucian turned to Captain Warwick. From his previous mind scans, he knew Warwick was the most talented captain in the Warden fleet that had remained behind. Not only was he talented, but he had a good grasp of tactics, to where Commander Carthen had overlooked his abilities.

Even if both men were mind-controlled and loyal, knowing

who should command was a simple decision. Warwick was better for that job, while Carthen was better at overall administration. While Carthen would not turn on Lucian, Lucian still felt better about putting Carthen in a less dangerous position.

"Captain Warwick, I'm promoting you to Grand Captain. While the fleet is in battle, you have supreme authority, second only to me. Commander Carthen will keep control of the stations in Psyche's orbit while administering the fleet's noncombatant staff. Grand Captain, I trust you can get the fleet into position?"

The newly minted Grand Captain went ramrod straight as he gave a stern salute. "Of course, Sorcerer-King."

Commander Carthen did not seem peeved thanks to Lucian pulling on his brand to ease the anger that would have burst forth. It was time to put Carthen out to pasture in a position where he could never harm Lucian or challenge his authority. Lucian's brand would do the babysitting.

"Congratulations, Grand Captain," Carthen said.

Grand Captain Warwick gave a slight nod. Now, there was no question about who had the higher rank.

"That's enough," Lucian said. "Let's save Psyche."

LUCIAN COULD ONLY IMAGINE how the Wardens were reacting to the sudden shift of management. Right before a major battle, no less. Such an action could only devastate the fleet's morale, especially in a fight where they were outnumbered almost ten to one.

But Lucian knew how to deal with that. None of them knew who he was or what he was capable of. They only knew him as the terrorist who had assassinated the League Hegemon and somehow blackmailed Commander Carthen and Captain Warwick. Those actions made him worthy of fear, but fear was a limited motivator.

He needed to win their respect, loyalty, and admiration. So that was why he flew at the head of the tiny Warden flotilla, wholly exposed to the vacuum of space. He would have been impossible to miss with his bright blue Binding aura while pulling himself with a Gravitonic brand. An electromagnetic brand using Dynamism kept him safe from radiation, while an Atomic brand continually fluxed his air into an optimal atmospheric composition. Thermalism kept the temperature comfortable within the aura. It was far more magic than even an advanced mage could perform, but Lucian was no mere mage. He was the Chosen of the Manifold, and the men under his command needed to see that. If they saw how powerful he was, they wouldn't begrudge Warwick and Carthen for deferring to him.

He opened himself to the radio spectrum using Radiance and listened to the Wardens' chatter. The general tone was one of disbelief and awe. It was what he had intended.

With minutes left until the Swarmer fleet arrived, Lucian began the next stage of his plan, creating a massive Psionic ward that covered the entire Warden fleet. He inspired feelings of bravery and confidence within that ward and smiled at the confident banter of Warden crews. It was like listening to the pre-fight monologues of boxers and their managers. They were energized and terrified, knowing they were about to enter the ring. They weren't thinking about who they were or what they had done. They weren't thinking about their families or even their dreams. They were thinking about the upcoming fight, of being heroes against impossible odds. They dreamed of glory.

If they believed in him now, how much more when they saw him destroy the Swarmer carriers? His position would be secure. He might still need to use Psionic brands for a few malcontents, but he would have the undying loyalty of the rank and file. And that was all he needed.

Lucian became a conduit of ether. An unreal amount already flowed through him from all the wards he had active. But that ether was only a fraction of what was available in the surrounding space. When the time came, he would exhaust everything for kilometers to accomplish his goals. For now, he was using but a drop at his total command. Rather than reach inside himself to find the ether, he could call for whatever he wished for at will, no matter the Aspect. The Orbs would respond to his need instantly.

Point Beta lay exactly one thousand kilometers above the center of Psyche's Voidside. The moon behind him was like the violet pupil in the eye of the white gas giant Cupid. The larger planet lay about five hundred thousand kilometers away, large enough to loom in the distance because of its Jovian size. As a fallback, if any Swarmer vessels broke through, the tachyon lance crews were on standby to shoot down anything that tried to enter Psyche's atmosphere.

The Radiance ward surrounding Lucian picked up a message from Captain Warwick. "Time to engagement: one minute. I'm detecting three carriers."

Lucian was glad that he had confirmed that number. It was less than the battle at Hephaestus, but Admiral Yang had over a thousand ships at her disposal. They had a fifth of her number, no battleships, and only one heavy cruiser. In short, no vessel in the Warden fleet had the firepower to challenge the stalwart crystalline shells of the carriers.

But now, they had something worth more than ships: the Chosen of the Manifold who held the Eight Orbs of Starsea.

Lucian transmitted a message back. "Grand Captain, all I need is for you guys to buy time and stay alive. It'll be some time before I've gathered enough ether to destroy the carriers. But once I do, the battle should end quickly."

Warwick chuckled. Even he was feeling the effects of Lucian's morale boost. "In our favor, I assume?"

"That's the idea."

"I have every confidence, Sorcerer-King."

Lucian cut off the communication as soon as he spied three ovoid masses approaching from deep space. They were small at first, undetectable by normal human vision. Already, his Radiance-enhanced sight could make out the shells of those ships coming apart, allowing streams of *Alkasen* fighters to pour out by the dozens.

Lucian began gathering ether as quickly as he could, his Orbs easily holding what should have been an overwhelming amount of power. As he slowed his advance, a line of ripsaw fighters streamed overhead, followed by a contingent of heftier javelin-class corvettes loaded with torpedoes. Those javelins would be useless against the thick, rocky hulls of the Swarmer carriers, fortified by Binding Magic, but they would be essential in targeting the interceptors. A few larger destroyers followed behind, whose entire purpose was shooting clouds of flak designed to eviscerate the Swarmers' tiny strike craft while shredding hostile torpedoes. Swarmer interceptors engaged with the ripsaws, shooting powerful green lasers in answer to the ripsaws' concentrated railgun fire.

Last came the Orion-class heavy cruiser *Barbarossa*, the flagship of this ragtag fleet. It was a mighty ship in its own right, loaded with a deadly array of railguns and one hundred and twenty torpedoes. Still, it was nothing compared to the giant battleships and dreadnoughts of the League First Fleet, which carried powerful tachyon lances capable of blasting entire ships to smithereens.

The small Warden fleet was dwarfed by the force facing it, primarily composed of interceptors zipping forward at incredible speed. Lucian knew that against that mass, there could be no hope of victory by conventional means. Without him, every sailor heading into battle only had minutes of life left; perhaps that assessment was generous.

Lucian intended to show them that wouldn't be the case. Even though he didn't know the limits of his powers, it seemed he could do almost anything.

It was time to put that idea to the test.

He was a beacon of light. Within the Ether, millions upon

millions of magic streams infused his body, making him shine like a newborn star. It was all compressed and held within his Focus. He didn't stop drawing ether until he had emptied it for ten klicks around him in a perfect sphere. At such distances, the ether accumulated slowly into his Focus. He *could* draw more, but it would take more time and effort. He realized this was the only hard limit he had.

But what he had was sufficient for his purposes. Already, the first flashes of destroyed ships lit the backdrop of space. Sailors were dying, and stories were ending. It was time to attack before any more perished.

Lucian began by creating a gravity point right on the surface of the central carrier, unleashing almost all of his ether into it. The gravity point intensified until it was beyond even Jovian levels. Such was its power that it even pulled Lucian toward it, along with every Warden vessel.

But if the gravity point were pulling Lucian and the League ship, it was positively *yanking* the *Alkasen* carriers. Already, it was pulling the two closest vessels toward it. There was a moment of resistance as the ships' Binding fields flashed at the point of contact with the gravity point. Lucian only increased the intensity of his stream, channeling as much ether as he could, unleashing it in a relentless flood.

At last, the gravity was strong enough to overcome the shields protecting the ships. Their hardened, rocky shells buckled into each other as the gravity point increased in power.

Lucian realized that this wasn't as simple as it first seemed. Even the League ships were being pulled in, and their engines were far too weak to escape. But if the League ships struggled, the Swarmer interceptors were being decimated. Most were relatively close to the carriers, and such was their disarray that the Wardens quickly dealt with those not pulled in, limited as their numbers were.

It had become a race against time. The *Alkasen* carriers had to be crushed before the Warden flotilla suffered a similar fate.

But Lucian had already drawn as much ether as he could, and he didn't have the time to siphon more.

He instantly saw the solution, though it would risk his life. It was a simple enough decision to drop the Psionic ward that boosted the Wardens' morale. But dropping that ward didn't free up enough ether. He also had to drop the surrounding shield, exposing him to the vacuum of space. He had to accomplish his task in a few seconds before he blacked out, never to wake up again.

There was no other way out. This action was the final, most dangerous key to his prophecy.

First, he exhaled all the air from his mouth and lungs. If too much was in his body, the force of it leaving could tear his lungs. Lucian next allowed the Psionic ward to dissipate.

Before he could think about it too much, he dropped the shield surrounding him.

Almost instantly, whatever breath remained was expelled from his mouth and lungs. His skin immediately dried as all moisture was dispelled, bruises and frostbite settling in within seconds. Within the deepness of his Focus, he hardly felt the pain. The fresh infusion of ether was more than enough to finish the job.

With a final push, he significantly increased the strength of the gravity point. He crushed the carriers into a sphere. It would only be a matter of time before a reactor failure led to a chain reaction, obliterating them all.

Already, he felt himself going numb while sunburn covered his exposed skin. The saliva boiled off his tongue.

He was fading. The only thing that kept him going was an image of Serah, the promise of seeing her again and holding her close. It was enough to marshal whatever ether he had left for one last stream.

Just before he lost consciousness, he warped himself to the bridge of the heavy cruiser *Barbarossa*. The rest was up to the Manifold.

AS SOON AS the warp was complete, the bridge crew jumped at his sudden appearance, but Lucian ignored them. Lucian wanted nothing more than to sink to his knees because of the unreal pain of being covered with radiation burns and bruises from head to toe. Lucian ground his teeth. His muscles seized uncontrollably, causing him to fall to one side. It felt like someone was pressing a red-hot iron on every inch of his body.

He clung to his Focus because he had to show strength in front of the Wardens. They had to see him as more than a man, someone unstoppable. It wasn't just about this battle, but the coming war. The prophecy had to be fulfilled.

Despite his pain, he raised his head long enough to see that the Swarmer carriers were thoroughly destroyed while the Warden ships, from *Barbarossa* down to the tiny ripsaw fighters, were mopping up what few interceptors remained.

"My King," Grand Captain Warwick said, finally recovering. "We must get you to the medical bay at once!"

Lucian held up a defraying hand. Already, the Ether had regenerated around him to a large extent. He could use that ether to heal himself. The only way to recover from injuries of this magnitude was to send his entire body back in time. However, his memories needed to be stored in the Ether temporarily so they weren't lost.

He combined every Aspect, focusing it all on his body. Within the Ether, his mind could exist while his body returned to the state it had existed in only a few minutes before. He accomplished this action in mere seconds.

When he opened his eyes, he was as good as new. The pain was gone, though he still remembered that fire burning on his skin.

Grand Captain Warwick marveled, clearly not knowing how to react. The rest of the bridge crew was similarly stunned. Healing like this wasn't supposed to be possible with magic, yet none of them could deny what had happened before their eyes.

Lucian ignored their reactions, walking toward the forward viewport as every pair of eyes followed him. He regarded the scene before him. Only a couple of dozen of the Swarmer interceptors were left, so they were not the actual threat. At any moment, the reactors powering the carriers would fail, causing an explosion of debris that would be fatal to every ship that didn't get out of the way.

"It's time to evacuate," Lucian said. "Get to a safe spot. At any moment, what's left of those carriers will create an explosion that will destroy this fleet. We need to get as far from this place as we can."

Warwick cleared his throat. "What of the remaining Swarmer vessels? If we leave them, they will harass our rear. We are certain to lose a few ships that way."

"Better than losing *all* our ships," Lucian said. "Retreat, Grand Captain. Leave any ships that are foolish enough to attack us to me."

Warwick's face was questioning, but he wasn't going to

disobey a direct order. Warwick was already raising his slate to his mouth. "Great work, men. Victory is ours. However, the Sorcerer-King has ordered our retreat to a safe location. At any moment, the reactors aboard the Swarmer carriers will fail, creating an explosion of debris that could overwhelm our shield systems. Retreat to Point Alpha at full speed."

Grand Captain Warwick was already veering the heavy cruiser around, bringing Psyche into its sights. The other ships of the fleet wheeled around in tandem.

As a Swarmer interceptor zoomed past *Barbarossa*, the bridge shook as it ate a line of laser fire. Lucian reached out with Gravitonics, crushing the ship like a bug in a fist. Even that seemingly simple action took an insane amount of ether, something only the most powerful of mages could accomplish, and Lucian had done it with barely a thought. Another ship flew by, which Lucian blasted apart with a shattering dualstream.

Despite his power, Lucian felt a heavy weariness. His Focus was exhausted, unable to stream otherwise boundless magic. He saw a third Swarmer interceptor incoming, and it was only with great effort that he destroyed it.

Still, it seemed it was enough of a deterrent to keep the other interceptors from following too closely. The last few that remained were heading for Psyche in some pointless bid to escape. Most of them were shot down by the ripsaws' railgun fire and the corvettes' torpedoes. Only a few slipped out of firing range. The interceptors were amazingly fast—far faster than any vessel humanity could bring to bear. Assuming the carriers had access to the same technology, it explained how this surprise fleet had gotten from the Gradene Gate to Psyche itself in just a few days.

These last few ships would never make it to Psyche's surface. Almost at once, a barrage of blue tachyon lances fried each vessel. It was beyond overkill and seemed a fitting finale to ensure ultimate victory.

Lucian refocused his mind, attempting to remain standing after such exertion. The amount of concentration required to pull everything off was beyond anything he had so far attempted, except perhaps his battle with Xara Mallis. Everyone on the bridge crew was still looking at him in wonder. They had witnessed his power and knew he was the reason they were alive.

Lucian knew, reaching out and feeling their general state of emotions, that they were loyal to him far more than they had ever been to Carthen. He had not only saved them, but had proved himself a worthy commander. A Sorcerer-King not only in name but in reality.

By the time they entered Psyche's orbit, *Barbarossa's* sensors had registered a massive explosion from behind. Still, by the time the debris reached them, they would be safely behind the moon, and Psyche's thick atmosphere would be enough to break up the rest.

"None of our primary stations will be in the path of the debris," Warwick commented, watching a data readout flash by on his terminal. "We stand to lose a dozen tachyon platforms but nothing more."

"Tell the men on board those platforms to eject to the surface," Lucian said.

"At once, my king." Warwick raised his slate to his mouth. "Defense platforms thirty-six through fifty-two: this is Grand Captain Warwick. By order of the Sorcerer-King, abandon your stations and escape to the surface. Once there, remain in position, and we will pick you up later."

Lucian nodded his approval. "And how long until we can pick them up? The surface of Psyche is dangerous. I wouldn't want to lose any men unnecessarily to monsters."

"The process will take some time, Sorcerer-King," Warwick said. "We have assault transports, each of which can hold two hundred Warden marines. If we send one to each crash site, there will be more than enough space to save everyone."

"I see. They will have to be integrated into the main part of the fleet. We can't take the defense platforms with us, after all."

"That's true," Warwick said. "Among the tachyon crews, a thousand sailors can pilot. Our assault transports have a capacity for tens of thousands of men, enough for a surface invasion of Psyche." He smiled apologetically. "Of course, I don't suggest an invasion, my King. I only mean there is a way to combine our forces. When the Warden fleet left, they left the transports behind. There should be enough room for the Wardens and your soldiers on the surface."

"We are still not at that point yet, Grand Captain. But that's good information to have."

"In the interim, perhaps we should start thinking about establishing your firm control on Psyche itself. Many parts of the moon remain outside your control. If I might be so bold as to say."

Lucian scanned his mind and realized that he and Commander Carthen, along with most of the higher-ups in the Warden fleet, were well aware of the recent chaos on Psyche's surface.

"Where are these troop transports based, Grand Captain?"

"Most are stationed on Warden Prime, in the lower dockyards. But dozens more are docked around the twelve major stations orbiting Psyche. It would take some shuffling around, but we can have boots on the ground in less than twenty-four hours."

"Any more Swarmer fleets in the system?"

"None that our alert buoys have picked up. However, our

latest data download alerted us to major mustering points in the Pontus and Astravan Systems."

"Astravan," Lucian mused. "That would cut off Admiral Yang from the Alpha Centauri fleet."

"I'm afraid so. If need be, Yang has a retreat point to the Archea System, but it would seem even that system's days are numbered."

Already, a plan was forming in Lucian's mind. He was confident in Warwick's loyalty and even Carthen's, who would remain relegated to general fleet maintenance. With luck, he wouldn't have to deal with him too often.

But even with such a grand victory and incredible display of power, there could still be some of the higher officers that were less than thrilled with Lucian's ascension, especially when it had happened so suddenly. He had to nip any potential rebellious thoughts in the bud.

"How soon can we have every commissioned officer, of the rank of captain and above, assembled before me on Warden Prime?"

"Within hours, Sorcerer-King," Warwick said.

"Good. See it done."

Warwick smiled. "It would be my pleasure."

At least for the moment, their loyalty was not in question, though he got the sense that they were curious about what was going on. Lucian intended to share some of that with them. Just the right amount to not overwhelm them.

By now, he was going by his instincts. The details he'd gained from his future delving were petering out. They had seen him through the battle, which was more than enough. The tool would always be available to him later, if he needed it. At least, that was what he hoped.

Lucian surveyed the officers. Besides these officers, about forty-five hundred additional Warden sailors were at Lucian's disposal. Had Rear Admiral Lowell remained behind with his forty-five thousand troops and eight hundred ships, taking over the Warden fleet might have been impossible, at least not without a tragic loss of life.

The men and women stood utterly silent and at attention, and as time dragged on, Lucian could feel the mood shift from nervousness to fear. Lucian was waiting for a good reason, however. He was placing brands on every officer, one by one. Each brand took about a second to create and wasn't designed for outright psychic control. It was more to keep tabs on them. It was the same brand Ansaldra had used to keep up with the nobles of Psyche. Of course, if the need presented itself, it gave Lucian a foothold in their psyches. He could change the nature of the brand on a case-by-case basis, should the need arrive.

After he had set the brands, Lucian created a Psionic stream combined with Reverse Thermalism to calm their emotions. Visibly, he could see their faces relax, though they did not break their attention.

At last, Lucian cleared his throat, and the officers' collective sharpened on him.

"This battle was just the first of many," he began. "I won't speak of glory. Because no matter how hard we fight, billions will die. Most of the Worlds will fall before ultimate victory is attained. Already, the Border Worlds are under assault, and the Mid-Worlds will fall soon. The Swarmers are attacking humanity from every angle. Saving everyone is an impossibility."

Lucian stared at the officers to make sure that point sank in. He knew that many of them were from worlds under direct threat. Maybe they were from worlds that had already fallen. There was a collective fire in their bellies to fight back, to unite behind someone strong enough to mount a resistance.

Lucian had to channel that strength and let them recognize the truth independently.

"The Hegemon plans to protect the core worlds only," Lucian said. "She will fail. Over a million Earth years ago, the *Alkasen* destroyed an empire called Starsea. You may have heard of Xara Mallis's attempt to recreate that empire. Starsea was an empire of over a thousand suns, with an armada that made the combined might of humanity look like a group of cavemen holding sticks."

The men and women watched him, and from their eyes, Lucian saw they were wondering where he was going with this.

"According to the Transcend Arian's prophecy, the Chosen of the Manifold would gather the Aspects of Magic. These powerful artifacts come from the time of Starsea. When wielded, they give a mage nearly unlimited power. A single mage gathering all these Orbs heals magic itself, meaning mages are no longer in danger of fraying." Lucian knew he was simplifying things, but the explanation would suffice. "These Aspects, called the Orbs, were lost to time. But those Orbs have now been found, thus fulfilling Arian's prophecy." He clenched his fist. "I am the Chosen of the Manifold, having gathered all the Orbs. There has never been a mage in history as powerful as me. No mage will fray and die as long as I hold the Orbs."

The officers' eyes widened at this revelation. Lucian didn't even have to tamper with their brands to inspire them to believe. They *already* believed. They had seen his power during the battle.

"Only the Chosen can stand against the Swarmers and be victorious," Lucian said. "The Worlds will soon recognize that, just as all of you do now. So, what can we do? How do we stop them? Our resources are small. Not even Psyche is under our control yet. However, my forces on the surface include many mages, many times more than the academies hold, not to mention conventional soldiers. Working together, imagine how powerful we will be! With this force, we can unite humanity. I will lead you to victory, to the salvation of humanity!"

Lucian could feel the zeal radiating from their brands. They were restraining themselves, the force of their discipline the only thing holding them back from shouting their enthusiasm.

"Many of you have families who are under threat. Many of you have lost loved ones. If I could bring them back, I would. I would be lying if I said I could save those directly in the Swarmers' path. That's why speed is important. The faster we move, the more we can save. We are fighting for our very survival as a species! Humanity has faced many trials over tens of thousands of years. So long as I live and breathe, this will not be the end of our story!"

Now, the officers *were* shouting their agreement. Lucian could ask them to do anything, and they would. Grand Captain Warwick and Commander Carthen watched him, pride written on their features.

Lucian continued. "You are the only ones outside my closest friends who know this. You know things the wider Worlds do not. I did not want to be a leader. A king. But that's the path the Manifold laid before me—the Manifold that is the ultimate reality behind all existence. I am the Chosen of the Manifold.

Only I can stop the *Alkasen*. Single-handedly, I destroyed three *Alkasen* carriers and the hundreds of ships they sheltered."

Lucian paused, realizing for the first time that these people didn't even know the *Alkasen* by that name. They only knew them as the Swarmers. But they were dealing with an intelligent race, not a mindless enemy. It was best to remind them of that.

"I'm ordering you to pass on what I've said to those under your command. It's important to know *why* we are fighting. Make no mistake. The Swarmers will not stop until every human has been hunted down. Whether that person is from the League, a Oneist, or one of the dozen planet-states that have declared independence lately, the Swarmers don't care. They outnumber us and outgun us. They want us dead. And they will succeed in their goal unless we fight back."

He could see the questions written on their faces, but Lucian knew it was time to wrap things up. He needed to find Serah, Emma, and his mother. It was something he had put off far too long, but now he could go, since his position was secure.

"Our priority is securing Psyche with as little bloodshed as possible and bringing it under our control. The role of the Wardens will be that of support and assistance. The entire moon has been rocked by war, and it's up to us to clean up the mess. Commander Carthen and Grand Captain Warwick will oversee this action. We need to marshal Psyche's manpower and resources and load as many fighting soldiers as possible onto the transports. That fleet we fought is just the first of many. That means we must ensure Psyche's people are as safe as possible. Food, supplies, and people must be moved to the Riftlands, where they can use the vast cave systems for protection. In the Riftlands, they will stand the best chance of holding on long enough for us to achieve victory."

When that victory was, Lucian couldn't say. He knew the

Alkasen couldn't be truly defeated until he returned the Orbs to the Heart of Creation through the First Gate. No one in the Worlds knew where that was, and any journey there would take months, if not years. By then, the Swarmers would have exterminated most of humanity.

He wondered whether he should focus on that rather than trying to gather a fleet large enough to challenge the *Alkasen* directly. But he had to find out where the First Gate was, and no one could tell him that. Searching for it system by system was doomed to failure.

It was then that a new thought struck him. An idea that was so obvious that it was a wonder he hadn't thought of it before.

The *Alkasen* Emissary, Silumko, might know. There was something Silumko had said during their meeting that might be the key, but it was difficult to recall that conversation, which seemed ages ago.

It was something he had to consider when he had the chance.

"That's all for now. Orders will be forthcoming. As you were."

Immediately, Carthen and Warwick approached Lucian.

"Excellent speech, my king," Carthen gushed. "And I'm thankful for your faith in my abilities. I will not fail you."

If Lucian could have used anyone else, he would have, but Carthen would be helpful, having expertise in logistics and command. "That's good to hear, Commander. The next item is assembling the ground troops to secure Psyche while uniting the two armies. We must do so without bloodshed."

Carthen frowned. "Well, there will be *some* conflict, but probably not much. Sorcerer-King, I have never seen a group of soldiers so devoted to their leader, including myself! These men and women will gladly fight and die for you if you were to give the order!"

Grand Captain Warwick nodded his agreement. "Getting the Wardens on the ground shouldn't be difficult. The officers are already privy to a general invasion plan."

"Can that invasion plan be converted into a humanitarian initiative?" Lucian asked.

Warwick nodded. "Not only that, Sorcerer-King, but it would make things much easier. We can establish landing zones at every major population center. Set up assistance areas where we can marshal people, assess their skills, and separate the wheat from the chaff. Everyone of legal age can undergo basic training. We are not lacking in weapons or ships. Only soldiers."

"Will there be enough pilots?" Lucian asked.

"Every transport comes equipped with a backup pilot droid," Warwick said. "They're not as good as a human pilot with academy training, but it will serve for basic maneuvers, like interplanetary transit, docking, and orbital insertions."

"I see," Lucian said. "And how long will it take to recruit from the population of Psyche and give them some basic training?"

"Ideally, we'd have three months to do that. But in periods of war and emergency, we have a program that can be shortened to ten weeks."

Lucian knew even that was too much. "That's impossible."

"I'm afraid so, Sorcerer-King," Carthen said. "Our surface scans show a force of forty thousand soldiers gathered north of Malia. Perhaps we should focus our efforts there. It would be a perfect fit, as far as our transport capacity goes. Such soldiers, who already have some military training, might be trained in as little as two weeks."

"That's far more doable, Commander," Lucian said. "They can undergo training while in transit, too."

Admittedly, Lucian didn't plan to travel between star

systems in the traditional sense. He would use portals to move his fleet far faster than the Swarmers could react. However, there would inevitably be some downtime for his soldiers to sharpen their skills. Some men would play planetary defense roles, defending worlds from orbital attacks on the ground. In contrast, others would have to be trained in the various positions on the Warden ships.

"We have exhaustive training modules," Commander Carthen said. "No matter what role we assign, automated instructors can teach them."

"And fuel?"

"We have multiple fuel stations around Psyche and four fuel tankers that can travel with the fleet itself. We are supplied from a fuel forge in Cupid's orbit. So long as that infrastructure stays in place, we won't want for fuel."

Lucian nodded. "There's also the matter of the mages. We need Atomicists and Gravitists especially. In tandem, they'll allow our ship to move faster and farther. Stationing at least one per ship would go a long way."

"A good point," Carthen said. "Both Gravitists and Atomicists were a key advantage for the Starsea Mages during the Mage War. They allowed Xara Mallis's smaller fleets to punch above their weight because they could travel faster and farther than League ships. We estimate Psyche alone has a full two thousand mages on the surface. Perhaps even more. The Volsung and Irion Academies can only bring half of that number to bear."

"Yes," Warwick said. "If what you've said is true, Sorcerer-King, then we have the most powerful fighting force in the Worlds. No one has as many mages as we do. At least, assuming we can get everyone to work with us."

"We will," Lucian said. "Here's what I want you both to do. Come up with a plan to take control of the surface. The key is getting the word out. The important thing is getting every mage gathered into a single fighting force and having a system of organization and a chain of command. A Mage Division, if you will."

"I concur," Commander Carthen said. "I recorded your rousing speech. I hope I didn't do anything wrong. But I can allow that video to be disseminated, setting up holo-projectors in key points. This could be a way to educate the populace on the threat we face quickly."

Carthen was already proving his usefulness. Lucian was glad he hadn't taken the more violent route with him. "Good idea. See that it's done."

Carthen smiled, pleased at the praise.

Warwick nodded. "I can speak with my captains about how to instigate the landing plan. We should have something drawn up for you within twenty-four hours, if not less. And, ah, it might be prudent to share slate details on our private Warden network."

Lucian saw the sense in that. These men were not mages, so he couldn't communicate with them Psionically. Of course, he could use Radiance to speak to them by radio, but it was far simpler to use a piece of technology everyone had access to.

After they exchanged slate details, Lucian nodded. "That's it for now. We'll reconvene later. I hope the transports will be underway soon. For now, I have some business to attend to."

"Of course, Sorcerer-King," Commander Carthen said. "We will be here."

Lucian took a few steps back and brought his cabin aboard *Blood Wyvern* to mind. Within a moment, he had vanished.

10

AS SOON AS Lucian appeared in his and Serah's cabin on *Blood Wyvern*, a sudden impact rocked him. The cabin's interior was bathed in red light, and he could hear the hiss of air escaping from the corridor outside.

Perhaps they weren't as safe in Kandi's orbit as Lucian had thought.

A tendril of fear snaked through his stomach, not for his sake, but for the others. He surrounded himself in a Binding aura and hacked the door with a Radiant stream.

What air remained in the cabin blasted out into the central passage. Looking up, Lucian found the source of the leak—a breach about half a meter wide that was open to the blackness of space. Lucian scanned up and down the corridor to find all the doors were firmly sealed.

He reached out a hand, shielding the breach with Binding Magic. Almost immediately, the corridor pressurized. Lucian advanced toward the bow.

Serah? Are you all right?

Lucian! Where the rotting hell have you been?

Is everyone okay?

Get to the bridge, and you tell me!

When Lucian opened the door to the bridge, it didn't open automatically, probably because the air pressure was still too low on his side. Someone must have manually overridden the doors because they slid open, letting out a rush of air.

Serah, Emma, and his mother all stared at him in shock and perhaps even a bit of panic. When Lucian looked at the LADAR screen, he could see why. There were easily a dozen ships chasing *Blood Wyvern,* though by now, they were distant, and the vessel was on a new trajectory that should lose them in a few more hours. The ship was well out of range of Kandi, but that hadn't stopped their pursuers.

"You dropped us into the middle of a war zone!" Serah said. "And then you took off like it was nothing!"

Lucian blinked. "I'm sorry. It didn't look bad earlier."

"Well, things changed fast," Mira said. "As soon as you left, it was like kicking an anthill."

"Sorry. I'll get you guys out of here soon. Is the breach in the main corridor the only damage to the ship?"

"As far as I know," Mira said. "We got grazed by some flak. We nearly lost all our air. Luckily, the doors closed on time before we could get sucked out."

That image only reminded Lucian of his vision. Perhaps there was still a chance for it to be fulfilled.

"We'll talk about it in a minute," he said.

He gathered his ether, and after a few seconds, he had enough to create a portal in front of the ship. It slipped through, instantly jumping back to Psyche.

"There," he said. "We should be safe." He turned to face the women. "So, what happened?"

"Well," Emma said, "as soon as you warped us, we were almost immediately bombarded with hail requests. Seems like there's a bounty on this ship, and everyone wanted to be the one to take us down."

"Seriously?"

"Yes, seriously. As Mira said, some flak found us before we could go off LADAR with the cloaking screen. But by then, it was too late."

"I'm just glad everyone is safe," Lucian said. "Must have been a big bounty."

"Yeah, ten thousand credits," Emma said. "Put out by the Wardens themselves!"

Lucian would have to have a chat with Commander Carthen about that.

"What took you so long?" Serah asked. "I don't appreciate you just leaving us hanging by a thread. We could have *died*."

"I'm sorry. I would have warped you somewhere else if I knew it would be dangerous. I couldn't think of a place far enough from Psyche but also close enough that it wouldn't take too much ether. Warping an entire ship isn't as easy as warping people, especially under pressure."

"I see your point," Serah said begrudgingly. "Luckily, Mira is an expert pilot."

"Yes, we owe her our lives," Emma said. "How did things go with the Wardens?"

"Better than expected. They're on our side now, and I'm in charge."

"Seriously?" Serah asked. "How did you manage that?"

Lucian shrugged. "A lot of magic and a lot of luck."

He explained the whole thing, their eyes wide as they hung on his every word.

Once done, Emma was the first to speak. "Well, I suppose

you *were* busy. Still, you need to be more careful next time. You could have easily died when you let your shield drop."

"Yeah," Serah said. "That sounded scary."

"I'm fine. All's well that ends well, right?"

"Son, I've got a question for you," Mira said. "Are you going to go around calling yourself the Sorcerer-King?"

Lucian felt slightly uncomfortable as all three women stared at him as if defying him to say "yes."

"It's the only title that means anything to the nobles," Lucian said. "I don't like it, but you have to admit it's useful."

"Well, Mira has something of a point," Serah said. "Sorcerer-King might work with the nobles, but that name has a lot of baggage among commoners. All you're teaching them with that name is to fear you."

"What do you suggest, then? Maybe just Chosen?"

"No," Emma said, "Absolutely not. That makes you sound like you're full of yourself."

Mira shrugged. "Well, it's very clear about who and what he is. It's what Arian called him, right?"

"Well, do you have any other ideas?" Lucian asked. "Who says I can't have *multiple* titles?"

The three women just stared at him. Lucian knew what that collective look meant. While others might be afraid of him, he would always be Lucian to them.

"You guys don't have to call me any of that stuff. That much should be obvious. It's just for people outside the inner crew."

"The inner crew," Serah said. "I like that. I've always wanted to be in a club."

"All right," Emma said. "Different titles, depending on who you're talking to. Makes sense. We should probably have one title that's a cut above the rest. A sort of catch-all title, if you will."

"I'm sure we can think of something," Mira said.

"Yeah," Serah said. "Just leave it to your PR team!"

"PR team, huh?" Lucian asked.

"Yes," Emma said, nodding. "Every leader needs one, right? Even my parents' company has a PR department. Controlling the narrative is important." She considered for a moment. "Our first task will be figuring out an appropriate title for you. There's a lot in a name, and picking the wrong one will lead to a poor impression."

"Okay, makes sense," Lucian said.

"We need something that people will understand instantly. A title with authority that doesn't sound too evil or esoteric."

"Got it," Lucian said. "Hero vibes, not dark lord vibes."

Serah chuckled. "So I guess Third Immortal is out the window?"

"*Definitely* not Third Immortal," Emma said. "You can't call yourself the Third Immortal or even the Chosen of the Manifold. The Chosen will work with mages, but it might lead to blank stares otherwise. It's not exactly common knowledge."

"Well, how about just Sorcerer-Ascendant?" Mira asked. "Before the Mage War, when all the mages were united, they had a Sorcerer-Ascendant who led them all. After the war, the title fell out of favor, though they kept up the tradition on Mako. But if we brought it back, it could go a long way. The Sorcerer-Ascendant was an office held by the most powerful mage in the Worlds. That demands respect from mage and non-mage alike. It would also imply all the mages should be subservient to him."

"Transcend White won't like that," Lucian said.

"Who cares what she thinks?" Serah asked. "Lakhmu himself named you his successor, and he was the Sorcerer-Ascendant. Not even she can argue with that, right? Why would he give you that title if he didn't want you to use it?"

"You might have a point there," Lucian said. "I'll admit, it sounds better than Sorcerer-King. And the people of Psyche should be able to stomach it, too."

"Should we go with that, then?" Emma asked.

"I think we have a winner," Serah said.

"I'm still not calling you that, son," Mira said. "There should be a rule that anyone who has changed your diapers doesn't have to grovel."

"I already said you didn't have to, mom. I don't want that, anyway. You guys are on my council, so you're exempt."

"So, that's what we're calling it now, not the inner crew?" Serah asked. "I've never been on a . . . *council* before."

"It'll be like Xara Mallis and the Council of the Wise," Emma said. "Except less evil, of course."

"Let's just call it the Council for now," Lucian said. "Maybe the Mage Council. Anyone who has joined me at any point can be a part of it. Sound fair?"

"Good enough for me," Mira said. "Although I'm not a mage."

"We'll make an exception," Emma said.

"So, do we get titles, too?" Mira asked.

"I've got one for you," Lucian said. "How does Fleet Admiral sound?"

Mira laughed. "*Fleet Admiral*? Of what?"

"Psyche. I admit, you only have two hundred ships right now, but we'll get more. You're the only one of us with combat experience, and I trust you more than any of the Wardens. Is it really so crazy?"

"I don't know. You think I can do that?"

"If you can't, no one will."

"That's not too encouraging."

"You'll be great," Emma said, apparently having a more appropriate response. "You have a lot of experience under your belt."

"Maybe," Mira said. "Well, we'll see." She turned to Lucian. "What comes next?"

"The next phase is bringing Psyche under our control. Trust me, there's a lot of mess to clean up."

ONCE THEY DOCKED on Warden Prime, Lucian gathered everyone in the newly minted Mage Council for a catch-up session. Everything in the station was humming along nicely. Commander Carthen was reshuffling the fleet and soldiers to prepare for the landing, while Grand Captain Warwick was busy with the officers laying out the overall strategy. Lucian sent them a message, letting them know that his title, now and into the future, would be Sorcerer-Ascendant, and instructed him to pass that along to the officers.

All that was left was for Lucian to ensure the Mage Council was on the same page.

After about an hour of catching up, Lucian concluded that his mother would lead the Warden fleet.

"Fleet Admiral Mira Abrantes," Fergus said. "It has a nice ring to it."

Her face flushed. "Well, hopefully, I can live up to it. I haven't captained anything larger than a destroyer."

"You'll be fine," Lucian said.

Mira seemed ready to change the subject. "If this Mage

Council is going to be a thing, maybe we should decide what everyone's role is."

Everyone looked at Lucian for direction. Nothing in his prophecies told him what to do once he got this far. While delving the future was a helpful tool, it wasn't foolproof. After all, it hadn't warned him that his mother would take *Blood Wyvern* into orbit. He had to be careful when using it in the future.

"I don't know what comes next," he began. "Getting this far would have been impossible without the future delving. As discussed, we can't count on it to lead our plans."

"What do you mean?" Serah asked.

"If I told you guys that *you would surely* die if you followed me, you might have stayed. If you had stayed, we would have met heavier resistance on our way to Warden Prime. But since I *didn't* warn you, you had the boldness to go your own way."

"Damn right we did," Mira said.

"That's a good thing, but it also proves something important. While delving the future is a useful tool, it has blind spots. It helped get us where we are, but we can't rely on it completely. With that said, here's how I'm reading the situation here. We have two goals. The first is to stop the Swarmers from destroying humanity. That's obvious enough. And the second is to return the Orbs to the Heart of Creation. That should solve the first goal, except we have no idea where the First Gate is. That's what we have to find if we're going to stop the Swarmers at the source. After all, they were sent here by the Ascendant Beings to get the Orbs back. They won't stop until they accomplish their goal."

Everyone at the table was watching him. Their expressions showed no one knew where to start.

"We have something of a lead," Lucian said.

"Silumko, right?" Emma asked.

Lucian was surprised she had guessed it. "Yeah. How did you know I was going to say that?"

"I still remember what you told us about him. He said you'd know the way to the First Gate as soon as you gathered the Orbs, right?"

And like that, the conversation came back to him. Emma's words triggered other memories. "Yeah, that's right. He said once I had the Orbs, the Seven-Sealed Path would reveal itself."

"What is this Seven-Sealed Path?" Fergus asked. "I don't remember that bit."

"Silumko said something about the Seven-Sealed Path showing the way. I assume that means it would lead to the First Gate."

His mother asked the obvious question. "Well . . . have you tried looking for it?"

Lucian cleared his throat. "No. Not yet."

"Well, what are you waiting for, boy?" Jagar asked, his expression one of disbelief. "This could be the key to everything!"

"Right now?"

"Yes," Emma said. "Is it dangerous or something?"

"I don't see why it would be," he said, standing and reaching for his Focus. "Let me see if I can sense something."

Everyone watched him as he reached for every Orb and streamed their collective power into his Focus. Immediately, Lucian was elevated to the Ether, where he could see the magic flowing around him, coalescing as a single eddying path in a rainbow of colors. Armed with all Eight Orbs, he could see that the ether flow wasn't random. He'd never considered detecting from what direction the ether was flowing.

For the first time, he realized it was all streaming from one direction. The First Gate, from which all ether entered the Shadow Realm.

This was it, he realized. The Seven-Sealed Path.

He reached along it as far as he could, the grasp of his Focus crossing hundreds of light-years through dozens of Gates. By the time he'd reached the extent of his influence to some nameless world deep in Dark Space, he could draw no more ether. However, he could see that the Path *still* hadn't ended.

The First Gate was far. Much farther than he could have possibly imagined. The prospect filled him with a horrible despondence.

There was no way he could make it there in time. Even if they went on the fastest spaceship, it would be years before they arrived.

Lucian released his Focus and returned to the Shadow Realm. After the brightness of the Ether, this reality seemed dark and grim indeed. Everyone must have seen his disappointment, because no one was saying a word.

"I . . . saw it," he finally managed. "I followed it as far as I could. Well over a hundred Gates, with no end in sight."

He went quiet, watching everyone's reaction as they collectively reached the same realization. Even if it was "only" a hundred Gates, and they had the fastest ship ever created, the journey would take years to accomplish.

They didn't have years. They had months and probably not even that. Now that Lucian held all the Orbs, the Swarmers would redouble their efforts to destroy humanity. He would become a target, just like the First and Second Immortal.

But unlike those two, he was committed to giving up his power if it meant the salvation of humanity.

"There's no way around it," Lucian said. "The journey to the First Gate will take years. And since I don't have a memory, it's not like I can portal to it. The farthest world I can reach is Nai Shairen, which would only save six months. Whatever the case, there's no way we can save Earth *and* return the Orbs on time. It's physically impossible."

The silence stretched. It didn't feel like it could be true.

"There *has* to be a way," Serah said, breaking the silence. "Why can't you talk to Silumko? Maybe they'll be willing to have a truce if they know you have all the Orbs and want to return them."

"Yeah," Fergus said. "You've been on his ship before. Why not just warp there and talk to him?"

"Wait a second," Mira said. "If they're hunting for the Orbs, wouldn't their natural reaction be to take them? I won't have Lucian be put in that kind of danger."

"It would be dangerous," Lucian agreed. "All it would take is one mistake. The First and Second Immortals fell to the *Alkasen* eventually and had the same powers I do. Warping right into that ship would be risky, especially if Silumko is hostile. He only refrained from attacking last time because his best hope of finding the Orbs was to let me and Xara duke it out. We did, and I ended up winning. Now, all bets are off." Lucian paused as another point came to him. "Hell, that ship might not even *exist* anymore, for all we know. And, of course, Silumko might not even be on it."

"If not that, then what?" Fergus asked. "I just don't see any other option."

Lucian didn't have an answer for that. He supposed anything was worth a try, even if talking to Silumko was risky. Hell, it was probably a suicide mission.

But Fergus was right. They needed answers, and Lucian couldn't think of a better person to ask than Silumko.

"I'll do it," Lucian said.

Mira looked at him worriedly. "Lucian . . ."

Lucian realized she didn't want him to go, but she couldn't stop him. She could only hope he knew what he was doing.

Lucian saw the fear in her eyes as much as the concern. She realized he wasn't just her son anymore, but a man of his own. He was someone she could no longer protect. It was hard letting go, remembering that he had to make his own decisions.

And maybe that was why she never finished her sentence.

She cleared her throat. "We . . . can run things while you're gone. Just introduce me to the men, and I can take care of things here."

Lucian nodded, his resolve firm. "One other thing. We need a system of organization for the mages. A Mage Division. I touched on it briefly already, but we have representatives for practically every Aspect around this table. Maybe everyone here can be the leader in their primary Aspect. Something that can integrate with the Wardens seamlessly to create a new fighting force. We would be the members of the Mage Council, in charge of that division."

"Like the Transcends, only different," Emma said.

"I mean . . . *not* like them," Lucian said. "Okay, maybe a *little* like them, but less stuffy."

"Transcend Serah," Serah said. "That just sounds wrong." She paused a moment, considering. "So, is this really what we're calling ourselves now? The Mage Division?"

"Well, we *are* building an army and navy, are we not?" Fergus said. "It would make sense to separate the mages from the non-mages. Mage Division is simple and right to the point. Each Aspect would be considered a brigade. These brigades would comprise mages and non-combatant support staff, such as medics, engineers, logistical support, et cetera. Anything to service the mages and get them what they need. There could be a brigade for each Aspect, and altogether, they would make up the Mage Division."

"Exactly," Lucian said. "And I want everyone around this table to be the leader of one of these brigades. You guys are the only ones I can trust. As for titles, maybe just Chief Radiant or whatever your Aspect is."

"Make sure that rank is higher than anything in the Wardens," Serah said. "I wouldn't want someone like Carthen thinking he could boss me around."

"That's a good point," Lucian said. "Of course, the Mage Division would be separate from every other part of the navy's organization. Every chief would be fully autonomous, answering only to me."

"So, I would be Chief Gravitist?" Serah asked. "I can live with that." Her face suddenly brightened. "Does that mean I get to be the boss of all the other Gravitists?"

"Yes. You'll be the highest-ranking Gravitist in the fleet. Selene would be the highest-ranking Atomicist. And so on."

"We're still missing Aspects, though," Fergus said. "We don't have a Chief Thermalist, Dynamist, or Binder, for example."

"Yeah," Emma said. "Fergus and I are Radiants, so who will get the role of Chief?"

"Maybe the two of you can duel for it," Serah said.

"No, none of that," Lucian said. "I didn't think this part through, did I?"

"Well, I don't want to be in charge of *anything*," Emma said. "I still consider myself a Talent of the Volsung Academy first. If I were to take on a new role, I would break my oath."

"What oath?" Serah asked. "Transcend White didn't require me to give an oath."

"Probably out of expediency more than anything," Fergus said.

Emma nodded. "Yes. Upon ascension, every Talent must give an oath to the Transcends and the League of Worlds. That she didn't require it of you means you aren't *technically* Talents. You may have been entered as Talents to avoid committing

"I know just who to ask," Lucian said.

"Plato?" Emma asked.

Lucian nodded. "With luck, he hasn't taken his Talent vows yet."

"And what about Linus?" Serah asked. "Seems unfair that *he* wouldn't get a position."

Truthfully, Lucian couldn't imagine Linus wanting to have a position of authority. While he was content with his role as mayor of the Isle of Madness, that wasn't an actual job. He was always more interested in watching holos than anything else. Besides, Serah already had the Chief Gravitist position.

"I'm sure we can find something for him if he wants it," Lucian said diplomatically.

"That leaves a Binder," Fergus said. "And no one here is a natural at that."

"I can take the role for now," Lucian said. "I have a lot of experience with Binding. It might as well be my natural primary. We can have them take the job when we find a suitable replacement."

"One more thing," Fergus said. "We also have a new Aspect of Magic to consider."

From the expressions on everyone's faces, it seemed everyone had forgotten that not-so-minor detail.

"That begs the question," Emma said. "Has anyone tried to use Space-Time Magic yet?"

Heads shook all around.

"What if someone *else* discovers it?" Serah asked. "Some other mages, I mean. That could be a disaster!"

"They won't know to look if they don't know it's there," Lucian said. "We have yet to let that cat out of the bag. There's still a lot we don't understand about Space-Time Magic. It takes a *lot* of ether to pull off. And the streams are far from simple. It's impossible to say how it'll affect things, at least for now. Either way, the fact that it exists should never leave this room."

"People will find out about it soon enough," Fergus said. "Count on it."

"Well," Emma said, "how can we prepare for that eventuality?"

"First," Fergus said, "maybe each of us can try to access it. Arian said it would spread once Lucian had all the Orbs. It would be best to confirm that fact."

"I agree," Lucian agreed. "But it'll have to wait until later."

"Going after Silumko?" Fergus asked.

"Yes. But first, I need to announce my mom's promotion." He turned to Mira. "I'll order Carthen and Warwick to gather the officers, and then you can introduce yourself."

"Still not too late to change your mind," Mira said.

"You're thinking about it too much," Lucian said. "You're perfect for the role."

"All right," she said, not entirely convinced. "Let's do this."

12

ALL THE WARDEN officers had gathered in the main mustering hall. Mira stood next to Lucian, dressed in her gray admiral's uniform. Carthen had printed a new insignia to be donned on her lapel, a circle of five stars set above a shining sun. The symbol was that of a fleet admiral, the highest rank in any navy in the Worlds. The sun represented Sol, the home system of humanity. Though they were far from Sol, Lucian still found the symbol fitting. It is what they would protect in the coming months.

The hundreds of officers in their ranks and files stood respectfully silent, looking smart in their gray uniforms and long ceremonial silk coats. Mira stood proudly as Lucian pinned the five-star insignia on her lapel. A murmur rippled through the officers then ebbed. She nodded as if accepting an impossibly heavy weight the tiny symbol bore.

"Congratulations, Fleet Admiral," Lucian said.

Mira's expression became even sterner. In her new uniform, she looked every inch an admiral. It was not just the uniform but her bearing, as if she had been born to it.

Lucian turned to the troops arrayed before him. "From now on, you will answer directly to Admiral Abrantes. She is at the top of the chain; the only person she answers to is me. She can organize the navy as she sees fit, including promoting new officers." *That should motivate them to lick her boots.* He nodded toward his mother. "You had something to say, Admiral Abrantes?"

She gave a curt nod. "Thank you, Sorcerer-Ascendant." She turned to face the crowd of officers, and every man and woman stood at even sharper attention. "I'm Admiral Mira Abrantes. Why should you follow me? I can give you a list of reasons, but words don't mean a damn thing. Anybody can say words. I will show you with my actions that I'm worthy of being followed. I've seen action in every Swarmer War there's ever been and have fought in multiple engagements. I served as a captain on the *UNS Barcelona*, a League heavy destroyer, and the *UNS Refuge*, a League carrier, both of which were destroyed at the Battle of Alpha Centauri."

Some officers shifted their feet at that. It had been the first significant engagement of the current war and had a heavy loss of life.

"I was presumed dead, but survived in an escape pod. I made my way back to civilization. I'm now here with my son, the Sorcerer-Ascendant. I have led many brave men and women, first as an ensign and then as a lieutenant, a captain, and a fleet commander."

Lucian knew the last role was no League rank, so it must have been during her time with the Golden Armada. None of the officers seemed to raise an eyebrow at it.

Mira continued. "And now, I sit before you as a fleet admiral. I am ready and willing to serve this fledging navy and see it soar. My orders will be backed up by years of experience. I've always served on the front lines, never from behind a desk. I

While there were no discernible doors in the white walls surrounding him, Lucian remembered the walls would "retract" circularly, allowing him to pass. With this in mind, he walked toward the carrier's stern, holding his Focus so that he would be ready to stream at a moment's notice. For good measure, he willed Lightspear into his hand. Its ethereal light formed and solidified, stretching about two meters from base to tip. Lucian strengthened his seven-sealed shield, making him all but impervious to magical attacks. Lightspear would deal with whatever resistance there was.

As he thought, the wall retracted as soon as he approached, creating a circular hole through which to pass. A long corridor was revealed, a passage that seemed to stretch down the ship's entire length, no less than a kilometer. There were no doors or openings on either side. If Lucian wanted to explore the ship, he'd have to guess where the gaps would emerge.

Lucian had only taken a few steps when the corridor ahead closed off. Not a second later, it also closed from behind. Meanwhile, a side passage opened up, revealing four gray robed *Alkasen* warrior mages bearing shockspears alight with electricity. They were the same beings that had attacked them on Mako and Nai Elyn, long-limbed, with grayish blue skin and a heavy brow ridge bearing small horns. But what caught Lucian's attention were the eyes, violet-tinged, as if they were under Psionic possession.

Lucian turned to face them just as the closest *Alkasen* sprang into action, thrusting his spear with lightning speed. But Lucian was ready, phasing to his left and cutting the being down as he transitioned. Two fireballs were absorbed by his shield and redirected into his ether pool. Lucian twirled with his weapon, meeting no resistance as he sliced another two warriors straight through the abdomen.

One *Alkasen* was left, his robe billowing as he cradled a ball of energy. He had gathered that magic during the fight, using Binding and Dynamism, while the others took the hits. As Lucian strode forward, the being let out a garbled cry and released a mighty fork of lightning. The electricity sizzled toward Lucian, but Lucian merely raised Lightspear, absorbing the magic. He redirected it back toward the *Alkasen's* chest. It overpowered the being's flimsy shield, instantly disintegrating him into a pile of smoking ash.

Lucian waited, sensing all around him with Radiance. There were more mages on the ship. *Hundreds* of them, all of which were lurking behind the walls in hidden corridors.

Just as he was about to begin his hunt for the rest, every wall around him retracted, revealing a vast space that probably took up the entire area of the ship, at least a thousand meters in all directions. And in that space were dozens of *Alkasen* with shockspears at the ready and, to Lucian's shock, an equal number of humans with violet-glowing eyes. They also held shockspears and were surrounded by magical auras that told Lucian they were mages.

Lucian had no time to question, because every single one attacked Lucian at the same time. He used all his available ether to strengthen his shield. Lucian became one with Lightspear and his Focus. He didn't think. He *acted*, dodging, striking, and phasing any time his shield needed a break to recharge. His mind became divorced from the act of killing as dozens fell to his ethereal weapon. Magic assailed him on all sides, but Lucian's shield never wavered. With the Orbs, they stood no chance against him, even if there were well over a hundred. He was practically a god in the Ether, using sorcery and the Orbs.

Time seemed to stretch, and Lucian fought until he was the only one left, standing alone in a white space filled with dead *Alkasen* and humans. He saw that the blood of the Ancients flowed red just like theirs.

He turned, sensing someone behind him.

The Emissary was much the same, tall and imposing, with scaly blue skin and a flowing white robe, on which the Septagon was decorated, including the Aspect of Space-Time in its middle. A golden cape stretched to the deck below him, just short of being soiled with blood. He held an intricate scepter in his right hand, which gave off an aura of ethereal light. It regarded Lucian with red, slitlike eyes, seeming to judge him intensely for the slaughter he had caused.

"Chosen," Silumko said grimly. "We meet again."

13

THERE WAS a long moment as the two sized each other up. It had been about half a year since their meeting in the space above Nai Elyn, though it seemed much longer to Lucian.

Lucian decided the best action was to get right to the point.

"I've done what you've asked, Silumko. I've found the Eight Orbs and the Seven-Sealed Path. The path is so long that it will take at least a couple of years to reach the First Gate. Maybe longer."

Silumko watched Lucian, a silent sentinel.

"By the time we reach the First Gate, the *Alkasen* will have killed humanity. So tell me. Why should I return them? Why not take everything I have, all my power, and use it to fight back against you?"

The Emissary continued to regard him silently.

"Nothing?" Lucian asked. "I've done the impossible, and you have *nothing* to say?"

Silumko's voice escaped his long, solemn face, deeply resonant. "What would you have me say, Chosen? Do you want my congratulations? My praise?"

"Yes. The Manifold will die if this continues. If the Manifold dies, so does the Light Realm. It ceases to exist as if it never was. And, of course, if the Light Realm dies, so will this one. A higher dimension casts your reality. If the higher dimension goes away, the shadow also disappears. This may take only a century, or it could take eons. It may even happen today, for all we know. But it *will* happen, given time. It is inevitable."

"Our scientists already say the universe is going to die out someday. Death isn't anything new to us."

"A foolish notion. The universe doesn't die out, Lucian; it is an iteration of infinite cycles. Eternity lies ahead of us. As well, eternity lies behind us. How many loops have we gone through? How many realities? How many times have we had this conversation? None can say."

"I don't understand," Lucian said. "The Oracle Rhana talked about the Starsea Cycle. Is that what you're referring to?"

"I hid this knowledge from you before, but now that you've proven yourself, you must understand things from our point of view. Why we're attacking you, and what you can do to stop it."

"That's all I want."

"The difference is this. The Starsea Cycle can be thought of as the Cycle of Magic. The cycle is active when at least one Orb is held in the Focus of at least one mage. When no Orbs are held, the Cycle is defunct. This is simple enough to understand. But I'm speaking of something greater, something you can think of as the Cycle of Creation. The purpose of the Heart of Creation is to instigate the Cycle of Creation, to keep reality from dying. To do this, the Heart requires the Seven Orbs and a sufficient amount of ether. You can think of the Orbs as the keys to the Heart. Instructions and intelligence, if you will, which ether will obey. This intelligence becomes yours, and it's how you know how to perform advanced magic without prior training. More than that, when you hold an Orb, ether obeys you as if *you* were the Heart of Creation, at least regarding that Aspect. Ether flows toward the Orbs, sensing the power of the Orb-holder; this is how, when you hold the Seven Orbs, you can sense the Seven-Fold Path. You merely have to follow the opposite direction of ether flow. When you hold all Seven, the path is harmonized."

"What about the Orb of Space-Time, then?" Lucian said. "Is it not required to follow the Path? To keep the Manifold from dying?"

"That Orb . . . is a special case. I will speak no more of it. It's not for you to know. Not now."

"What do you mean?"

"There is knowledge I have been allowed to say and knowledge that must remain hidden. The knowledge you're asking must be sought from one higher than me."

"Your masters, then. The Ascendants. As if that's ever going to happen."

Silumko was silent at that point. Lucian wondered if he should force the information out with Psionics, but something told him Silumko would be prepared for that. Besides, that action might be interpreted as dishonoring their temporary truce, undermining the chance of peace, however slim.

So, Lucian did the only thing he could do. He thought about the information, doing his best to absorb it. Everything about it made sense, and he felt many connections being made. The Manifold was almost like a living thing; ether was the blood, the Heart of Creation the heart, and the Orbs the intelligence directing it all. The Heart cycled ether through the Light Realm, which held reality together. But the First Gate was a wound through which ether escaped, like air from a breached spaceship. Even if the overall breach was minor, it could purge the Light Realm of ether over a long enough time.

Considering this realization, some of the Ascendants' motivations made sense. This madness would not end until the Orbs were returned.

"I still don't understand one thing," Lucian said. "If I know what I'm supposed to do, why are you attacking me? Wouldn't that mean we're on the same side?"

"Unfortunately, it's not so simple. I represent the Ascendants. They do not believe in the Chosen's ability to complete his appointed task. The First Immortal stole the Orbs from the Heart, while the second clung to power. Perhaps you are different. Even now, the Heart is the calling, and it is up to the Chosen to answer, no matter the circumstances."

"So you want me to abandon humanity when it needs me the most? Do you want me to let billions of people die, all for a shot of returning the Orbs? Maybe a few people might hide out for a few years and survive. But most would die because of the *Alkasen*." Lucian remembered the Preserved human mages he had just fought. "Or worse."

"Returning them is the *only* choice."

"I refuse to believe that. Otherwise, what am I fighting for?"

"You already prove the Ascendants' fears are valid. Why would they ever believe you would do the right thing? First, you must give up your power. That is hard enough. But you would also have to give up on magic existing in your reality. Magic, which your society depends on, *especially* regarding the Gates. If they cease to function, the collapse of interstellar trade will consign millions, if not billions, to death. If those millions or billions exist by the time you finish your task. In your case, you would never know the answer to that. Another impediment to you doing the right thing. And finally, you would have to give up your life, at least in this reality. Of course, you will have no means of escape as soon as you pass through the First Gate and into the Light Realm."

Silumko watched Lucian closely for a reaction. With everything laid out before him like that, Lucian understood the dilemma. It was a lot to sacrifice, all for an idea that was, on its face, quite difficult to grasp. After all, all he had was Silumko's word that all this was true. Lucian's hunch was that it *was* true. If so, sacrificing almost everything to return the Orbs would doom billions to death and lead to his demise.

Who had a will strong enough to see that through?

"I think I get it now," Lucian answered. "It's a lot to ask. You have no way of knowing if I'll go through with it. No way of trusting me."

Silumko nodded. "If I had a thousand mages and my fleets with me, we would not even be having this talk. I would have killed you long ago."

"And you would be the one to return the Orbs?"

"Yes. Assuming I survived the encounter. Of course, I have my own will, but it cannot supersede the Ascendant Beings' holy mandate."

"Why share any of this with me at all?"

"One simple reason. Despite the mandate of my masters, you have endured many tribulations. So many that there is the possibility, as slight as it is, that the *Alkasen* cannot stop you. So, I want you to know these things if you somehow emerge victorious from this impossible war. I wish to be the voice of reason when you stray from the proper path. It is probably pointless, but it is better than not saying anything."

That made a strange sort of sense. Silumko made no move to leave, so Lucian decided that now might be the time to learn more.

"Tell me more about the *Alkasen*. How did you get humans to fight for you? Human mages, no less. And how are you still alive after so long?"

"The *Alkasen* is not just a single race. We make up a greater whole. The Preserved are *Alkasen* mages who hold the Bond of Unity."

"The Bond of Unity?"

"A Psionic brand, potent and impervious to all Psionic interference. Every Preserved has one, including me. It is magic from the Light Realm, given to us by the Ascendants. The Bond awakens us when at least one Orb is held in the Focus of at least one mage."

"You awaken when the Starsea Cycle is active," Lucian said in realization. "Which means you would have woken up when Arian held the Orb of Space-Time all those years ago." He frowned. "Wait. Where were you for all those years that magic was dead?"

"We sleep in a sort of stasis. Our minds. Our bodies. Our fleets. This stasis is controlled by the Bond and cannot reach outside our bodies."

"Arian found the Orb of Space-Time about two centuries ago," Lucian said. "A little less than that, come to think of it. What took you guys so long to find us?"

"We knew where you were," Silumko said. "We can sense the Orbs when they are being held. After a million of our years, our fleets from the Age of Starsea had disintegrated into dust. We had to rebuild an entire society in the place you call Dark Space. It took us many decades, but in the end, we rebuilt in sufficient numbers to ensure our victory, even against a potential Third Immortal who had gathered all Eight Orbs." Silumko looked at him intensely with his red eyes. "Against you, Chosen."

"Then why not just end us in the First and Second Swarmer Wars?" Lucian asked. "You could have eradicated us."

"For two reasons. Those minor invasions were sent to test your strength and abilities. And the second reason is more important. The Orbs were lost to us. From the awakening of the

Starsea Cycle, we knew it was only a matter of time before the Chosen would come and gather the Orbs. Such was in the Prophecy of the Seven, known to us in the Age of Starsea. The Prophecy that impelled the Last Vigilants to become the Seven Oracles."

Lucian understood all this, though it was bewildering. It was unsettling to imagine the *Alkasen* going into stasis for hundreds of thousands of years, then rebuilding their fleet to find the Orbs. All of this was made possible by the Bond of Unity. That Bond "preserved" the *Alkasen*, the Servants of Light, to ensure they never failed in their mission to find the Orbs.

"What is your history, then?" Lucian asked. "Are you the leader of the *Alkasen*?"

"Over one million of your years ago, I was born. I fought under the banner of the Second Immortal as a Lower Admiral in his Infinite Armada." His throat gave a strange, low warble. "I was at the Battle of Holy Xama, the first of the Core Worlds to fall. Victory seemed inevitable, but internal rebellions significantly weakened us. Pushed by the *Alkasen* on the outside and torn by uprisings within, the Immortal Emperor fell. And with his fall, what hope we had of standing against the *Alkasen* perished. The First Vigilants, the Emperor's closest sycophants, each claimed one of his Orbs. Our fleets might have been a match for the *Alkasen* were it not for the Bond of Unity. Our ships, mages, and soldiers became theirs. Even with all this, we beat back the first wave over five of your years. But by then, Starsea was ill-prepared to survive the coming darkness. Many kingdoms arose from the empire's carcass, feebly and pointlessly fighting for a few centuries more. Orbs traded hands, the Madness became rampant among the mages, and billions more died. Even without the return of the *Alkasen*, a second wave far mightier than the first, the Ancients would have destroyed each other." Silumko stood silently for a moment. "Of course, as you know, the *Alkasen* never got what they sought. Rather than let them have the Orbs, the Seven Vigilants agreed to protect them, inspired by a mutual prophecy from the Manifold that you know as the Prophecy of the Seven. Following the prophecy, they imparted their Focuses into each of their Orbs. This action killed them, but it allowed what few *Alkasen* remained to survive. For with the silence of the Orbs, the *Alkasen* slept. Their lot was to await the Chosen of the Manifold, as spoken by the Prophecy."

"If the Manifold gave them the Prophecy, it must not have wanted the *Alkasen* to find the Orbs."

"Something I've thought of, too. Many times. But the Manifold is above even the Ascendants; who knows what it wants? It is pointless to speculate on its goals. Indeed, it doesn't *have* any. The Manifold merely responds to the will of its supplicants, they being the mages and sorcerers."

That reminded Lucian of something Vera had told him long ago, along with Lakhmu: that belief made magic. The Manifold responded to one's truth. That was the essence of sorcery, the highest kind of magic.

"Tell me more about the Bond of Unity."

"The Ascendant Beings devised the Bond to ensure the loyalty of the Servants of Light, not just their preservation. Such was their desperate need to obtain the Orbs. They feared that if the *Alkasen* found them, they would want to keep them out of lust for power. This was not an idle fear, given the behavior of every mage who has ever gained an Orb. The Bond serves two purposes. The first is to protect the mind of any *Alkasen* who happens upon an Orb so they would not keep it. And second, to spread itself to every sentient creature, making them a part of the *Alkasen* collective whole."

"Collective whole," Lucian said. "So the Bond unites the

Alkasen?"

Silumko nodded. "Yes. That is why there are humans here. Our Preserved spread the Bond of Unity to conquered worlds. Humans who can't use magic join our fleets and invasion forces. The process is not instant, of course; it takes a few months of your time for the transition to complete."

"These weren't just humans, though," Lucian said. "They were mages."

"The Bond also can awaken the Focus in any sentient who has the potential," Silumko said. "Far more are capable of magic than you realize; they merely will never have their powers emerge naturally. In short, the Bond is an advanced Psionic brand, a sorcery of the Light Realm that cannot be undone from within the Shadow Realm. You might do so, as the Chosen holding the Orbs. But even for you, it would not be easy."

"So there are the Preserved, which are your mages. And then there is everyone who isn't a mage."

"We call them the Devoted. Whether Preserved or Devoted, all who carry the Bond are *Alkasen*. None is greater or lesser than the other. Of course, there are other complexities and roles, but that will suffice for an explanation." Silumko's red eyes seemed to narrow. "In short, there is no hope for you or your race, Chosen. The numbers against you are unimaginable. Already, the Bond of Unity spreads like a virus. Millions have been absorbed by now, including those with the spark of magical potential. Millions more will join our ranks before the end."

"You're nothing more than a slave, then."

"You can think that way if you wish. We cannot do anything against the Ascendant Beings' will. That includes keeping the Orbs for ourselves, giving up our mission, or even ending our lives. But there is one comfort. Although the Bond of Unity makes us immortal, our thralldom is only temporary."

"What do you mean?"

Silumko stared at Lucian with his red, unblinking eyes. "When the Orbs are returned, the *Alkasen* will be released from the Bond."

Lucian got the sense that Silumko very much looked forward to that day. If he had been alive for a million years, or *Preserved*, Lucian supposed losing the Bond might be a relief, especially when it meant freedom. It was an incredible incentive to find the Orbs and return them. It also explained why the *Alkasen* fought with such ferocity. If Lucian had been enslaved for a million years, he would want nothing more than to be on the front lines, hoping to get taken out by railgun fire.

"Well," Lucian said, "I tried to make peace."

Again, Silumko gave that strange, low warble of his. "Between our two kinds—Light and Shadow—there can only be war. We of the Light will not consider this done until the Orbs have been returned to the Heart of Creation. It's simple as that." Silumko gave a gracious bow. "We will meet again, Lucian. Above the skies of Earth."

Before Lucian could say anything more, at that very moment, Silumko was surrounded by a black aura of Space-Time Magic, then was gone.

Lucian just stared at the space Silumko had occupied, an icy dread overtaking him. It proved what he and his friends had long feared: Space-Time Magic was now useable by anyone with the power to stream it.

He reached out in the vain hope he could trace the Emissary's path. But after a moment, there was nothing to detect. He was the only one left aboard this vessel, not counting the dead.

Lucian had learned some new things, but those new things only led to more questions. He was especially curious about the

Orb of Space-Time and why Silumko had said it was a special case. There was more, but he would not learn the answer today.

It was hard for Lucian to absorb the horror of it all. The *Alkasen* were not destroying humanity; they were *absorbing* it, just as they had the Ancients. As Silumko had mentioned, the *Alkasen* had to number in the millions by now. Perhaps even in the *billions*. By now, the Swarmers had taken over dozens of League planets, not to mention the Ancient Worlds from a million years ago. And who knew just how many of *them* there were? It was an empire of a thousand suns, making it many times larger than the League of Worlds.

He couldn't just stand here speculating. He had to get back to the others.

14

AS SOON AS LUCIAN RETURNED, he gathered the Mage Council and explained everything he had learned from Silumko. Only his mother was absent, since she was getting the Wardens ready to land on Psyche. He recorded the conversation on his slate to send to her later.

Once finished, everyone remained silent as they considered the news.

Serah was the first to speak. "It'll be war, then. I'm thinking these Ascendants are the bad guys."

"That goes without saying," Emma said. "Although I'm more worried about what Silumko said about the Bond of Unity."

"The question is, how to stop it?" Fergus asked.

Everyone waited for Lucian's response, as if *he* knew the answer. But he was just as worried as them. The potential of a few *Alkasen* converting entire worlds was nothing short of terrifying, especially if spreading the Bond caused new mages to be born. Mages that would be loyal to the Ascendants rather than humanity.

"If what Silumko said is true," Selene said, "then even Starsea and the Ancients couldn't stand victorious against the *Alkasen*. If they lost, what hope do *we* have?"

He didn't need to be reminded of how stacked the odds were against them. Selene had a knack for telling the truth to the point of extreme bluntness. He didn't want that despondence to infect the rest of the Council.

He didn't blame her for saying it. On its face, this *was* a pointless war. They were so outnumbered that Lucian wouldn't have been surprised if humanity got destroyed within a matter of months. Starsea, at least, had held on for five years.

Selene pressed on. "There is one other thing that confuses me. The Swarmers, or *Alkasen*, seem to be an amalgamation of anyone controlled by this Bond of Unity. *Someone* controls the Bond itself and anyone possessed by it. The question is, who?"

"The Ascendants," Serah said. "That much is obvious, right?"

"Not necessarily," Selene said. "They are in the Light Realm, after all. It would have to be powerful magic indeed for a few of them to control millions upon millions of soldiers, even if they are godlike. I have a theory some of that power is delegated a bit. Perhaps the being that spreads the Bond is in charge of whoever they convert. That incentivizes them to keep spreading it because it would build their power."

"That makes sense," Fergus said. "For now, though, the theory needs testing."

"Of course," Selene said. "Just thought I would offer my thoughts."

Lucian also thought the idea intriguing, but Fergus was right. It was just speculation until it was proven fact. "One thing I know. Silumko said the Bond is required for someone to become *Alkasen*. There are the Devoted and the Preserved. The

Preserved, the mages, seem to have a higher ranking, despite Silumko saying they are all equal."

"That makes sense," Fergus said. "And you said there were over a *hundred* on that ship? And they all attacked you at the same time?"

Lucian nodded, trying not to think about it too much. "I had my shield set with every Aspect. Lightspear took care of the rest."

Though Lucian didn't go into further detail, it was clear from the blanching of the others' faces that he didn't need to.

He changed the subject. "There's still a lot we don't know, and I don't know how to find out more. It's up to us to figure out the rest."

"One thing we *do* know," Emma said. "Space-Time Magic is possible to stream. At least by Silumko and possibly any mage who has an affinity for the Aspect."

There was a long, almost solemn, silence after this as everyone thought of the implications. The *Alkasen* could use Space-Time Magic and were aware of its existence. Lucian couldn't help but imagine these "Preserved" creating portals at will, showing up where they were least expected. Entire fleets could travel instantly, perhaps even to Earth. All the Swarmers would have to do was send a single Preserved scout to form a memory of a particular location. That scout could return to its fleet and, using that memory, create a portal for the entire fleet. It meant bypassing the Gates was possible. It made static defenses worthless, such as Starbase Centauri and Sol Citadel. Even fleets would be useless if they were out of position. The whole point of a fleet was to destroy an enemy fleet. How could wars be waged if fleets could jump past each other without being bottlenecked by the Gates or fuel reserves?

It was a terrifying future. A future humanity might not live to see.

"There is one consolation, backed up by my experience," Lucian said. "Space-Time Magic is difficult to stream, and it becomes even more complicated when creating portals to move entire fleets. Simply, even a powerful mage can't make a giant portal capable of transitioning something as immense as a Swarmer carrier across light-years of space. Yes, Silumko can warp, but that was just him, and he had time to gather ether during our conversation."

"What about mages working in confluence?" Emma asked.

Lucian nodded. "That's what I was about to say. To create fleet portals, the ones we have to worry about, the *Alkasen* would have to pool dozens, if not hundreds, of Preserved. The amount of ether required to make a portal like that would take hours, if not days. I can do it easily because I have the Orb of Space-Time, but even I feel the strain. It depends on portal size and distance."

He looked around at the table before him, at their worried faces. He had hoped to allay their fears, but just the fact that it was possible was sobering. The *Alkasen* would use the tool as soon as possible.

Serah sighed. "We're so screwed, aren't we?"

Selene nodded. "For all we know, the Swarmer armada could be surrounding Earth right now. Space-Time Magic is one of our key advantages. Knowing the enemy can do it too is more than a bit concerning."

"Perhaps it can be defended against with a ward," Emma said. "Is there any reason to think it *couldn't* be?"

"None that I'm aware of," Lucian said. "Perhaps if you had enough Space-Time mages, you could make a ward strong enough to make it impossible for another mage to warp into it. That would be a way to protect our forces. Honestly, I'm more worried about a few Preserved warping and causing mayhem.

That's far more possible to do than the massive fleets jumping around all over the place. It would keep our fleet and soldiers safe if we can ward against that."

"Makes sense," Fergus said. "We just have to find out if it's possible."

"We need to test things out, for sure," Lucian said. "And we also need to find out who is capable of Space-Time Magic. That goes for everyone around this table and the mages on Psyche."

Emma nodded. "We should find out who's capable of doing it."

"Add it to the list," Serah said. "I know this is probably the wrong reaction, but I'm pretty stoked to try it out! I've always been jealous of Lucian's abilities."

Lucian remembered what Serah had said back on Psyche. If she had the power, she would change the past and bring people back to life. Hopefully, she hadn't *really* meant that, because Lucian didn't know if that would change *their* reality. Time Magic was not something he wanted to toy with. He'd done so a few times, but the scope had been limited. Lucian didn't even want to think of the implications of jumping around in time, forward or backward, causing chaos. For all he knew, it would require an impossibly large amount of ether, even for him.

"We'll figure out this Space-Time stuff later," Lucian said. "There's one last thing we have to consider. I want to go to *Resplendent* to recruit Linus, Plato, and Khairu for the Council. That would mean talking to Transcend White and getting her blessing."

"You think she would go for that?" Serah asked.

"If I explained things, yes. It would be great to get the entire Volsung Academy on our side. Besides, I need to tell her about the Orbs and Xara Mallis. She will be interested to know."

"That's true," Emma said. "That would be good for *every* mage to know. Not just the mages, but the entire League of

Worlds. It would do a lot to unite the mages and non-mages against the Swarmers, with you as the leader. The Sorcerer-Ascendant."

Lucian nodded. "The fraying is over, which opens up many possibilities with magic that weren't there before. The first one we share this with should be the Transcends. They might have already figured it out, but we can help them make sense of it."

"As for myself," Fergus said, "I immediately noticed the difference when fighting on Warden Prime. I could draw ether far more quickly than before."

"I've noticed the same thing," Emma said. "As incredible as it is, we must remember that magic is still dangerous."

"It's a miracle," Selene said. "Something I would have never dreamed possible!"

"I wonder," Emma said. "What's happened to the mages who have already shown signs of fraying? Will they heal?"

"That's a good question," Lucian said. "I'm sure we'll find out soon. After all, there are probably many mages on the surface of Psyche who are frayed. But back to the subject of the Volsung Mages. I want to enter a treaty with them. The Irion mages, too. Despite our differences, the mutual survival of humanity is our most important concern. Magekind needs to be united. A single force to counter the thousands of Preserved the *Alkasen* surely have."

"Behind *you*, you mean," Selene said.

Lucian nodded. "Yes. I never thought I'd be the leader of anything, but I'm the Chosen of the Manifold. If not me, then who?"

"You misunderstand me," Selene said. "You shouldn't be shy about taking charge. As you said, you are the Chosen of the Manifold. You hold the Orbs. We need to follow the person who has power. That's you."

The others nodded their agreement.

"If I may speak on the Irion Mages," Fergus said. "Despite Vassar's and my history, I have friends there. And being where they are in the Border Worlds, they are under direct threat from the Swarmers. It's only a matter of time before they're overrun if they haven't been already."

"Irion *is* a Border World," Emma agreed. "They can't have much time left."

"Let's figure out the situation with the Volsung mages first," Lucian said. "But of course, we'll rescue Irion, too. I want to complete this Council first. That way, we can organize the mages on Psyche. The Chief of each Aspect will be in charge of that Aspect for potentially hundreds of mages. The chain must be established to gain control."

"We still don't know if they'll want to be on the Council," Fergus said.

"That's why we need to move soon," Lucian said.

Fergus chuckled. "I never imagined it would turn out like this when I left Kiro Village. All this trouble over a few shiny stones."

Lucian smiled, thinking the observation was apt. He faced everyone at the table. "I know the situation looks impossible, but we ended up getting this far. Who says we can't go farther? All the way to the end, even? After everything, we can't give up. Our strength is in our unity. Transcend White and the rest need to know what's going on. They need to know Xara Mallis is dead. They need to know about Sharo Khalin, too. He's the last avatar of the Ancient One, and as long as the Ancient One exists, he'll always be a threat. Once Sharo is dealt with, the Ancient One will have no hold on this reality."

"It's a lot to clean up, lad, that's for sure," Jagar said, coming out of his silence. "But I'm willing to follow you to the end. Whatever that end is. Life here's more interesting than back in my hut, that's for sure."

Once again, they looked to Lucian for the next move. He reached for his slate and sent the recording to his mother, along with a text.

Going to see the Volsung Mages soon. Is everything okay?

It only took a few seconds for her to acknowledge the message. *Will listen later. You wouldn't believe how much they've let things slide. If this were the First Fleet, they would have been on head duty until the death of the universe! But not to worry, I'll have them whipped into shape by the time you return. Their structure has good bones, even if the meat is rotting.*

I believe it, Lucian responded. *Good luck. This shouldn't take too long.*

With that, he pocketed his slate. He wasn't sure whether the Volsung Mages were still on *Resplendent*, but he had nothing else to go on.

"All right," he said. "I want all of us to go. There's strength in numbers, and I want them to see that we are a united front."

Heads nodded, though Emma seemed a little nervous at the prospect. Technically, she was still part of the Volsung Academy, even if she was more aligned with Lucian now.

Lucian decided not to wait a minute longer. He reached out with his hand, creating an oval portal next to the table. Through the portal's vertical plane came the warbled refraction of *Resplendent's* bridge.

The task ahead of them wouldn't be easy, but it would be necessary. Lucian had to win over the Volsung Mages and convince them he hadn't assassinated the League Hegemon, as reported by every major news outlet. Though Transcend White knew his innocence, he wasn't sure about the others.

One by one, they stepped through the portal and onto the bridge of the mage ship.

15

WHEN THEY APPEARED on the bridge of *Resplendent*, it was a scene of chaos.

All at once, Lucian and his companions became the focus of magical attacks from an unknown number of assailants. Thunderbolts, fireballs, and ice spears were all hurled in their direction.

Lucian entered the Ether and shielded it by instinct, creating a seven-fold shield large enough to cover himself and his companions. The magic attacks were absorbed quickly, and as he drew more ether, he reached out to the offending mages with Psionic Magic, blocking their access to their Focuses, all while summoning Lightspear.

Among these mages, however, a single voice cut through the madness.

"Stop!" Transcend White ordered. "Stop at once!"

Instantly, every attack ceased. Lucian and his companions found themselves surrounded by a large group of mages, perhaps thirty or forty Talents, along with five of the eight Transcends. Transcend White stood at their fore, flanked by

117

Transcends Blue, Red, Violet, and Orange. Talents and Novices of various Aspects stood around them, as many as a hundred, ready to attack at a single command, with the gray-robed Talents brandishing electricity-infused shockspears. Many had singed robes and injuries.

Lucian had done nothing to do with that. He had merely blocked their attacks. Something was going on here, and he wanted to figure it out.

But from the looks on their faces, it was as if *Lucian* were the actual threat, even if they outnumbered his group almost ten to one. Lucian could understand why. After all, he had shielded attacks from every one of them. And from their eyes widening, the sight of Lightspear was like nothing they had ever seen.

Eventually, the mages collapsed their shockspears one by one. The action did little to lower Lucian's guard. Still, he allowed Lightspear to dissipate from his hand. As soon as the weapon disappeared, the Volsung mages drew a sharp intake of breath. Even Transcends Blue and Orange looked flustered. Transcend Violet's pale face was strangely serene, given the situation, while Transcend Red glared at Lucian in challenge.

"What's going on here?" he asked. "Why did you attack me like that?"

"In case you haven't noticed," Transcend Red said, nodding toward a pair of injured mages lying on the deck before her, "we are in a bit of a situation here."

"That doesn't explain anything," Lucian said. "Don't tell me you believe that rot about me killing the Hegemon. I'm here to help."

The mages looked at each other, though some looked at Transcends Red and White for direction.

"Well," Transcend Red, with a prim smile, "perhaps you didn't pull the trigger, but it's undeniable that *your* actions got him killed."

Lucian didn't counter the point.

"Enough," Transcend White said. "This isn't becoming of you, Transcend Red, nor you, Talent Lucian. We need to work together if we are to survive this situation."

Talent Lucian. Was she trying to put him in his place at a time like this?

"I'm not Talent Lucian anymore." Now, everyone was looking at him, including Transcend White. "I'm the Sorcerer-Ascendant, appointed by the Sorcerer-Ascendant Lakhmu himself."

To almost everyone, this information didn't seem to mean much. The Talents looked to the Transcends for direction, though Lucian noted the expressions of the older ones paling. The Transcends' faces were grave. Transcend Orange's countenance was scornful, openly mocking as he scoffed.

"*Sorcerer-Ascendant*? What is this nonsense? Lakhmu is an old ghost best known for dancing naked in the trees. Your title, even if rightfully conferred, is moot. The practice of sorcery has been dead since the end of the Mage War. There is no faster way for a mage to fray than to aspire to sorcery. The Path of Balance must be adhered to!"

"Have more respect, Transcend Orange," Lucian said. "Sorcerer Lakhmu did something even the combined power of the Transcends couldn't. He removed Vera's brand."

At the mention of Vera's name, there was a collective gasp, mainly from the older Talents and the Transcends. Not everyone knew who she was or her significance.

Lucian continued. "To erase that brand, he had to give his own life. But before doing so, he conferred his title on me. One time long ago, Lakhmu was the recognized master of all magekind. He would not confer his title lightly. He only did it because he recognized who I was."

"Which is?" Transcend Orange asked.

Lucian ignored him for now. Now was not the best time to reveal who he was. He would, in time. For now, the only one whose opinion mattered was Transcend White.

"I . . . am very sorry to hear that, Lucian," she said, her face solemn. "However, Transcend Orange is correct. The practice of sorcery is dangerous, which is why it's forbidden. Already, we are seeing drastic effects of the fraying playing out. The Volsung Mages are evidence of that."

Lucian frowned. "What do you mean?"

Transcend Red seemed to be fast losing patience. "We are at war with ourselves, Lucian. Approximately forty-eight hours ago, a third of our mages instantly fell to the madness of the fraying, while another third are dead or missing."

Lucian could not hide his shock. But looking at the haunted faces around him, he knew it to be true. But how could it be possible? Gathering the Orbs was supposed to *cure* the fraying.

"A third has *frayed*, you said?"

Transcend White gave an affirming nod. "Yes. This very ship is under quarantine by order of the League of Worlds. We only control a small portion of the ship, meaning we can't reach the escape boats. The rest is controlled by those who have . . . *turned*. It's even worse than what I've described, however."

Lucian could detect a slight shakiness in Transcend White's voice. That unnerved him more than anything else because, up to this point, she had been nothing but unflappable.

"Tell me," Lucian said.

"It happened during the night hours. They took the stern, and we lost control of the engines. We fought for a time, but whatever magic possesses our old compatriots . . . it *spreads*."

Lucian felt a coldness spread over him. The Bond of Unity couldn't be here *already*. That would mean *Alkasen* mages had infiltrated the Volsung Mages' ranks. But Transcend White had mentioned no such thing, and indeed, an *Alkasen* mage would have no means of warping directly on board *Resplendent*. They would need a memory of it, which was exceedingly unlikely.

Transcend White continued. "It's like nothing we've ever seen. This madness seems to be communicable. When we realized this, we saved who we could and retreated to the bridge. We control about a quarter of the vessel. *They* control the rest."

Emma came out of her silence. "Do you have control of the ship's network?"

"Nominally," Transcend White said. "The Green Talents are quartered close to the bridge, and it's only by their constant efforts that the life support systems haven't been shut down."

"Who's with the frays?" Lucian asked, feeling dread even to be asking the question. "Psion Khairu? Linus and Plato?"

"All three are safe," Transcend White said. "They are currently patrolling the upper deck and should be back soon."

"Well, we don't have to stay here a minute longer," Lucian said. "Let's get out of here as soon as we've gathered everyone."

"Not so fast," Transcend White said. "I haven't even explained the most important part. We don't have control of the ship, outside of the life support systems. The frays do."

Transcend Blue cleared his throat. "Must we call them *frays*, Transcend White? These are our friends, our colleagues. And some on this very council have fallen to this dark sorcery. We have heard nothing from Transcends Green, Yellow, or Gray."

"The fraying is irreversible, Transcend Blue," Transcend White said. "Once it sets in, there is no known cure. As difficult as it is to admit, our friends and colleagues are no longer that. They are something else. A horror not even seen in the darkest days of the Mage War."

Everyone went silent at that.

"I don't understand," Serah said. "What's the important part? If the fraying is irreversible, let's save who we can. Lucian can create a portal to get us out of here."

"Well said," Transcend Red said. "We had better go while we still have the chance."

"It isn't so simple, and you know it," Transcend White said with vehemence. "As I've just said, we don't have full control of the ship. That includes the navigation system."

"Meaning?" Lucian asked.

Transcend White turned to the vast, forward viewports, which revealed a commanding view of space beyond. There was a bright planet that lay in the exact center of the screen.

"In four hours, this ship will crash at three percent light speed directly into Archea. We are the only ones standing between this ship and the death of millions on the surface."

Everyone went silent as they considered the gravity of that statement. The damage would be indescribable, far worse than any extinction event that had afflicted Earth's history.

"I don't understand," Emma said. "Where's Archea's Planetary Defense Force? Aren't they supposed to stop this kind of thing from ever happening?"

"Admiral Lowell's fleet absorbed the defense force to bolster his forces. He's training his men on the pirates occupying the system's outer part. In short, he's too far to help."

Serah whistled. "This Lowell guy seems to be a *real* forward thinker, huh?"

Transcend White ignored her observation. "Our estimates show that if we can't turn *Resplendent* aside within one hour of impact, we'll have to destroy the ship ourselves with our magic. If we scuttle the ship any closer than that, the ship's debris will still cause widespread devastation. Not as bad as a direct hit, but almost as bad. An hour will give the planet enough time to get out of the way. Before you came, we were discussing battle plans. And . . . contingencies."

"And yet," Transcend Orange interrupted, "we have another option with Lucian here. We can preserve ourselves to ensure the future success of the war effort. Just as Transcend Red suggested."

"How could you say such a thing?" Transcend Violet asked. "You would consign millions to death! You heard Transcend White. The planet has no defenses capable of shooting down a ship moving as fast as us."

"And yet," Transcend Red said, with a small, superior smile, "Archea is already doomed. Even if this unfortunate situation never occurred, Lowell will undoubtedly withdraw his fleet when it becomes clear Archea will be lost. There is absolutely no possibility of it being saved. Hegemon Madi clarified she would only defend the core worlds. Some say she will defend only the Solar System. If that's so, then there is no hope of saving Archea. We would sacrifice our lives needlessly. And for what, honor? The harder choice is to leave, to abandon Archea to its fate because we would also deprive the League of our unique talents. This is not selfishness. It's practicality. If we stayed, we could doom the entire human race. The lack of our help could be what decides whether the Swarmers win."

"Nice speech," Transcend Blue said. "Only it reeks of self-interest. Our order was founded long ago to help people, not to abandon them to certain doom. We *know* we can save these people if we act now. Ultimately, we don't know if our survival will truly make a difference for the League."

"It only makes sense to fight when you know you can win," Transcend Red said. "Even our most optimistic projections show a few of us surviving this. Or have you forgotten? Somehow, this version of the fraying spreads where it never has before." She gestured toward Lucian. "And now the Chosen of the Manifold has come, quite providentially. Almost as if the Manifold wants to provide us with a means of escape. I'm sure he's wise enough to see that this fight is hopeless. Lakhmu judged him a worthy successor. Even he must see the sense of living to fight another day."

Lucian gave an ironic smile but said nothing to support this.

"I agree," Transcend Orange said tentatively. "Lucian's arrival is most fortuitous, and we would be fools not to take advantage of it."

Everyone started arguing. Lucian just shook his head, raising his hand. Within moments, every mage had grown silent.

"Don't worry," Lucian said. "We'll fix the situation, as bad as it is. Transcend White, can we bring everyone to the bridge who's currently on patrol? I want to share my plan."

"Who are *you* to order Transcend White about, Talent Lucian?" Transcend Blue scoffed.

Much to Lucian's surprise, Transcend White didn't contest it. "Done. Psion Khairu and the patrol should be back within minutes."

As good as Transcend White's words, the Yellow Psion returned that minute. Her eyes widened slightly upon seeing Lucian and the others, but her face then assumed a stony expression. Her shockspear was alight with electricity, but she retracted it upon stepping up to Transcend White.

"Corridor is clear. The brands on the inner doorways are still holding."

Among Khairu's party stood twelve mages, half of which were Psions. Linus and Plato were among them, wearing gray robes and the colored sashes of Talents, each gray and red. Their faces were sterner and leaner than Lucian remembered. He wondered how each of them had been raised to Talent so quickly, but there was no time to question.

Linus beamed a goofy smile while Plato nodded more formally, but neither said anything.

"Psion Khairu," Transcend White said, "and Talents Linus

and Plato. Lucian has informed me he is here to help, though the nature of that help is still up in the air. He has a plan he wants us all to hear."

Every face turned to Lucian.

"Now that everyone's done arguing, I can tell you a little about what's happening. Not just here, but outside this spaceship."

"What do you mean?" Transcend White asked.

"Earlier today, I traveled onto an *Alkasen* carrier to speak with someone I believe to be their leader. He calls himself the Emissary, an Ancient from the time of Starsea."

The Volsung Mages seemed shocked at this revelation, and for a good reason: no one had ever spoken directly with an *Alkasen*. To learn that, plus that it was a being from the Age of Starsea, might even stretch credulity.

Transcend White, however, was nodding. Likely, Khairu had told her about Silumko after they had found the Orb of Space-Time on Nai Elyn. From the unsurprised expressions on the Transcends' faces, they knew as well.

He continued to tell the basics of the story, about how the *Alkasen* grow using the Bond of Unity, a kind of brand that spreads from mage to mage and can unite all sentient beings within their collective. Mages within that collective are themselves capable of spreading the Bond.

"So, that's what happened here," Lucian continued. "One of these *Alkasen* mages—a Preserved—started spreading the Bond on your vessel. When you realized what was happening, it was too late."

All waited silently for Transcend White to speak. She just seemed confused by Lucian's explanation. It wasn't the reaction he was expecting.

At last, she shook her head. "No, that's not what happened."

Lucian frowned, realizing that he'd almost slipped up. Of

course, the *Alkasen* could have warped on board. But Lucian had said nothing about the Orb of Space-Time, as they had agreed at the Mage Council Meeting. Of course, the mages would know something strange was happening since they had just witnessed him using a portal. So far, no one had asked him to explain himself.

"Then what else could be the source of the Bond?"

"We know the answer to that. It is none other than Transcend Gray."

16

NOW LUCIAN WAS EVEN MORE confused. Was it possible that an *Alkasen* warped on board, spread the Bond to Transcend Gray, and then warped away? Or was something else going on entirely?

"I don't understand," Lucian said. "If Transcend Gray is the source of the Bond, why couldn't an *Alkasen* have infected him?"

"Because," Transcend White said, "many mages witnessed when he turned. Transcend Gray was training some of his Talents when he began attacking them with a strange form of magic that caused them to fall under his spell. Only a few escaped to warn the rest. All of us knew his condition, but the speed of the transformation took us aback. And yet, such a quick *snapping* has happened before, even if it is rare."

Lucian nodded. He remembered learning about "snapping" during his lessons at the Academy. It was one reason the fraying was deemed so dangerous. A mage with the condition could suddenly, without warning, go mad, although the phenomenon was rare. That was why it was necessary to nip the potential in the bud. The fact they had let Transcend Gray live among them for so long only exposed their hypocrisy. Any lesser mage would have been shipped off to Psyche years ago.

And now, because of that hypocrisy, the future of their Academy was in peril.

"What is unknown," Transcend White continued, "is how he spread the fraying. We've never seen this, though the characteristics you listed about this Bond of Unity seem to match. As for an *Alkasen* coming on board, that's simply impossible. We monitor all traffic entering and leaving this ship; none has come on board since we left Oceanus."

Lucian didn't bother explaining about warping, something Transcend White knew about, anyway. If mages witnessed the transformation, the source likely wasn't an *Alkasen*.

"The point is," Transcend Red said, "we need to sort this out soon because we have less than three hours before we will be forced to destroy the ship."

"Don't worry about the ship," Lucian said. "I can warp it away if needed. To another star system, if need be. That can buy us time to figure things out."

"Okay," Transcend Red said. "If it wasn't an *Alkasen*, and if Transcend Gray has this Bond of Unity, how could he possibly get it?"

The question hung in the air, and it was clear no one had the answer. Lucian didn't relish fighting people who had once been his fellow students. Many of them were of a similar age to him. There had to be a way to save them. "Let's just focus on getting this ship back."

"Any ideas, *Sorcerer-Ascendant*?" Transcend Red asked, her tone ironic.

Lucian ignored her glibness. "Maybe we can isolate one of the turned mages. I can reach out to the Bond. See if there's a way to undo it. We aren't sure if we're even dealing with the

Bond, but I would be surprised if it were something else. If I can understand how it works, I can unravel it."

Transcend Violet's face was solemn. "I've already scanned the mind of a young Novice. Briefly, mind you. The brand is unlike anything I've ever seen. I would need hours, if not days, to figure it out. I might not even be capable of that much, such is its complexity."

Lucian nodded. He was even more sure of his theory. "The Bond of Unity was created with sorcery. It doesn't follow the same rules most mages follow. What was done by sorcery cannot be undone by magery. It's a higher kind of magic."

Transcend Orange scoffed. "What do you know of these things? You are a Talent of this Academy, raised by necessity. We only have your word that Lakhmu conferred his title upon you, and even then, Lakhmu is not highly esteemed by any reputable mage."

Lucian held his Focus to keep his cool. "I've seen things you would never believe, Transcend Orange. You know nothing. You've spent almost your whole life on Transcend Mount, only reading the teachings of the old masters. So what do you know about sorcery?"

Everyone's eyes widened at the insult, including the Transcends'. Transcend Red raised a hand to her mouth to hold back laughter while Transcend Orange's face darkened.

"Why, you insolent pup! You are a young, foolhardy, brainless lump of . . . of . . . *ordure!*"

"Be silent, Transcend Orange," Transcend White said. "This is unbecoming of you. You are strong in Atomic Magic, but is it hard to conceive that someone might know something you do not, whatever their age?"

Transcend Orange shut his mouth, silent for now at least.

Lucian shrugged as if Transcend Orange's outburst had been of no consequence. "That's my idea in a nutshell. Find one of these mages, isolate them, and try to figure out how this Bond of Unity works."

"If you need help," Khairu said, "you have my spear and my magic. You'll need someone to watch your back."

"I can help, too," Linus said. "You need someone with expertise. That's most definitely me."

"You have me, too," Plato said. "It'll be like old times again, eh?"

Lucian nodded, grateful for their support.

Fergus was next to talk. "I think I speak for everyone. We will do whatever we can to help."

"That's admirable," Transcend Violet said, "but can we allow the risk? The safest course is for Lucian to move this ship entirely first. Somewhere far away, where it can't be any danger."

"I can only move this ship someplace I have a clear memory of," Lucian said. "Most of those places are close to planets and moons, so that wouldn't be good. And we can't just leave the ship; the lifeboats are guarded. Even if I warped *Resplendent* deep into Dark Space, we might find ourselves in the middle of an *Alkasen* fleet." He shook his head. "I won't risk that."

"You're right," Transcend White said. "We must take this ship back however we can. Escape is the last resort."

Everyone went quiet as they looked to Lucian for direction. From the thunderous expression on Transcend White's face, she seemed aware of the shift in balance. Lucian was the only one who could get them out of this mess, even if he hadn't revealed his identity.

But much to Lucian's surprise, her disposition softened as she turned to regard the rest of the assembly of mages.

"There is one thing left unmentioned," Transcend White said. "Knowledge that has only been known by us Transcends. It will come to light eventually, so I might as well say it now. We have wasted enough time already, especially with so much at stake. So I'll do my best to make this brief." Transcend White looked at Lucian. "The Prophecy of the Seven, written by Arian in the days before the Mage War, is completely true. I have verified this and welcome anyone to test me on it."

Everyone looked at each other, clearly shocked by this news and not knowing what it meant.

"When Lucian and I last spoke, he had gathered Five of the Seven fabled Orbs of Starsea." She paused. "Plus another, which was lost to time."

"A lost Orb?" asked a woman wearing a talent's gray robes and a violet sash. Her long gray hair was tied back, and her skin wrinkled from the years.

Transcend White nodded. "Yes, an entirely new Aspect long lost to time. What kind of magic do you think allows Lucian to create his portals? It's not any magic we know. It is of a different Aspect, one lost since the time of the Gate-Builders, long before the time of even the Ancients and Starsea." She paused for a moment to collect her thoughts. "That makes for six Orbs—five of the original seven prophesied by Arian, plus the lost one, that of Space-Time, the knowledge of which was hidden from us until recently."

"So, what?" another male Talent asked, bald and swarthy in appearance. "You're saying the Chosen of the Manifold is real, too? I'm sorry. I refuse to believe this tripe."

"You dare challenge me?" Transcend White asked, a dangerous edge in her tone. "I stake my position as Transcend White upon it."

From their collective silence, that let them know the utter seriousness of her convictions.

Transcend White continued. "Since then, Lucian has received training from Sorcerer-Ascendant Lakhmu, the leader of the Mako Academy. And yes, in times of old, such as during the Mage War, he was the leader of all magekind." She frowned. "The former Sorcerer-Ascendant and I had our disagreements. But anyone would be a fool to admit he wasn't the greatest sorcerer in the Worlds. His powers were far beyond anyone who has ever undergone our training, which was always limited." Transcend White looked at Lucian. "But as powerful as Sorcerer Lakhmu was, he will now only be remembered as the second strongest. Lucian Abrantes far exceeds Sorcerer Lakhmu's abilities. I know Lucian's nature, and he would not lie about receiving the title of Sorcerer-Ascendant. Lucian is no mere mage, limited in power by rules designed to curtail the fraying. Rules to which most mages are bound because they aren't capable of the highest mysteries of magic. Lucian is a sorcerer of the old way, stronger than any the Worlds have ever seen. He is stronger than Lakhmu. Stronger than Vera Desai. Stronger even than Xara Mallis. Yes, he knows the practice of magery, as all of us do. But under Lakhmu, he learned the art of sorcery, of streaming from within the Ether itself, an act that dooms even the most powerful mages to the fraying. His Orbs give him power beyond imagination. He has only two to find, that of Gravitonics and Atomicism." She swallowed. "Both of which are held by Xara Mallis."

From the reaction of the Talents, this was the greatest revelation of all. All of them started arguing and protesting, and their speech was only stilled when Transcend White raised her hand.

"Yes, it's the truth. Mallis is still alive and wants the same thing as Lucian: to control the Orbs of Starsea. As in the days of the Mage War, she seeks the Orbs to cement her power on the Worlds. To become immortal. But allowing her to gain access to the Orbs would be a complete disaster." She nodded, firming herself to go on. "As soon as Lucian has helped us out here, I will fully support his claim."

There was a silence that seemed to go on forever. Transcend White saying such a thing was nearly unimaginable. It would mean giving up her power, not to mention changing the entire trajectory and purpose of the Volsung Mages. It might even be considered a betrayal to the League of Worlds, who oversaw the workings of their institution.

That Transcend White would put all that on the line spoke to her seriousness.

"Preposterous," Transcend Orange said at last. From the expressions of the other mages, it seemed he wasn't the only one who thought as much. "He might have a few Orbs; I concede that. But *six*? Last we spoke, you informed us he only had two, and even that much, I doubt!"

"We met more recently on Oceanus," Transcend White said. "There, he informed me he held six. I have no reason to doubt him."

"You would place yourself under him, Transcend White? I've followed you through everything, but you've gone too far this time!"

All at once, all the mages started arguing again. Lucian resisted the urge to sigh.

Fergus scoffed and raised two fingers to his mouth before giving a sharp whistle. Much to Lucian's surprise, that got everyone's attention. It gave Lucian an opening to speak.

"You're right, Transcend Orange. I don't have Six Orbs," Lucian said.

Transcend Orange gave an asinine smile, even tittering a bit.

"I don't have Six Orbs because I have all of them. That makes me the fulfillment of Arian's prophecy. I'm the uncontested Chosen of the Manifold and, by all rights, the leader of all magekind."

17

EVERYONE STARED at him in awe and perhaps even fear. Even Transcend Red's eyes registered surprise and maybe a bit of disbelief. But she didn't dare challenge him, nor did Transcend Orange. In their minds, what he'd just said was so outrageous that it could be true.

Transcend White, at last, found her voice. "And what of Xara Mallis?"

"Dead," Lucian said. "We fought in the skies of Psyche. On the plains of Isis. The wastes of Hephaestus." He decided not to go into further detail. Perhaps he could do so with Transcend White later. "I drove Lightspear into her heart and destroyed the Shadow possessing her. Her Orbs are now mine."

"Wait," Transcend Red said, her face dawning with recognition. "When did this occur?"

Lucian shrugged. "I don't know. Two days ago, maybe?"

"That coincides with when Transcend Gray went mad," Transcend Blue said.

Lucian frowned, confused. "What do you mean? Arian's

prophecy said the fraying would end once I got all the Orbs. I did that."

Could Arian have been wrong? And yet, Lucian couldn't deny it. The timing was uncanny. Had it all been some massive trick? Had Arian's prophecy been corrupted somehow?

"This can't be right," he said. "There's something we're missing."

"No, I don't think there is," Transcend Red said. "Your actions, Lucian, have caused the sure death of the Volsung Mage Academy. Yes, you have gathered the Orbs, but somehow, that has probably caused everyone with the fraying to go mad simultaneously. Not only that, but to become pawns of the *Alkasen* capable of spreading the disease."

"How could I have possibly known?" Lucian asked. "I set out to find the Orbs to *stop* the *Alkasen*."

"You are still the responsible party," Transcend Red said. "You must fix this."

The deck went quiet as everyone felt the gravity of Transcend Red's words. Even if they agreed with her, they were afraid to go against Lucian, knowing his power. Transcend White had said he was the most powerful sorcerer in the Worlds.

Thankfully, Fergus stepped up to take control of the situation. "Now, wait just a minute. I think Lucian is right. There's more to this than meets the eye."

Transcend Red spread her hands. "Please, share your thoughts."

"There's no reason to think Arian's prophecy is wrong. It was misinterpreted. Lucian *has* cured the fraying—in mages who have yet to fray. Surely, you've noticed the difference in streaming magic in the last couple of days. Gathering ether is easy. That's because it's pure now. It even *tastes* clean. Though that is strange to say, you'll know what I mean. We have Lucian to thank for that. With the Orbs joined in one Focus—*his* Focus—magic functions properly."

Much to Lucian's relief, heads were nodding all around. It wasn't just Lucian's friends experiencing the purity of magic for the first time.

Fergus continued. "Though the jury is still out, I'd hazard a guess that there is no risk of fraying from any mage who survived this event. No immolations, no rotting skin or organs. And no risk of insanity when the disease reaches the brain." He surveyed the crowd. "*None* of that should happen now."

"You can't prove that," Transcend Orange said. "For all we know, any of us could fray and turn on the others at any moment!"

"That won't happen," Lucian said. "Fergus is right. This *event*, as Fergus called it, only affects those who were already frayed, plus anyone the *Alkasen* spread the Bond to. If we fight back and don't let them replicate the Bond, we can stop its spread."

"We must fight back," Transcend Blue said confidently. "If this Bond can be undone, we can save the rest."

"I agree," Transcend Violet said. "If there's even a chance we can save the others, we should do so."

"You can't be serious," Transcend Red said. "All of this is conjecture! Rather than risking everything, we should get out while we can. I know I can't be the only one."

Transcend White nodded. "We've been speaking for an hour now, which means we only have two hours left to take control of the vessel." She turned to Lucian. "What is your plan, Sorcerer-Ascendant?"

That made everyone go quiet. If Transcend White recognized Lucian's legitimacy, they had no choice but to do the same or be openly insubordinate. Even Lucian didn't know which way things would go.

So, he stood straight, realizing he had to play the part. To his surprise, he found it came quickly. He'd been through too much to be intimidated by anything.

"I'm going to take a small team." He gestured toward his friends. "Everyone around me, plus Psion Khairu, and Talents Linus and Plato. People I'm familiar with."

"And what about the rest of us?" Transcend Blue asked. "It seems too small a group."

"Keep the bridge safe and the network secure. Sometimes, a well-honed team works better than an army."

Transcend Orange scoffed. "You expect to take back the entire ship with just *eight* people?"

Lucian was tired of dealing with him, but he figured others might have the same question, so he answered. "Yes, I do. With everyone here, we have all the Aspects covered. All we need to do is find one Preserved mage and see if the Bond can be undone. That's it for now."

"How can you isolate just one without risking yourself or the others?" Transcend Blue asked.

"There's always a risk. The only other option is a ship hijacked by the Preserved. That's not an outcome anyone wants." He nodded toward the doors leading out from the bridge. "We better get moving."

Thankfully, no one tried to challenge him further as he gathered his friends and headed for the corridor.

When the bridge doors shut behind him, the quiet of the central passage was eerie. Many of the lights were out while the rest flickered. There probably wasn't enough power to keep them on thoroughly. Lucian reached with his Focus, finding that dozens of Preserved mages were lying in wait beyond the doors at the end of the corridor.

Lucian immediately saw Transcend Blue's point. It wouldn't

be easy to grab just one because they worked as a unit. But Lucian already knew how he might get around that.

He paused a few meters from the doors, which were branded with a seven-fold shield that must have taken multiple mages to create.

"Still holding," Plato said. The red-sashed Talent turned to Lucian. "I want to ask what's happened since you left us high and dry. I still haven't forgiven you for that, you know."

"No one told you what happened?" Lucian asked. "We *wanted* to take you. Things were moving fast."

Linus shook his head. "Excuses! We've had it hard, Lucian, just so you know. Here I was, relaxing in the waiting room, catching up on my backlog of holo-films. And then Transcend White comes barging in, telling Plato and me we would be inducted into the Volsung Mages! You can imagine the fit I had. Absolute hysterics! However, Transcend White insisted it be so, and it was that or starve." He shrugged his shoulders. "Next thing I know, I'm a Novice again. Admittedly, that phase didn't last long, and both Plato and I were quickly raised to Talent. And then we were given *responsibilities*. Horrible stuff. And after that, despite our positions of authority, all we ever heard were rumors. There was the Hegemon's assassination, of course. I never believed you did that, my boy. Not your style, though maybe you had a hand in it somehow. They said you were consorting with pirates and even helping the Believers in the Spinward Worlds. It's hard to know fact from fiction! And I'm positively flummoxed at everything you said on the bridge."

"Who's this fellow?" Plato asked, eyeing Jagar.

Jagar grunted. "Jagar Tengiz Ashiz."

"Ah, I remember Lucian talking about you." He turned to Selene. "And you must be Selene."

She gave a regal, queenly nod.

Linus gave a boisterous laugh. "Fancy that! Glad to see both of you are alive and well. We have a lot to catch up on!"

"Introductions and stories can wait," Lucian said. "We have an hour and a half to save everyone on this ship." He clapped his hands. "All right, here's the plan. I want everyone to ward their primaries as much as possible. Really go all out. Stay close to me, and set a range of about five meters on those wards. None of you will stream offensively. Use every bit of ether you can, and do any potential fighting with your spears. That should neutralize every magical attack, leaving me free to deal with the Preserved."

"How do you plan on capturing just one?" Khairu asked. "Seems iffy."

"We aren't going through those doors. At least a dozen Preserved are on the other side. I plan to use a portal to get to Transcend White's cabin. The Preserved will probably not be interested in it. From there, we can see if we can nab one of them and bring them back here."

"And the wards will keep us safe from magical attacks," Fergus said.

Lucian nodded. "Exactly. Now, stream your wards."

Everyone hurried to do just that. As each ward was set, Lucian could feel their collective presence around him. Each was powerful and would not be quickly shattered. Around him were some of the most powerful mages in the Worlds.

"That should do it," Lucian said.

Already, Lucian was opening a portal to Transcend White's cabin. He stepped through, finding it empty. The others followed behind.

He kept the portal open with a brand. They might need to escape quickly. He reached out to the corridor beyond the cabin door, sensing with Radiance a few Preserved lurking out there. With luck, Fergus's Radiant ward would keep them undetectable.

"Don't move a muscle," Lucian said.

He floated toward the door, then quickly phased through it. He appeared on the other side, right next to a young male Novice with violet-shrouded eyes.

Perfect. Before the Preserved Novice could react, Lucian surrounded them with Space-Time Magic, warping the short distance back to the cabin.

The Novice instantly attempted to stream, but it was like trying to light water on fire within the collective wards. He was utterly powerless as he tried to back away toward the door. Lucian streamed a Binding shield over the threshold, preventing escape.

The door opened, revealing two Preserved Red Talents streaming fireballs and one Green Talent streaming a laser. Their magic was neutralized by Fergus's and Plato's wards, while the Binding shield kept them in the corridor.

"Get through the portal!" Lucian ordered.

As a unit, they retreated. Lucian tethered the Novice, withdrawing with the rest.

Once back in the main corridor, Lucian let the portal disappear while allowing the Binding shield to fall.

The Novice skulked away, backing away toward the door. For the first time, Lucian got a good look at him. His pale face gave a deadened stare, while his eyes were utterly violet and glowing. If he was merely frayed, that would not be the case. Lucian knew now that they were dealing with the Bond.

The Novice didn't speak or show any fear. He looked to be about eighteen.

"Novice Zacharias," Khairu said. "Can you hear me?"

Zacharias's only response was a low snarl.

"He's gone," Linus said. "Better get this over with quickly."

Lucian reached out for the Novice's Focus. He found a brand of dizzying complexity composed of all seven primary Aspects. Dispelling the Bond would require proficiency in every Aspect, plus the power to back it up.

Lucian was the only one who could do it. Despite the brand's intricacy, it would not be beyond Lucian's abilities to unravel. But it would be difficult to do it for every single afflicted mage. They didn't have the time. There *had* to be a better way.

Lucian continued delving into the Bond, even as the shielded door came under increased assault. There were a significant number of Preserved Red Talents attempting to melt it. Plato added his strength to the shield to buy extra time. He was dangerously close to becoming overwhelmed. His face was strained as both of his hands glowed red.

"Should we drop our wards to help him?" Fergus asked.

Lucian nodded, even as he continued to wrangle with the Bond. "Do it. I'm almost done here."

Lucian refocused his attention. The Bond was connected to *something*. If he could cut off the Bond from that something, Zacharias would be lifted from the effects of the brand.

At last, Lucian had it. He streamed from every Orb, connecting each stream to the right spot within the Bond.

The effect was instant. The violet aura dissipated from Zacharias's eyes, which were a brilliant blue. He blinked a few times, clearly perplexed.

"Where am I?" he asked.

Lucian nodded. "You're safe. Go to the bridge. If you remember anything, tell Transcend White."

"Who are you? What did you do to me?"

The Novice's voice was entitled, and something told Lucian he was a rich, spoiled brat.

"Just go," Khairu said. "That's an order."

Zacharias didn't want to argue with her, at least. He complied, running down the corridor with long, lanky strides.

"It's possible," Fergus said, marveling.

"I can't do it for every mage," Lucian said. "We have what, an hour left? But there is a better way. I understand how the Bond works now."

"What do we do, then?" Emma asked.

"Transcend Gray is the source. If we take him out, the rest will dissolve."

"Is it that simple?" Serah asked. "Let's get him then!"

"Unfortunately, we will have to kill him," Lucian said. "No way around that. And he's likely guarded."

"Any idea where he is?" Fergus asked.

"Finding him won't be easy," Khairu said. "These Preserved are working together. Perhaps controlled by Transcend Gray directly."

"I assume Transcend Gray is a Gravitist?" Selene asked.

Lucian nodded. "A powerful one, though I've never seen him in action."

"He doesn't stream much anymore," Khairu said. "Though some say he's second only to Transcend White and Transcend Red."

"Do what you have to do, Lucian," Jagar said. "Hundreds of lives are in your hands. Don't lose the flock for one stray sheep."

Lucian nodded, seeing the wisdom of this.

"Perhaps there is a way to get him on his own," Fergus said. "Like you did with that young Novice."

Lucian knew Transcend Gray would not allow himself to be so easily overcome. He wondered if there was a way he might detect his presence. It wouldn't be easy if Transcend Gray were actively warding himself. Still, Lucian had enough power to brute force it, especially using sorcery and the Orbs of Psionics and Radiance. Lucian had never connected Psionically with Transcend Gray, so he wasn't sure if it would be possible to find him.

He would have to force a path.

"There's one thing we're forgetting," Khairu said. "We don't know where Transcends Green and Yellow are, either. If they've been turned, we could face three Transcends rather than one."

That was something to consider, and Lucian knew that even now, the Preserved were probably preparing for an attack.

"There's no more time to waste," Lucian said. "The plan is the same. I'm going to find him using the Orb of Psionics. Assuming I can locate him, we'll head into the ship. Once the portal opens, redirect your magic to ward your primaries, like before."

The others nodded their understanding.

Lucian entered the Ether, expanding his Focus to include the entire ship. Combining Psionics and Radiance, he created a vast ethereal field encompassing the vessel. At once, he realized the general position of most mages on the ship and felt a powerful presence emanating from the engine room. He didn't know whether it was Transcend Yellow, Green, or Gray, but it was undoubtedly one of the three. Such was the power that it could be all three standing relatively close together, the option he thought most likely.

Lucian remembered the engine room, so he could open a portal there. But the consequences of such a direct attack could be disastrous. If the three Transcends were working together, they could do significant damage, especially if they were expecting him.

Lucian withdrew from the Ether. "They're in the engine room."

Before anyone could respond, the magical shield edifying the door winked out. Before Lucian could stream his own to replace it, the door blasted open. The corridor beyond was filled with a large group of Preserved mages, their eyes glowing with eerie violet light.

Lucian acted before thinking, sending a kinetic wave barreling down the corridor, scattering them like bowling pins. It bought enough time for his companions to activate their wards.

As more Preserved filled the passage, Lucian knew their position would soon be overwhelmed.

"Get back to the bridge!" he ordered. "Keep those wards strong!"

Their wards activated, providing a defense against the sudden assault. Lucian's magic gave them enough reprieve to retreat to the bridge.

Lucian, however, would not be going with them. "Hold the line."

"Lucian!" Serah shouted. "What are you doing?"

Lucian gathered enough ether to warp himself to the ship's engine room. It was time to face Transcend Gray.

18

AS SOON AS HE APPEARED, Lucian was surrounded by Preserved on all sides. He phased down the corridor to avoid the barrage of magical attacks. As soon as he reappeared, he raised a shield that changed its Aspect depending on the magic that struck him. He summoned Lightspear as he floated toward a power source directly ahead of him, not bothering to kill the turned mages around him.

Lucian phased past a closed door, entering the ship's central corridor. Before him stood a small Preserved army, a mix of Novices and Talents with violet-glowing eyes. They surrounded the three Transcends, facing him side-by-side in their vibrantly colored robes. Transcend Yellow stood on the left, her eyes shining violet. On the right stood Transcend Green, his hands glowing with Green Radiance. Both of their expressions were deadened, lacking humanity.

In the center stood Transcend Gray, surrounded by a thick shield composed of all Aspects. Within the Ether, Lucian could see lines entering that shield from the surrounding mages. It seemed every mage was working in confluence with Transcend Gray, who had an insane amount of power at his fingertips.

Lucian continued gathering ether, knowing this would be no easy fight.

Transcend Gray's eyes shone with amethyst radiance, while a power-hungry smile stretched across his wasted face. Every inch of his skin was covered with fraying wounds.

Despite the strength of Lucian's shield, he was yanked with incredible force. And as he was pulled, infinite darkness manifested, surrounding him and Transcend Gray. There, they floated, with endless black in all directions.

Whatever Transcend Gray was doing, Lucian could sense that it was using both Gravitonic and Space-Time Magic. Lucian found his thoughts muddled and confused, unable to make sense of things in a logical progression. He strengthened his Space-Time shield, which allowed him to see things sequentially.

Lucian immediately understood Transcend Gray's intention. He had meant to swallow him with this darkness from which Lucian couldn't escape and then allow the void to collapse, essentially crushing him. Once Lucian understood Transcend Gray's goal, he could reverse it. First, he counter-streamed Gravitonics and Space-Time, fighting the expansion of space. The void withdrew, bringing Lucian back to the deck, with Transcend Gray buckling under the pressure, despite the ether he was drawing from his thralls.

Lucian faced Transcend Gray, who was using his ether to power a seven-fold shield. The Transcend smiled maniacally, utterly sure Lucian could do nothing against it.

However, there was something Transcend Gray hadn't counted on: Lightspear.

Lucian phased forward with the deadly weapon so fast and so suddenly that there was nothing Transcend Gray could do to

stop it. Lightspear passed through the seven-fold barrier as if it didn't exist, impaling Transcend Gray's chest. The Transcend's gray, broken face registered surprise just a moment before letting out a bloodcurdling scream. Lightspear's radiance consumed him, and after a long moment, his remains collapsed into ash.

The effect of his death was immediate. The violet sheen in the Preserved mages' eyes winked out, and they blinked as if waking from a dream. Bemused, they noticed Lucian standing there, his white spear radiant. Transcend Yellow's eyes widened as she took him in.

"Lucian," she said. "Where did you come from?"

"What's going on?" Transcend Green asked. "How did I end up here?"

From the confused expressions on everyone's faces, none knew what was happening. It would take a lot of explaining. Something he didn't have time to do. Everyone was looking at the pile of ash at his feet, realizing it had once been a person.

Before they could ask him anything more, Lucian decided this mess wasn't his problem. He warped back to the bridge, only to find himself in the middle of a crowd.

Lucian found Transcend White. "Transcend Gray is dead. The Bond is undone, and everyone is safe."

"What of Transcend Yellow?" Transcend Red demanded. "And Transcend Green?"

"Both are safe," Lucian said. "Though they might be loopy."

"Very good," Transcend White said. "Now, we can—"

One of the Yellow Talents, the pilot, called from the front of the bridge. "Your High Eminence! We have control of the navigation again!"

Transcend White hurried to the helm, the Talents parting for her. Lucian followed behind.

"Excellent, Talent Horace. Slow the ship as much as possible. How much time until impact?"

"Five minutes."

She turned to Lucian. "How soon can you move this ship?"

"Faster than that. However, we need to slow down as much as possible first. Can you do that?"

"Sure thing," Horace said.

"Slow the ship," Transcend White said.

Talent Horace followed the command. Everyone grabbed hold of something, as the inertial dampeners could hardly compensate for the slowdown.

Lucian set to work, even as Archea grew ever more prominent in the forward viewscreen. The mages on the bridge gave him a wide berth as he began drawing ether into his Focus. He lost all sense of time and was only marginally aware of what was going on outside himself as a shell of black magic surrounded him, swirling and infusing into his body.

He waited until the planet dominated the viewscreen, mere seconds from impact. Lucian streamed the portal right before the ship. *Resplendent* passed through, reemerging tens of light-years away in the Cupid System.

———

THE VIOLET-TINGED MOON of Psyche floated before them, only a short distance away. Such was *Resplendent's* speed that the moon was rapidly growing in the forward viewport.

Khairu muscled Talent Horace aside and took up the helm. "Two minutes to impact! Veer to starboard, reverse thrust full!"

"Hold on to something!" Talent Horace called.

Almost instantly, Lucian felt the force of inertia increase. There was no way the dampeners would keep up. Every Gray Talent began streaming against that force, but it was like trying to stop the wind with one's hands. The hull creaked and groaned as the ship turned to avoid crashing into Psyche.

Even with all the mages' powers combined, something was going to give.

"It's not turning fast enough!" Talent Horace wailed. "She's going to rend asunder!"

Lucian reached for the Orb of Gravitonics, covering the entire ship in its aura. He began drawing deeply, streaming against the force.

Almost at once, the entire force was canceled out. The mages, one by one, dropped their streams as Lucian took on the entire load with ease, his body coated with silvery brilliance. They watched him, eyes wide and mouths agape, as the ship turned even more sharply, far beyond what should have been possible.

Soon, the rim of the moon slipped beneath the ship, and a vast field of stars spread before them. There was a moment of stunned silence, then a chorus of relieved sighs.

"Calibrate the slowdown at maximum dampening capacity," Khairu said.

As her orders were followed, Lucian allowed his gravity aura to dissipate.

Lucian turned to the five Transcends still on the bridge, all watching him in silence. Even Transcends Orange and Red seemed to have nothing to say.

"Welcome to the Cupid System," Lucian said. "The domain of the Sorcerer-Ascendant."

Transcend Red's expression was dark. "You would have us throw ourselves at your mercy?"

"This is simply the safest place in the Worlds for you," Lucian said. "The League still believes frays control your ship, and it would be difficult to convince them otherwise."

Transcend Blue shook his head. "I hate that you're right . . ."

"So, what?" Transcend Red asked. "Are we supposed to recognize your authority or something?"

Lucian gave her a level gaze. "Yes. I just saved your life, and even Transcend White recognizes me as the Sorcerer-Ascendant."

"We did not discuss this!" Transcend Orange said, turning to Transcend White. "How dare you speak for all of us? I, for one, refuse to follow this traitorous upstart!"

"I just saved your ship and your entire Academy," Lucian said. "Shouldn't you be a bit more grateful?"

Transcend Orange whipped back toward Lucian. "It's your job to serve us. You swore an oath to follow the order of the Transcends upon your ascension!"

"I made no such oath. You even witnessed that when I was ascended." Lucian smiled. "What excuse will you come up with now?"

Transcend Orange huffed, turning to Transcend White once again. "Your High Eminence, are you *really* going along with this codswallop?"

Everyone looked at her for a reaction. Her eyes met Lucian's and gave him a level gaze.

"I've already spoken my mind on the matter. I will work with the Chosen so long as he doesn't require me to kneel on these old knees."

The Transcends drew a sharp intake of breath. Their reactions varied: shocked, afraid, and even furious.

Transcend Red's face was the color of her namesake. "Because of the emergency before, I was silent when perhaps I should have spoken. Transcend White, you may be in charge, and your post may be for life. However, there *is* a way to depose you if the rest of the Transcends agree. Since two of the seven Transcends still alive cannot be considered of sound mind, a unanimous vote among the Transcends here should suffice."

"What are you suggesting, Transcend Red?" Transcend White asked dangerously.

She smiled, her canines appearing sharp. "Let it be known that I call for a vote of no confidence in our esteemed leader. This outrage has gotten too far out of hand!" She looked at Lucian with vehemence. "I refuse to follow this . . . this . . . *child!*"

"I second the motion," Transcend Orange said, his expression grim.

A long silence stretched across the bridge, which no one dared to break. When Lucian cleared his throat, everyone turned to look at him.

"Do we have to go through all these theatrics? You are welcome to go your own way, Transcends Red and Orange."

He reached for the Space-Time Aspect, and brilliant dark energy covered his body. He opened a portal directly next to Transcend Red, leading to an isolated alley he knew in Miami. Seeing that exit caused her eyes to almost pop out of her head. She watched him, not sure if he was being serious.

Lucian nodded toward the portal. "That will take you to Earth, along with anyone who doesn't want to fight with me, because that's what following me means: fighting for humanity. If you want to fight with me, you must recognize my supremacy and follow my orders. I don't care *what* your title is. I'm the Chosen of the Manifold and the Sorcerer-Ascendant. I hold all Eight Orbs, and you are in *my* domain."

She glowered at him, probably because she didn't like him calling her bluff. Now it was on her to decide what to do.

In the end, she didn't budge. No one else did, either. Not even Transcend Orange.

At last, she licked her lips and spoke in a soft, almost meek, voice. "We cannot decide to follow you so suddenly and so quickly. The Spectrum must convene and vote. Even the others, if they are determined to be of sound mind."

"You were ready to speak for everyone before," Lucian said. "And now, it requires a vote because things got too real for you?"

Transcend Red just gave him a deadened glare, her blue eyes icy. Her back was against the wall, and there was no way to escape. Lucian was sure she would have killed him if she could.

"There is one matter we are not discussing," Transcend Blue said. "We are short one Transcend, and we still haven't consolidated the ship. Let's pick up the pieces before making any rash decisions."

"That's the wisest thing I've heard so far," Transcend White said. She faced Lucian. "We will speak of this at a later time, Lucian. We appreciate your help, but clearly, we must set our affairs in order."

Lucian nodded. "Of course. You guys talking it out and making sense of things isn't a bad idea. I'll return later." Lucian remembered the original purpose of his coming. "And, ah . . . one other thing. There was the original reason I came here."

"Yes?" Transcend White asked, her voice holding a slight edge.

"I would like to take a few of your mages to help establish order on the surface of Psyche. Xara Mallis caused a lot of chaos down there. There might also be some Bonded mages down there, causing mayhem. I was going to send the Wardens down there to help keep the peace."

Her eyes widened, clearly in shock. "The Wardens?"

"Yes. They're on our side now."

"You've been busy, I see. Very well. Who would you like to take?"

"Psion Khairu, along with Talents Linus and Plato."

"Done and done," Linus said. "When do we start?"

Transcend White shot him a warning look, but Linus just smiled.

"You can have the Talents. However, at least for now, Psion Khairu is the de facto leader of the Yellows. I cannot spare her."

"Let me go with him," Khairu said.

Lucian watched her in surprise. It was not like her to go against Transcend White. He chose not to say anything, though. Given his and Khairu's tense history, anything he said might cause her to change her mind, and he wanted her on the Mage Council as Chief Dynamist.

Transcend White looked at her curiously. "And what can be more important than leading your Aspect in the absence of your Transcend?"

"What is the Volsung Academy in the grand scheme of things?" Khairu asked. "We are important, but we all know the awful truth." She looked around at her audience. "The Academies are prisons, only marginally better than Psyche. As mages, we have no rights and have no choice but to serve the League. The entire purpose of the Academies and Psyche was because of the fraying. But now, the fraying is gone, meaning it's no longer necessary to be under the League's purview."

Heads nodded all around. Even the Transcends were listening to her.

"We could go crawling back to the League. And maybe that's what we would vote for if it weren't for the Swarmers. I've traveled with Lucian for a long time. When we first met, I was not impressed. He was whiney, impulsive, impatient, and far from the perfect candidate. He only got into the Academy by sheer luck, as far as I saw it."

Lucian would have countered her, except what she said was accurate. He no longer felt the need to defend himself.

Khairu continued. "At the Academy, he struggled for a long time. Until something inside changed. His potential became more apparent. But that potential outpaced his readiness. We can throw around blame all we like, but the decision was made. He was exiled. And against all odds, he returned, having escaped *Psyche*, something no mage has ever done. And not only that, but he has since found all Eight Orbs, a journey that began on the Isle of Madness, where he found the Orb of Binding."

At this information, the mages broke into an excited buzz. That an Orb of Starsea had been *there*, a mere one thousand kilometers west of the Volsung Academy, was simply unfathomable.

"After everything he's gone through, I don't see how anyone can look at him and judge him unworthy of being followed," Khairu said. "Circumstances in the Worlds have changed. I . . . don't know all the details about Hegemon Palmer, but I know Lucian would not have killed him in cold blood."

"I can confirm that much, at least," Transcend White said. "Vera Desai possessed Hegemon Palmer. My sister." She looked at Lucian. "Who has since died, along with her Psion."

Lucian nodded his confirmation. He hadn't outright told Transcend White about Vera, but she had already guessed it when they met on Oceanus. On the surface, she looked calm and collected, but Lucian knew she must be a storm of emotions within.

However, most of the focus was not on her but on Lucian himself as the mages exclaimed their incredulity. Almost everyone knew the name Vera Desai, outside perhaps the freshest Novices. But it was not common knowledge that Vera and Transcend White were siblings.

Transcend White raised a hand, getting their attention back. "Many things are coming to light that were once in darkness, known only to a few. There is still a lot more to sort out. However, one thing is clear. The time has come for Lucian's status as the Chosen of the Manifold to no longer remain hidden. He is the only one who can stop the *Alkasen*. We must do what we can to help him . . . or perish." She let the weight of those words set in. "No one on this bridge has been tested more than him. I'll be the first to admit I was wrong about him. He isn't the Novice some of you know. He rescued this ship and every life upon it, an impossible task. A fact some of my colleagues seem to have forgotten, though it happened not thirty minutes ago."

Transcend White looked at Khairu and then gave her a nod. "It seems I've done my own convincing. Normally, this is a matter I'd leave for Transcend Yellow, but given her absence . . . yes. That would be best, Khairu. Go with the Sorcerer-Ascendant. We will set our affairs in order here."

Lucian nodded his understanding. He was sure they would make the right decision once they made sense of things. And once they agreed to follow him, they could work out the logistics of integrating them into the Mage Division.

Lucian checked his slate to see a missed message from his mother. He looked up at his friends.

"The transports are ready. We should head back."

19

IN THE COMING WEEKS, order was established. Lucian's primary fear that there would be Preserved among Xara's force of mages spreading the Bond of Unity turned out to be almost for nothing. Ansaldra's army had been quite stringent on expelling frays. There were a couple of isolated cases of mages transforming into Preserved, but in each case, the mages knew the signs and followed previous orders to kill them on the spot before they ever became a threat. After that, there was no further sign of trouble, much to Lucian's relief.

With that question settled, Lucian's next task was to make sure boots were on the ground so that the entire surface of Psyche could be brought under his control. Every settlement with more than a few hundred people received a Warden presence. The smaller towns got only a squadron of a dozen troops, while the larger cities, like Dara, Malia, and Kalm, might get a battalion numbering five hundred. Whatever the case, each contingent spread the relevant news across Psyche. Ansaldra was dead, along with Xara Mallis, and Lucian Abrantes was her successor.

The Wardens also warned the people about the coming Swarmer invasion. Once law and order were established, Lucian's next task was to separate those who could fight from those who could not. Those who could fight were assigned either to the Army or the Fleet. Those who couldn't fight were required to seek shelter in the Riftlands to protect themselves from the inevitable Swarmer invasion.

Lucian knew sheltering in the Riftlands wasn't the perfect solution, but it was far better than being exposed in the Golden Vale.

Of course, some resisted these sudden changes, those who didn't believe in the coming invasion. But with Lucian's limited time, all he could do was save those who wanted to be saved. If they fled into the wilderness, out of reach of the Wardens, there was little he could do about it.

Lucian didn't know the exact population of Psyche, but it was probably under half a million. Only a tiny fraction of that number would be qualified to serve in the military. According to his highest Warden officers, he could expect fifteen percent of Psyche's population to be marshaled into his army as fighters or support staff, but that was a pie-in-the-sky estimate. He was far more likely to get five percent enrollment, especially given how little time they had to arrange their affairs.

Assuming a population of five hundred thousand meant they could expect twenty-five thousand from the general population. Including Xara's old army, numbering about forty thousand soldiers, and the Wardens numbering five thousand, it would bring Lucian's total manpower up to seventy thousand soldiers. Not a bad start, but those numbers meant nothing unless he could position them correctly. Captain Warwick informed him that fifty thousand troops could be carried by the assault transports, which meant Lucian would have to garrison twenty thousand soldiers on the moon to defend against invasion. It seemed a fair balance to strike.

The days passed, and using the transports, Lucian marshaled most of his forces north of Malia, which the remnants of Xara's army still occupied.

The Warden officers were quite busy setting up the new chain of command. Monitoring their brands, Lucian saw they were obeying him without question. There had been no need for the brands, though Lucian kept them in place, since they weren't causing him any harm.

The Mage-Lords and Mage-Knights of Ansaldra's old empire also integrated into the military, and the soldiers under their command began training under the Wardens. Most had never even used a gun. Lucian combined Ansaldra's airships with Xara's. They would be all but useless to Lucian's efforts, but would probably have their uses keeping order here on Psyche while he was gone. Many of the airmen retrained into roles in the Warden fleet. With Admiral Mira Abrantes in charge, the transition happened quickly.

Lucian was not only organizing his forces. He was scouting the Riftlands for likely places to house the people who would remain behind. Psyche's rifts were filled with dozens upon dozens of cave systems that would, in tandem, provide adequate shelter for the thousands who would need them. They had to be filled with enough food to survive the coming storm. The people and Psyche's garrison would be better prepared to resist a potential Alkasen invasion in the rifts.

Lucian also began reorganizing Xara's mages. He found that once he had proven himself, most of the Mage-Knights and Mage-Lords accepted the change of management quickly enough, especially once they learned of Lucian's plans to resist the *Alkasen*. Those on the Mage Council promptly stepped into their roles, organizing and training their respective brigades.

Lucian was functioning as Chief Binder, though he planned to find someone else to take on the job. Fergus was Chief Radiant, Khairu Chief Dynamist, Selene Chief Atomicist, Plato Chief Thermalist, Serah Chief Gravitist, and Jagar Chief Psionic. There was also the Aspect of Space-Time, but Lucian would get to that later. He wasn't ready to advertise that Aspect's existence, at least not until he could control how it was used.

He learned Xara was calling her fledgling state "Starsea," and Lucian had difficulty changing the name. The idea had taken root, capturing the imaginations of mages and non-mages alike. It was easy to see why. On Psyche, the days of Xara's Starsea were romanticized. It had been a time, however brief, that the mages had been independent against a cruel League of Worlds. Or at least, that was how their version of things went.

Lucian knew it would be almost impossible to call his growing state anything *but* Starsea, even if it had a bad connotation elsewhere. In the end, he called it that. After all, the idea had momentum. Better to take control of the name, make it his own, and use that wind to fill his sails. And who knew? With the mages in no further danger of fraying, perhaps the idea of Starsea could be accepted in the Worlds, especially once Lucian started enacting the next stages of his strategy.

Three weeks after the first transports landed on Psyche, the transition of power was complete. There were only a few matters to attend to. Lucian had been so busy consolidating Psyche's surface that he still had to figure out where the Volsung Mages fit into it. This entire time, they had remained in orbit, debating whether to join him. Every time he visited Transcend White for an update, she asked for more time to shift the mindset of some of the more stubborn Transcends. Though Transcends Green and Yellow were both of sound mind, Transcends Red and Orange kept insisting more time was needed.

With everything almost under control, he decided it was time to settle things. He opened a portal to the bridge of *Resplendent*, not intending to leave until he had an answer.

THE SCENE on board was far more peaceful than last time. About ten Talents staffed the bridge's control panel, with Talent Horace at the helm. However, there was little need for him to be there since the ship was locked in geosynchronous orbit above Psyche, where it could easily communicate with Lucian and his ground forces.

At his appearance, a few of the Talents gave him acknowledging nods, which Lucian returned as he made his way down the ship's central corridor. The Transcends were spending most of their time in debate these days, so Lucian knew precisely where to find them.

Within the minute, he was standing in their meeting chamber. It was similarly appointed to the one on Volsung, though gleaming metal surfaces replaced the stone of the Academy. They had eight seats arranged in a line, all the same color as their respective Aspect. The Gray Seat was filled with an overweight man of late middle age with a halo of gray hair. Lucian remembered him as Psion Gray, who had scolded him when he had returned to Volsung after escaping Psyche. How long ago that seemed.

They sat in the same order as on Volsung, from left to right: Red, Orange, Yellow, Green, Blue, Gray, Violet, and finally, White at the very end. All watched him solemnly as he approached, though there was a hint of animosity in Transcends Red and Orange. Lucian could read nothing from the others' expressions.

Transcend White sat still as a statue, and Lucian sensed she was exasperated.

"Anything?" he asked.

"Nothing much to report, I'm afraid," Transcend White answered. "How goes the progress on the surface? Our Talents inform us that a substantial amount of work has been done."

Lucian nodded. "Yes. Things are almost ready." He cut right to the chase. "I need to know which way the Volsung Mages will go."

"We are still at an impasse, though some of us have changed our allegiances. Some for, some against."

That was different. "All right. Who stands with me, and who is against?"

Transcend Red gave a small smile. "Transcends Orange, Blue, Violet, and Gray are against joining forces. The rest of us are for joining."

That was a surprise. "I'm grateful for your support, Transcend Red. May I ask what spurred it?"

"It has less to do with you and more to do with a lack of alternate ideas. Where will the Volsung Mages go if not follow you, Sorcerer-Ascendant?"

"I have many ideas," Transcend Orange said. "But all you fools refuse to listen."

Transcend Red laughed. "Have you been keeping up with the Swarmers' movements, you blustering oaf? There *is* nowhere to go!"

"I will not submit this esteemed institution to a mere boy," Transcend Orange said. "He hasn't the right to call himself Sorcerer-Ascendant. How can we even verify his story is true?"

"I've explained already," Lucian said. "You're just choosing not to trust me."

Lucian looked at Transcend Blue, who had once supported him, along with Violet. Transcend Green had been against him at first, but it seemed he had switched allegiances.

"Transcend Blue," Lucian said, "why the change of heart?"

"You have yet to tell us what happened after meeting Transcend White on Oceanus. We need details, boy."

Everyone watched Lucian to see how he would react to the slight. From the smirk on Transcend Blue's lips, calling him "boy" hadn't been a slip.

Lucian ignored him. "I've given you more than enough time to figure things out. But now, you are in *my* domain. Your presence and disrespect of my office will no longer be tolerated."

Transcend Blue continued smirking, believing Lucian wouldn't do anything to him.

"You wouldn't dare go against us," Transcend Orange said. "We are the Spectrum of Transcends, and you will accord us the respect we're due if you wish for our help."

Lucian shrugged. "I don't have time for you to keep dragging this out. I don't need you. You need *me*. After this audience, I will speak with Vassar on Irion. If you've been keeping up with things, you'd know they're in imminent danger from the Swarmers. I'm sure they'll see sense in joining Starsea."

"Starsea?" Transcend Violet asked. "The rumors *are* true. You would become another Xara Mallis!"

"Why would you think that?" Lucian asked. "I've already achieved far more than Mallis ever did. If I wanted to rule the Worlds, I could set out to do that with or without your help. That's not my goal, though. All I want to do is stop the *Alkasen* before they destroy Earth. I want your help with that, though it's not needed." He faced the entire Spectrum, ensuring all of them were included in what he said next. "You are in Starsea space. For three weeks, I've let you hem and haw about what you're going to do. That ends now. You will tell me by the end of the day whether you'll join us. If not, you have one day to be out of Psyche's orbit and two weeks to be out of this star system."

Transcend Blue looked at him challengingly. "And if we're not?"

"Then *Resplendent* will be possessed by the Starsea navy."

"You have no right!" Transcend Blue said.

"I invoke my right as the Sorcerer-Ascendant, as the leader of all magekind. You may challenge it, Transcend Blue. If you dare."

Transcend Blue's silence clarified that he didn't want to do that.

"One day," Lucian said before turning and creating a portal back to the fields north of Malia.

"Sorcerer-Ascendant," Transcend White said. "Wait one moment. Please."

Lucian allowed his portal to wink out and gave her a chance to speak.

Transcend White turned to face the others. "The Sorcerer-Ascendant is right. We've wasted far too much time with this. The time for action is now. I will not allow the Volsung Academy to be ripped apart. I hoped to accomplish this in an agreeable, unanimous manner, as we have almost always done. However, certain individuals on the Spectrum cannot set aside their interests for the sake of humanity." She gave a firm nod. "Lucian has made himself clear. Whether or not you like it, he is the Sorcerer-Ascendant. Lucian inherited the title from Lakhmu and fulfilled Arian's Prophecy of the Seven. He doesn't just have the Seven Orbs, but also the one that was lost. His age is of no consequence. He has been tested in more ways than anyone on this council, including me. Rather than waiting, let us go forth now, boldly. We *will* commit the Volsung Mages to this cause. We will begin now."

Transcend Orange slammed the armrest of his chair. "Pre-posterous! Did you not hear him, Your High Eminence? *Starsea.* After fighting in the Mage War against your own flesh and blood, no less, you would give up everything to join them now? To become one of *them*?"

"This is not the same, Transcend Orange. The fraying is no more, and we must stand united. I will hear no further talk of disunity. Humanity is more important than your bloated ego."

Transcend Orange puffed himself up. "We must return to the First Fleet. If we only explained the situation, they would understand fully. Let us fight under the League, as we always have."

"We've already sent three messages to the First Fleet, Tran-scend Orange," Transcend Green said. "Either they never arrived, or worse, they were ignored. How much would you prostrate yourself before them?" All eyes went to him. "Look at it from the Hegemon's perspective. Infighting broke out on our ship. The Preserved sent out several threatening messages during the crisis. We are alone in a great storm, and Lucian Abrantes—the Chosen of the Manifold—is our only lifeline. Even if we *wanted* a different outcome, as I did, there *is* no other outcome. And I might add, Transcend Orange, that you have failed to come up with a single idea that wouldn't guarantee the death of every mage aboard this ship!"

Transcend Orange retreated into silence. His allies, Tran-scends Violet, Blue, and Gray, were not coming to his defense. Perhaps their opinions had even been swayed.

"I will follow you," Transcend Blue said. "But I require the Volsung Academy to keep its autonomy."

"Of course," Lucian said. "We have our own Mage Division, but if it helps grease the wheels, I will concede that. Transcend White will lead you; she'll only answer to me."

Transcend Orange stubbornly set his jaw while Transcend

Gray's face assumed a stony silence. The only softening came from Transcend Violet, who sadly shook her head.

"That it has to come to this," Transcend Violet said. "I've just realized something. I believe in the Prophecy of the Seven. And here you stand before us, its fulfillment. I, a Psionic, cannot accept the fulfillment of a prophecy." She gave a bitter smile at the irony. "It's true, though. If you are the Chosen, then what does our opinions matter? If the Manifold wills it, anyone standing in the way will get steamrolled. Even when we exiled you to the Isle of Madness, it was the will of the Manifold because it led you to the Orb of Binding. Even when we thought we were being wise, preventing the next Xara Mallis, here you stand before us, the head of a new Starsea that is fated to rise above its predecessor." She laughed. "What fools we are." Finally, she nodded. "I'm tired of going against the will of the Manifold. I will follow you, too, Sorcerer-Ascendant. To the ends of the galaxy."

All eyes now went to Transcends Gray and Orange. Transcend Gray cleared his throat.

"I will bow to the will of the majority."

Last of all was Transcend Orange, now alone. His expression was dark, but he had dug himself in and didn't want to back down.

"I see I have no choice," he said. "So long as you don't violate our sacred traditions."

"The Volsung Mages' affairs will remain untouched," Lucian said. "Your training might change since the fraying is no longer dangerous."

At that moment, Khairu's voice entered Lucian's mind. *Lucian! We have trouble.*

What's going on?

Well, it's the caves in Snake Rift. The one you told us to explore. There are Preserved here! Hundreds of them.

Lucian frowned. That was something that had slipped his mind. The frays of Psyche had long called the Darkrift their home. And, of course, none of that had changed in the last few years. That would mean hundreds of mages in the caves, all bearing the Bond of Unity.

If Lucian intended those caves to be used as a shelter, they would have to be cleared out.

Where are you?

In Blood Wyvern *now. Right above Snake Rift. How are we going to deal with this?*

An idea was already forming in Lucian's mind. *Stay there for now and stay out of range of their magic.*

He let the connection go and opened a portal back to the surface of Psyche.

20

ONCE LUCIAN HAD GATHERED ALL the members of the Mage Council and shared the news, he opened a portal to *Blood Wyvern*. They found Khairu on the bridge, surveying the entrance to the Darkrift about five hundred meters below the hovering spaceship.

The scene was much as Khairu described. About a hundred human figures stood eerily still in front of the entrance. With Radiance, Lucian could see their glowing violet eyes and frayed skin. He sensed a collective Psionic ward of surprising strength when he reached out for them. Lucian could force the issue and break the ward, but they could easily withdraw within the cavern by the time he'd gathered more ether to undo their Bonds.

There was a more straightforward way they could deal with the issue.

Lucian looked down at the Preserved grimly. "It's going to be a fight."

"It's a rotting shame," Serah said. "But I guess nothing can be done about it."

"Are we sure about that?" Emma asked. "Wouldn't we need to find the one controlling all of them? That's what you did with Transcend Gray."

Lucian shook his head. "It's not so simple. Transcend Gray was the only fray on board the ship, and the only source of the Bond." He nodded at the frayed mages below. "However, the people in the Darkrift were *all* frays. That means *all* are the source of the Bond."

"They're decentralized," Selene said. "It's harder to attack something that doesn't have a single source."

"That's right," Lucian said.

"So I *was* right," Serah said. Everyone looked at her as she smiled. "Remember way back in *Ethereal*, when we talked about these Preserved?"

The conversation came back to Lucian. "Space zombies?"

She nodded sagely. "That's right. Space zombies. In a manner of speaking, of course. I doubt they have a taste for human flesh."

"I should hope not," Plato said, patting his belly. "I'd be the main course."

"So, we have no choice but to kill them," Emma said.

"Yes," Lucian said. "And *we* need to clear out those caves. If we don't, they'll be a thorn in our side, and our people could use the shelter." He toggled a topographical map of the rift below them while the others gathered around. "Looks like we can use a plateau a couple of kilometers up the rift from here. That would make a good staging point to gather the mages."

"I've got an idea," Linus said. "And we wouldn't have to risk a single mage."

"If you're going to say a few torpedoes, I've already thought of that."

"Oh. Well, it certainly *would* make things easier, you must admit."

"Maybe," Lucian admitted. "But it could risk burying the entrance. It would be a shame to lose such an important asset. Bullets and even railgun fire can be blocked. They have enough mages to shield just about anything. Which means we need to fight with *our* mages."

"I have to agree with Lucian," Serah said. "This place is the ideal shelter. Tens of thousands of people can live in shallower parts. The frays cultivate lots of crops, too. *Fields* of them. There are lakes as well, chock full of fish."

"I'm sure all that can support a population of a few thousand," Fergus said. "We're talking about tens of thousands of civilians here, which still have to be moved."

"No, the food sources won't last forever," Serah said. "But the people of Kiro village will know how to stretch the supplies. Plus, they'll be able to plant more fields. There are many hidden valleys, and the best part, if there's trouble, people can always escape underground."

Lucian had to agree; the Darkrift was the safest option for the civilians of Psyche. Only time would tell if it could hold out against the Swarmers. And, of course, there would be those who would refuse to be moved, so there might be fewer people to support than they thought.

"We're taking over these caves," Lucian said. "No question about that. I want the troops to get some experience, too. I doubt this will be the last time we fight these Preserved."

"Well, looks like there's two hundred down there," Fergus said. "We have about fifteen hundred Psyche Mage-Knight and Mage-Lords at our disposal. Two thousand, when we add the Volsung Mages, though not all are battle trained. As long as we have enough shielding Psionics, I doubt the Bond will pass on."

"Yes, Psionics is the chief Aspect we need to defend against," Lucian said. "However, the Bond uses *all* the Aspects in some form. We need to ensure every Aspect is covered."

Linus cleared his throat. "Should be no trouble with the number of mages we have. Say, that reminds me. Who here actually knows *anything* about fighting battles with magic? From what I understand, things change drastically when large numbers of mages are on both sides. We wouldn't have seen that since the Mage War, and I was only a lad around that time."

Khairu answered. "As a Psion, I've received some education on the matter, but my training is far from complete."

Everyone looked at Jagar, the only one with any experience of the Mage War. He had fought for Xara's Starsea Mages over five decades ago, holding a position of authority as a member of Xara's Council of the Wise.

He cleared his throat. "War is horrible, however one tries to justify it. Just thought I'd say that. It seems there's no road around it in this case. The only road through war is paved with lives."

No one responded to this because it was true. All they could do was move forward with eyes wide open.

"As you probably know," Jagar said, "mages changed warfare forever. Conventional weapons are practically useless when there are enough mages on both sides. There are so many shields and wards going on that the effect of guns is largely nullified. Heavy armament can still bust through mage shields, but they have to be rotting strong." Jagar withdrew his shockspear, giving it a few adroit twirls. "That's why they invented the shockspear. You'll get used to using it because magic's good for rot when there are over fifty mages on either side."

Khairu nodded. "Yes. Until now, we've only experienced duels and smaller skirmishes. Battles with mages are won in one of two ways: one side overwhelms the magical defenses of the other. If enough mages fall, wards and shields can be cracked. Or, in the event of a stalemate, it comes down to a physical brawl until one side is too weak to resist the other."

"So what does this mean, practically speaking?" Lucian asked.

"It depends," Jagar said. "If two sides are of equal magical power, it's going to come down to hand-to-hand butchery. Any magic you stream under the enemy's wards will be blunted. You'll be able to attack relatively close to you, but it becomes a lot harder at a distance. You won't be able to shoot a fireball at fifty meters and hit something, for example. Thermal wards dissolve that fireball long before it hits its intended target."

"Okay, what about us?" Lucian asked. "We have two thousand mages. There are probably two hundred down there. We could overwhelm them, right?"

Jagar nodded. "The proper strategy is to have enough mages to ward all the Aspects and then to use your surplus to counter-stream the enemy's defenses. Once those are down, the rest of your mages can take out whatever's left."

"Sounds simple," Emma said.

"It is. Bloody, but simple."

Emma looked down at the Preserved. "Most of them don't even *have* weapons . . ."

"Don't be fooled," Fergus said. "They are dangerous. We don't even know how they spread the Bond. Or even if the Bond can be countered with magic."

"We need to learn how to fight them," Lucian said. "But maybe you have a point, Fergus. Maybe I should only commit a thousand mages to start with."

"If you're going to fight," Jagar said, "do so with overwhelming force. It minimizes your losses and brings the battle to a swift conclusion. That's how Xara did it. Though her fleet and armies were smaller, she concentrated them on where the

League was weak, winning victory after victory. She'd take their ships, supplies, and sometimes even their soldiers."

"He's not Xara Mallis," Serah said.

"Aye, that he's not. But that doesn't mean he can't learn a thing or two from her."

"How did she lose, anyway?" Lucian asked.

"The League finally stopped squabbling and recognized the threat she posed. At her height, everything outside the First Worlds was under her domain. But once the League got its act together, the First Worlds held ninety percent of the Worlds' population. Even Xara couldn't stand against that. It all turned around in Archea. The first time she took a fight she probably should have avoided."

"What happened?" Serah asked.

"I was there on her flagship," Jagar said. "It was the first time the League consented to use mages on their vessels. That was something Xara hadn't expected. Nor did she expect a pincer movement to come from around Archea, with ships filled with Atomicists and Gravitists that allowed a speedy attack. The battle was hard-fought, but at last, Xara gave the order to retreat. It would be the first of many as the League's industrial capacity kicked into overdrive. Three years later, the Starsea Mages had been reduced to a single planet, Isis. And we all know what happened there."

"She was so close to winning," Emma said. "Scary . . ."

"We can learn from that battle," Jagar said. "Assume nothing in war. Xara was sure the League would never use mages. She was sure the Volsung Mages would never throw in their lot with them. She was convinced the League planned to purge the mages following their victory, so in her mind, no mage would ever consent to help the League. From the number of mages who flew under the banner of Starsea, many believed it to be so." He nodded grimly. "But she never counted on the Mage-League Concordat. It guaranteed their safety when the war ended as long as they served the League as an unofficial branch of its military." He nodded grimly. "The rest is history."

Lucian watched the Preserved in the entrance of the Dark-rift below. "I don't want to leave anything to chance. We'll gather every available mage we have on the plateau. Have a third of each brigade committed to warding, another third counter-streaming, and the final third attacking offensively."

"A sound strategy," Jagar said. "Little room for error."

"I can try to remove the Bond," Lucian said. "If I can find one mage who's the source of everything. I just don't think that's going to happen."

"Either way, these Preserved must be dealt with," Selene said. When she looked at Lucian, it was hard not to feel like Ansaldra was looking at him. Her expression and green eyes were the only difference, whereas Ansaldra's had been perma-nently violet, perhaps from constantly streaming Psionic Magic.

"There is something I was hoping to say," Selene said. "I'm not sure when I'll get the opportunity again."

"What's that?" Lucian asked.

"After the battle, when you leave Psyche, you'll need someone to keep things in order here while you're gone. I'm not sure how much use I'll be off this moon. I understand I'm the Chief Atomicist, but Psyche is my home. I've also kept some key memories from my time as the Sorceress-Queen."

Lucian frowned. "Memories? What do you mean?"

"Don't worry," Selene said. "The Queen is completely gone."

"I know that," Lucian said. "I dealt with her myself."

"Of course." She cleared her throat somewhat nervously. "What I meant was, I remember certain things, like details regarding her administration, the names of the lords and ladies of her court, finances, the movements of its politics. That will be useful when handling whatever nobles have remained behind."

"What are you trying to say? That you want to be in charge while I'm gone?"

"*Someone* has to be in charge. And since Ansaldra ruled from my person, and I have noble blood, although of a minor house . . . the Mage-Lords and Ladies would come to accept me as your representative. If you want someone who can get things done, it's me."

There was only one question Lucian had. Could he trust her? And would the people of Psyche accept her or come to understand the complexity of the situation that she *wasn't* the Sorceress-Queen, just the person the Queen had possessed?

Lucian doubted that greatly. But he needed someone to watch over Psyche, and her knowledge would be helpful.

"Are you sure about this?" Lucian asked.

"I am."

"Give me some time to think about it. I would need a new Chief Atomicist. Right now, though, let's focus on the battle."

Selene nodded graciously. "Of course."

"Anything else?" Lucian asked.

Heads shook all around.

"Then let's begin our battle plans. Jagar . . . would you be willing to advise me?"

"Advise, yes. But if you want me down there leading the charge, I'm too old for that."

"I understand. You have the most experience with these things."

"What you outlined earlier should work."

"It just seems . . . too simple. Lives are at stake."

"You want my opinion? It's important not to make things

too complicated. You'll confuse your soldiers. If it were me, I'd do what you already said. Ward with a third, counter-stream with another third, and blast them to bits with the last third."

"But if they can be turned, it's a tragic loss of life," Emma said.

"A complication," Jagar said. "A complication that could see lives on your side lost. Decide whose lives are more important. The mages will watch for that."

Emma went quiet, but from her expression, this troubled her.

"Let's set up the mages," Lucian said.

21

THE NEXT DAY, Lucian floated before the Mage Division and the Volsung Mages, each separated into their separate Aspect Brigades. Over two thousand men and women faced him, their faces stern and ready to receive orders. Though their modes of dress were different, they all wore colored sashes similar to the Talents of the Volsung Academy. It was the easiest way to tell what division they belonged to, essential for maintaining confluent streams in the middle of battle.

Lucian reached for the Ether and modulated his voice, so it was loud enough to boom across the landscape.

"Today is a new beginning. History will reflect on this day and say this is where Starsea began."

The mages looked at each other before returning their attention to Lucian.

"They called you mad, but all I see are warriors! Not since the Mage War has there been such a gathering. From the rifts of Psyche, from the sands of the Westlands. From the Mountains of Madness and the Golden Vale. From the coasts of the Sea of Eros, from the northern forests. Together, we are all

Psycheans, and they will know us from Terminus to Sulisto! From Fringe to Core, Trailward and Spinward. The galaxy will know you as saviors. It all begins here."

The Starsea Mages shouted their agreement while the Volsung Mages shifted their feet uneasily.

"They had the gall to call this the Mad Moon. Soon, they will learn the hard truth. The only thing we're mad for is freedom!"

The mages roared, almost as if they could taste that freedom now.

"Your captains have laid out the battle plans already. I don't intend for this to be a fair fight. We will fall upon them without warning, with thunder, lightning, and fury! The Preserved are a fearsome force, but one of you is worth more than any of them! We will win the Darkrift for Psyche, the salvation of our citizens. And if you are afraid, remember . . . you have the Chosen of the Manifold on your side! The *true* Chosen who holds *all* the Aspects of Magic, and not some pretender who only had *two rotting Orbs!*"

This got a laugh. Lucian smiled, utterly confident in the loyalty of his troops.

"I am the Sorcerer-Ascendant, named by Sorcerer Lakhmu himself. I'll be there with you on the front lines, as will the Chief Mages. None of us is a coward, hiding behind the battle lines while you risk your lives."

The mages were already reaching for their shockspears, properly riled up before battle began.

"The Darkrift is our last bit of business before we reach for the stars! So fight with bravery and honor. To victory, now and forever. For Starsea!"

"Starsea!" came the unified response, along with some shouts of "Chosen!"

Lucian noted a few familiar faces in the crowd: Elder Ytrib

from Kiro Village, along with Elders Jalisa, Gia, and Erymmo. He even saw Morgana, the young woman he had met in the village so long ago, now more grown, her face stern and ready to battle.

"I see you, Kiro Village!"

They shouted back at his acknowledgment.

The faces of the Volsung Mages remained neutral, the speech having far less effect on them. Clearly, they didn't fully recognize Lucian for who he was yet. That would come in time.

Already, the mages were arranging themselves on the plateau and setting their wards, the collective power pulsating in the surrounding air. Lucian flew to the front of the lines, finding the Preserved still milling about the wide entrance into the Darkrift with little to no organization. They didn't even seem to know that his mages were there. Several Warden gunships hovered overhead for additional air support, if the situation called for it.

There was only one disadvantage for the Starsea troops. Only a narrow trail led from the plateau to the field of battle. It would allow the Preserved to defend easily from that direction, and would undoubtedly cause casualties among Lucian's mages. Lucian wanted as few deaths as possible on his side. A crushing victory was the only acceptable outcome.

He already had a plan in place. He would open not one but *two* portals, one directly in front of the Preserved in the Darkrift, and another from the right side. Combined with the trail which snaked down the left side, it provided three angles to attack. More than enough to deal with the threat.

Lucian hovered near the left side of the rift, where the first troops were readying themselves to march. The only job of this third of the army was to ward every Aspect, to nullify the effect of the Preserved magic.

Lucian settled down near Fergus, who led that contingent to the rift floor.

"Go?" Fergus asked.

"Forward march," Lucian confirmed.

Fergus turned to his column. "Ten-hut!"

The mages drew themselves up proudly, spears at the ready.

"*Forward . . . harch!*"

The soldiers gave a unified grunt as they stepped forward down the trail. It would take them about ten minutes to reach the rift floor. Lucian flew above them for a minute to inspire confidence. When he peered down at the entrance of the Darkrift, the Preserved were still unmoving, but Lucian could see various weapons held in their hands. Usually, nothing more advanced than bronze spears and shields and even a few clubs fashioned with sticks and stones.

After a few minutes, he flew back to the plateau to prepare the rest of the troops. He began gathering the ether to create the two portals, something he had never tried before. After a few minutes of collecting ether, the portals opened in the middle and side of the plateau.

The Preserved reacted almost instantly as soon as the portals appeared before them. They formed ranks and shot massive fireballs into the openings. Plato's brigade strengthened its ward, causing the fireballs to be absorbed harmlessly.

By now, Fergus's brigade had reached the rift floor. They fanned out, forming ranks and sticking their shockspears out, most of them forming blue binding shields on their shield arms.

This action caused the Preserved to draw back and create their own battle lines in eerie unison before the Darkrift entrance. Once the line was firm, the Preserved shambled toward Fergus's brigade, falling upon the line of Starsea Mages. Already, the first of the Preserved went down. He waited until the Preserved were locked into battle with Fergus's brigade, so they couldn't easily withdraw.

"Go into the portals!" Lucian shouted. "Now!"

The mages, led by Lucian's friends, poured through the open portals, joining the melee. The mages that went through the second portal counter-streamed the Preserved wards, while the mages of the third portal used offensive magic to take down their foes. Lucian was the last to pass through, allowing them to close behind him.

He flew above the melee, entering the Ether to find a potential source of the Bond. From the Light Realm, he could see the Focuses of the Preserved mages fighting below him. But unlike the Preserved on *Resplendent*, most of the Bonds didn't point toward any mage being the source. It was much as he had suspected; they had each succumbed to the Bond. There was no choice but to fight and kill them all.

Half of the Preserved had fallen five minutes into the battle, with Lucian's mages forming an impenetrable wall around them.

Lucian spied a pair of Preserved shambling up on an unsuspecting Volsung Talent that had trailed away from the main battle line. One of the Preserved fought the Talent while the other hung back, its body surrounded with violet luminescence as a stream of violet magic began eddying toward the Talent. He knew he was witnessing the spread of the Bond and had seconds left to prevent it.

Lucian shot forward, Lightspear extended, driving the weapon clean through both mages. The Talent looked at him in shock, and Lucian knew he hadn't succumbed from the clarity in his eyes. Lucian left him there, charging into the Preserved mass with a roar. The Starsea Mages around him responded quickly, rushing to fill the gap.

Lucian held his Focus, fighting like a madman as the

Preserved fell upon him from all sides. He snarled as he stabbed a huge one, after which he phased a short distance to avoid the swing of an axe. It seemed these Preserved were drawn to him far more than anyone else. That made sense; they were *Alkasen*, and he held the Orbs, something they would be attracted to like moths to a flame. He surrounded himself in an aura of Dynamistic Magic, causing any Preserved who got too close to be thrown back by lightning. Such was Lucian's power that the Preserved had no shot at warding his magic, especially considering the counter-streams of his own mages.

Lucian knew the battle would be easy, but it almost seemed *too* easy.

His suspicions were confirmed when some of the Starsea Mages began shouting in alarm, looking toward the cavern.

"There's more!" he heard someone shout.

Lucian turned to watch this development. Indeed, a mass of new Preserved was charging out of the caverns. *Hundreds* of them.

Lucian had to get ahead of this before his soldiers panicked. He floated above the battle again, pointing Lightspear toward the new enemy. He created a Psionic ward to encompass the entire battlefield, inspiring feelings of bravery and calm in his troops. Almost instantly, he saw it take effect. Where mages had been looking left and right, wondering what to do, now those closest to the Darkrift turned to meet the new threat while the rest focused on mopping up outside.

Lucian floated toward the Darkrift entrance. He reached for the Orb of Gravitonics, creating a large gravity amplification disc across half of the cave entrance. That slowed the pace of the *Alkasen* considerably, causing their line to become uneven. The wings of Lucian's mages quickly crushed the advancing Preserved, allowing them to surround the slower ones in the middle.

Within half an hour, the battle was over. Hundreds of dead bodies, mainly of the Preserved, littered the entrance of the Darkrift. Even though the Bond had turned them into senseless monsters, it was hard not to feel a sense of loss. It would have been an enormous boon for his forces if Lucian could have cured them.

For now, however, all that was left was to clean up the mess.

22

THE STARSEA MAGES worked to bury their dead.

In the end, over six hundred frayed mages had charged out of that cave, so including those on the surface, it was an army of almost one thousand Preserved—over five times the expected number. The Starsea Mages' casualties were just over a hundred soldiers. That was a hundred more than Lucian wanted, but given the surprise ambush, it was probably the best Lucian could have hoped for.

Lucian left Selene in charge for now. It would be an excellent test of her abilities. While she set things in order, Lucian went with Serah and Fergus to meet the Kiro mages, who survived the battle. It was a reunion that made him nervous. There was no telling how Serah would react to the father and village that had exiled her. Fergus would be glad to see the Elders and update them on how things had gone.

They found the Kiro mages on the rift's edge, cooking food over a fire in their camp. There were only ten of them, including the Elders, and all stood at Lucian's approach. Every eye went to Serah, seeming to note her healthy appearance.

Elder Ytrib looked much the same, except now he bore new lines that bespoke additional worries. It was much the same for his wife, Elder Gia, Serah's stepmother. Elder Erymmo gave Lucian a respectful nod. Lucian remembered long ago when he had learned simple wards from him. What would the man think of Lucian's abilities now? He wanted to spill out everything, but he knew there wouldn't be time, and this was Serah's moment, not his.

Serah watched her father, and none of the villagers spoke as the two eyed each other. Elder Ytrib's face looked almost grieved. As much as he wanted to embrace her, he knew that Serah still hadn't forgiven him for her exile. So, he hung back, fumbling for something to say, not knowing how to shatter the silence between them.

"My daughter," he began, somewhat formally. "You look as young as the day you left Kiro. Almost three standard years have passed since then. I would have thought, surely, you would have been . . ."

He trailed off, not completing the thought.

Serah just cracked a smile. "What can I say? I have a good skin regimen."

Ytrib frowned as if he doubted that was the reason. "Be serious, Serah. How did it reverse?"

Serah nodded toward Lucian. "You have him to thank for that."

Elder Ytrib's eyes widened as he looked at Lucian. "*You*? What happened?"

Lucian decided he'd rather not get into it. "It would take too long to explain."

"I . . . see. A shame. We had a mage from the village that frayed right after the Battle of Malia. Horrible business, that. But we did what we had to do."

Lucian didn't want the details.

Ytrib once again faced Serah. "I won't make any excuses, Serah, for what I did."

"You don't have to defend yourself. All's well that ends well, right?"

"You can't mean that. You have every right to be angry at me!"

"Oh, I am," she said. "You chose Kiro over your own family. Mom would have beaten you silly."

"Please don't bring her into this."

"I am. She'd want you to know that, too." She watched him closely. "Maybe that's enough punishment, though."

Ytrib sighed. "Yes. Maybe so."

Elder Gia just watched Serah pityingly with her soft brown eyes. Serah was practically ignoring her existence. It was clear Serah didn't much care for her.

"Still," Serah said, "maybe there's a reason things happened the way they did."

She looked at Lucian, and Elder Ytrib seemed to read the closeness of that expression. His eyes went back to him. "Lucian, I'm glad you and Serah are both thriving. I suppose you found the Orb of Psionics, plus a few more, eh?"

"Not only that," Fergus said. "The mission expanded beyond the salvation of Psyche to that of all the Worlds. We are the only ones who can stop the *Alkasen*."

"Yes, I know. I'm glad you're alive too, Fergus. Seems I chose the right man for the job." Ytrib frowned. "That reminds me. What became of Cleon? He didn't abandon the mission, did he?"

Fergus shook his head solemnly. "Far from it. He fell in the Burning Sands. We fought the Queen herself and about twenty of her Mage-Knights and Lords. I survived the encounter, but the same cannot be said for him. I'm only here because of his sacrifice. Without him, the quest for the Orb would have failed."

"Odious news indeed," Elder Ytrib said. "And yet, I feared that all of you had died. It's a shame that we are only speaking now, but I suppose such things cannot be helped. I have lived with the guilt of sending all of you to your deaths. That you have survived and risen to lead the fight against these *Alkasen* is a testament to everyone's enduring strength."

Fergus's chest swelled with pride. It was almost as if he were the captain of the Kiro Watch again.

"We can talk about all this later," Ytrib said. "Serah. Will you consent to speak with me?"

She sighed. From her face, it seemed like she didn't want to, while a part of her did. "Fine. Just don't expect forgiveness."

"Fair enough."

They went off together, and Elder Erymmo approached Lucian. The man looked older than when they'd last met, his beard more white than gray. "We meet again, Chosen," he said, giving a slight bow. The movement was slow, as if it caused him discomfort.

"No need for that," Lucian said. "Without you, I'd probably be dead."

"What do you mean?"

"You taught me about wards," Lucian said. "I can't tell you how many times that saved my life on Psyche."

"Well," Elder Erymmo said, somewhat flustered, "I'm glad my lessons were of use."

"Seriously," Lucian said. "Thank you." He took out the carbon alloy shockspear Elder Erymmo had given him. He still carried it, although he had Lightspear now. "And this has saved my life more than a few times, too." He held it out. "You told me your friend made it. So, I think it's fitting for me to give it back."

Elder Erymmo held out his palms, shaking his head. "A gift

given is given for life. Keep it, Lucian. May it remind you of your time among us, as short as it was. I gave it to you in friendship. I'm glad it was useful, but now, consider it a gift from the people of Psyche, who have accepted you as their own. It was not your fate to be confined to this world. And now, we Psycheans will follow you to the stars, a place most never dreamed of going."

"I have a feeling all this is going to lead back to Earth," Lucian said.

Elder Erymmo said. "I haven't gazed upon Earth's blue skies since my youth. It would be fine to see that one last time."

"With me, Erymmo, you will," Lucian said. "I wish I had something of equal value to give you."

"You have already given it. Though Psyche is my home, I have longed to see the Worlds again for many years. When I was younger, I was very bitter about my fate. Like Captain Fergus, I was a young mage at Irion, brash and bold. That was before his time, though. The Academy life was never for me. I had five years of travel and adventures before the mage-hunters caught up with me."

Lucian smiled. He couldn't imagine the sedate Elder as a reckless young man. "Was it worth it?"

"Oh, yes. I did more living in five years than most do in five decades." He heaved a heavy sigh. "I wonder . . ."

"Wonder what?" Lucian asked, unable to help his curiosity.

"This is probably too much to share. But before coming to Psyche, I was forced to leave someone behind. Someone very dear to me." He shook his head as if coming out of a daydream. "Ah, foolishness! We will see, Lucian, we will see . . ."

Before Lucian could ask anything more, Erymmo hobbled off.

Lucian looked at Serah and her father, who were now a fair way off and in deep conversation. Fergus was talking with Elder

Sina and Elder Jalisa. Lucian was about to go off on his own when Morgana approached him, the few extra years lending her face a profound beauty. There was still a mischievous glint in her eyes, but something told Lucian she now had the discipline to temper her impetuous nature.

"Lucian!" She gave him a quick hug before pulling back suddenly, as if remembering herself. She gave an embarrassed laugh. "Or I guess I should say, Sorcerer-Ascendant." She giggled again. "It's good to see you."

"How have things been in the village?"

"We're alive, if that's what you mean. Things have been *insane*." Before Lucian could even ask, she was getting into it. "Just a few days after you left, we got attacked by some of the Queen's guards! We beat them back, though, and things were peaceful for a long time. At least until Xara Mallis came. Before we knew what was happening, we were being put in this giant army, leading a resistance against Ansaldra! It was *wild*. Except it wasn't anything like what we imagined. She gave some evil orders. I . . . saw some bad things. She would kill entire villages and tell the Thermalists to burn down cities that put up a fight. Sometimes, she forced the mages to do those things with magic. And of course, she would . . ." She swallowed. "She would kill anyone who stood up to her and absorb their Focus. That's the rumor, anyway."

Lucian nodded. "That's right. That's what she was doing."

"Anyway, we just went along with it because we had no choice, you know? If you were a mage, you had to fight for Xara. We were too scared to refuse. And she always promised that she would give us land and riches, especially when we left Psyche to spread her domain. Honestly, it didn't feel like a resistance against Ansaldra. That's when you came in. It was a bit confusing because everyone was saying *you* were the evil one, but I knew that couldn't be true. I knew you! I couldn't speak much in your defense because it would've killed me. But as soon as Xara was gone, the Kiro mages made sure the rest of them knew you were on our side and that you weren't like Xara. I'm not sure how much good it did, but we spread the good word, anyway."

"It probably helped more than you know. Every bit helps."

She bobbed her head almost furiously. "Oh, I agree! Within a day, everyone knew everything about you, how you saved the foraging party in the Greenrift, how you took down those wyverns all by yourself, how you volunteered to seek the Orb of Psionics, something hundreds of mages have died doing over the years. Everyone knows Jalisa's prophecy about the Orb of Psionics in the Burning Sands. That only the Chosen of the Manifold would find it. I'll be honest; many Starsea Mages didn't want to follow you at first. Either they liked Xara and believed *she* was the Chosen, or they thought you would be just as bad as her. But then, we found out everything else. Like how you stopped the Wardens from destroying Psyche, stopped the Swarmer fleet, and everything else besides that! All the Starsea Mages have been brought around. We'll follow you to the ends of the galaxy!"

Lucian had already learned much of this over the last few weeks, but didn't want to burst Morgana's bubble. "Thanks for doing your part, Morgana."

Her cheeks flushed. "Of course!"

Serah sidled back. "Hello, Morgana. You've grown. You were fifteen standard years the last I saw you?"

Morgana's face quickly erased its obvious infatuation, though Serah would have had to be blind not to see it. "Yes. I'm a Starsea Mage now. A Binder, just like Lucian!"

"Well, Lucian is *actually* a Psionic," Serah said. "But I get your point." She took his arm. "He *is* pretty great, isn't he?"

Morgana, at last, seemed to get the point. "I'll leave the two of you be. Captain Pavan had some duties for me." She gave Lucian a warm smile. "It was good catching up, Lucian! I mean, Sorcerer-Ascendant."

Once Morgana left, Lucian and Serah watched the milling soldiers. Most of the gruesome work of burying the dead was done, while now most were setting up camp and cooking their evening meals.

Serah looked around approvingly. "Congrats on your first victory, Chosen. I had to admit I was worried there for a second."

Lucian nodded. "I'd never tell the soldiers this, but so was I. I didn't expect that surprise ambush." He considered for a moment. "It's a little worrying, to be honest. They were more coordinated than I expected."

"I know," Serah said. "It shows that our enemy has at least a modicum of intelligence."

"That seems to be the case. We still don't know how the Preserved work, but the Bond allows them to fight together more closely than we thought. It's just a shame I couldn't save them. They were people. Once."

"You can't blame yourself. You did what you could to protect the ones under your command. You can't do everything. You can't *be* everything, even if you have all the Orbs."

"I'm the Chosen. I should be able to save whoever I want. Just like I saved you."

"That's not the way it works."

"I know. It's just . . ." He sighed. "And I gave that speech like this battle was going to be glorious. I'm a hypocrite. This was a slaughter."

"You were inspiring your soldiers. It's not easy to kill, but it has to be done. So what if what you say isn't honest all the time? Remember the goal. We need these caves to save tens of thousands of people, and there was no way of saving these Preserved. Whoever they were before is gone."

Lucian knew Serah was right, but it was hard not to feel he could have done more. "If there was just a way to find out which ones to take out, that way I could have saved the rest..."

"Until that day comes, stop feeling guilty. We need your head in the game. This is just the beginning, and it won't be the last time we face these Preserved."

"You're right." He paused. "What do you think of letting Selene run things here?"

It was a while before she responded. Lucian wasn't sure if that was hesitancy or her just thinking.

"I . . . think she will do well. For the reasons she stated. Of course, no one's a perfect fit, but she's willing to do the job, which is more than any of us. She's committed to helping you, and she is cool under pressure. That'll be useful. Her only job is keeping Psyche safe so you can return the Orbs. As long as she can do that, she's a good fit."

"That could be years," Lucian said.

Again, he was reminded of the hopelessness of his mission. Selene was the least of his problems.

"We need to get moving," he said. "As soon as tomorrow."

Serah nodded. "Yeah. I figured that would be the case."

"How'd things go with your dad?"

Serah looked over in Ytrib's direction, who was watching her from beside the fire.

"I . . . think I've made peace with him. What he did was wrong, but I understand why he did it. It's been tearing him up for a while. I . . . can't make myself stay mad at him. Not with the Worlds going the way they are." She sighed. "I just don't understand why things must be so complicated."

"I know what you mean," Lucian said. "What I wouldn't give

to go back to the days before the Orb of Space-Time, where we could just hang out on the spaceship together." He smiled. "Even Psyche was nice, even if we were fighting for our lives." He gave a sudden laugh. "Remember that first night on Archea Station?"

Serah laughed in memory. "My first bar *and* bar fight. How could I forget?"

Lucian laughed. "Things are always simpler when you have one goal. Find the next Orb. Easy enough, right?" He shook his head. "Now it's not so simple. We have to choose between fighting back against the Swarmers or going after the First Gate. The goal isn't obvious anymore. There's no room for mistakes."

"Yeah, it is more complicated. But I don't think I would go back."

"You wouldn't?"

She shook her head and smiled. "We have each other. As long as I have you, nothing else matters. Things might be complicated, but being with you isn't. If that makes sense."

Lucian smiled. "Yeah, I feel the same way, too. When things are complicated, it's easy to think about simpler times. I'm afraid we won't see those days again. We're fighters now. We're going to spend the rest of our lives saving people. And you're right. When you can't be yourself anymore, when you have to be strong for everyone else . . . it just makes that other person more important. You're the only thing about my life that's simple. Nothing else matters." A moment of silence passed between them. Lucian took her hand. "I love you."

Serah looked into his eyes and smiled. "I love you, too. Look, I know things are complicated now. But think of it this way. The sooner we end this, the sooner we can have a life together."

Lucian nodded. "You always give me the right perspective."

"Of course. A little optimism is the cure for just about

everything. I've been thinking. After this is over, there's nothing we *can't* do. There are so many worlds out there . . ."

Serah stopped short, clearly realizing what she had been saying. Lucian just watched her, smiling.

"What?"

"I'm . . . sorry. What you told me about the First Gate, that you would have to pass through it . . ." She shook her head. "Silumko said it would . . ."

She trailed off, not wanting to finish. Her face softened, and it looked as if she might cry at any moment.

Lucian just smiled and held her face in his hands. "Look. I know what Silumko and Rhana said. What returning the Orbs means. I don't believe a word of it. There *has* to be a way to do it without dying."

"Maybe," Serah said. "I hope so. I don't know what I'd do without you. We'll find a way."

Lucian nodded. "Of course we will."

Deep down, though, Lucian wasn't sure. Even if he was the Chosen of the Manifold, some things were beyond him.

He kissed her, but the feeling in his heart was still a distant contrast to how it used to be. It felt as if the future wasn't sure, as if they might never get their simple life back, even after everything was over. And Serah was right. There might not be a way to come back from the First Gate.

But they still had each other. They were in this together until the end.

23

AFTER LUCIAN'S talk with Serah, it was hard to snap back to reality, but almost immediately, Lucian was bombarded with things to do.

He first portaled to *Wayfinder* and then jumped the entire ship, along with its attendant droid, to Snake Rift. After they landed, he called Selene to come on board.

Once they had gathered in the central wardroom, Lucian explained what was happening.

"Selene, you're in charge of Alistair and *Wayfinder*. You'll need both to get around Psyche quickly."

"I am happy to serve," Alistair said.

"You're leaving, then?" she asked.

Lucian nodded. "We can't wait any longer. Every day we wait, it's more time for the *Alkasen* to advance. The Darkrift should be safe. At least this part of it. But you'll have the people of Psyche and twenty thousand soldiers at your disposal. You'll have mages, too. I've put the Elders of Kiro Village in charge of them so that you can focus on the big picture."

Selene nodded. "I'm ready, Sorcerer-Ascendant. I trust you'll find someone to become your new Chief Atomicist?"

"I'm sure somebody will turn up. Will you be okay?"

"I've already got some ideas for setting up the defenses. I've already talked to the Mage-Lords and Ladies. There will be no trouble from them, I assure you. If Ansaldra could handle them, so can I."

Lucian was glad she was confident. She would need that. "You'll be on your own soon."

Selene didn't seem fazed by the prospect. Lucian realized she was the right person for the job.

"Don't worry about me, Lucian. And . . . I suppose I should thank you. For including me when no one else would have. And saving my life twice, even if the easier thing would have been to kill me."

Lucian nodded. "Of course. If you need anything, you'll have the data relays to send us something. They should last a good while before the Swarmers destroy them."

"We'll be fine, Lucian. Trust the Manifold. It chose you, after all. So whatever it wills, you won't be led astray."

Lucian realized she was right. It was a thought that had never occurred to him. "Good luck, Selene."

They went their separate ways. Lucian paused on the boarding ramp a moment before he spied *Blood Wyvern* lowering to the plateau below. Once it landed, Mira came down the boarding ramp. Lucian went up to her as she was getting out, the rest of the Mage Council also joining him. She was all about business as she began her report.

"Everything's a go with the fleet. We can get underway as soon as you send the transports up."

Lucian nodded. "Good. Any news on the *Alkasen's* movements?"

"The large Swarmer fleet in Pontus is splitting up into

dozens of smaller forces. My guess is they mean to siege every Trailward System outside Archea."

"I suppose that would include Psyche."

Mira nodded. "Yes. Psyche and a couple of dozen others. I estimate three months before every one of these systems falls under the Swarmers' control. Psyche will probably come under threat soon."

"There is no way to save these worlds?"

Mira's face was grave. "Lucian, I've fought the Swarmers, and this is what they do. First, they destroy anything that's putting up a fight. Once that's dealt with, their fleet splits up, one for each system they intend to conquer. Though the individual fleets are small, they are large enough to overwhelm most planetary defense forces by a long shot. If you try to hunt one of these fleets down, they'll draw back and join the others until they are large enough to challenge you."

"There's no way to stop them from doing that?"

"I'm not saying there isn't. But if nothing can be done, tens of millions will die in the next few months. If not more. My reports show the same thing is happening in the Spinward Worlds. The League only has three fleets right now. The First Fleet is still in Alpha Centauri, and there's talk of it withdrawing to the Solar System to join the reserves around Jupiter. There are thousands of ships fresh from the Jovian Yards that aren't assigned to a proper fleet yet. The Second Fleet is still in orbit above Oceanus, but they are moving to reinforce Archea, where the Third Fleet is. That one you already know about, led by Admiral Lowell in Archea, comprises the bulk of the Wardens. It's also the smallest fleet by far."

"What about the Believer fleet?"

"It's in the Arion System, currently in transit to Nessus. Its numbers are comparable to the Golden Armada in the Hephaestus System. A little over a thousand ships."

"Is Zheng's fleet staying put?"

"Seems that way. The Pirates and the League don't trust each other, and no one trusts the Believers."

"That's it, then. All the ships in the Worlds."

"We need to get all these people working *together*," Serah said. "What's the Hegemon doing?"

"She's trying much the same thing," Mira said. "Her goal is to secure everything in the Solar System, leaving the rest to burn."

"Serah's right," Lucian said. "We've got to bring everyone together. The League. The Pirates. Even the Believers, once we will deal with Sharo. When he's no longer a threat, the Believers should follow me easily enough. Even if Khalin called me a false messiah, they would have to accept me as a true one if I'm standing, but he's not."

"I can only hope it's that simple," Mira said doubtfully. "There's a lot on your plate."

"Our first task is to head to Archea," Lucian said. "We need to take control of the rest of the Wardens' ships before the Second Fleet bolsters them."

"I'm sure Admiral Lowell will be perfectly accommodating," Fergus observed.

"Yeah," Serah said. "Seems impossible to do this without there being a fight."

"I'm willing to work with him," Lucian said. "I doubt *he'll* want to. They think I killed Palmer when it was every pirate on the bridge of *Stars' Blood*."

"Well, you have to admit," Emma said. "You had a bit of a hand in it."

"Yes, to stop Vera," Lucian said. "In retrospect, maybe I jumped the gun a bit." He looked at Mira. "What's Lowell like? He *has* to see reason, right?"

"I know of him. He has a reputation for being a hardass.

You've got to be to make it to admiral. And as a Warden, he's not a fan of mages."

"Of course," Serah said.

"We have to prioritize," Khairu said. "Archea can wait. We still need to talk about the Irion Mages' Tower. We haven't heard anything from them, and we know Swarmers are in the system. That's a few hundred mages there we might recruit into our ranks."

"Yes," Emma agreed. "We have to get there before the Swarmers do."

Everyone looked at Fergus for his reaction. It was apparent he didn't like the idea of going back.

"Vassar won't bend easily," he finally said. "Even when he's backed into a corner. He always tries to cut a deal."

"They might have a few Preserved among their ranks," Emma said. "It would only take a few to change the equation entirely."

It was a good point. As Khairu said, hundreds of mages were there, all of which could be a boon to the Mage Division. Assuming they could get them to agree to work with him.

"Let's just focus on one thing at a time," Lucian said. "Perform triage. First, we need to get the fleet into space. Then we can deal with Irion. After, we can figure out what to do about Lowell."

"We're ready when you are, Sorcerer-Ascendant," Mira said.

Lucian nodded. He had to give his mother credit for adhering to the chain-of-command and calling him by his title. That couldn't have been easy for her.

"Right," he said. "Let's rock and roll."

Just as he was about to board *Blood Wyvern*, everyone's eyes went to the three Transcends approaching them from across the plateau—Transcends White, Red, and Violet.

"Looks like trouble," Serah said.

Lucian turned to meet them. Transcend White wasted no time in addressing him.

"*Resplendent* just received an encrypted communication from Irion."

"Speak of the devil . . ." Fergus said.

"Let me guess," Lucian said. "They're under attack and want our help?"

"You've foreseen this?"

"No," Lucian said. "Admiral Abrantes just gave me a report about it. When did the message come in?"

"It's dated to forty hours ago," Transcend White said. "They were still under evacuation procedures."

"Do you think Vassar will work with us willingly?"

"Willingly?" She gave a short, bitter laugh. "We'll have to drag him by the scruff of his neck. We must go there immediately."

Transcend Red gave a small, almost sadistic, smile. "I *so* look forward to putting that sniveling weasel in his place."

Lucian frowned. "Wait. You all want to come with me?"

"Yes," Transcend White said. "If he sees we've thrown in our lots with you, it will change the equation."

"I see." Lucian looked at the others. "Are you guys all right getting the troops into space?"

"More than all right," Mira said. "Do what you need to do."

"I would like to come," Fergus said.

Lucian wasn't sure how to respond. In this situation, Fergus might spark Vassar's powder keg. Or perhaps it was the other way around.

Lucian cleared his throat awkwardly. "Given your history with Vassar, perhaps it would be best—"

"I insist," Fergus said. "I know Vassar better than anyone here. We were best friends once. Almost brothers. If he's playing us false, I will know beyond a doubt."

Lucian could find much the same information using Psionics, but he wasn't going to press the point. Fergus didn't ask for much, so when he did, Lucian knew it was important to him.

"All right. Fergus comes, too, along with the Transcends. Serah as well."

"There's one other matter," Transcend Violet said, looking him up and down. "If you wish to be taken seriously, perhaps you should wear something more . . . *befitting* your rank and title."

"Why?" Lucian asked, looking up and down at his Talent robes, which showed severe signs of wear. "What's wrong with these?"

Transcend Violet gave an understanding smile. "In the days of the Mage War, and even before, the office of the Sorcerer-Ascendant had its own robes. No one has claimed them since then, not since Lakhmu went into isolation on Mako."

"I see," Lucian said. "You think I should wear them?"

"Yes," she said. "Beyond a doubt."

"All right," he said. "If you have the robes, I'll wear them."

"Leave it to us," Transcend Violet said. "Our Transcend robes have been passed down since the first Transcends of Volsung, fabricated with magic sealed with the Seven Aspects. Though we no longer have the occasion to create them, the art of their making has not been lost. I know how to make the same robes the Sorcerer-Ascendant would have worn in the old days. And it will befit your rank and send the right message to Vassar and the rest of the Irion Mages." Transcend Violet gave a mysterious smile. "It will require an hour of the Transcends' time, for it must be forged with all Seven Aspects. That way, it can last and sustain itself without our influence."

"Do we have time for this?" Lucian asked. "The Mages Tower could be under attack right now."

"One thing is for sure," Transcend Violet said. "Vassar will not take you seriously if you show up wearing *that*."

Lucian saw he wasn't going to win this one. "All right. You win."

"Leave it to the Spectrum. I already have the design in mind."

Lucian nodded. "All right, then. New robes first, and then we head to Irion."

24

THE TRANSCENDS HAD BEEN in their meeting chamber for over an hour. Lucian was nearly at the point where he considered barging in to see what was happening.

When they emerged, they filed out with Transcend Violet at the fore, cradling the folded robes almost reverentially. She held them aloft, allowing them to unfurl, and everyone's breath seemed to catch at their majesty.

They were immaculately white, much like Transcend White's, though there were a few key differences. The first, emblazoned on the chest, was a depiction of the Septagon, with each point of the shape blazing with the color of its respective Aspect, with ethereal lines connecting the nodes one and two spaces apart. But besides that, a single black Aspect shone in the middle. It had lines connecting all seven around it. Lucian knew that couldn't have been the original robes because of the recent discovery of Space-Time Magic. It perfectly depicted the Septagon. The white of the fabric glimmered with an iridescent sheen. A cape hung from the collar that shifted between all the spectrum colors, a never-ending kaleidoscope.

Lucian wasn't sure what to think at first. It looked like the costume of a superhero. But he supposed that was kind of what he was at this point. And it seemed like something the Sorcerer-Ascendant of all Magekind might wear.

"Rotting hell," Serah said, her breath catching. "It's magnificent!"

Transcend Violet gave a pleased smile. "We worked hard to get the colors working just right. The fabric is seven-sealed and will never stain or tear."

"Thank you," Lucian said, taking the robes from Transcend Violet.

Lucian found a nearby room and quickly changed. He used a bit of Radiant magic to create a reflection before him and was shocked at his transformation. The robes were a perfect fit. Not only that, but he *did* look like a rotting superhero. Transcend Orange must have begrudgingly created the colored jewels of the Septagon, and they each shone with ethereal light. A gravity brand within the cape made it undulate about a meter off the deck. Seven-sealed magic was difficult to stream, even with the combined might of the Transcends. It only revealed to Lucian how committed they were to his cause.

For effect, he willed Lightspear into his right hand. As soon as the weapon formed, the picture was complete. This was who he was now. The Chosen of the Manifold and the Sorcerer-Ascendant of all Magekind.

He returned to the corridor outside. The Transcends paused their conversation and stared at him in awe. Fergus's and Serah's jaws dropped at the change.

"Sorcerer-Ascendant," Transcend White said, pleased. "It seems you've stepped into your role."

For once, she seemed happy to see him. To Lucian, it seemed strange how clothing could change others' perceptions.

Even Transcend Orange's eyes were wide, as if seeing something that hadn't been there before.

Lucian supposed no matter how powerful, intelligent, or wise a person was, they could not escape the influence of clothing. If this ensemble made his job easier, he would wear it every day until he accomplished his mission.

"Let's move," he said.

To his surprise, everyone's feet shifted, eager to be off. They were ready and willing to follow him, much to his surprise.

"Err . . . Sorcerer-Ascendant," Transcend Orange said awkwardly.

"Yes?"

"What are the Transcends staying behind supposed to do?"

Lucian looked at Transcends Green, Blue, Yellow, Orange, and the newly minted Transcend Gray. All of them were eagerly awaiting orders.

"Transcend Green has the seniority among you, so he leads until Transcend White gets back. For now, remain in orbit and coordinate with Admiral Abrantes. Follow her orders regarding fleet movements."

"Of course," Transcend Green said. "I thank you for your vote of confidence. We will hold down the fort."

"One other thing," Lucian said, turning to Transcend Orange. "With Selene remaining behind on Psyche, I'm looking for an Orange Talent to elevate to the position of Chief Atomicist. I want your list of recommendations once I'm back."

"Of course, Sorcerer-Ascendant. Anything else?"

"Yes. Transcend Blue, send me a similar list of your top, most capable Binders."

"It shall be done."

Lucian turned around, recalling a memory of Vassar's waiting room in the Irion Mages' Tower. As soon as the picture formed, he began drawing ether. After a few seconds, he had collected enough to create the portal. A sinuous line stretched and rotated, and through the portal's warbled plane lay the luxurious waiting area beyond.

He was the first one through, and it only took a few seconds for everyone else to cross—Transcends White, Red, Violet, and Fergus and Serah, their expressions stern.

The reception desk was empty, and the enormous double doors leading into Vassar's office were ajar. Lucian headed there. As soon as he stepped past the threshold, he felt it was empty. He flew to the upper level, finding Vassar's desk much as he had imagined, in a state of disarray, as if he'd left in a hurry.

But it wasn't only the desk that caught his attention. Through the vast floor-to-ceiling windows above the massive mountains of Irion, Lucian spied four Swarmer fighters swooping in for an attack run on the Mages' Tower. Their rocky, crystalline exteriors shone light blue under the light of Irion's bright yellow sun.

Immediately, Lucian reached for his Focus. He wouldn't have time to ready an attack that would destroy the ships in the few seconds he had left.

"Get around me!" he shouted.

He just had to trust his orders would be followed as he formed an image of Irion's hangar level. Just as the ships' cannons lit with green laser lines, Lucian warped the surrounding others into the hangar of the Tower, where hopefully, the surrounding mountain would serve as protection.

The very foundations of the building trembled as bits of rocks cascaded down from the ceiling. The lights flickered a few times in the vast space.

Lucian took a quick look around to find they weren't alone. Six ships were docked here, all heavy transports. There were dozens of mages hustling and bustling to get themselves loaded. Evacuations were underway, but if the Swarmer ships out there were unopposed, they had almost no chance of escaping.

At first, they weren't noticed, just six more among a crowd focused entirely on survival. Lucian wasn't sure where to look for Vassar until he saw a familiar face. The beautiful, blonde-haired Delphine had led Lucian, Fergus, and Khairu to the Skyloft to speak to Quentin Vassar all those months ago. If anyone knew where the First Mage was, it would be his executive assistant.

"Delphine!" he called.

The woman turned, and her blue eyes widened upon seeing him. She scanned his sorcerer's robes up and down, not knowing what to make of them, and quickly took in the Transcends on his left and right, along with Fergus and Serah. It was almost too much for her. "Lucian? Fergus? Transcends White, Red, and Violet?" Each question became more alarming as she asked it. "How in the Worlds did you get here?"

Lucian ignored the question. "I need to speak to Vassar. Take us to him."

"The First Mage is not taking visitors. Hell, we've got to get out of here before they bring the whole Tower down around us!"

Transcend White took a step forward. "Delphine, was it? I'm Transcend White of the Volsung Academy, and he specifically requested our help. Take us to him unless you want everyone here to die to the Swarmers. Or worse."

Delphine watched her with widened eyes. "Transcend White. Be welcome here. If you had only told us you were coming—"

"We don't have time for pleasantries," Transcend White said. "Vassar. Now."

Delphine's cheeks reddened. "Of course." She raised her slate to her mouth, the stress of the situation causing her once-perfect hair to become disheveled. "Vassar? A Volsung Academy delegation is here."

When he didn't respond, she pocketed her slate and blew a stray hair out of her eye. "Madness! All right, follow me. We don't have much time before Irion goes the way of Pontus."

She threaded through the crowd as Lucian and the others followed. Others cast curious glances, and from their widened expressions, they recognized the Transcends, if not Lucian himself, though just as many were marveling at him.

Delphine drew up before a massive transport, almost as large as a conventional interstellar liner. She took a moment to straighten her hair before scanning the door open.

She led them into a spacious atrium, a sort of cafeteria or central hub of the ship. It was crowded with both Irion mages dressed in suit-robe hybrids and office workers wearing business attire. This attack on the Tower had been quite sudden from their shellshocked expressions. But if Transcend White had gotten a message from Vassar a little over forty hours ago, they would have had to know it was coming. Perhaps they had kept it secret to prevent panic.

"This way," Delphine said quietly.

She led them down a central passage and scanned them into a room on the right. The door slid back, revealing an elegantly appointed suite. Vassar lounged on a luxurious sofa, sipping a glass of wine with a perfectly calm demeanor, as if the Irion Tower hadn't just been blasted with laser fire two minutes ago.

Upon seeing Lucian standing before him, along with the Transcends, Fergus, and Serah, he drained his glass. There was a small wine stain on the upper right breast of his robe.

"Enjoying yourself?" Lucian asked.

Vassar smacked his lips. "The Tower is doomed. Might as well enjoy myself a bit before all of us bite the dust."

Delphine gasped, but Vassar just gave an insolent smile.

"What, Delphine? Afraid to die? After everything the Tower's been through, after the mages we had to put down like mad dogs?"

So, the Irion Academy *had* dealt with Preserved, too.

"No one's going to die, Vassar," Lucian said. "Not if I can help it."

He frowned, noticing his appearance for the first time. "What's with that get-up?" He laughed. "Don't tell me they promoted you."

Lucian realized the man was beyond drunk. He turned to Delphine. "Delphine, Vassar is compromised. If you want the Irion Mages' Tower to survive, you will answer to me, not him."

Vassar stood, swaying for a moment and almost stumbling. "Like hell you will, Delphine!" He puffed out his chest. "Give the order as we talked about before. All ships into orbit and ahead full to the Thor Gate. With luck, maybe a few of us can survive."

Delphine looked from Vassar to Lucian, unable to decide who to follow. Vassar's executive assistant held the keys to the proverbial kingdom. From the shadows under the eyes, Lucian got the sense she did ninety percent of Vassar's job anyway, if not more. While she was usually quick on her feet, she now stood frozen.

"Delphine, you know the right thing to do," Fergus said. "This institution isn't just about Vassar and his ego. It's about you, me, and every mage and person who depends on Irion and its subsidiaries. There is still a chance to save everyone. You will serve Vassar best if you disregard his orders."

"Don't listen to him, Delphine," Vassar said nastily. "You would listen to this consort of pirates, this prisoner of the Mad Moon, this honorless contract breaker? *I'm* the First Mage of this Tower, and I *will* be obeyed!"

At that moment, something in Delphine seemed to snap. She stood straight as her cheeks colored. "Vassar, hundreds of people are looking to you right now to lead them, and you've been hiding in this cabin drinking. Even when you're sober, I constantly clean up your messes. This Academy used to stand for something other than making money, and now that it can't do that anymore, you've gone off the deep end. Whatever authority you have is gone!"

"Delphine," Vassar said, "you're fired!"

"Better than being dead! I have nothing to lose; you will *not* leave this cabin until I deem you no longer a threat to this institution."

"You ungrateful, magicless . . ." He stopped himself just short of cursing her out. "I made you who you are! Without me, you'd be nothing!"

"You're a sad man," Delphine said. "Do you really think I'm nothing without you? It's the opposite. Deep down, you know that's true. Maybe I'm better off without you. You can't get to an appointment on time without my help!"

"Speaking of time," Transcend White said, "we're running out of it."

"Traitorous scum!" Vassar spat at Transcend White. "You have no authority here! I'm the First Mage of Irion. You're violating the Academy Charter of 2276 that recognizes the separation of magical powers! Irion is *mine* to command!"

"That charter is null and void," Transcend White said. "A supermajority of magekind now recognizes a Sorcerer-Ascendant. Surely, you knew of this provision?"

That provision was news to Lucian, too. He wondered why Transcend White had kept that from him, but perhaps she had assumed he already knew. The title had been Serah's suggestion, per Lakhmu's wishes. Maybe the old sorcerer had known it would come in handy down the line.

Instantly, Vassar's eyes widened and went to Lucian. "Who, *this* whelp? Sorcerer-Ascendant of all Magekind? Bah!"

"It's true," Lucian said. "And as Sorcerer-Ascendant, I'm ordering you to stand down."

"You don't have that authority." He turned to Transcend White, almost imploringly. "You put yourself under this fool?" He turned to face the other Transcends, his face snarling. "All of you are false! Traitors!"

Transcend White looked at him with distaste. "Volsung recognizes his legitimacy, as does the entire Moon of Psyche. That is over two thousand mages, Vassar. Soon to be three thousand when Irion joins us."

"Ha! Do you think the opinion of those frays matters? Do you think the League will accept them as a supermajority? You are a greater fool than even I thought, Vivienne."

Transcend White did not take kindly to him using her name. She nodded to Transcends Red and Violet. "Block him."

Together, the Transcends streamed a Psionic brand around Vassar's Focus. The man railed against it, but in his current state and against two powerful Transcends, there was nothing he could do.

"Madness!" he cried. "Scum! Villains!"

Seeing her old boss's state nearly made Delphine's eyes pop out of her head.

"Listen here," Lucian said. "You're a mean drunk, and your days of leading the Irion Academy are over. You should be out there taking charge, not hiding in here drinking your sorrows away."

"There is nothing *but* sorrow!" Vassar wailed. "There is no way to escape this Tower. They are attacking us from every angle. The planetary defense force was overwhelmed! What hope have we of escaping? Those idiots on the board are calling for us to take off and try our luck." He chuckled darkly. "I'm just giving them what they want."

Lucian ignored him. There was no point in arguing with the blowhard.

Delphine looked at Lucian. "What is your plan, Sorcerer-Ascendant? Is there a way out?"

"Yes. I can open a portal to the Cupid System from here, allowing every ship in this hangar to escape."

"Seriously?" Delphine asked. "I've never heard of such magic . . ."

"It's a new kind," Lucian said, not wanting to go into detail.

"Sorcery," Vassar said. "Sorcery is forbidden at the Irion Academy."

Lucian ignored him. "Are the ships ready to go, Delphine?"

"Stop, foul usurper!" Vassar said. "Stop at once!"

Lucian bound his mouth shut. Vassar groaned as he tried vainly to get another word out.

Delphine nodded, satisfied. "Great. I'm out of a job, though."

"That's all right," Lucian said. "We're hiring." Lucian turned to Transcend Red. "Could you and Transcend Violet stay to ensure he doesn't cause any trouble? It's time we headed to the bridge."

"It would be my pleasure," Transcend Red said.

"You need not worry," Transcend Violet said. "My block on him is sure. He cannot match me in Psionics."

Lucian let go of the Binding that kept Vassar's mouth shut. The First Mage breathed heavily as if that magic had nearly suffocated him.

"Try to update him on all the pertinent details," Lucian said. "Once he sobers up."

Vassar remained silent for once, a fact for which Lucian was thankful.

Delphine cleared her throat. "We should move. I've just gotten a security alert from the Tower. It's been breached by drop pods."

"Drop pods," Fergus said. "The Swarmers could break into the hangar at any moment!"

Delphine nodded. "If you would, follow me to the bridge. The entire crew is there and ready."

25

DELPHINE RAISED her slate to her mouth. "Attention, mages and employees of the Irion Academy. Members of the Board of Mages. This is Delphine Moneaux. I have some good news and some bad news. Bad news: the First Mage of Irion is three sheets to the wind right now, perhaps even four, and is in no state to lead or save our lives. The good news is that the new Sorcerer-Ascendant of Magekind has joined us and plans to get us all out of this. It's our only chance, so you better listen up and trust him at his word. A supermajority of magekind has recognized his leadership, even if no one on Irion has yet. Here he is."

Delphine handed her slate over. Lucian nodded his thanks.

"This is Lucian Abrantes. Sorcerer-Ascendant of Magekind, Sorcerer-King of Psyche, and Chosen of the Manifold. Everything Delphine said was true, and if we follow Vassar's original plan of blasting into the sky and heading for the Thor Gate, every ship will get shot down. None of that matters, though. I have a way to get us out. I'll open a space-time portal right in front of the hangar doors, large enough for every ship to pass

213

through. That portal will take you to the Cupid System, where my fleet is waiting. This is the only way to save yourselves. But you should know that if you go through that portal, you agree to follow me and recognize my claim as Sorcerer-Ascendant, just as every mage on Psyche and every mage at the Volsung Academy has done. I earned the title from Sorcerer Lakhmu and hold all Seven Orbs of Starsea." He left out information about the Orb of Space-Time, at least for now. "All of this will be explained in more detail later. Head into the portal as soon as it appears. You better be inside a ship because the portal will instantly suck all the air out of the hangar. I'll everyone exactly two minutes to get inside the closest ship. Good luck."

He handed the slate back and immediately began gathering his ether. He knew it would take a lot to create a portal because of the distance and size.

Delphine's eyes widened as she watched the central screen, which showed a live camera feed of the corridor leading into the hangar. Lucian noted much the same thing as her: a dozen of Preserved all pouring in from the central elevator of the Tower, a mix of humans and Ancients all bearing shockspears.

"Who are they?" she asked.

"Preserved," Lucian said. "They fight for the *Alkasen*."

"Lucian?" Transcend White asked.

Lucian drew ether even faster, and with a last pull, he had the right amount. The portal opened, revealing a vista of stars along with Psyche in the distance. Anything that wasn't nailed down instantly flew through it. As Lucian held the portal, every Preserved was sucked into the darkness of space, quickly lost to sight.

"Holy shit," Delphine said, her face pale. "We're going into *that*?"

"Well," Fergus said, "we'll have a ship around us, at least."

"Go ahead," Lucian said.

"Into the portal, Mage-Captain Winters," Delphine said to the captain, a middle-aged woman with spiked black hair and a geometric face tattoo. The captain nodded in acknowledgment of the order.

She pushed the control stick forward, causing the ship to lurch forward. The transports behind followed suit. Within moments, they were in the Cupid System. Once Lucian was sure everyone was through, he allowed the portal to shut.

With that action, these six ships were all that was left of the Irion Mages, besides those that might be dispersed into the broader Worlds.

Mage-Captain Winters's eyes went wide at the vista before them. "Is that Psyche?"

Lucian nodded. "It is, Captain. It's where the rest of our fleet is based."

"What fleet?"

"The fleet of Starsea. We control Psyche now."

"Starsea?" Delphine asked. "What do you mean?"

"He doesn't mean the Starsea of Xara Mallis and Vera Desai," Transcend White said, stepping in. "He means a new resistance whose vision is to unify humanity in its fight against the Swarmers."

Delphine blinked. "I see how that might be useful, but . . . *Starsea*?"

"It's a name many Psyche mages are ready to rally behind," Lucian said.

"You mean *them*?" Delphine asked, looking pale as she nodded toward the moon before them.

"That's right. As Sorcerer-Ascendant, it's my job to gather as large a fleet as possible to stop the *Alkasen*. We already defeated a fleet of them here. Now that we've rescued what we could of Irion, we need to move on to the next objective."

"Which is?" Delphine asked.

"The Archea System. It's a key crossroads for both the Swarmers and the League. The League is already sending their Second Fleet to reinforce the Third that's already there."

She looked aghast. "You're going to fight the League? I want no part of that!"

"Not to war," Lucian said. "I mean to recruit them."

"How?"

"In the same way I recruited the Wardens. My powers of persuasion."

Delphine was about to respond when her slate chimed with an incoming call.

"I have to take this," she said. "It's the Mage Board."

"Perhaps we should all be on that call," Transcend White said. "Do you have somewhere we can speak in private?"

"Yes, we have a conference room not too far from here. I'll lead you there."

Lucian stepped over to Captain Winters. "Head for Warden Prime. Don't dock there. Just get the ship on the same orbit."

"Will do, Sorcerer-Ascendant."

Lucian, Serah, Fergus, and Transcend White followed Delphine toward the back of the ship.

Once settled into a finely appointed conference room, Delphine streamed the holo-call from her slate. Instantly, seven holographic projections of men and women of middle and elder ages stood atop the table. They were glaring down at Lucian and Transcend White. Lucian supposed this board was Irion's version of the Spectrum.

One of them was a brown-skinned woman with vibrantly purple hair. She wore rich green robes and looked to be in her late fifties. She was the first to speak.

"Who the hell do you think you are?" she asked of Lucian. "Where's Vassar?"

"Under guard," Lucian said. "He was a threat to the safety of the Irion Academy."

"We are . . . *aware* . . . of Vassar's vices," the woman said. "However, the board should have been consulted on this!"

"First Radiant Velma," Delphine said. "If I may?"

The First Radiant nodded. "Go ahead."

Delphine cleared her throat nervously. "First Radiant, there wasn't time to consult the board. We had to act fast. As First Mage, Vassar has an executive privilege during emergencies. It would have been risky to take the time for the board to discuss the situation and overrule his veto."

The mage next to Velma, a balding older man with a stick-like figure and rich yellow robes, turned his head toward the First Radiant. "She has a point, Velma. It would have required all seven of us to overrule him, and that could not have been done quickly."

"Maybe so," Velma admitted. She faced Lucian. "What of this . . . Sorcerer-Ascendant, then? Is all that you said true?"

"It is," Lucian said. "If you don't believe me, just ask Transcend White here."

Every head turned to her High Eminence, and she confirmed Lucian's words with a nod. "As of three weeks ago, the Volsung Academy follows the Chosen of the Manifold. That's Lucian. He holds the Seven Orbs of Starsea and, thus, is the subject of Arian's Prophecy of the Seven. He is the Worlds' only hope of stopping the *Alkasen*. It behooves us to follow him to the very ends of creation if need be."

"Bold words," Velma said. She turned back to Lucian. "And are you up to the task?"

"If I'm not, no one is. I'm the holder of the Seven Orbs of

Starsea. The Chosen of the Manifold. The King of Psyche. The heir of Sorcerer-Ascendant Lakhmu ..."

"About Lakhmu," Velma said. "We thought he'd passed away long ago."

"It happened about a month ago," Lucian said. "Right after he had trained me and conferred his title. You can ask anyone who was with me."

There was a long silence where none of the board members spoke. All seemed to look at Velma for direction.

"You have put us in a precarious situation," Velma said. "Our loyalty is to Irion and the First Mage. However, we are aware of his faults. There is much behind Irion that is rotten, and Vassar was the source."

At this, the other board members looked at Velma in shock.

"What of it?" she asked, seeing their reaction. "Can't you see the Worlds are at risk? We can no longer look past Vassar's many crimes. We've allowed him to get away with it for various reasons. Reasons of profit, reasons of convenience, out of fear, or perhaps the fact that he was the only one who could grease the wheels with the League." She shook her head as she looked back at Lucian. "However, this much is clear. A new era is dawning in the Worlds. We cannot allow his corruption to stand any longer. As you all know, I have been the leader of the investigation into Vassar's crimes and have held back bringing my evidence to the board for the sake of the Academy. As unfit as Vassar is for leadership of the Irion Mages' Tower, it was better than dividing us. Or so my thinking went."

The board's silence made it hard to know what they thought.

"What crimes are you accusing him of?" Fergus asked. "If you need a witness, I have quite the list of grievances."

The hint of a smile twitched on Velma's lips. "There are many, Radiant Fergus. Many indeed. However, I was hoping for a more practical solution than an impeachment trial." She turned, appealing to her fellow board members. "As you all know, we can vote Vassar out of office for good with a simple, unified vote of no confidence. We can instate a new First Mage as soon as he's out."

A man with wild white hair at the edge of the table, with the blue robes of the First Binder, addressed the First Radiant. "Do you have any suggestions, First Radiant?"

"Yes," Velma said. "Someone outside this board since all of you are power-mad fools."

This comment elicited a few chuckles.

The white-haired man spoke again. "Surely, you don't mean this Sorcerer-Ascendant to be First Mage of Irion as well? It seems even the esteemed Transcend White has kept her post."

"No, not the Sorcerer-Ascendant. I will nominate the man who should have been lifted to the board in the first place had it not been for Vassar's influence: Fergus Madigan."

26

"FERGUS MADIGAN?" the First Dynamist asked. "Fergus Madigan was exiled to Psyche. Fergus Madigan broke his contract with Zheng Yang. Fergus Madigan—"

The First Radiant completed his sentence. "—is the most egregiously and unfairly treated mage to step foot into this academy, First Dynamist Shor. We would be fortunate if he accepted my nomination and my forgiveness for not having the courage to call out Vassar's villainy earlier."

"That is the First Mage you speak of!" one man thundered in a deep baritone.

One woman, the First Psionic, judging by her violet robes, snickered. "First-rate *drunk*, more like."

At that moment, the board devolved into an argument. It took all of Lucian's willpower not to tell Delphine to turn them off.

But it wasn't Lucian who stepped up to address them. It was Fergus.

"Quiet, the lot of you."

To Lucian's surprise, they did pipe down as they looked at him.

Fergus cleared his throat. "Vassar is unfit to lead the Irion Academy. First Radiant Velma, I'm grateful for your support, but this is not a posting I want."

"That is why you must take it, Fergus," Velma said with conviction. "Are you forgetting what happened last time?"

"Assuming this board votes to remove Vassar, then it's not my problem anymore."

Velma scoffed. "The First Mage was *always* your posting! You would walk away from it now, even after everything that's happened? Will you *ever* learn?"

For the first time, Fergus looked unsure, as if comprehending something for the very first time that had long eluded him. Lucian realized the First Radiant was right. Fergus had told them how the First Mage position could have been his had he not bowed to Vassar's ambition. That choice had been almost fatal on his part. Even when Fergus escaped Psyche, Vassar betrayed him again, consigning him to a contract under Admiral Yang's thumb.

Lucian realized Fergus *was* the right man for the job. And from the expressions of most of the board members, it seemed they thought so, too. The only person who didn't fully realize it was Fergus himself.

Finally, after a long, contemplative silence, Fergus nodded. "Velma . . . you're right. I hate to admit it, but you are."

"So, will you accept my nomination?"

The First Radiant was ready to get down to brass tacks.

"Yes," Fergus said. "Contingent on the vote of this board regarding Vassar."

The First Radiant turned to the others. "I'm calling to order a meeting to discuss the question of Vassar's leadership. A unanimous vote of no-confidence, followed by a simple majority vote to raise Fergus to the mantle of First Mage of Irion."

The white-haired First Binder cleared his throat. "This is all moving rather fast. Could we not have an hour or two of discussion first?"

"Is there a need for that?" Velma asked. "All the facts are before us and cannot be denied. All of you are familiar with the contents of my investigation, even if I haven't brought them formally to the board. A few of you still refuse to acknowledge the implications, despite the truth staring you in the face."

"Let's just vote," the First Psionic said. "All this board does is squabble. The need to remove Vassar is clear. There is no time for partisan quibbling. The Worlds are at stake, and if we cannot oust him, the death of this Academy is not off the table."

The First Binder guffawed. "Such hyperbole, Marta. We have defeated the Swarmers in two wars, and we will drive them back into Dark Space in this third one!"

"Who are you performing for, Sergei? Don't you see how recent events have changed the equation entirely? We must come together behind a strong leader. That leader is Fergus Madigan."

"And what of this *Sorcerer-Ascendant*?" First Binder Sergei spat. "Who is he? Why should we trust him? He claims to be leading a new Starsea. We'll have another Xara Mallis on our hands!"

"I killed Xara Mallis," Lucian said.

Every head turned to him. It was clear from their reactions that Vassar had never shared his meeting with Xara and Vera when they visited the Mage Tower. The only one who *wasn't* shocked was Velma. She knew something of it, and the other board members noticed.

"You know of this, Velma?" the First Psionic asked.

Velma gave a regal nod. "Yes. Though Vassar and I

disagreed on many things, he sought my advice when Xara and Vera showed up. It happened about eight standard months ago. Vera Desai and Xara Mallis came to the Irion Tower with a proposition."

"What?" Sergei asked. "And the board was not apprised of this? How did they survive the Tragedy of Isis?"

"It's beside the point, but they escaped. And they never abandoned their search for the Orbs of Starsea. Vassar would not have told me of their meeting, but I kept a close eye on him, and he had no choice."

"You openly admit this?" Sergei asked.

Velma ignored him. "Vassar made a deal with both that was completely off the books and enriched himself. He sold our Dark Space Gate data."

"Do you have proof?" Shor asked. "This wasn't part of your original investigation."

"Yes," Velma said. "I have all the evidence."

"Vassar told us the same thing," Fergus said. "We were using Transcend White's spaceship to hunt Vera and Xara. Our search led us to Isis and the Starsea Sanctum. After leaving that planet, we received a message from Vassar himself. He all but said Xara and Vera had passed through the Irion Tower. So, we went there, and he confirmed the same thing the First Radiant told you."

"It's hearsay until I see hard evidence," Sergei said.

"How is it hearsay?" Lucian asked. "I've known Fergus for a year and a half now, and he's probably the most honorable man I know. My entire crew, plus myself, can vouch for the message. So can Psion Khairu of the Volsung Academy. These charges are established by credible witnesses. We can also dig up the transmission in *Ethereal's* log."

"Though it's been many years," Fergus said, "I know Velma is honorable. Any reasonable person would say that this happened, and that Vassar needs to answer for it. We didn't realize the map data release wasn't sanctioned by the Board of Mages."

"Like hell it wasn't," Shor said. "I've heard enough. Sergei, you seem to be the only holdout. After all this evidence, are you going to defend Vassar?"

"It's moving too quickly," Sergei said. "Does Vassar have no chance to speak in his defense?"

"I don't have time for this," Lucian said. "You guys need to settle your own affairs."

"I would like to hear from this Khairu," Velma said. "If she can't speak in person, then perhaps she can give a holographic deposition."

Lucian wished he could snap his fingers and have everything be done, but he realized that wasn't how things worked. Things had to be done by the book before any significant moves could be made.

"You guys can send a team to *Resplendent* to speak to her." He looked at Sergei. Lucian was sure the man was in Vassar's books and was doing everything he could to gum up the works. The man even had the gall to give a cunning smile.

Lucian didn't have time for this. He turned to Fergus.

"Can you handle this, Fergus? If you need me for anything, you can reach me by slate or Psionic link."

"Trust me; I'll see this through to the end."

Sergei's smile faltered a bit at that.

"And what about Vassar in the meantime?" Lucian asked.

"For now," Velma said, "placing him under house arrest would be appropriate, achievable with a simple majority vote."

"Do you bring the measure before us, First Radiant?" Shor asked.

Velma nodded. "I do. All in favor, say *aye*."

Well over half did, five of them by Lucian's count. Sergei

remained silent, along with a red-haired woman who stood next to him, whose robes announced her as the First Gravitist.

"Let it be known that First Mage Quentin Vassar is being placed under house arrest, unable to leave this ship until the completion of the investigation."

Shor chuckled. "Should be easy enough if we keep him drunk."

"This council is dismissed for now."

Delphine stopped the stream from her slate, and all the figures disappeared but Velma.

"I stayed on because I want to speak with you further, Radiant Fergus. There was much left unsaid during that meeting, and I would like to keep you updated."

"Of course," Fergus said. He turned to Lucian. "I can update you later."

Lucian nodded gratefully. "Will you be all right here?"

"I'll be fine. As you said, I'll contact you when the investigation is completed. Not even the likes of Sergei will wriggle his way out of this one."

"That he won't," Velma said. "And, Sorcerer-Ascendant. Thank you for your fast decision-making. I apologize for politics gumming up the works, but these things are rarely simple. If we do this the right way, the loyalty of the Irion Mages will be cemented to your cause."

"I understand and trust your judgment," Lucian said. "For now, have your ships follow the Starsea Fleet in orbit around Psyche. We will depart for Archea soon. I don't expect you to conclude your investigation so quickly, but I will remain hopeful."

"We'll see. I've long been preparing my case against Vassar, and I only require the depositions of certain knowledgeable individuals of his crimes. Truly, Sorcerer-Ascendant, all the pieces are in place. It will be a matter of days or sooner."

"That's good news. Keep Vassar under guard with some mages you can trust implicitly."

"Of course. Good luck, Sorcerer-Ascendant. I'm sure you have duties to attend to."

"Good luck yourself. A pleasure to make your acquaintance."

Velma smiled graciously and disappeared off the table's holo-projector.

Delphine heaved a sigh. "I imagine I'll be a part of this deposition, too . . ."

It occurred to Lucian that as Vassar's executive assistant, Delphine was probably very knowledgeable about many of his crimes. She was perhaps even complicit in them.

"Just tell the truth, and you'll be fine," Fergus said. "You showed your true colors back there on Irion."

"It took me long enough," she said. "Well, I have some matters to see to as well. This place would indeed fall apart without me. Mr. Madigan, perhaps it's best if I orient you to what's been going on the last six months." Delphine looked at the three Transcends. "And if your Eminences would like to stay, you would be most welcome."

"I'll remain here until we can be relieved by Velma's mages," Transcend White said. "I don't want Vassar to escape. Sorcerer-Ascendant, it would probably be best if you returned to *Barbarossa*. Let us take care of this mess."

"Will do. Good luck with everything."

With that, he and Serah stepped through a portal to *Barbarossa's* bridge.

27

WHEN LUCIAN and Serah arrived on *Barbarossa*, they found everyone on the Mage Council, except for Fergus, was already gathered. The fleet was arrayed and ready to depart, and all the bridge officers were standing by at their stations.

Lucian and Mira stood shoulder-to-shoulder on the bridge, staring at the modest fleet outside the front viewports composed of a mix of two hundred guardian-class heavy destroyers, javelin-class corvettes, and ripsaw fighters. It couldn't *really* be called a fleet, but Lucian wanted to think of it as such. He knew that one day soon, it would be. *Barbarossa* was the largest ship by far. Combined with the sixty heavy assault transport ships and twelve fuel tankers, this fleet was shy of three hundred vessels.

It was a start, however humble. And, of course, Lucian had nearly three thousand mages on his side now, including those of Irion.

Former Warden officers, now officers of Starsea, were busy at their terminals, ready for departure. There was an air of expectation and excitement that they were about to get underway.

This moment, long built toward, was finally happening.

"Is everything in order?" Lucian asked.

"Everything is ready," Mira said. "Our orbit will place us on a trajectory to the Archea Gate in just a couple of minutes."

Lucian knew that with his powers, it didn't matter which way they were facing. They would be in the Archea System within the hour, where Admiral Lowell had taken most of the Warden fleet. Lucian didn't want it to come to blows, but he doubted Admiral Lowell would be amenable to working with him.

"Did our message to Lowell get sent?" Lucian asked.

Mira nodded. "Days ago. They've had plenty of time to respond. That they haven't is telling."

"You believe they will react in a hostile manner?"

"I wouldn't put it off the table."

"The key is taking control of Lowell, then."

If Lowell could be controlled, so could his fleet of five hundred ships and crew of forty-five thousand battle-trained Wardens. With such a force, Lucian could challenge the smaller Swarmer fleets, especially with his magic powers. The trick was getting to him without blood being shed on either side. A difficult proposition.

Lucian raised his slate and linked it to every ship's intercom system. "This is the Sorcerer-Ascendant. All of you have fought hard to get to this point. I can't tell you how proud I am of every person here. All of you will be at the core of the resistance against the Swarmers. That resistance will grow by the day as we gather more to join us."

A thought came to Lucian, an idea so obvious that he wasn't sure why it hadn't occurred to him earlier.

He continued with a smile of realization. "I know we told

you that our next aim is Archea. However, the confrontation might not be peaceful, based on Admiral Lowell's silence. While I'm confident in the Starsea fleet's abilities, we still need to undertake one action before we meet Lowell head-on."

His mother looked at him questioningly. He muted his slate for a second. "Trust me."

"This isn't the plan, son."

"Trust me."

Mira looked tense for a moment, seeming to want to argue, but she gave a slow nod, allowing her son to take the lead.

Lucian unmuted his slate. "Our next destination will not be Archea. It will be Hephaestus. That's where Admiral Yang and the Golden Armada are stationed. Since we've already worked together, we can convince her to work with us. That said, there's no telling how Admiral Yang will react when our ships are logged on their sensors. But we're going to need her help. Once she's on board, we'll have a larger force than Lowell's, giving us more negotiating power."

Mira's face paled at this change of plans. She motioned him to mute his mic, which he did.

"Son, are you crazy? Zheng is unpredictable. For all we know, she'll open fire without regard for who we are!"

"If that's the case, I can open a new portal back to Psyche so we can reassess. We might lose a few ships while I gather enough ether, but I don't think it's in Zheng's interest to attack us. She will want to know who we are first; once she finds out, she won't attack. Especially with Fergus in the fleet."

"Fergus," Mira said, her face darkening. "Yes, I'd forgotten about their history. If you're sure about this, I'm ready when you are."

Lucian nodded. Whatever her reasons, Lucian was glad she was on board.

Mira took up her slate. "Admiral Abrantes speaking. I want

all sailors to their battle stations and all ships in attack formation as soon as we go through the portal."

Over the following minutes, the fleet maneuvered, the corvettes flying point with the destroyers hovering watchfully behind. *Barbarossa* hung back to provide support fire against larger ships. In an equal fight, such a small force would be slaughtered by the Golden Armada. But at least arrayed for battle, they would be better able to take a fight while Lucian gathered his magic.

"Engage the flight path, Helmsman Morales," Mira ordered.

"Aye-aye," Morales said, his voice firm. He was a tall, muscular man with bronzed skin and intense brown eyes. Those eyes were focused and intent on carrying out Mira's orders. His hand grasped the control stick tightly as he steered the ship into position.

Grand Captain Warwick was also present, content to remain on standby. With Admiral Abrantes present, he was more of a backup in case she needed to delegate something.

As a single force, the Starsea Fleet left Psyche's orbit, heading into the darkness of space. Lucian let the fleet pick up speed, burning as fast as *Barbarossa* could manage. It was the slowest ship, given its mass. The smaller and speedier corvettes had to hold themselves back like dogs fighting their leashes.

Lucian began gathering ether, knowing it would take a long while to have the proper amount. He had to bridge an incredible distance and make the portal large enough to fit *Barbarossa* and *Resplendent*. It would be several minutes before he had the requisite power.

"Needle position," Lucian ordered.

The ships flawlessly formed a single line to enter the portal seamlessly. Lucian streamed the portal open directly at the head of the fleet, and one by one, the ships slipped through. He knew those vessels were already fanning out into the battle formation on the other side. It was only a few seconds for *Barbarossa* to follow. Lucian allowed the portal to close.

The barren, molten globe of Hephaestus stood in the distance, large enough to be covered by one hand. This had been the site of the battle with the *Alkasen* several months back, though now the space was empty.

But the Golden Armada lurked somewhere, likely in orbit around Hephaestus itself.

Almost immediately, the ship's bridge was lit with a hail request. Lucian hit accept from his slate.

He recognized the voice of Zheng's First Quartermaster, Altan Gan Baatar. "Oi! This is Golden Armada Space! What're you doing here?"

"Greetings, *Stars' Blood*," Lucian said. "This is Sorcerer-Ascendant Lucian Abrantes with the Starsea Fleet. How are you holding up?"

"Lucian Abrantes? Sorcerer-Ascendant? Bloody, rotten *Starsea*? They've been dead for five decades now! What kind of joke is this?"

Zheng's voice came on next, annoyed. "Give me that." There was a brief cry of surprise and a scuffle as Altan was pushed aside. "Lucian Abrantes. Give me one good reason I shouldn't blast your tiny, pathetic, impotent fleet into a billion pieces for throwing me to the League on a silver platter back in Alpha Centauri."

"I can explain," he said. "Any damage done wasn't intentional."

"Wasn't *intentional*? You're going to have to do better than that. And what's the deal with this *Starsea*? Don't tell me you've built your *own* little kingdom, like half the bloody League!"

Lucian smiled. "No, not a kingdom. I'm gathering a fleet to stop the Swarmers."

There was a moment's pause, and then Zheng gave an

ironic laugh. "Cute. Our scopes are detecting around two hundred vessels, all in poor condition. If I gave the order, I could blast you into dust with just half of my mighty armada. Since you know that, you probably didn't come here to fight me. Which means you've come to beg for my help." She paused. "What makes you think *I* would work with *you*, especially after you've treated me poorly?"

"Poorly? You're the one who assassinated the rotting Hegemon! That started the entire battle to begin with."

"Wrong. *You* whisked us away to Alpha Centauri. Without Transcend White securing peace, we would have destroyed ourselves on the League. She deserves all the credit for cleaning up your mess."

"Transcend White is with us," Lucian said. "I can put her on."

There was a moment's pause. Lucian could sense Zheng's surprise. "She's with *you*?"

"Yes. She will vouch for me. She knows I'm the best chance of stopping the Swarmers and saving humanity. So do all the Volsung Mages and the people of Psyche."

There was a moment of recalculation on Zheng's end before she spoke again.

"All right. For the sake of entertainment, I will entertain *you*. What exactly do you want from me?"

"Tell me this," Lucian said. "Would you rather play guard duty with Hephaestus, waiting until the Swarmers inevitably overwhelm you? Or would you rather come with me and make a difference?"

Altan was the one who answered. "Go with you, of course."

"Quiet, you!" Zheng said. "I thought I had you scrubbing the deck!"

"Sorry, Admiral."

There was a moment of silence, apparently for Zheng to gather her thoughts.

"Tell you what," Zheng said. "You have to give me a reason to help you, Lucian. I'm a pirate. There's got to be some treasure at the end of this road, or I'm not interested."

"How much is the League paying you?"

"They're giving me some of the tax revenue from Hephaestus. That comes out to about one hundred thousand credits a day."

"Damn," Lucian said.

"Yes," Zheng said. "Very much *damn*. If you can beat that, which I know you can't, then perhaps I might follow you."

"What about honor and glory?" Lucian asked. "What about being a rotting hero for once? Some things can't be valued in credits."

"You don't know me *at all*," Zheng said. "You realize I killed three of my husbands just to get where I am?"

"No wonder Fergus is scared of you."

Zheng laughed. "Funny. Which begs the question. Where is my Fergus?"

"Busy," Mira said, stepping in. "Admiral Yang, this is Admiral Abrantes."

"Mira! You were so quiet. I must congratulate you on your promotion. Although, *Admiral* seems too grand a title for so tiny a flotilla."

Mira ignored her. "Small things can pack big punches."

"Was that a threat?"

"Not at all. It's just not smart to ruffle the feathers of the Chosen of the Manifold. You've seen what he's capable of, so unless you want him to open up a black hole in the middle of your precious fleet, maybe you should try being more polite."

"Mira! Perhaps I underestimated you. Crude, but sometimes crudeness is effective." She paused for a moment to consider. "Well, I *have* been thinking about that . . . *thing* . . . Lucian created that destroyed that Swarmer fleet three months ago. A powerful weapon, that. With power like that, Lucian, you could conquer the galaxy!"

"I could," Lucian said. "And anyone who helped me would get a share of the spoils."

"Would they? Well, you have my undivided attention, although I don't think you have the stomach for such wanton destruction. Pillage and plunder is my game, not yours."

"You sure it's your game? Looks like you're on guard duty to me. What's the point of pillage and plunder when you have a stake in the League's success? Hephaestus is a nice little cash cow for you. Probably ten times more valuable than whatever your little pirate queendom was worth in the Border Worlds, especially now that the Swarmers are overrunning everything. If you want to keep the credits rolling in—more than that, if you want credits even to be *worth* something —then join us. You can't spend anything if you're dead."

"Hmm. I admit you may have a point there. The question is one of leadership. Why you?"

"Admiral Abrantes said it herself. I'm the Chosen of the Manifold. I've gathered all the Orbs of Starsea. The mages recognize my legitimacy as Sorcerer-Ascendant. I have a fleet of two hundred ships and fifty thousand soldiers."

"So do some of the larger pirate warlords I know, at least as far as ship count."

"What he's not telling you," Mira said, "Is that almost three thousand of that number are mages. Imagine what can be done with that kind of power."

There was a brief pause of surprise. "So many? Why should I believe you?"

Lucian considered for a moment. "Proof can be sent if you

require it. I need your help with Lowell and the Wardens in Archea."

"You're going to attack him?"

"Not attack. I will have the same conversation with Lowell I'm having with you now. My position will be stronger if you're backing me up. I want him to join me, too."

"Lowell will never cave to you," Zheng said. "I've spoken with him myself. He wants nothing to do with me. He's old school. No pirates. No magic. And certainly not both put together."

"I will turn him," Lucian said. "Whatever it takes."

"You seem . . . confident of that."

Lucian smiled. "Completely confident."

"I don't know, Lucian. *Chosen*, as you seem to love calling yourself. You've done a lot to destroy my trust. I would never follow your orders. Imagine what my men would think, their fearless leader coming to heel like an obedient dog. I shudder to think of it!"

"You've already done that with the League. So, you'd rather stay here working for them, waiting for the end to come?"

"It's better than being under your command."

"Zheng," Mira said, "you're going to die anyway, so why not throw everything for at least a chance at winning? Would you seriously rather die here than work with Lucian?"

"I don't work with *anybody*. I'm Zheng Yang, the Terror of the Stars. How can I be the Terror of the Stars if this kid can order me about?"

"I'm asking you to work with me, not under me, Admiral Yang."

"Under you," she said. Lucian could hear the smile in her voice. "Now *that* I wouldn't be opposed to."

"I'm about to kick your lecherous ass," Mira said.

"Oh? Relax, Abrantes. You should be grateful good looks run in the family."

"I don't have time for this," Lucian said. "So I'm taking this as a *no* on your part?"

"I'm sorry, Lucian. I don't work for free."

"What do you want, then?"

"You said it yourself. Pillage and plunder." Lucian could sense her smile. "I want *Archea*."

Lucian thought about the first time Fergus mentioned Zheng in that dingy bar on Archea Station. That was where she had risen to her inglorious heights, beginning in the bordellos in the station's lower reaches. Through deception, cunning, and more than a bit of murder, she rose to become the Pirate Empress.

Fergus had also mentioned another detail since then, which he was only now remembering. When she offed her third husband, she hid his death and gave orders as if she *were* him. By the time the Golden Armada realized what was happening, Zheng had secured her power. Just as she kept his fleet, she kept his name, fusing it with her own. Eventually, the League ousted her from Archea, forcing her into exile to Brennus.

Of course, control of the planet was what she wanted. And it was the only thing that would get her to help Lucian.

"Well, fight with me until the end of this, and you'll get Archea. If we win, you can have the entire system. If we lose, well, at least you would have fought for something worth dying for. At least you would have felt Archea's sun on your face one last time. That's where we're heading after this. Are you going to stay behind while we take it back?"

She was silent for a time, clearly thinking of Lucian's offer. He knew that pause was for effect. He had her.

Zheng sighed. "All right, *fine*. I must admit that guard duty is boring, even if it pays handsomely. Assuming I say *yes*, how are we going about this?"

"We'll leave immediately. Admiral Abrantes can send you the location for the portal I'm going to make to Archea."

"Just like what you did from Hephaestus to AC?"

"The same. "

"All right. I'll help you. But I don't just want Archea. I want every system surrounding it."

Mira growled. "You're moving the goalposts, Zheng."

"Well, *you* are talking about uniting the entire rotting galaxy, to borrow a curse word from Psyche that I've grown quite fond of. I'm contributing most of the ships, so I should get a fair reward."

"You can't have Psyche," Lucian said. "That's mine. And you can't have Halia. That's too close to the First Worlds."

"I want Halia, Hephaestus, Alsan, and, as mentioned, Archea. You can keep Psyche."

Mira scoffed. "With just Halia and Hephaestus, you'll own some of the most promising mineral deposits in the Trailward Worlds."

"Yes, that's the idea. It's my price. Take it or leave it."

Lucian resisted the urge to curse. "All right, fine. It's yours. But you won't get any of it until we're done with this war. That means sticking with me until the end."

"And what's the end?" Zheng asked.

"When Earth is safe. Otherwise, I will not vouch for you at the bargaining table."

Lucian knew his word would be worth a lot, especially if he were the one who helped save the League. Of course, he could force the Hegemon and the League to give him whatever he wanted with Psionics, though the execution of that might be a little messy.

"How do I know you'll keep your word?" Zheng asked.

"I'm a man of my word, and I've never broken a promise to anyone," Lucian said. "Anyone in my fleet will tell you as much. Likewise, how do I know I can trust you?"

"You have no choice but to trust me."

"Same. If you want to be anything more than a guard dog for a planet you don't even own, then come with me."

Zheng sighed. "All right, then. Send me the coordinates, and we'll organize our fleet maneuvers. Of course, I'll keep full autonomy of my fleet. This won't work otherwise."

"Sounds good," Lucian said. He was just glad that she was on board. "Talk soon."

He closed the channel, and his mother looked at him, impressed. "I can't believe you managed that. Are you really going to hand over those planets to her?"

"Honestly? It's a small price to pay for the salvation of humanity."

"Still . . . feels wrong to promise them planets that aren't even ours by right."

"Let's be real. There probably won't even be a League by the end of this. They only control seven systems now. We can let the Pirates and the League figure things out once all this is over."

28

LUCIAN HAD TO ADMIT, the size of Admiral Yang's fleet spread before them was impressive and would have been intimidating if he had no confidence in his abilities. In the three months since the battle outside Hephaestus, Zheng's numbers had only grown. She had not been idle and had put her skilled shipwrights and the industrial capacity of Hephaestus to good use.

However, some things could not be replaced.

"Twelve battleships," Mira said. "She used to have fifteen."

"They took a pummeling against the Swarmers," Lucian said.

"Still, an imposing force. Most of what she's added is on the smaller side, but no one builds ships like the Golden Pirates. You can bet they'll be fast and pack a punch. It's a different power than the League uses."

"I'll take your word for it."

Lucian hailed *Stars' Blood* from his slate. After a moment, Zheng picked up.

"What's the plan?" she asked.

"I'm going to create a portal to Archea, and then we will hunt for Lowell's fleet and convince him to join us."

"And if this *convincing* doesn't work?"

"It will."

"You sound sure of that."

"I have the Orb of Psionics. I can force him to see reason."

Zheng went silent at that. If Lucian could do it to Lowell, he could do it to her, too.

"Your move, Sorcerer-Ascendant," Zheng said. "We'll be right behind."

Lucian began gathering ether to open the portal. It would require more than the one from Psyche to Hephaestus because it would need to be wide enough to fit *Stars' Blood*, a carrier almost as massive as the ones fielded by the League. He would also have to hold it open longer to allow all the ships to pass.

Rather than hold an active stream, he branded it. As he entered the Ether, the Shadow Realm before him was replaced by a matrix of multi-colored lines. All those lines infused into him. Time disappeared as Lucian became a conduit of incredible creative power.

After some time, he opened the portal wide enough to accommodate *Stars' Blood* comfortably. He branded the magic. He couldn't stream as long as this brand held. But at least this way, he was not continually streaming. The portal would dissolve as soon as he let go of the brand.

"Go," Lucian said.

"Ahead full," Mira ordered. "Into the portal."

Lucian watched the Pirate fleet outside the viewport. He recognized they could hang back, letting the Starsea Fleet go to their doom in Archea. Lucian didn't know what they would have to gain from that, but he was aware of the possibility.

As the first Starsea corvettes slipped through, the Pirate fleet got in line behind *Barbarossa*. They were following.

"It's on now," Mira said.

The portal was directly in front of Starsea Fleet, and through its warbled plane, he could see the arid surface of Archea in the distance. *Barbarossa* slipped through.

Warning klaxons wailed, sending high-pitched tones echoing through the bridge as the heavy cruiser immediately came under fire. They had stumbled directly upon the League fleet.

"Fire at will!" Mira orders.

The cruiser's torpedo tubes emptied at once, blasting forward toward the massive fleet arrayed before them in front of the planet. Swarms of League corvettes unleashed railgun fire upon the portal. Lucian was shocked at the reception. How had they known they would come out here at this very point?

It had to have been simply bad luck. This was the only point in the Archea System Lucian could have portaled to, and it was close to Archea Station. Naturally, Admiral Lowell's fleet would have been nearby.

The Starsea fleet was already forming its own battle lines, the javelin-class corvettes moving to engage the enemy while the guardian-class destroyers began their hunt for smaller vessels.

But despite the chaos of battle, Lucian noted one crucial detail. The League fleet had very few large vessels. He counted only four battleships and one supercarrier hanging behind those, well out of range. Zheng's battleships were already slipping through the portal, enough to challenge their firepower.

"Their battleships are out of position," Mira said. "This is our chance! Push forward!"

"Hail Lowell," Lucian said.

"I'm trying, but he's not accepting. He's aboard *Mekong*, that carrier."

Lucian could see it in the distance. The longer this took, the more casualties both sides would take. The goal wasn't winning a battle; it was recruiting a navy. Already, ships were lighting up in brief fireballs quickly extinguished by the vacuum of space.

Once the last ships went through the portal, Lucian let go of his brand. Most of the ether locked in the brand returned to his Focus. He redirected it to create an aura around himself, combining Binding, Atomicism, Dynamism, and Thermalism to make a bubble that would make it impervious to the vacuum of space.

"What are you doing?" Mira asked.

"Going to find Lowell."

Lucian warped himself outside the ship onto the hull of *Mekong* itself. Combining Space-Time with Radiance, he phased through the ship's hull and hit the upper deck.

All that streaming had almost completely exhausted his ether. Thankfully, this area of the ship was abandoned, despite the blare of warning klaxons.

Lucian ducked into an open crew cabin that was currently unoccupied. There, he drew ether into his Focus. He re-entered the corridor, bending light around his body to become invisible as a troop of League marines clomped past. He drew more ether to maintain the stream and flew down the corridor at breakneck speed. After rounding a corner, he found the primary thoroughfare a hive of activity, filled to the brim with League sailors. Such was the strength of his magical aura that none detected his presence.

He entered the elevator that would take him to the bridge, hacking the terminal with Radiant Magic. The elevator shot up the central tower of the ship.

A moment later, the doors opened onto *Mekong's* massive bridge, filled with at least fifty Warden officers. Some glanced his way, but he was still wrapped in his Radiant invisibility stream. Several soldiers ran over to investigate, but Lucian was already floating above them, toward the man who had to be Admiral Lowell, a man with receding gray hair and a mustache. Lucian could see the Starsea fleet through the wide forward viewport, a frightening force wreaking havoc on the League's front lines.

Lucian was burning ether at an alarming rate. He drew more, allowing the Gravitonic stream to dissipate as he fell to the deck steps away from Lowell, redirecting the flow into Psionics. He didn't waste time; he formed a Psionic brand designed for pure mind domination. Nothing less would serve. A simple, separate Radiant brand hid the violet of Lowell's eyes so that none would suspect his condition.

Lucian wrangled with the admiral's mind for a moment before he gained firm control. Lowell shuddered, then grew still, drawing a few curious glances.

"Admiral?" a nearby officer asked with concern, the name Alexander stamped in bold letters across his gray uniform.

"Accept the hail from *Barbarossa*," Lowell said.

"Sir?" Alexander asked.

"Do it!"

"We will destroy them in time, Admiral. The rest of our battleships will be in range in just fifteen minutes. If you are trying to negotiate their surrender . . ."

Lucian increased the Admiral's anger until his face became pumice. "Get off my bridge, Captain Alexander, and that's an order!"

The captain's face went ashen. "Yes, Admiral. Forgive me."

As the captain turned and left, Lowell answered the communication himself in a huff.

"Admiral Lowell speaking."

"Admiral Lowell," came Mira's voice. "This is Admiral Abrantes of the Starsea Fleet. Stop firing at once! We are not the enemy."

Lowell turned to his soldiers. "You heard her. Cease fire!"

The men and women on the bridge looked at him in disbelief, but they consented without delay because of what he'd said to the captain earlier. Within moments, the entire League fleet had ceased fire. At almost the same time, the Starsea fleet also went still.

Lucian drew more ether, maintaining his invisibility. He set it as a brand and continued to puppet Lowell.

"That's better," Mira said. "We aren't here to fight, Admiral. The Swarmers have already shed too much blood for us to turn on each other."

Lucian made Lowell soften. "I concur, Admiral Abrantes. However, you can imagine my surprise to find a fleet right on my doorstep."

He couldn't make Lowell agree too readily, or his officers would feel something was drastically wrong. Lucian delved deeply into the man's mind to better understand how he might respond. Lucian felt like a puppeteer still learning the ropes. Or perhaps a puppeteer with butterfingers. There was more to Psionic control than just brands. It was a lot of gentle poking and prodding. He realized that he probably should have tested things out first.

"However," he made Lowell say, "my actions were completely in order. You are violating League space. I've never heard of you, Admiral Abrantes, but you are a part of Admiral Yang's fleet. Where is she?"

"She's working with us. We are not trying to harm the League. We're trying to help it. Our goal is to gather a force capable of fighting back against the Swarmers. If humanity is to survive, then the last thing we should do is fight each other."

Lucian felt the realization dawn in Admiral Lowell's mind. "Wait. *Resplendent* is among your ships. We are also getting reports of Warden ships, including *Barbarossa*."

"That's right," Mira said. "We come from many backgrounds, Admiral. Some of us are from the League, like me. Some are mages from Irion, Volsung, or even Psyche. Some are Wardens, and many are from the Golden Armada. We are over fifteen hundred ships strong, and should you join us, Admiral Lowell, we will be over two thousand."

Lucian could sense this man's natural reaction: to refuse to join and go down fighting. Lowell was nothing if not a stubborn man. But with his Psionic brand, Lucian could fill the man's mind with doubt and weaken his backbone.

"So," Lowell said, "you are requesting my unconditional surrender?"

"Not surrender," Mira said. "I am requesting you to join us. As you no doubt know, they'll fall upon this system in a matter of weeks. If we fight together, we stand a better chance of survival. We can save humanity with two thousand ships and thousand mages working together."

"Three *thousand*? Admiral Abrantes, let's be clear. The mages are going mad! Reports from all over the Worlds say they are fraying, only adding to the chaos. One ship in your fleet, *Resplendent*, is a terrible danger to you and your ships—"

"That's been taken care of," Mira said. "They have gained control of the ship, and all the frayed mages have been dealt with."

"Yes, but more of them can go mad. Believe me, as the Admiral of the Warden fleet, I know just how dangerous mages can be."

Lucian found it uncanny that Lowell was saying all this while being mind-controlled by a mage.

He decided it was time to warp back to *Barbarossa*. He could keep the brand running even if he wasn't physically present. Ansaldra had likely maintained well over a hundred brands at the height of her power. Perhaps even more. If she could do that with sorcery, how much more could he?

With the last ether he'd gathered, he warped from *Mekong's* bridge and appeared next to his mother. She gasped when he allowed his invisibility stream to drop.

"Damn," she said. "I can never get used to that."

"Admiral Lowell," Lucian said confidently, "this is Lucian Abrantes, Sorcerer-Ascendant of Magekind, King of Psyche, and ruler of Starsea."

From his brand, Lucian felt the admiral's confusion and his instant inclination to perceive Lucian as a threat. Lucian allayed his fears by tinkering with the brand.

"Sorcerer-Ascendant," Admiral Lowell said. "What is this I hear about Starsea?"

"Starsea is the resistance against the Swarmers. A resistance you and your fleet must join."

"So I can help you in your conquest of the Worlds? Ha! As if that will ever happen."

Lucian increased the strength of his brand. "You are outnumbered and outgunned, Admiral. The League's Second Fleet is still a week away from reinforcing you. Even if you escaped, I could use my magic to keep up with you. How is it you think we fell upon you with no warning?"

There was silence as Admiral Lowell considered all this. It was clear the man was having doubts, to where Lucian didn't need to reinforce them with the brand.

"More than that," Lucian said, "I have almost three thousand mages at my command. That's Thermalists who can melt the hulls of your ships. Atomicists who can create new fuel for my fleet or overload your fusion reactors. Dynamists who can shield the tachyon lances of your battleships. Radiants who can garble your communications. Binders who can draw your ships together or shatter them entirely. Psionics can devastate you during boarding operations. Gravitists who can offset your fleet's movements." Lucian let his point sink in. "You did the wise thing to call off your attack on us. We never meant to fight you. We were responding in kind. But now is the time to accept your defeat and turn over your ships and crew to the Starsea Fleet."

"The Starsea Fleet?" Lowell spat. "Starsea died over five decades ago! The League does not recognize your authority."

Lucian smiled. "It will. Beginning with you."

Silence was Lucian's only answer. He realized he could demand Lowell to bend to him, and even without the Psionic brand, he would have no choice but to agree.

"I . . . must speak to Admiral Thorin and the Hegemon about this. On my own, I don't have the proper authority to—"

"Gather your top officers and come to *Barbarossa*. There, we can discuss the terms of your unconditional surrender."

"Sorcerer-Ascendant, I—"

Lucian pushed on his brand, forcing him into compliance.

Lowell cleared his throat. "I will come immediately."

"Good. We will receive you in the hangar."

Admiral Yang rang him up on his slate. Lucian answered.

"What's going on?"

"Negotiations. Come to the hangar on *Barbarossa*. Bring your top officers."

"Negotiations? Are they surrendering so soon? The rest of their battleships are just minutes away from being in range!"

"It's over, Admiral Yang. It would seem Starsea has won its first major victory."

29

ABOUT AN HOUR LATER, Lucian waited for Admiral Lowell's arrival in the reception area next to the ship's hangar. Everyone among his Mage Council was with him, including Talent Isaac, who Transcend Orange had recommended as Chief Atomicist. Also included were the Transcends, the Mage Board of Irion, Admiral Yang and some of her top officers, Commander Carthen and Grand Captain Warwick, and about a dozen other Starsea officers.

They watched as a sleek transport ship entered the hangar and settled in the middle. After the hangar pressurized, Lucian and the rest of his entourage entered.

They stood waiting a couple of minutes before the transport's door opened, revealing the gray-haired Admiral Gavin Lowell, who walked down the boarding ramp with the straight bearing of a military man. Lucian had to hand it to him; the admiral was facing this situation as bravely as anyone could be expected, especially considering Lucian wasn't doing anything to influence his brand. With him were twelve other officers, all captains from the look of it, all wearing trim, gray Warden uniforms. Lowell gazed at Lucian's party, his eyes lingering on Carthen and Warwick.

Probing his Psionic brand, Lucian could feel the man's anger at his two former underlings, followed by a quick realization that he was about to follow in their footsteps and swear allegiance to the Sorcerer-Ascendant. Lowell drew up a few paces from Lucian, hatred burning in his small brown eyes, while the expressions on his officers' faces remained impassive.

"Thank you for joining us," Lucian said.

"Just get to the point."

Lucian arched an eyebrow, ignoring the disrespect, at least for now. "Admiral Lowell, you fired on us when all we wanted to do was talk. We've been trying to reach you for weeks to no avail. In short, your actions have caused hundreds of needless deaths when we can't afford it."

Lowell just watched Lucian with an air of insolence. The older admiral clearly didn't think much of him.

Lucian was about to change that.

"Admiral Lowell, these are Starsea's terms. You must surrender your entire fleet to the command of Grand Admiral Abrantes. You are to resign from your post as rear admiral of the League fleet and remain in confinement. You must also give up the Archea System. Your officers, staff, and sailors can remain in their current positions as long as they swear oaths of allegiance to the Sorcerer-Ascendant of Magekind."

Lowell's brown eyes became mocking. "You think this is some game?"

"I don't. Gathering all of humanity to resist the Swarmers is the furthest thing from a game I can imagine. You will accept these terms without protest if you have the same mindset."

"This is an offense to the League of Worlds! You would become a new Xara Mallis!"

Lucian smiled at the accusation he had heard many times

in the last few weeks. "Xara and I are very different. For one, my power far surpasses hers. It's safe to say no one in the Worlds can stand against me. I would let you work under me in my fleet, but I can't worry about when you might try to stab me in the back. The only safe place I *can* keep you is in a cell until the end of this war."

Lowell's eyes widened at the suggestion. He immediately dropped his affronted demeanor. "Now, let's not be hasty. Perhaps I can be of use to you."

Lucian did his best to look bored. "The effort isn't worth it, frankly. You will always hate me, and I can't have that liability. You must sign the treaty we have prepared for you if you truly want to make a difference. After you sign, you can forward it to your command staff and fleet officers. The best thing you can do is to ensure a smooth transition of power."

Admiral Lowell chewed his lower lip as he thought about this. Lucian could read his every thought. Though his expression was strangely calm, inside the man was roiling. He was afraid, angry, and confused all at once. How could this Sorcerer-Ascendant come out of nowhere? How could the mages of Irion and Volsung *both* be following him? How had even the Pirate Empress, the Terror of Stars, bow to him? Despite this young upstart's youth, there was more to him than met the eye. That much was clear.

Lowell, at last, saw there was no way to wriggle out of this. He was an excellent tactician and knew his way in a fight, with his fists and with a fleet. He'd received top marks at the Luna Space Academy, but a drinking problem in his younger days had kept him from rising as high as his instructors had predicted. In the end, in his late fifties, he'd been relegated to the relative backwater of Psyche and could expect to rise no higher.

Perhaps, with a shift in attitude, this young mage—this

Sorcerer-Ascendant—might be persuaded to trust him. Maybe there was room to ascend to heights he never dreamed possible. It would take some humility, but clearly, the young man had a good read on him, and he couldn't expect to outplay him. After all, his only other option was to be relegated to a prison cell.

Lucian read all this and more as he awaited Lowell's response.

"Sorcerer-Ascendant, you must forgive my former transgression. You surely understand that I acted in the best manner I could. When your fleet appeared out of nowhere, I couldn't think of it as anything *but* hostile. I could indeed have responded to your earlier hails; however, I was under orders not to engage with you and was told that a League delegation would contact you first. Indeed, you have a powerful weapon in your magic, the likes of which the Worlds has never seen. The way you can move entire fleets instantly will change warfare forever. I wish to be a part of that. If you'll have me."

Lucian read the brand, and to his surprise, detected no deceit. It was strange to him that the admiral could have done such an about-face, but he seemed to have come to this new conclusion after realizing Lucian's strength and abilities.

But it was still up to Lucian to decide how to use him—and *if* he was going to use him.

Lucian sighed. "I have many reasons not to trust you, Admiral. So tell me why I should?"

Lucian already knew the answer to that. Lowell *had* done what he thought was best with the information he had. The League admiral was defending the system he'd been tasked with guarding. Of course, he could have stopped when Mira hailed him, but Lowell hadn't wanted to take any chances.

Lowell watched Lucian closely. "As I previously said, I did

what I thought was best. Nothing more or less. If you have no further need of me—"

"I do," Lucian said. Everyone looked at him in surprise. "I know you were doing your best, Lowell. That's what you do. It's who you are."

Lowell frowned. "I don't see how you could know that."

"You are a dutiful man. You have your vices, but who doesn't?"

Lowell's eyes widened at that, and from that widening, Lowell didn't think Lucian was bluffing.

"You're . . . you're in my head. Aren't you?"

From the paling on Lowell's face, Lucian knew he didn't need to do any more convincing. It was impossible to stand up to somebody who could read every thought and understand one's entire history with a simple streaming of magic.

"I'll do whatever you ask," Lowell said. "I place myself under your command. Under the Grand Admiral's authority, if need be."

"Good," Lucian said. "Whatever she says, goes. Make yourself indispensable, and you will do well. Your old colleagues, Carthen and Warwick, are also working with us."

Both men nodded to their old master.

Next, Lowell regarded Mira, who gave Lowell a hard stare that Lucian could only describe as terrifying. It was the look she had given him when he'd gotten into a bit of mischief in his younger days, only a hundred times worse. Lucian watched as Admiral Lowell swallowed a nervous throat lump.

"You get one strike before you're out," Mira said. "Are we clear on that?"

Lowell cleared his throat. "Perfectly, Grand Admiral."

Transcend White's voice entered his mind. *Are you sure he can be trusted?*

Yes. I've read his thoughts, and he won't betray us. He started wanting to stab us in the back, but now that he knows who and what I am, he won't.

Lowell looked at Lucian, giving a stiff salute. "The Third Fleet is yours to command, Sorcerer-Ascendant. I am ready and willing to sign any official documents you have."

"Of course. First, we have to make sure Archea is secure. And the fleet codes need to be entrusted to Admiral Abrantes. As a sign of good faith. You need not worry; the terms are all drawn up."

Lowell's smile faltered for a moment. With those codes, Mira would have the power to do whatever she wanted. It was typically something only the highest-ranking officer had access to, and Lowell would lose access as soon as Mira received ownership of the codes. It was the ultimate test of his seriousness.

"Of course," he said. "I will send them as soon as everything is signed."

Again, Lucian read Lowell's brand and detected no deceit. He nodded at his mother to continue the negotiations.

Everything had been signed within the hour, and the fleet codes were transferred. And the Starsea Fleet was five hundred vessels stronger, rising above two thousand ships.

With the addition of the League's Third Fleet, Lucian now had access to the giant battleships that would allow him to go toe-to-toe with some of the Swarmers' larger vessels. With focused fire, he wouldn't have to deal with every carrier personally.

Lowell would be relegated to a smaller fleet wing directly under Mira's authority as a rear admiral.

Lucian nodded, satisfied. This conclusion was the best he could have hoped for.

THE FOLLOWING week was spent bringing the Archea System under control and retrofitting every ship capable of fighting. This included civilian transports, freighters, leisure craft, prospecting ships, ice haulers, and dozens of other vessels. Anyone with spacefaring experience was recruited into the war effort and paid a wage.

It was not only the ship's codes Lucian got access to. It was also the money entrusted to the fleet, over ten million credits, an unimaginable sum to Lucian.

With the fleet's money, Lucian paid his soldiers and gave them some shore leave on Archea for the week while he got things under control.

Within hours of Lucian's takeover, the League declared war against the "Starsea insurrection" and vowed to end it with violence if necessary. Hegemon Kirsten Madi denounced Lucian on all the newsfeeds and anyone following him. This included the Volsung and Irion Mage Academies, the "faithless" Admiral Yang, and the "useless" Wardens who had failed to contain the outbreak from Psyche.

Lucian knew it was all just words. The League was powerless to do anything against him, especially given the state of the Worlds. Lucian sent a message to the First Fleet and Hegemon Madi, detailing his plans for stopping the Swarmers. However, his transmissions went ignored.

What wasn't ignored were his broadcasts to the various media. They were happy to get his message out, if only to get eyeballs. That was, until the League censored his voice on all official channels.

He would deal with the new Hegemon in time, but now, he had to set his affairs in order. There seemed to be no reaction from the Swarmers to Lucian's actions; their fleets were still dispersing to siege the Trailward Worlds. Besides the fleets already in League Space, countless *Alkasen* ships were pouring in from Dark Space. Communications from the farthest systems had already gone dark. It was an ominous feeling, waiting for the coming storm.

The Believers were entering the Nessus System with little to no resistance, as if all the rest weren't bad enough. They were just days away from claiming the planet. Lucian had a hard decision to make; to save Nessus and win points with the League or to remain in place in Archea and meet the Swarmers' advance head-on. He could not do both.

Lucian had just come from a meeting with the top brass to discuss this question, about fifty of the highest-ranking officials in his fledgling fleet. This meeting included the Mage Council, the Transcends, and the Irion Board of Mages, who had finally sent Vassar packing. Lucian trusted Fergus, the new First Mage, to make the right decision regarding the Irion Mages.

Fergus was already integrating the Irion Mages into Starsea's Mage Division, with the full approval of the Board. Most agreed that things had been shaken so much that adopting a new system would be far more manageable. After the process was complete, Fergus would continue his role as Chief Radiant, thus ending the Irion Academy, at least until the war's end. For now, the Volsung Mages remained separate and had no desire to be absorbed by the Starsea Mage Division. True to his promise, Lucian would grant their wish.

During the meeting with the top brass, there was no consensus on the right move. The mages leaned toward meeting the Believer fleet head-on to win points with the League. The Pirates and aristocracy of Psyche wanted to remain in Archea, building a larger fleet to deal with the Swarmers.

There were problems with both plans. For one, humans wasting lives on each other was counterproductive. Lucian could never forget who was in charge of the Believer fleet: Sharo Khalin, the last remaining avatar of the Ancient One. While he wasn't on the side of the *Alkasen*, he wasn't the League's ally, either. His only goal was to kill Lucian and claim his Orbs.

With nothing decided, Lucian withdrew into meditation. He found an isolated viewing room and locked the door behind him. Before a panorama of Archea's arid deserts, Lucian sat and assumed his Focus. As he had on Psyche, he would need to delve the Manifold for answers.

When he combined Psionics with Space-Time, dozens of futures spread before him, most of them disastrous. This process required an abundance of both patience and ether. Lucian sat for untold hours as time slipped away, exploring the various future realities of confronting the Believers. Some scenarios involved attacking them head-on, while others had Lucian warping to *Holy Fire* to assassinate Sharo Khalin directly.

Only with this option, things became . . . muddy. The Manifold wouldn't allow Lucian to see a way to attack and defeat Khalin. If he went forward with the attack, he'd be flying blind.

He increased the flow of ether to force the issue, and again, the resistance rose to match.

Lucian opened his eyes, recognizing the truth. His Space-Time Magic was being blocked.

Lucian remembered Silumko, who had actively used Space-Time Magic right before him. Did Sharo Khalin have the same access? If so, could he use it to defend himself?

Lucian cut off the connection immediately. No answers had come, although he recognized a crucial weakness in his fleet that he had put off for far too long.

Lucian didn't know if it was possible for any mage besides him to portal entire fleets, but he knew a single mage could warp themselves. Silumko had done it, after all. Many Space-Time mages working in confluence *might* create a portal large enough to attack them. It was a possibility Lucian had to plan for immediately.

He opened a Psionic link to Transcend White. *Meet me in Barbarossa's conference room.*

WITHIN TEN MINUTES, Transcend White was standing before him. Lucian shared his visions with her, along with what he expected the Ancient One was doing. From the paling on her face, it was clear she also recognized the danger.

She took a moment to process the information before speaking.

"You're right that this needs to be defended. Likely, the Ancient One is using a Space-Time ward to prevent you from delving any futures that end in his defeat."

"That's what I think, too. If he's warding Space-Time or having some other mages do it, it would be impossible for me to warp onto the High Prophet's flagship."

"That means they're training their Prophets in Space-Time Magic."

Lucian nodded, having come to the same conclusion. "We need to train our mages to use Space-Time Magic. We can't put it off any longer."

"That risks a great deal," Transcend White said. "When this knowledge goes out, there's no getting it back."

"It already *is* out," Lucian said. "In the hands of our enemies. Our only saving grace is that the amount of ether required to create a long-distance portal is extreme. As far as I know, I'm the only one who can do it single-handedly. The Ancient One might also be capable of it. It's hard to say."

"That begs the question," Transcend White said. "How many Space-Time mages do you think we'll need?"

"Let's test every mage in the fleet for potential. Space-Time occupies the central node of the Septagon and connects all of them. It allows combinations of streams that were never possible before, but it can also be streamed independently." Lucian watched Transcend White closely. "Would you be willing to try?"

"Me?" Transcend White laughed. "I'm too old to mess around with a new Aspect."

"If anyone is capable of Space-Time Magic, it would be you. Would you at least try?"

Transcend White seemed tired for a moment, and Lucian understood her hesitancy. Such magic would drain her physically. By now, Lucian wouldn't have been surprised if she were over a century old. She was a powerful mage, but she had to be judicious in using her magic.

"It's all right," Lucian said. "Come to think of it, I can figure it out without you having to stream."

"How?" Transcend White asked.

"I can use Psionics to see your Focus. From there, I can tell if you have the ability."

"You make something quite advanced sound so simple."

"It's really nothing. Anyway, could you organize a way to test all the mages? It will only take me a few seconds to see whether a mage has the potential."

"I will see it done, Sorcerer-Ascendant."

————

EVERY MAGE in the Starsea Fleet had gathered on *Mekong* within the hour. As the largest ship in the former Third Fleet, Lucian decided it would make for the perfect flagship, a place for the Starsea Fleet to base all its ripsaw fighters. The transition would only take about a week, and already, Commander Carthen had moved all the command staff over.

Lucian stood at the head of a mustering hall in the barracks, where men and women filed one by one. Holding the Orb of Psionics, he took a few moments to examine each of their Focuses.

It immediately became clear that most did not have the potential to use Space-Time Magic. That meant it was rare, and there might not be many fleets or assassins warping around the Worlds willy-nilly.

It took about four hours to go through all the mages, of which forty-nine were separated from the rest.

Included in this number was Emma. She seemed to have solid potential, which was serendipitous since he had not yet assigned her to his Mage Council. Now, she would be in control of her own brigade, though at only forty-nine mages, it was less a brigade and more of a platoon.

He dismissed the remaining mages to their former duties and took stock of the forty-nine mages before him. Thanks to

Transcend Violet, the Mage Division wore similar garb: uniform black robes with the Septagon on the chest. Each mage had their own cape, colored according to the mage's Aspect. It seemed every Aspect was represented among them, but soon, they would all wear the black mantle of a Space-Time Mage. They eagerly waited for Lucian to speak.

"I've set you aside," Lucian said, "because each of you has a rare gift."

Their eyes collectively widened at this, but they did not interrupt him.

"As many of you may have guessed, there is a new Aspect of Magic. And all of you have the potential to use it."

There was a mix of reactions. Some looked afraid, others excited, and others were wary of what Lucian would say next.

"There's no reason to be afraid. When I gathered the Seven Orbs, I left out crucial information. There's an Eighth Orb, which I found on the distant moon of Nai Elyn. This moon orbits the planet that was once the homeworld of the Ancients. This Orb controls the realities of space and time."

To prove his point, Lucian warped a few meters ahead until he was face to face with a young woman who was once an Irion Talent. She gasped at the sudden movement.

He took a few steps back. "All of you have the power to use this magic. It is a powerful Aspect. Maybe even *the* most powerful. You will train with me daily to learn how to use it." He gave a firm nod. "We will begin now."

The first thing Lucian did was teach them how to isolate the Aspect of Space-Time. Emma was the first to find it, taking only a few minutes, but everyone could single it out by the end of the lesson.

The next day, they were already performing basic streams, and by the third, all of them could ward Space-Time, an essential thing Lucian wanted them to do.

On the fourth day, Lucian stood at their fore. "Your progress so far has been amazing, to where I trust all of you enough to practice on your own. As you've learned, active Space-Time streams require a lot of ether. Most of you will not be capable of warping even a short distance, much less a portal that can span star systems. Combining Space-Time with your primary might also prove challenging, though if you *can* do it, it will give you an advantage few other mages in the Worlds will have. Of course, mastery will take many years." Lucian looked at the assembly, all watching him almost reverentially. "You come from many backgrounds. Psyche. Irion. Volsung. But now, you are a unit with one purpose. From now on, you will be known as the Space-Time Sentinels."

Lucian watched as they absorbed this information. There was a proudness to their bearing, but also confusion. They had fully expected him to call them the Space-Time Brigade, in line with every other brigade in the Mage Division.

"I call you the Sentinels," Lucian said, "because your number one task will be to guard this fleet. Space-Time Magic is loose in the universe. Just as you can use it, so can our enemies. The Preserved can use it. The Oneist Prophets can use it. Wards must be streamed around our fleet at all times, preventing any distant attack."

The newly minted Space-Time Sentinels looked at Lucian with dedication. He opened a nearby crate he had taken, filled with new capes Transcend Violet had created, as black as the void of space itself. He handed them out. One-by-one, the mages dropped their colored mantles and donned their new black ones. Once done, they faced him again.

"What's more," he said, "you won't be defending just the fleet. All of you are to become my bodyguards. An elite force that will come with me to wherever the fighting is thickest. The Space-Time Sentinels will be known and feared by our enemies. The Swarmers. The Oneists. And darker forces than even those."

Lucian motioned Emma to stand before him and had her face the general assembly. Lucian pinned a golden Septagon on the lapel of her robe.

"This is your Space-Time Captain, Emma Almaty," he said. "You follow every one of her orders as if it came from me. I trust her with my life, as I hope to trust every one of you."

Lucian had already spoken to Emma about this appointment, which she agreed to.

"That's the end of today's training," Emma said, taking control. "All of you can resume your former duties. If I need you, I'll let you know."

Once everyone was gone, Lucian faced her. "You've got this?"

Emma took a moment to respond. "It feels . . . right. *The Sentinels* is the right name. It captures what we're supposed to do. Yes, I think I'm up to the task. I can keep the fleet safe. You as well. You might be the most powerful mage in the Worlds, but even you can't see everything." Emma gave a firm nod, as if to confirm that. "As captain of the Sentinels, I will make sure nothing bad happens to you or this fleet."

Lucian nodded. "I'm glad to hear it. When I asked if you wanted the role, I thought you'd say no."

"A part of me wanted to. I've come to realize that choice is a bit of an illusion. If not me, then who?"

It was a question for which Lucian didn't have the answer.

"I'll leave you in charge of setting up the Sentinels. However you want to organize or use them, I trust your judgment."

"Leave it to me."

"I can continue training everyone until we get moving again. After that, you'll be in charge of training."

"I hardly know anything about Space-Time Magic," Emma said.

"But you have the greatest potential in it. Of everyone here, you're probably the only one powerful enough to warp yourself across light-years, though that'll take practice. More than that, as a Radiant, you can combine Space-Time and Radiance to phase, at least for brief moments. That's something none of the others can do. You'll have to figure out many things, but if anyone can, it's you."

She smiled. "Thanks for the vote of confidence. I can have the mages duel a bit to hone their skills. But at all times, I'm going to have mages keep a ward up. There's forty-nine of us, so maybe seven at a time is enough to keep it running."

"That's a good idea," Lucian said. An idea suddenly came to him. "One more thing."

"Yes?"

"Take a poll of all your mages, asking them what star systems they've been in. Once they're done, send me the results."

Emma frowned, confused. "Sure, I'll do it. But why?"

"A project I plan to work on later."

"That's cryptic."

"Sorry, I've got to run. Talk to you soon."

Lucian created a portal for the command deck of *Mekong*.

LUCIAN STOOD on the bridge of *Mekong*, taking a sip of coffee. He was monitoring his command staff busy at their stations when an alert chimed from the central monitor.

Immediately, Mira went to stand before it. "What've we got, Karlsen?"

Karlsen served as the ship's Chief Sensors Officer. She towered over Mira, and her long black hair pulled back in a ponytail only accentuated her height. "Looks like one of our alert buoys around Nahar. Picking up several Swarmer strike craft on a trajectory from the Alsan Gate."

Lucian recalled his research on this system. Nahar was the smallest and outermost gas giant of the Archea System, and its current orbital position placed it quite close to the Alsan Gate. It also was a vital source of helium-3 and held most of the system's orbital fuel refineries.

"Strange," Mira said. "There was no sighting of them passing the Gate?"

Karlsen cleared her throat. "I assume they magically shielded themselves."

"Of course," Mira said. "How many were logged?"

"There appear to be two dozen."

"Were those the exact numbers?"

"Yes. Twenty-four exactly."

"Simple enough to deal with. Probably a bombing run to take out our fuel source."

"Orders, Admiral?" Chief Helmsman Morales's voice was deep and resonant.

"Nothing for now, Morales," Mira answered. "Seems like a job for a small task force, not the fleet at large." She raised her slate to her mouth. "Admiral Lowell."

The rear admiral's response was nearly immediate. "Yes, Grand Admiral?"

"Did you receive the alert about the Swarmer vessels?"

"I did."

"Think you're up for a little job? Take a hundred ships and hunt them down before they cause too much damage."

"That would be simplicity itself," Lowell said. "However, I would hesitate to send so many after such a small force. This aggression on the Swarmers' part seems rather obvious. A feint to weaken the main fleet. However, it cannot go unanswered."

"My thoughts exactly."

Mira clasped her hands behind her black Starsea admiral's uniform, a color which was now outfitted amongst all their sailors. More and more, it felt as if they were becoming a real navy.

"This system's gas mines are under threat," she said. "If we lose them, we'll have no other way to refuel. Our Atomicists can only stretch our reserves, not manufacture them endlessly."

Lucian listened attentively. He trusted his mother to make the right call.

At last, she nodded. "Admiral Lowell, you will take one hundred ships to deal with the threat. I want you to take five heavy cruisers, thirty destroyers, and sixty-five corvettes." She paused, considering for a moment. "Make sure each ship is outfitted with a Gravitist and an Atomicist to ensure maximum speed. I want to hit them fast before they know what's coming."

Lucian broke his silence. "I want to go with this task force."

Mira arched an eyebrow but refrained from asking why. "And the Sorcerer-Ascendant will accompany you."

There was a moment's pause on Lowell's end. "Of course. His presence would be most welcome."

Though the rear admiral said this easily, Lucian detected a note of strain in his voice.

"Thank you, Admiral," Lucian said. "I trust you to do your job properly. I like to see these Swarmers up close any chance I can."

"Of course."

The rear admiral had been especially testy ever since Lucian had requisitioned the carrier *Mekong* for his mother and had given him *Barbarossa*. He seemed more annoyed about that than turning over the fleet entirely. But *Mekong* rightfully belonged to the Grand Admiral.

"I'll see you on board *Barbarossa*," Lucian said. "I want that task force ready to set out within the hour."

"Of course, Sorcerer-Ascendant. It shall be as you say."

———

Lucian stood with Admiral Lowell on the deck of *Barbarossa* as it led the task force to the edge of the Archea System. Even with the Gravitists warding each ship, Lucian could feel the strain of the deceleration. The Atomicists were streaming overtime to replicate fuel units as quickly as they were depleted. An exhausting task, but one that would see them reaching the cold outer system in just four hours, whereas the journey without it would have taken ten times as long.

About ten minutes from the Forge of Nahar, the primary gas mine, an alert chimed from the central monitor.

Lowell cleared his throat as he scanned the data. "Nahar Station is under assault. It will be impossible to attack the Swarmers without damaging it."

"And when will we be in range?" Lucian asked.

The Chief Systems officer, a man named Barnett, responded. "Five minutes for torpedoes, if not sooner."

Lucian spoke into his slate. "Battle stations, all. I will not risk the station or the forge."

Lowell sidled over to Lucian, speaking in a confidential tone. "If you truly wish not to risk the station or forge, we cannot engage the fleet. They are remaining close to the station, hoping you won't risk the civilian population."

Of course, there would be a civilian population. Lucian nearly cursed at the oversight.

"They haven't attacked the station at all?"

Lowell shook his head. "I'm sure they would also like to use the fuel forge. They plan to wipe out the life on board the station before requisitioning it for their use. Of course, the most prudent course would be to destroy the station, along with the Swarmers. This will ensure the least loss of life among our crew. Especially considering the Swarmers will kill all those on the station, anyway."

"I won't destroy the station," Lucian said. "We can save the forge, the station, and the civilians, all while keeping our fleet intact."

Lowell chuckled. "Respectfully, Sorcerer-Ascendant, sometimes a sacrifice of life is needed to ensure the greater good."

"And how many lives are on the station?"

Lowell shrugged. "Two thousand, perhaps. But the lives of our sailors are far more valuable to the war effort."

"We need the fuel," Lucian said. "How can we use it if we risk the station?"

"Then what do you propose, Sorcerer-Ascendant?"

"One minute until torpedo range," Barnett said.

As much as Lucian hated to admit it, the rear admiral might be right. There was no way to attack the Swarmer vessels without risking the station. It was easier to destroy them and be done with it. The station was likely doomed, anyway. Any attempt to save it would only risk Lucian's ships and sailors. He had few enough of those to spare.

By now, the royal blue gas giant of Nahar dominated the viewscreen. An immense, rotating world-sized storm churned like a whirlpool along its equator. Nahar's swirls and cyclones were a varied mix of reds and deep blues, punctuated with islands and archipelagos of jade green.

And against that massive backdrop was a tiny black dot, what Lucian assumed to be the station. It grew larger with each passing second. For now, the small Swarmer strike force was not visible.

"Raise shields and power weapons," Lucian ordered.

Lowell arched an eyebrow, but didn't question the command. "Raise shields and power weapons!"

Energy shields covered every vessel large enough to generate one. Even with the action, the Swarmer vessels remained rooted, not even maneuvering to defend themselves.

"We are now in torpedo range," Barnett said.

"Your orders, Sorcerer-Ascendant?" Lowell asked.

"Stand by," Lucian said.

"Sorcerer-Ascendant . . ."

Lucian had done his best to be patient with the admiral. However, he was questioning him far too much.

"Get ready to fire on the hostiles," Lucian said. "But only on my word."

By now, the station was quite prominent in the viewscreen, and Lucian could pick out a group of *Alkasen* strike craft circling it but not firing. The Starsea task force had slowed to where the station was no longer getting larger. After waiting a moment, the Swarmer vessels did not change their behavior.

Lucian reached the Orb of Binding. If the Swarmer vessels weren't going to move, he would have to move *them*. It would take time, but it could be done with patience.

He drew as much ether as he could, using Radiance to enhance his vision enough to lock onto a smaller Swarmer vessel, a craft comparable to a League corvette. Lucian's body became surrounded with blue light as a shining tether formed between his outstretched hand and the ship, a tether that went directly through the viewscreen as if it weren't there. As Lucian increased the tether's strength, the ship attempted to counter the pull with its powerful engine. However, it proved no match against the Orb of Binding and Lucian's Focus. With each passing moment, his tether grew stronger and stronger. Despite the insane amount of ether required, the Swarmer corvette was reeled toward the Starsea task force.

Admiral Lowell watched slack jawed. Lucian's body was practically alight with blue magic, the thick beam of blue light pulsating with magical energy. The ship was moving quickly, powerless to resist the Orb. Lucian could feel the strength of its engines, far more potent than anything the League fielded for a ship this size outside of the prototypical quantum engine found on *Blood Wyvern*.

As soon as it was far enough from the station, he nodded. "Blast it."

Immediately, the space ahead was lit with the white-hot

streaks of unleashed torpedoes. The crystalline Swarmer lit in a brief explosion, quickly snuffed out by the surrounding void.

"One down," Lucian said, "twenty-three more to go."

Next, Lucian set his sights on bigger prey, one of the larger Swarmer vessels, about the size of a League cruiser. It must have gotten missed in the initial report, though Lucian couldn't see how. It had the same crystalline exterior as the smaller corvette, except it was much larger, probably enough to hold five hundred or more crewmembers.

Lucian wouldn't allow himself to be daunted by the size of it. He grabbed hold of its bow and streamed.

The ship immediately responded, powering its engines to counter the pull of the tether. All it could do was match the tether's power, hoping Lucian couldn't overpower the engines.

It was futile. It took about five minutes, but eventually, the tension and power of Lucian's tether were such that the ship couldn't resist it. The tether was a thick column of pulsating blue light, almost blinding. The vessel was dragged toward the fleet.

"Almost too easy," Lowell said with a smirk.

"Take it out," Lucian said.

But as soon as torpedoes were launched, the pressure suddenly released. The Swarmer had cut off its engines, causing it to fly toward the fleet at breakneck speed. The ship's captain meant to use it as a weapon, knowing the vessel was going down, anyway.

"Brace for impact!" Lowell shouted.

Lucian redirected his mighty flow of magic. With just a few seconds to spare before the cruiser crashed into *Barbarossa*, Lucian opened a portal directly in its path, pointing it to the vicinity of Archea. When the Swarmer vessel slipped through and disappeared, Lucian closed it. The main fleet would deal with it as soon as it lit their LADAR terminals.

"That was quick thinking," Lowell said.

Lucian didn't answer as he set to work tethering the next vessel. But as soon as he performed that action, the entire Swarmer squadron, at last, responded.

"Shoot them down as soon as they clear the station," Lucian said.

But before his order could be followed, the LADAR monitor blared as it logged new hostiles.

"Admiral!" Barnett said. "A fleet has dropped right on top of us!"

Almost at once, the Starsea task force became the focus of countless attacks. Just from the blips on the LADAR, Lucian could tell it was a lot of ships. Perhaps two hundred, which would outnumber his task force two to one.

"Engage," Lowell said. "Give them everything we've got!"

As *Barbarossa* turned to face the oncoming fleet, Lucian immediately saw how they had gotten there. A portal had opened, and through it, ship after Swarmer ship issued forth.

It was a trap. As Lowell had suspected, the small Swarmer group attacking the station had been bait meant to draw them out of position.

Lucian reached out his Focus, reversing the stream holding the portal in place. This action only took a few seconds, but by the time Lucian had fully extinguished it, there were two hundred Swarmer vessels to deal with, not to mention the ships next to the station.

"We're completely out of position," Lowell said. "Fire on the fuel station!"

Before Lucian could counteract the order, the concentrated fire of the Starsea task force obliterated the smaller Swarmer attack group, along with the station itself. A massive flash of light emitted from the disintegrating machinery housing the volatile refinery. Within microseconds, thousands were dead.

Lucian wheeled on the Admiral. "I could have destroyed those ships! You didn't have to attack the station."

Lowell set his face grimly, seeming to have no regrets. "There was no time, Sorcerer-Ascendant. If you could have done something, you *would* have by now." As if the matter were concluded, Lowell turned to the Chief Helmsman. "Make for that carrier on the Swarmers' left flank. Concentrate all fire there."

"You can't break that ship with conventional weapons," Lucian said. "You'll need lances and lots of them. No ship here has them equipped."

"Then I'm afraid this task force is as good as lost."

"You're done. Another word from you, and I'm sending you to the brig."

The senior staff watched wide-eyed, and from the anger on Lucian's face, they knew he meant it. Admiral Lowell opened his mouth, but in the end, he decided it was better to keep silent. Instead, his smug expression invited Lucian to extricate them from this impossible predicament.

So, that was what Lucian would do. Extricate them.

He took up his slate. "Target the smaller vessels. Leave those carriers to me."

Without further explanation, Lucian formed a Gravitonic mass in the distance, in the center of the three carriers that had slipped through the Swarmers' portal. As Lucian added to the gravity point, increasing its power, he watched various Starsea ships go down. Within seconds, three corvettes lit the darkness of space, only to be eternally snuffed out. That was about fifty lives right there. A squadron of Swarmer bombers ran over a destroyer, splitting it down the middle with a rain of green lasers. Another hundred souls lost. Lucian was tempted to divert his stream to attack the smaller ships, but he knew that what he was doing would save more lives. The carriers were the source of the fighters and bombers laying waste to his ships, and if they went unchallenged, they would only spew out more interceptors until Lucian's smaller force was overwhelmed.

At last, Lucian could see the effects of his magic. The three ovoid carriers were pulled inextricably toward the gravity point and began crashing into each other. The Gravitonic tide began towing the smaller Swarmer vessels, making their movements sluggish.

Senior officers were watching the display in shock. Unlike the rest of the Wardens, they had yet to see the Sorcerer-Ascendant's magic in action. Lucian only increased the Gravitonic pull. Swarmer ships and vessels were falling toward the gravity point at incredible speed, circling it like a vortex before being compressed into a ball of metal and crystalline rock.

Within minutes, the battle had completely turned around.

Helmsman Barnett was the first on the bridge to speak. "Putting the ship into orbit around the gravitational . . .disturbance."

Lucian raised his slate to his mouth, straining from holding the stream. "All ships follow *Barbarossa's* lead. Don't get too close to the gravity point."

Once most of the Swarmer vessels had been consumed, Lucian let go of his stream. Almost at once, the ball of metal and rock began breaking up, some at high speed. Thankfully, the task force sped away, missing most of the exploding flak.

Lucian's shoulders sagged, but he did his best not to let it show. The senior officers looked at him as if he were a god, watching the phenomenon with amazement outside the viewports.

It took five more minutes to mop up what few Swarmer vessels remained, but the victory seemed hollow. The whole reason they had come here had been to save the station. But the fuel supply was as good as lost, and it would take months to reestablish the station with a working crew. Not only that, but a couple of thousand lives had needlessly been lost.

There was no point in pointing out the fact, however.

"Set course for Archea Station," Lucian said wearily.

As Barnett set the course, Lucian turned to Admiral Lowell, whose face was paler than usual. He was not the only one who recognized the gravity of his error.

"Sorcerer-Ascendant. Forgive my lack of faith. I promise in the future—"

"—Never question me again, Admiral. Never. I will give you one more chance. Now, get the fleet back in one piece."

Admiral Lowell swallowed. "I will never doubt you again, Sorcerer-Ascendant. I swear it."

Lucian gave him a baleful glare before warping back to the bridge of *Mekong*.

AS SOON AS Lucian appeared on *Mekong's* bridge, Mira approached him.

"Everything all right? How'd it go?"

Lucian looked around to see that the black-uniformed senior officers of *Mekong* were arrayed before him, about twenty in all. Also present were most members of the Mage Council, including Serah, Khairu, Plato, Isaac, and a new Binder from Irion Fergus had recommended, a man named Aldric. He had the powerful presence of a warrior about him, tall and proud with shoulder-length blond hair, his frame broad, and his blue eyes keen.

"Admiral Lowell is on his way back right now," Lucian said. "Unfortunately, the forge station was lost."

There was silence as everyone processed the news. It wasn't just the thousands of lives that were gone, but the Starsea Fleet's ability to refuel itself. While almost all major ships had an Atomicist on board, it wasn't every ship. And no Atomicist could regenerate fuel as quickly as their respective ship could use it. They were a boost, nothing more.

"Anything else?" Mira asked.

"Yes," Lucian said. "We were ambushed. It was all a set-up."

Silence fell over the bridge. Sensors Officer Karlsen went especially pale. Not logging the ships would have been her mistake.

"Ambushed?" Mira asked. "The sensor data hasn't come in yet. How many?"

"The force was at least twice as large as us. They had three carriers with plenty of fighters and bombers. Some larger ships were mixed in, probably the equivalent of our cruisers."

Mira's face paled as she realized how dangerous the situation had been. "I should've sent half the fleet."

"I'm speechless," Karlsen said. "We can go over the data. I did everything according to the proper parameters . . ."

She trailed off, her bewildered expression seeming to question her very sanity.

"It wasn't your fault," Lucian said. "They used a portal once we had engaged with the strike force you logged. There were twenty-four ships exactly, as you said. The portal you couldn't have possibly predicted."

"What are our losses?" Mira asked.

"Maybe half our ships. But considering the situation, we're lucky. Once I set up my magic, we crushed them."

"What kind of magic is as powerful as that?" Aldric asked.

Lucian looked at him. "I created a gravity point several multiples stronger than Jupiter's gravity. Just for long enough to attract their ships. It gave us the edge to wipe out the rest."

"Impressive," Aldric said.

"I'm glad the battle was won," Mira said, "but strategically speaking, the Swarmers scored a major victory in wiping out the forge station."

"You have Admiral Lowell to thank for that," Lucian said. "He open-fired on the station when I ordered him not to."

"He *what*?"

"He panicked. He gave the order before I could counteract it."

Mira's face reddened. "Well, I'll deal with him as soon as he returns; you can be sure of that." She heaved a heavy sigh. "Now, there's no way we can hold the Archea System against the Swarmers. Without fuel, our fleet will be a sitting duck."

"We can't defend Archea anyway," Lucian said. "They used a portal to ambush us. Which means everything we feared is true. Like us, they can use Space-Time Magic."

"What can we do about it?" Serah asked.

At that very moment, a swirl of black magic appeared in the center of the bridge. Everyone backed away in alarm as Lucian was already summoning Lightspear. When the swirl dissipated, it revealed Emma standing in her black Sentinel uniform and cape.

He wondered how she would have known he was back until he realized that as a natural Radiant, she was already adept at detecting the Focuses of other mages.

Lucian allowed Lightspear to dissipate. "Impressive."

Emma ignored the praise. "I just came here to tell you something. I have the Sentinels warding the entire fleet, as you specified. We're detecting a lot of interference. I'm guessing someone is trying to portal to us."

"We just fought a battle at Nahar," Lucian said. "A large Swarmer fleet ambushed us using a portal. So yes, it would seem they are trying to attack us. From now on, we need Sentinels to cover all of our fleet actions, however small."

Emma's eyes widened at the news. "Yes, that makes sense. Still, our wards can only stretch so far, but they should keep us safe from ships dropping in too close."

"As long as they know where we are, we'll always be playing

defense. We need a more secure base to operate from. Something the Swarmers don't know about."

"Forget about us," Mira said. "They could coordinate a major attack on Earth! The League defenses at Alpha Centauri would mean nothing."

Lucian had already foreseen that, but until now, he hadn't been sure the Swarmers could portal entire fleets. For all he knew, Earth could be under assault, and none of them would know it. Space-Time Magic was a pandora's box. Things would never be the same.

Still, he knew there were some limits. Without the Orb of Space-Time, it took many Space-Time mages working together to make a portal capable of moving entire fleets. And once those fleets had moved, they would be committed and unable to withdraw. Even with the Orb of Space-Time, it took Lucian time to gather the required ether.

That meant the Swarmers probably wouldn't use a portal unless they were sure of victory or dropping in at a distant location where their presence wouldn't be noted. The *Alkasen* had believed they could take the Starsea task force by surprise at Nahar. Perhaps they hadn't counted on Lucian also being there. Without Lucian, the task force would have been annihilated.

Lucian regarded the officers. "We need to make the League aware of this danger."

"Are we moving out?" Mira asked.

Lucian nodded. "Our presence here is useless. No world is safe. Any Swarmer fleet with Preserved can travel wherever they want, assuming they can pool enough ether. I don't know how long it takes for them to do that. It could be hours or days, for all we know. But gone are the days when it would take weeks to pass between star systems. It can be done in much less time."

Everyone was silent as they considered the implications of

these words. From Lucian's tests, it seemed only five percent of mages could even stream Space-Time Magic. If those numbers held up elsewhere, then Space-Time mages were scarce. No one would want to risk them needlessly.

"Where is Hegemon Madi?" he asked.

"She's with the First Fleet in the Solar System," Mira said. "But if we go there, they will surely open fire."

Lucian nodded his understanding. "That's why I intend to go there by myself."

Emma stepped up. "Not alone, you won't. As a Sentinel, it's my job to guard you."

Lucian realized she was right. The Sentinels guarding him had been his idea, after all. "Okay. Captain Almaty will go with me, but that's it. This should be a quick trip."

Emma typed on her slate. "Making sure my soldiers know what's going on. Lieutenant Mwangi will hold down the fort while I'm gone."

Lucian looked at his mother. "You're in charge. When Admiral Lowell returns, deal with him as you see fit. We should be back soon."

A moment later, Lucian was opening a portal to the lounge deck of the *Volga*, the largest carrier in the League fleet.

―――――

WHEN HE AND Emma stepped onto the other side, the lounge was filled with cleaning droids tidying up a colossal mess. Empty glasses and platters were strewn about while the acrid tinge of smoke lingered in the air. There had been a wild party here just hours ago. The droids didn't seem calibrated to detect intruders, only to clean.

The first thing Lucian did was stream an invisibility ward around both him and Emma. The shield was extremely ether intensive, but it was nothing to Lucian. He also warded Thermalism to hide their heat signatures. While it was unlikely League sailors would be equipped to detect that, the various security cameras and droids would be.

With both wards active, Lucian felt safe from detection.

The Hegemon was somewhere on this ship. Since the former Hegemon Palmer had used it as his base of operations, Madi probably used it as hers, too. Lucian had an inkling that she was the source of this party. With a bit of luck, they could find her on their own, considering it was night hours.

Emma's voice entered his mind. *Fiddling while Rome burns?*

Seems like it. Where could she be?

Her stateroom, most likely. I looked at the schematics of this ship already. We'll need to head to the stern to find her room.

Nice work. Glad you're with me.

It's the main reason I offered to come. That, and to keep you from doing something you regret.

Emma took the lead, heading right for a wall. As if it were nothing, she phased through it to the other side, leaving Lucian alone in the lounge.

Lucian followed, combining Radiance and Space-Time to phase as well. He found her waiting in an empty corridor beyond. Thankfully, no one was there to see her for the moment she had become visible.

With nothing around, he felt comfortable enough to speak aloud. "Where'd you learn that?"

"Ever since you mentioned it, I've been practicing."

"We need to be careful. What if there had been people on this side?"

She smiled. "Lucian, I would have detected them. Trust me. I know what I'm doing."

"Of course."

"Come on. It's not far."

He followed her through the corridors. From the few blue-uniformed League officers walking around at this late hour, Lucian guessed this area was primarily cabins for the upper echelons. None of them noticed them in the slightest as they passed.

At last, they arrived at the stern and stood before a pair of ornate double doors that looked out of place on a military vessel. Two guards in thick red armor bearing heavy gauss rifles stood on either side. One of them stirred, seeming to detect their presence. Lucian realized they were probably loaded out with cybernetic implants, which gave them sharper senses. Cybernetics were a privilege that would be afforded to the Hegemon's Security Force, though illegal for the citizenry at large.

Lucian reached out to both of their minds rather than risk detection, creating mind control brands that instructed them to stand perfectly still and not to raise any alarms. He made one guard scan the doors open. Beyond lay a luxurious space, with a large viewscreen looking out from the stern of the ship. Lucian could see a panorama of stars, along with Mars floating far away, just large enough to be covered by a hand. They were near Sol Citadel, then. They both stepped inside and allowed the doors to close behind them.

The scene before could only be described as the conclusion of an afterparty even more epic than the main event. About a dozen men and women, all physically perfect from expensive genetic tailoring, were passed out around the stateroom, lounging on couches, in corners, and sprawled out on the deck, most of them in various stages of undress. Half-empty bottles, pills, and glasses littered the room profusely. Every single reveler was asleep or unconscious, save one, who stood facing them in front of a wide viewscreen.

Hegemon Madi was just as beautiful as the others, relatively young for a Hegemon in her late thirties. Unlike the surrounding partiers, she was fully dressed in a shimmering, pearlescent cocktail dress that complemented her form. Strangely, Lucian couldn't note anything unique about her face that lent her that beauty; in fact, he realized the source of her beauty was simply a lack of imperfection. Most people who opted for gene tailoring added minor flaws to make their beauty more natural, but Madi hadn't gone that route.

Her eyes were a warm, friendly brown, and a small smile played on her lips. She seemed to know they were there, even if she couldn't see them.

"If you're here to kill me," she said, her voice filled with silky confidence, "just make it quick."

33

LUCIAN ALLOWED the invisibility aura to fall, and the Hegemon smiled as she took them in. Unlike her guests, she seemed wholly sober and put together for such a wild night. She held a glass of wine and seemed at ease, despite the apparent danger to her life.

Her smile widened as she took in Lucian as if he were a new toy to play with. It was apparent she recognized who he was. She should've been frightened out of her wits. That she wasn't put Lucian on his guard.

"Hegemon Madi," he said. "We're not here to kill you. Just talk."

She inclined her head. "I figured as much. You must be Lucian Abrantes. I've heard a lot about you. Is there something I can do for you? Would you like some wine, perhaps?" Her eyes next went to Emma. "You look familiar as well."

"Emma Almaty," she said. "Former Talent of the Volsung Academy, now Captain of the Starsea Sentinels."

"Starsea?" The Hegemon frowned. "It would seem reports of Starsea's resurrection were not exaggerated."

Lucian did not doubt that the Hegemon had spies in his fleet. Such things were unavoidable.

Madi continued. "And why are you here? How did you get past my security detail?"

"Does it matter?" Lucian asked. "If you think security can hold me back, you don't know how dangerous I am."

She gave a light laugh. "Are you threatening me? I can have the entire First Fleet descend upon you with one word."

Lucian smiled. "Luckily for you, I'm not here to threaten you. I have other things in mind."

"Such as?"

"Saving humanity. I'm here to tell you that Earth is in imminent danger. We must work together to save it before it's too late."

"Is that so?" She took another sip of her wine, seeming almost bored. "And here I was, thinking that this day was over."

Emma surveyed the room and its occupants, some of whom were snoring. "Looks like it's been quite the day."

"Even a Hegemon needs to unwind. When you've experienced as much as I have, it takes a lot to scratch particular . . . itches." She cleared her throat, and her demeanor became all business. "Now, what was it you wanted, exactly? Why would I work with you, the leader of an outright rebellion? Even the faithless Golden Pirates have abandoned Hephaestus to aid you. In short, you have a lot of gall to come here into my stateroom, demanding things from me."

"I haven't demanded anything," Lucian said. "Not yet, anyway. I've come here for one purpose. If we don't work together, the League will die. Simple as that. Billions upon billions of lives are in our hands. Despite that colossal fleet you've amassed at the Jovian Yards, the Swarmers outnumber it ten to one, if not a *hundred* to one. We don't stand a chance unless we combine forces."

She smiled. "Lucian, I'll tell you something that I don't tell just anyone. I have a cybernetic implant that neutralizes the fear response in my brain. It's somewhat necessary when you're a woman like me in such a position of power. Many people make the mistake of thinking I'm incapable, and as a woman, even in these enlightened times, every mistake you make is magnified a hundredfold. I tell you this to show you that my thinking is quite clear and logical. That's why I'm not quailing in fear for my life. Not even you, Lucian, can intimidate me, even knowing what happened to my predecessor."

Lucian was surprised she would reveal so much. "Why are you telling me this?"

"To show you that the League Assembly made no mistake when they elected me Hegemon. I have certain mental advantages that make me particularly suited for this role. I'm ready to talk, Lucian Abrantes."

Lucian and Emma looked at each other, hardly believing it would be this easy. Maybe this Hegemon would be easier to work with than Palmer, but Lucian didn't make the mistake of letting his guard down.

Lucian nodded. "As long as you don't call for any guards, we'll be fine. We're not here to harm you. We want to talk about what's best for the League."

"I'm listening."

"This is the situation. The Swarmers can use portals to jump between entire star systems, just like me. Just hours ago, there was a surprise attack in the Archea System against our fleet."

"You mean the Third Fleet *you* absconded with?" Hegemon Madi asked with an amused smile.

"The Third Fleet has been repurposed," Lucian said. "Without me, they would have perished. You should be thanking me."

"I will do no such thing, I assure you."

Lucian ignored that. "What's more, I have healed the fraying, so the Wardens' role of guarding Psyche is moot. For now, they have been repurposed for the general defense of the League. Yes, they fly under Starsea's banner, but Starsea doesn't want to see the League fall. I intend to disband the fleet as soon as the League is saved."

"I see," Madi said. "I can tell you're not lying."

Something in her voice told Lucian she was sure of that fact. Her implants probably allowed her to read the microexpressions that people were powerless to stop. Cybernetic implants would let her see details that would slip by others. That meant the Hegemon was nearly impossible to deceive, at least when speaking face to face.

"Of course I'm telling you the truth," Lucian said. "They're far better off in my hands than anyone else's."

She laughed. "And what experience do you have of leading fleets? You haven't led so much as an escape pod."

Lucian had been in several escape pods, but he wasn't going to bring the point up. "I have talented admirals under my command. I didn't seek a leadership position, but I'm the only one capable of stopping the Swarmers."

Hegemon Madi nodded as if she were familiar with that line of reasoning. "Yes, Transcend White briefed me a few days after my ascension. You're this *Chosen of the Manifold*. She told me about these Orbs that must be gathered and disposed of."

Lucian hid his surprise. "Yes, that's right. Well, if she told you that, you must know I'm not the one to pull the trigger on Palmer. And you also know that he was possessed by a dangerous mage named Vera Desai, who has since died."

"I know that, too," she said. "I don't blame you for Palmer's death, although you are responsible in many ways. It was you who kidnapped him, after all. Transcend White was fairly exhaustive, but I'm sure she left a lot out, and she hasn't updated me in quite some time."

"Do you miss Palmer?" Emma asked. "After all, his death cleared a path for you."

She smiled, not even feigning regret. "Yes, that much is true if I'm to speak candidly. I can hardly fault you for that, and I am the more . . . *logical* choice for defending the League." She regarded Lucian again. "I only mention all this because what the League believes of you is an insurmountable obstacle. Even if I wanted to work with you, there is no way the rest of the League would accept you as its savior. Transcend White told me about your responsibility to end the Swarmers. I'm all for that. These Orbs, these artifacts of Starsea, must be taken back wherever they were found. And the League will ensure you have everything you need to accomplish this goal."

Lucian blinked. "Seriously?"

"Seriously. Let me know what you need, and we'll provide it."

"That's the thing. The place we have to go is so far away that there's no way we can get there before the Swarmers destroy Earth. We have to fight back this wave at least, and then that's when I can start my journey. Without my magic, it'll be impossible to face down such numbers."

"I see," Madi said. "Yes, the odds are truly against us. I've heard reports of your powers during your battle in the Hephaestus System and, more recently, in the Cupid System. As impressive as destroying entire Swarmer carrier squadrons is, you'll need something more than that when the Swarmers siege Earth itself."

By Lucian's estimation, she was being entirely frank. Publicly, Madi would never admit as much. But the League's fleet positions told him that Earth was the priority.

"Now," Madi said, "what was this about a surprise attack?"

Lucian gave her a brief description of his recent battle. As she listened attentively, it seemed strange that all of them could discuss something so serious, given the general setting of debauchery.

Once done, she shook her head. "This… is terrible news. As you've already said, these portals threaten to tear us from the inside out."

"That's why it's so important to work together," Emma said. "If the League falls, the Swarmers can wipe us from existence."

"I'm aware of the danger, Captain Almaty," the Hegemon said. "Here's what I'll do. I'll meet with Admiral Thorin. As soon as I explain everything, we'll arrange our fleets to protect Earth as best we can. If any portals appear near there, we can deal with them long before they become a threat. From what you've said, ships can only come out one at a time. Enough time to respond, no matter where they land."

"What about the other worlds?" Emma asked. "It's not just Earth at risk."

Madi nodded as if she had expected that question. "Earth is the priority. If Earth falls, it means humanity's extinction. Without Earth, it'll take thousands of years for humanity to rebuild. The same cannot be said for any other world."

"So, we're just going to give up everything else?" Lucian asked.

Hegemon Madi gave a stiff nod. "The math is simple. I will choose the lives of tens of billions on Earth and Luna over the billions spread out over the rest of the Worlds. We must protect who we can. Earth and its surrounding orbitals contain far more people than the rest of the Worlds combined. We must also defend other strategic points in the Solar System: Mars, the Jovian Yards, the Forge of Heaven, and Sol Citadel."

Lucian realized that the massive fleet the League was mustering near the Jovian Shipyards might have been the only thing keeping the Swarmers from attacking it directly. According to Lucian's intelligence reports, the League fleet by the Jovian Yards, commanded by Admiral Thorin, had swelled to almost five thousand ships, including two hundred battleships and carriers. Such a fleet had never been seen before in all the Worlds, and it was easy to see why the *Alkasen* hesitated to challenge it directly.

But eventually, they would; it was just a matter of time. For now, however, the *Alkasen* were focused on absorbing every system that was easy pickings, growing their swarm with the Bond of Unity while adding and retrofitting new ships.

For now, the Swarmer forces were fragmented. But one day, perhaps with portals, that fleet would gather in one location. From there, it would only take a few portals to launch a massive attack on the Solar System designed to end humanity forever.

"Can you abandon all the Worlds to their fate without the blessing of the League Assembly?" Emma asked, her face pale. "Many of them are not from Earth. They would never allow it."

"We're at war, Captain Almaty. I'm the commander-in-chief of the Consolidated League Fleets. This doesn't have to go through the Assembly." She looked from one of them to the other. "Here's what you need to do. Just get back to your ships and plan to head to the Solar System. There is still the High Prophet to contend with, yes. I don't know if he can be convinced to work with us. Right now, they are ignoring all official communications."

"Khalin has his own game," Lucian said, not wanting to go into specifics.

The Hegemon nodded as if she suspected that much. "Right now, the priority is defending Earth. We can figure out the rest later."

"If I move my fleet to the Solar System, do I have your word that you won't fire on me?"

"After this meeting, I'll summon Thorin and the rest of my admirals. I'll tell them what you've told me and give you free rein to move about in League Space."

"So we're not at war?" Emma asked.

Madi shook her head. "No. Officially, we don't condone your actions. But I believe in the Sorcerer-Ascendant's intentions."

"One more thing," Lucian said. "I will need you to give me a pardon for Palmer's death and an executive order recognizing my legitimacy as Sorcerer-Ascendant of all Magekind."

"I will do no such thing unless your so-called *Starsea Fleet* recognizes my ultimate authority as Hegemon."

"That's not happening. If I'm seen as your deputy, it undermines my authority. Starsea remains independent. End of story."

Madi gave him a hard stare, but in the end, she relented. "Very well. I will draft the orders as soon as I'm done with the admirals and staff."

"Until it's enacted and I see it on the news, my fleet stays put," Lucian said.

Her gaze was stony but accepting. "I'll make sure it's done, I assure you."

"In that case, I will join your forces in the Solar System. But it may be some time. We're making some important gains in the Mid-Worlds."

"You're allowed to do what you wish. However, if ever Earth comes under threat, you must come to our aid."

"Of course. Anything else?"

She shook her head. "I think we've settled the most important things."

Before Lucian created his portal, he placed a subtle Psionic brand on her mind. He read her thoughts, not sifting them too intensely so as not to give away his actions. He gleaned enough information to figure out that she was genuine about working with him, at least for now. This was simply a logical move for her, as she had said before. They could trust Hegemon Madi.

"Good luck, Hegemon. We'll be in touch."

Lucian gathered his ether and created a portal to *Mekong*.

34

SHORTLY AFTER LUCIAN and Emma appeared on the bridge of *Mekong*, he called his command staff and relayed the news. It took a few minutes to explain his meeting with the Hegemon so that everyone was on the same page.

Mira was the first to speak. "So, what's the plan now? Our scouts are reporting a massive Swarmer incursion from the Irion System. That's not all that far away."

Lucian frowned. "What about the *Alkasen* fleet in the Isis System?"

Mira nodded. "Yes, that one's new. Maybe they used a portal. There are a lot of fleet movements going on right now."

"Probably gathering for another offensive," Fergus said.

The Swarmers were playing a game Lucian could hardly keep up with. By now, anything further out from Archea and Psyche was as good as lost. And as soon as the Swarmers concentrated their forces on Archea, this system would fall.

"With Space-Time Magic on their side, nothing is stopping them from attacking Earth," Mira said. "That's where we need to be focusing our efforts."

"What about actually *stopping* them?" Serah asked. "Unless we can stop them at the source, what's the point of anything?"

Everyone watched Lucian for an answer while everyone else on the line was silent, perhaps fifty people in all.

"It won't be easy," Lucian admitted. "The truth is, we have to hold Earth. The Hegemon is right. I know it's not easy letting go of everything else. Wherever we *aren't*, that's where the Swarmers *will* be."

"Are you suggesting we give up?" Admiral Yang asked. "Archea is my home. Like hell I'm going to allow it to fall. Remember your promise. I have no reason to help if we're giving it up."

"Admiral Yang," Mira said, "even you must see the writing on the wall. It will be impossible to hold this system with the numbers we have, especially lacking the fuel forge. There are well over ten thousand Swarmer vessels in the Irion and Isis fleets combined, not to mention all the others closing in from everywhere else. I'm sure I don't need to remind you we only have about two thousand ships with inferior technology. Without Lucian, we don't stand a chance. Without Lucian—"

Zheng interrupted. "Ah, but we *do* have Lucian. And with our new Space-Time Sentinels, we have all the same advantages as the Swarmers. We just aren't using them properly."

"Admiral Yang is right," Lucian said.

Mira looked at him with surprise, along with the rest of the members of the Mage Council. The plan in the back of Lucian's mind was coming to fruition. He had been turning it over in his mind since they'd absorbed Lowell's fleet, meditating on it, even delving the Manifold for answers.

Now, with the Space-Time Sentinels trained, he was ready to share that plan.

"My strategy gives us control and will cause the Swarmers

to react to *us* for a change. Despite our lower numbers, we should be able to deal them damage."

Mira seemed willing to entertain the idea. "I'm listening."

"The best defense is a good offense," Lucian went on. "That's the League's problem. They are always reacting to whatever the *Alkasen* do." He paused. "Sitting on Earth like a turtle retreating into its shell will fail. The shell might protect for a while, but eventually, as more strength is piled on, that defense will crack. We need to come out of our shell. The key is movement and unpredictability. We have the opportunity and the resources to strike back."

"You should know better than anyone else my unpredictability," Zheng said, smiling. "I've been doing that all my life, so I'm all for hearing this plan."

Lucian toggled his slate, projecting a large holographic map of League Space before him. Everyone on the call was now viewing a similar map from their devices. The map detailed fleet positions for every player in the game: the League, the Starsea Fleet, the Believers, and all known Swarmer fleets. Over half of the map now was dark, a sign of the Swarmers' occupation.

"Now," Lucian said, "we have a mighty fleet. Two thousand ships. Even with my magic, we are probably doomed in a pitched battle against superior forces. But now, most Swarmer fleets are dispersed to siege every defenseless star system. I propose hunting down these smaller detachments, anything that's two hundred ships or fewer, where our victory will be crushing. We destroy these ships, liberate the worlds they're occupying, and recruit their population. And, of course, we take whatever ships they have. This way, we can grow our fleet while safely dealing damage to the enemy."

Lucian highlighted the Quassel System, which was in between Pontus and Irion.

"This is where I need your help, Admiral Yang," Lucian said. "Your network of pirates spans most of the Trailward Worlds. Assuming they're still in place, they should have reliable information on the Swarmers' numbers."

"They should," the Pirate Admiral agreed.

"I suggest Quassel as our first target," Lucian said. "There are no signs of a large Swarmer presence there, but they have been under siege for the past few weeks."

"Let me draw up the latest report I had from there," she said.

All went silent as she pulled the relevant information.

"The Quassel System," Admiral Yang said. "The last report I had from there was about a week ago. My sources estimate the Swarmers have one hundred and fifty vessels here, plus or minus fifty. The fleet is large enough to lock the system down and completely choke spaceship traffic and all civilian escape from the primary population center, a moon named Zegasi. Almost all the system's population exists on Zegasi and a few moons orbiting the gas giant Quassel. If we go in and eradicate that fleet, the system will be liberated."

"Can you give us similar information from other systems?" Mira asked.

Zheng nodded. "As Lucian said, the Golden Armada has a presence in almost every Trailward system, and most of these cells are well-hidden and still intact. The information will not always be current, but it's better than nothing."

"How can we be sure this information is reliable?" Khairu asked.

"We can't, in a lot of cases. These cells don't report to me every day. At best, I'll get a weekly update."

"I thought the Swarmers were destroying the mass relays at the Gates," Emma said. "That's why most Swarmer-occupied systems aren't sending out any information."

"We pirates don't rely on mass relays," Zheng said proudly. "Ours are much smaller and harder to detect. Since they only need to use our data, they will be almost impossible for the Swarmers to find."

"Guerilla warfare," Mira said. "I like the idea of it. However, there are some flaws in the strategy. We're not just carrying light and fast vessels like corvettes and destroyers. We also have heavy capital ships, armored transports, and fuel freighters. These ships are too slow; if they're left behind with no defense, they're vulnerable to attack."

"We will leave the slower vessels behind," Lucian said. "They need a safe spot to hang out. Some unassuming moon or distant planet would be best, with a fuel source that our Atomicists can stretch."

He already had the perfect place in mind. He highlighted the Cupid System, bringing up a star system map and underscoring the moon of Kandi, in orbit around the gas giant Ibbus, a deep oceanic blue with two thin green stripes around its equator.

"Kandi, huh?" Zheng asked. "I have a pirate cell there."

"Would it work?"

"I believe it would," she said. "It has advantages. It even has a small fuel forge in orbit around Ibbus and is relatively isolated."

"I've been there before, so I can portal the fleet there," Lucian said. "The only problem is bringing the moon under control. They aren't exactly friendly to authority."

"They will come to heel easily enough, especially with me on your side," Zheng said. "If two thousand ships above their port won't make them see reason, nothing will."

Mira nodded. "Once Kandi is secured, we can begin our campaign to liberate the worlds. Beginning with Quassel."

"If I may," Commander Carthen interjected. "I would

caution against any rash moves. If I might be so bold, Sorcerer-Ascendant, it would be safer and easier to join the League Fleet in the Solar System."

Lucian thought it over for a moment. He knew his decision, but couldn't be seen rushing into this.

At last, he nodded. "The Swarmers must be forced to react to us. If we're defending Earth, we're being predictable. With Space-Time Magic, we have a tool that has never been used in warfare. It's a tool the Swarmers are already using against *us*. The only thing that can prevent them from completely crushing us is if we take the fight to them. Taking out a few Swarmer attack groups here and there might seem inconsequential. As small as a single cut is, a thousand such cuts could cripple their war effort entirely. Taking control of these systems will hobble their supply lines and potentially save millions of lives. Most worlds are still being blockaded, and it seems the Swarmers are pushing inward as quickly as possible without consolidating their gains. This is an opportunity we cannot miss. A chink in their armor we must exploit."

"Another thing that hasn't been mentioned," Mira said. "If we keep the Swarmers busy Trailward, that will give the League time to prepare a defense."

"I'm sorry, but I'm with Carthen on this one," Fergus said. "It sounds damn risky."

Zheng smiled. "Sometimes, one must venture down the branch to pluck the best fruit."

Lucian wasn't sure if the metaphor worked, but he understood her meaning. It *was* risky, but the plan could slow the Swarmers down. That was something they sorely needed to do.

"One problem," Serah said. "Lucian can only portal the fleet to places he's already been. This limits us."

"I have an idea about that," Lucian said. "Emma, do you have the survey I asked you to send to your Sentinels?"

"Yes," she said. "Turns out between us, we've been to most of the systems in the League."

Lucian nodded. It was much as he thought. "Here's my plan. I will take each member of the Sentinels, having them lead a stream connecting us to a location they've been to. I would supply the ether, but it would be their memory to use. We would pass through the portal together in *Blood Wyvern*, allowing me to form my own memory of the location."

"And you would do this for every system?" Mira asked.

Lucian nodded. "I'll remember most systems in the League of Worlds. Then we can go anywhere we want. I'm calling it a *mental map*, if you will."

"Makes sense," Fergus said. "This idea makes the whole thing seem more concrete."

"I agree," Emma said. "The only kink I see is that none of the Sentinels can create a portal independently. While they wouldn't be supplying the ether, as the one controlling the stream, their Focus would have to be strong enough."

"If we create the portal quickly, it shouldn't be an issue," Lucian said. "At least, that's what I'm hoping."

"I hope so, too," Emma said.

"Assuming this *does* work," Transcend White said, coming out of her silence, "then when do we start?"

"As soon as possible," Lucian said. "I can have the Sentinels meet me as soon as we've finished here."

"There's one thing no one's mentioned," Serah said. "Eventually, wouldn't the Swarmers catch on to what we're doing? Wouldn't that force them to gather into bigger fleets?"

"It would," Lucian confirmed. "But this is a good thing. It would make it impossible for them to attack every undefended world. That would allow some breathing room for planets currently under siege. It might even allow them to strike back.

In the end, we *want* the Swarmers to bunch up. That's when my magic becomes most effective."

"Yes, I can see that," Admiral Yang said. "Well, this plan has my full support. Anything that might save Archea."

"In that case, meeting adjourned," Lucian said. "Unless anyone has further questions?"

From their collective silence, it didn't seem as if anyone did.

Lucian nodded. "We'll begin the campaign as soon as the Sentinels and I form the mental map."

35

LUCIAN GATHERED every Sentinel aboard *Blood Wyvern*, only leaving behind those whose locations were redundant to keep up the fleet's ward. Once out in space and safely away from the fleet, they began their work.

Lucian wished he'd had more time to train them properly, but they would have to learn the same way he did. It was necessary to secure the victory.

He went through the mages one by one. The portal stream required Space-Time and Binding Magic, and lots of it. Lucian would supply the magic, while the Sentinel would supply the memory.

They worked one by one, and Lucian was pleased to see, in every case, a portal opened up faithfully before them. It took less than a second for *Blood Wyvern* to pass through to the other side, at which point Lucian would note his surroundings. There was always something nearby to pin the memory to, whether that was a planet, moon, space station, or even an asteroid.

Using Psionic Magic, he made each memory permanent so

that he couldn't forget the location or the system it was associated with.

Lucian took about two days to form a mental map of most League Space. He was utterly exhausted by the end, having only taken brief breaks between each portal. He had to retreat to the engine room to meditate and rest his Focus. It was the only space aboard *Blood Wyvern* that wasn't crowded with Sentinels.

He was relieved that the monumental task was finished. When they returned, the fleet was ready to travel to Kandi.

Lucian stood on the bridge of *Mekong*, giving a single nod. "Creating the portal now."

Within a moment, a vast portal opened before *Mekong*, far more extensive than any he had ever made. Still, it was easy for him to power, and there was more than enough room for *Mekong* to pass through. Beyond the portal's plane, Lucian spied the icy methane moon of Kandi against the backdrop of Ibbus.

"Drop into orbit around the moon," Lucian said. "Broadcast the message I prepared to the surface."

Mira nodded. The message had been pre-recorded and communicated two things. The first was that Ibbus and its attendant moons were now under the purview of the Sorcerer-Ascendant of Psyche. The second was a general call for recruitment to fly under his banner, and any ship that did so would be rewarded handsomely. Lucian hoped the message would have the intended effect. He figured they might pick up a couple of hundred lighter vessels that way.

The message went out as soon as *Mekong* passed through the portal. All was silent as a host of Starsea ships, large and small, swarmed after him, streaming past *Mekong* and entering Kandi's orbit. Lucian knew that without firing a shot, the moon was his. No ship would challenge such an imposing armada.

Kandi was too small and unimportant to have planetary anti-space batteries.

"Grand Captain Warwick," Mira said calmly. "Secure the Forge of Ibbus."

His voice resonated from the communications panel. "Moving to engage."

A large detachment of the fleet, two hundred ships in all and including armored transports, veered toward the gas giant in the distance. They would reach their target within a couple of hours.

Already, the bridge of *Mekong* was being blasted with hail requests. Mira rerouted those requests to various captains she had designated to handle the influx. Most of the signals contained a code communicating interest in joining the Starsea Fleet.

"This is going swimmingly," Mira said. "Far better than expected."

Serah laughed. "Probably has something to do with the reward we promised."

"We'll get everything sorted out," Mira said. "Once things are settled, we can begin the counterattack."

———

WITHIN HOURS, Kandi fully recognized Starsea and the Sorcerer-Ascendant's supremacy. Dozens of ships joined their ranks, mainly for the generous sign-on bonus. It wasn't like the pirates of that moon had any better prospects, especially given the times.

By the next day, the Starsea Fleet was ready to begin its first operation: the liberation of Quassel and its attendant moons.

Lucian didn't have to draw from his new list of locations for this portal. He remembered the massive gas giant from their journey to Irion all those months ago.

Lucian homed in on that memory and created the portal. Within moments, the Starsea Fleet was passing into hostile territory. Humanity was taking the fight to the Swarmers, and Lucian was proud that it was happening under his leadership.

All was quiet as they passed into the new system. Given their luck in the past, Lucian almost expected to be ambushed right away. However, all was silent on their scopes as the massive, reddish-brown gas giant of Quassel loomed before them. Its size was nearly stellar mass, almost large enough to be considered a brown dwarf. As the main focal point of the system, the one who controlled Quassel controlled everything else.

Admiral Yang's voice exited the comms panel. "Sending an encrypted message to my cell for the latest updates."

While they waited for Zheng's information, Lucian watched the Starsea Fleet pass through the portal. As planned, the assault transports and fuel freighters stayed behind while the two thousand ships slipped through. Lucian included the carriers and battleships, knowing that his Gravitists and Atomicists would allow them to keep up with the rest. It was probably overkill, but he wanted to leave nothing to chance.

Seeing the massive fleet arrayed against the glowing backdrop of Quassel was a glorious sight. It was hard for Lucian to believe it was all under his command, though he was content to let his mother call the shots.

It took half an hour for the fleet to enter the formation of smaller ships in the front and capital ships behind the main lines. There was no sign of the enemy, nor any hails from other vessels. The system was silent, a testament to the Swarmer's effectiveness at quashing all space lane traffic. That lack of traffic could only work in favor of the Starsea Fleet.

"Thrusters on low," Mira said. "Stand by."

"Radiants, Thermalists," Lucian said into his slate. "Keep those wards steady. I don't want to take any chances."

Lucian felt the two massive wards surrounding the entire fleet strengthen. The Radiants, led by Fergus, were on board *Resplendent*, where they could work in confluence to keep the fleet off LADAR. Likewise, the Thermalists under Plato ensured this part of space was as cold as its surroundings. The fleet wouldn't be detected until they were on top of the Swarmers. All was going according to plan.

At last, Zheng's voice exited the ship's bridge. "Swarmer fleet is active and currently bombarding the capital of this system, on the moon of Zegasi. Coordinates uploaded."

Mira read the readout on her slate. "Just one hundred thousand klicks away. We'll get there fast."

"Zegasi is the primary population center of this system," Emma said. "The capital is on the other side of the moon. We should be well hidden even without the ward."

Mira gave an acknowledging nod. "They must be completely oblivious to our presence. All the better." Mira turned to her helmsman. "Morales, time to arrival?"

Morales cleared his throat. "Ten minutes at proposed vector, Admiral. This path keeps the moon between them and us as long as possible."

She reviewed the information on her slate. "Very good. Keep engines at the same power level for now."

The entire bridge was silent, as if a single whisper would alert the Swarmers to their presence. At some point, the Swarmers *would* recognize they were there, but if it weren't until the last moment, there would be nothing they could do to defend themselves.

The tension was palpable when, at last, the moon of Zegasi slipped into view against the backdrop of the massive planet behind. Lucian knew Zegasi was classified as an "Earth-similar" world, a step below "Earthlike." That meant someone couldn't stand on its surface without survival gear, such as a respirator or adequate clothing. From its appearance, it was a cold, gray world with generous ice caps and glaciation. Only a narrow band of greenery ringed its equator.

"Two minutes until arrival," Helmsman Morales said.

"Anything on the scopes, Karlsen?" Mira asked.

"Nothing yet, Admiral. Either we're undetected, or they're good at pretending."

"Entering attack vector in ten seconds," Morales said.

"Continue with the attack plan," Mira said.

Within seconds, the fleet was veering into the moon's orbit. Despite the inertial dampening and streams of the Gravitists, Lucian felt pulled by lateral force. They watched for about a minute as the moon's gray surface skimmed beneath them.

"Swarmer vessels detected," Karlsen said. "They're moving to engage."

"How many?" Mira asked. "Ship classes?"

"No carriers," Karlsen said, relief palpable on her features. "Mostly bombers and fighters, along with five cruiser-equivalent class ships. Scopes are logging one hundred and fifty-seven in all."

"Wipe them out," Mira said.

Within seconds, the battle was joined. The Starsea Fleet fanned out, coming at the Swarmer vessels from every angle, providing no opportunity for escape. From the harried movements of the enemy, it was clear they had been caught entirely by surprise. While the *Alkasen* fighters and bombers quickly reacted, the cruisers lumbered to meet the threat, turning broadside to point their bows at the Starsea Fleet.

"Fire on those cruisers!" Mira commanded. "Don't let them get any shots off!"

Instantly, the cruisers became the focus of intense Starsea fire. Hundreds of white-hot kinetic railgun streams blasted their rocky hulls while the bright blue tachyon lances of the capital ships lent their super-heated fury.

Under such a barrage, the cruisers cracked apart. Even as they disintegrated, the smaller Starsea vessels teemed around what few Swarmer ships remained, picking them off with deadly efficiency. Within a matter of minutes, every Swarmer vessel had been destroyed.

Mira Abrantes stood at the viewport, watching the one-sided slaughter with hands behind her back. After fifteen seconds of silence passed, she turned to Sensors Officer Karlsen. "Battle report?"

Karlsen cleared her throat. "We lost twelve ships. The new conscripts from Kandi, mostly. Two destroyers, four corvettes, and ten light ships. The Swarmers lost all one hundred and fifty-seven."

Mira nodded. "And Admiral Yang's losses?"

"The Golden Armada logged seven losses, all lighter vessels."

Twenty-three total losses. Lucian could hardly believe the number was so low.

"And there are no more Swarmer ships in this system?" he asked.

"None detected," Karlsen said. "We will learn more soon."

The dash lit with a hail request from *Stars' Blood*. Mira accepted.

"Admiral Yang," she said. "I suppose congratulations are in order."

"Flawless victory," she responded.

Lucian cleared his throat. "Are you detecting any more hostiles in the system?"

"If there are any, they haven't been logged. Most citizens of the Quassel System live on Zegasi. This is where the Swarmers would have concentrated. With that force blasted into oblivion, I think it's safe to say this system is liberated."

Another hail request lit the dashboard. Mira frowned, then looked at Lucian. "The code claims to be from the Syndic of Zegasi."

Lucian nodded. "Put them through."

Mira hit accept, and at once, a middle-aged female voice spilled out of the speakers.

"Unknown fleet. I'm Syndic Laine, and I speak on behalf of the humble people of Zegasi. Your violation of our borders is an outrage. If you are still a hundred thousand kilometers within the moon's borders after an hour, our planetary batteries will blow you to dust."

Lucian shared a skeptical look with his mother before returning his attention to the dashboard. "Syndic Laine, you're ungrateful for someone whose world was just saved."

"I'm warning you! I don't know how such a force of pirates and miscreants parked themselves above us, but that question won't matter if you ignore our request. Not even the infamous *Stars' Blood* can withstand our stockpile of nuclear warheads."

Lucian knew it was a bluff. They would have already fired them on the Swarmers if they had said nuclear warheads.

"You misunderstand," Lucian said. "We're not pirates."

"*Stars' Blood* has been logged on our sensors, and everyone knows that's Zheng Yang's flagship. Several other vessels of the Golden Armada have also been spotted."

"I can explain," Lucian said. "The Golden Armada is working with us."

"Who are you, then?"

"We are the Starsea Fleet, an independent power based out of the Cupid System. I'm Sorcerer-Ascendant Lucian Abrantes, the head of Starsea. And you are the Syndic of Zegasi, I presume?"

"I am," she said. "*Starsea.* There are many new kingdoms and empires to keep track of these days. Not that it will matter, anyway. Everything will soon go the way of flames, dust, and ruin . . ."

"Cheery, isn't she?" Serah muttered from beside him.

"That won't happen as long as I can help it," Lucian said. "Right now, Starsea is liberating the outer worlds, since the League is unable and unwilling. We have over two thousand ships at our command. When you join us, Syndic, we hope you'll add to our numbers."

"Join you?" The Syndic laughed. "If I did that, our little moon would remain undefended. I would never let the poor people of this world fall victim to alien scum, Sorcerer-Ascendant."

"You *can't* defend it," Lucian said. "If a small Swarmer fleet can give you so much trouble, then your only chance is to take every fighting ship you have and join us. Starsea plans to take the fight to the Swarmers. The best defense is a good offense."

"Look," the Syndic said, "I don't know who you think you are or even how you got here, but I will have you know that the Quassel System, of which I'm the steward, will *not* be absorbed by your so-called, illegitimate empire. Zegasi is, and always will be, a loyal League World. We do not recognize this *Starsea.*"

"You don't have to give up your independence. I'm just offering a lifeline to you and your people. I've already spoken with Hegemon Madi. Even she has agreed to join forces with Starsea."

"I haven't heard anything about that."

"It's a recent development. Just happened a few days ago. If you're a loyal League World, we need all the help we can get. Our job is to rescue every world we can. Let's say this is our way of punching back at the Swarmers and showing them we won't go down without a fight. Who knows? Maybe we can win. But it requires everyone chipping in to help."

The line was silent for a long time. Lucian realized then that he couldn't convince Syndic Laine. It would be nice to have her cooperation, but it wasn't required.

That was why Lucian was surprised at her following words.

"All right. I . . . suppose we have some resources you can use. Food, fuel . . . even sailors and ships, if that's what you need. We used to be a border system, you see. It's my instinct not to trust outsiders. We even have a pirate hideout on one moon of this system, if you can believe it. They've been a huge thorn in our side for nearly a decade."

Lucian cleared his throat awkwardly. "We are grateful, Syndic. If you can help us, that's great. We'll be setting out soon to liberate our next system."

"Which is?"

Lucian nodded toward his mother, who took over. "Syndic Laine, this is Grand Admiral Mira Abrantes. Our next COA is returning to the Cupid System to resupply."

"That has to be a one or two-month journey at least!"

"We can make that journey in minutes," Mira said. "The Sorcerer-Ascendant can create a portal that can take us directly there."

"I don't understand . . . how is that possible?"

Lucian smiled. "It's something you'll have to see to believe. When can I expect you and your ships to join us? And how many do you have? Of course, everyone will be paid a generous wage."

"I don't know. I'm afraid we can't offer much in the way of ships. Our defense force was wiped out a month ago. We can offer various civilian surface-to-space vessels, but not much else."

"Every bit counts. Do you have the resources to retrofit them for combat?"

"The devastation down here is pretty bad, Sorcerer-Ascendant. There's little that's useable. People are going hungry."

"We have spare weapons and plenty of food," Mira said. "We can base your ships at Kandi until they are combat-ready."

"In that case," the Syndic said, "I can broadcast a general call to arms. Every ship that wishes to fight will have twenty-four hours to join you."

"I'm afraid we can't wait that long," Lucian said. "Make it eight."

"Eight hours? Sorcerer-Ascendant, that will be—"

"Minimum of one hundred credit bonus to any ship that joins us, assuming it's in decent shape," Lucian said. "If that doesn't get them to come, I don't know what will. All fuel and maintenance expenses are paid. We'll offer more for larger and more capable ships." Lucian nodded at his mother. "The Grand Admiral will forward you the pay scale."

There was a moment before the Syndic responded. "That's . . . incredibly generous. Well, there might be some room for negotiation. Eight hours, you said?"

"Yes. Starting now. We'll see you in orbit, Syndic."

Lucian closed the channel. He couldn't stay on the line all day with her. He was utterly confident that by the end of the eight hours, his fleet would be hundreds of ships stronger.

36

WITHIN THE PRESCRIBED TIME, another three hundred ships had joined the Starsea Fleet, and the combined crew of those ships was somewhere around three thousand sailors. It was primarily personal vessels, cargo ships, and a few light surveyors, but there were also armored transports, including a few battle-hardened mercenary crews. Zegasi was a major hub for soldiers of fortune in the Trailward Worlds, so it was a happy accident that Lucian had suggested attacking here first. Now, those soldiers were his to command.

Once the ships had joined the fleet, Lucian created a portal back to Kandi to regroup. Lucian ordered twenty-four hours of onboarding for the new soldiers and sailors, followed by R&R.

Lucian stayed in orbit, opting to get some shuteye while leaving the management of the fleet to Mira and the command staff. For the first time in what seemed ages, he got an uninterrupted eight hours of sleep.

Once he awoke, the rest of the day was spent planning. At Mira's suggestion, their next target would be the Portua System. According to Zheng's pirate network, the Swarmers had about three hundred vessels here. The Starsea Fleet now numbered twenty-five hundred. It should prove to be another flawless victory.

"It'll be a quick fight," Mira said. "More than that, it forms an important passage through the Mid-Worlds. If the system is liberated, it cuts off the Swarmer advance from much of the Trailward Border Worlds. Seeing that so few Swarmer ships are there, I suggest it as our next target."

"I'm game," Admiral Yang said.

"I have a memory of the planet we can portal to," Lucian said. "It should be pretty simple."

"Go in guns blazing?" Serah asked.

Lucian nodded. "Absolutely. Portua is a pretty big world. That's a lot of population and ships to add to the fleet."

"Portua has several million inhabitants," Emma said. "Not a lot by First World standards, but it is for the Mid-Worlds."

"All the more reason to liberate it," Fergus said.

"I don't see any tactical reason it shouldn't be a resounding victory," Grand Captain Warwick said. "It would be great for morale."

"Yes, but we should go in with eyes wide open," Lucian said. He looked around at his senior staff. "Before any future attacks begin, I would like to portal in a scouting task force. To ensure we know what we're getting into." Lucian turned to Warwick. "Would you be willing to lead that?"

"More than willing, Sorcerer-Ascendant. Give me our most powerful survey vessel and ten ripsaws, and I'll see it done."

"And plenty of Radiants and Thermalists to mask your presence," Fergus said.

"Of course," Warwick said.

"It's settled," Lucian said. "I want that scouting party in Portua within the hour."

WHILE WAITING for the scouting force's return, Lucian interviewed Syndic Laine about the Siege of Zegasi. She met him in a well-appointed cabin he'd set up as his office. It felt strange to have an office, but Lucian needed *somewhere* he could be alone. And he liked this space in particular because it also had a cabin adjacent where he and Serah could get some privacy, along with another small area he'd appropriated as his meditation chamber.

But for the Sorcerer-Ascendant, there was no real privacy. Seven Sentinels stood behind him, his guard. While all were proficient in Space-Time Magic, each had a primary in one of the Seven Aspects. Emma had insisted on this; at all times, they kept up a ward in their respective primaries, and if the unthinkable ever happened, those wards could strengthen into active shields. Lucian could deal with the would-be assailant with his magic and have seven Sentinels backing him up with their shockspears.

Initially, he'd said seven Sentinels were far too many, but Emma had won that argument. She also had the support of the entire Mage Council, and even the Transcends agreed with her.

It felt strange to have them standing against the viewscreen, silent as statues. But when Lucian was busy, he hardly even noticed they were there.

There was a knock at the door, and Lucian buzzed the Syndic in. Laine strode into the office with the air of one who had been doing business for many years. Her hair was a medium brown, and she wore a suit that cost more than the average person could hope to make in a year. She noted the Sentinels, which seemed to take a bit of assurance out of her step, though she recovered quickly.

"Good morning, Sorcerer-Ascendant," she said with breezy confidence.

Lucian took a sip of his coffee, clearing his throat. "Good morning. Thanks for coming in."

She sat in the chair in front of his desk without waiting for an invitation. "Allow me to get straight to the point. I've been meaning to talk to you for some time."

Lucian appreciated her brevity; he knew she was trying to take control of the conversation, such as she could, by initiating the questions and making it seem like this meeting was *her* idea. He didn't care. It was a game, and he was confident enough in his position not to play.

"I want you to tell me about the siege," Lucian said. "From my understanding, your world endured the Swarmer blockade for almost a month. In that time, they never attempted to invade the planet?"

Laine shrugged. "No, they didn't. It seems to be their M.O. Send in their fastest, lightest ships to lock down the world and wait for the planetary invasion force to come behind. They sent enough to take care of our own meager planetary defense force. I ordered what ships we had to retreat to the various moons of the system; those ships are now part of your fleet, Sorcerer-Ascendant."

"I see," Lucian said. "It would seem your world was lucky. I'm sure you looked at the files I sent you?"

The Syndic nodded, her confident air betrayed by a slight paling of her features. "Horrible, that. That these *Alkasen* can spread this . . . *disease* . . ." She trailed off, then cleared her throat. "I'm sorry. I'm sure that's not the proper term. Indeed, we were fortunate. If you're planning on liberating more systems, you'll have to ensure the Bond hasn't contaminated the population."

Lucian saw what she meant. Undoubtedly, many worlds

had already been invaded, especially in the periphery. The humans Lucian had fought on Silumko's ship were evidence of that.

"Yes, we will have to tread carefully," Lucian said. "I just wanted to clear that up."

"Of course," Syndic Laine said, already rising to leave. She seemed keen to be out of Lucian's presence. Lucian was used to that by now. For anyone besides his friends, he was an object of intimidation. They knew what he was capable of, and Syndic Laine wasn't sure how far she could trust him.

"You can go," Lucian said. "And welcome to the Starsea Fleet."

Laine nodded gratefully, the heavy metal doors shutting behind her.

Lucian thought for a moment, wondering just how many worlds were left that were under siege but not yet invaded. He could only hope that most of the Mid-Worlds they were targeting were like Zegasi and less like worlds that had long fallen, like Sani and Kasturi.

———

Twelve hours later, the scouting party returned. Warwick informed Lucian that the system was quiet. No sign of Swarmers beyond a small force guarding the planet and a complete lack of assault transports or carriers, both of which would have been capable of carrying out invasion operations. For now, the planet was safe from Preserved spreading the Bond.

With that information in hand, the liberation of Portua could begin as planned.

Admiral Abrantes only brought half their forces, favoring fast ships and some lighter cruisers. Only three battleships would come along, in the unlikely case a Swarmer fleet happened to portal there at the last minute. If that happened, the battleships would train their lances on the opening, obliterating anything that emerged.

Lucian stood on the bridge of *Mekong*, feeling well-rested and well-fed for once. All eyes were on him as he began gathering his ether to open the portal.

It stretched before the vanguard of the fleet. As they had drilled, the ships slipped through with efficient grace.

By the time *Mekong* passed through, most of the fleet had already arrayed itself on the far side of the planet, an Earthlike world filled with snaky landmasses, blue oceans, and thick white clouds. Portua, like Earth, had a single moon. At the moment, it wasn't visible since the planet itself eclipsed it.

"No ships detected," Sensors Officer Karlsen said.

"Continue the attack plan," Mira said.

This time, there was less tension in the air. The Starsea Fleet was more confident, especially knowing what to expect from the scouting party.

Except when they rounded the planet, instead of finding the *Alkasen* fleet above the capital city, they saw only empty space.

"Nothing," Serah said from beside Lucian.

"They're here," Lucian said.

"Logging something on my sensors," Karlsen said. "Swarmer fleet located. They are inbound from directly ahead. They must have moved locations."

"How many?" Mira asked.

"Logging two . . . no, three hundred ships."

"That's more than expected," Mira said. "Should be no issue, though."

Warwick shuffled his feet nervously, but said nothing.

"Engage," Mira said. "Keep those battleships out of the fray and keep an eye out for portals."

The fleets clashed. Green lasers fired from the crystalline *Alkasen* vessels, while white-hot streaks shot from the Starsea Fleet's railguns. Corvettes launched swarms of torpedoes. Even if the numbers were more significant than expected, Starsea still outnumbered the Swarmers by five to one.

"New ships logged moonward!" Karlsen said. "Two hundred ships blasting hard for the planet!"

Mira held up her slate. "Admiral Yang, engage!"

"Already on it," Zheng's voice returned. "Clever little buggers. Using the moon as a shield."

Lucian looked at Warwick. "You didn't check the moon?"

Warwick cleared his throat, his expression pale. "I . . . deemed it too risky, Sorcerer-Ascendant."

The new attack force was already upon them, raining death and destruction upon the disorganized Starsea Fleet. Lucian reached out to some wayward Swarmer fighters and crushed them with a few well-placed Gravitonic streams.

"Face us toward the moon," Lucian said. "I want to see what we're dealing with."

Chief Helmsman Morales complied, turning the ship. Three Swarmer vessels were bearing down on them, including dozens of strike craft with movements so coordinated they might've been a school of fish. This attack group fanned out, flanking a large Starsea cruiser and lighting it with a barrage of laser fire that overwhelmed its shields. The cruiser ripped down the middle, exposing hundreds of Starsea sailors to a near-instant death.

Lucian crushed what he could with Gravitonics, ether ripping through him almost violently. He tried to push down his frustration. The Swarmers wouldn't win this fight, not by a long shot. They would inflict more casualties than they should have because of bad intelligence.

It was thirty minutes before every Swarmer vessel was eradicated. The fleet was on high alert for any change in the situation. After five minutes of silence, it seemed to be over.

"Battle report?" Mira asked.

"Five hundred twenty-two Swarmer vessels destroyed," Karlsen said.

"Were any transports or troop carriers?"

Karlsen shook her head. "No, Admiral."

"What about our losses?"

She cleared her throat nervously. "About the same. About half among the pirates, the rest with us." She paused. "I've also received word that Syndic Laine's vessel, *Everything Goes*, was destroyed."

Mira's expression was carefully neutral, though her brown eyes were hard. Even Lucian could tell she wanted to curse, but she had to put on a brave and controlled face for her crew.

A third of this Starsea detachment had been lost. All because they had been caught out of position. The Syndic's death would be a blow to morale as well, especially for the Zegasi recruits.

Lucian looked at Warwick, and from the paleness of his face, it seemed as if he feared for his very life. Lucian read his mind with a Psionic brand and soon discovered that Warwick had acted as he thought best, given the situation. The Swarmer patrols had been too thick in the cislunar space between the moon and the planet, so he felt it was too risky to explore the moon's far side. No one on board the survey crew had thought any differently.

It wasn't his fault; given an equivalent situation and resources, Lucian would have done the same thing. He wasn't going to point out the fact, however.

Lucian turned to face the crew on the bridge, all looking to him for guidance during this dark moment. How he responded could be everything.

"One thing is clear. The *Alkasen* knew about what happened at Zegasi and were on high alert. The Swarmers aren't just going to sit back and let us take them out. They will respond to everything we do." He nodded to the planet outside the viewports. "Yes, we took some losses. But we have liberated another planet. There are no transports, meaning the people of Portua are safe. We need to continue with the plan. Recruit these people and their ships. We will learn from our mistakes; we underestimated our enemy." He looked around at his crew. "Never again."

The men and women on the bridge nodded their agreement.

Lucian looked back at his mother. There was no time to wallow in self-pity.

"Send out our broadcast to the planet," he said. "Tell them they have eight hours to join us."

WITHIN THE PRESCRIBED EIGHT HOURS, the Starsea Fleet gained from Portua about the same number of ships it had lost. Much like Zegasi, however, most were not military ships. They were civilian vessels that could be retrofitted for combat.

They returned to Kandi to regroup, their numbers the same as when they left. It felt as if no progress had been made, and it was hard for Lucian not to sink into a certain despondency as he retreated to his quarters to meditate.

He delved the Manifold, seeking visions that would give him a clear path forward. While he saw many futures, those futures were muddy and grim. He let go of his stream just as there was a knock at the door.

Serah stepped inside, offering him a smile and a hot mug of coffee. "How're you holding up?"

Lucian rose and took the cup. "I'm holding."

He didn't want to get into his feelings. He had to be strong. A leader. But as she continued to watch him, he realized with Serah that just wasn't true. She had seen him at his best and his worst. She could see the real him, his struggles and frustrations.

"Let's sit down," he said.

They sat on the bed, and Lucian took a long sip. The brewing machine in *Mekong's* officers' wardroom was far better than any ship he'd ever been on. He closed his eyes, luxuriating in the taste. It took him away from the situation, at least for a moment.

"I'm sorry things didn't go as planned," Serah said. "But maybe it wasn't all a loss."

He looked at her curiously. "What do you mean?"

"Well, you gave the people of Portua a second chance. You saved them from becoming *Alkasen*."

"For now, yes. Not everyone could be saved."

Serah gave a slight nod, conceding that point. "Sure, most were left behind, but do you think the Swarmers will go after them soon, now that they know you can strike anywhere next? That goes for Zegasi, too."

"Yeah, maybe. We have to keep the momentum up. And not take things for granted."

"Exactly. We gained valuable information. Now we know the Swarmers are reacting to us. We know what to expect next time. We won't make the same mistakes. That's valuable, right?"

"We lost five hundred ships," Lucian said. "Yes, it was my mom's suggestion to send only half the fleet. Yes, we were working off bad information. But at any point, I could've over-ridden their suggestions."

"You trusted your advisors," Serah said. "There's nothing wrong with that. No one knows everything. Not even you." She looked back at the meditation chamber. "How did that go?"

Lucian shook his head. "I tried to see the future, but there's too much in motion. All I want to know is the next right thing to do, but even that's hard to see."

"The Manifold will show you what it wants you to know," Serah said. "It's the nature of the beast."

"Yeah. You're right."

"Of course I'm right." She touched his arm. "I understand how you're feeling. We always knew the day would come when you'd have to give orders. Sometimes, that means making the wrong call and losing lives. Every king, every general, and every admiral has to deal with that. You can't let the burden get to you. It's your job to see the big picture. Everyone understands that."

"They may not want to follow me anymore," Lucian said. "They know I'm not invincible."

"They see that you're human. In the battle, we traded fairly with the Swarmers ship for ship. More than fair, considering their technology is better than ours. We lost five hundred, and so did they, and many of the ones we lost were retrofitted civilian vessels not built for fleet combat."

"I led them to their deaths."

"They fought voluntarily. They knew the risks."

"I know. It's hard not to blame myself."

"There are many people who could blame themselves right now. Not just you." She took him by the hand and looked him in the face. "I don't see you as any less. I see you as *more* now. No one can win all the time, and in war, people die. It's just a fact. Mourn for the dead, yes. But sometimes, the best way you can honor the dead is by picking up and moving on. That's what they'd want you to do. That way, their deaths wouldn't have been in vain."

Lucian realized she was right. He was about to respond when there was another knock at the door.

"Come in."

One sentinel stood there, Emma's second-in-command, who also was in charge of his retinue today. Lieutenant Mwangi was a sharp-featured woman whose dark skin contrasted strangely with her platinum-blonde hair. Like Lucian, her primary was Psionics, and she had been a Mage-Knight in Ansaldra's army, though she had grown up on Terminus.

"Sorcerer-Ascendant," she said. "I know you said you didn't wish to be disturbed, but almost twelve hours have passed since you retired. You told me to get you if that happened."

"Has that much time passed already?"

Serah nodded in confirmation. When Lucian delved the Manifold, time had a way of slipping away.

"The next operation will begin soon," he said. He nodded gratefully to Mwangi. "Let's go."

The Sentinels fell in around him as he headed for the bridge.

———

THEY DID NOT REPEAT the mistake of Portua.

When they attacked, it was with the full force of their fleet. They scouted each system thoroughly beforehand, spending many days locating and logging Swarmer positions. They couldn't check every nook and cranny, but they could ensure the attack zone, which usually surrounded a system's most populated world, was safe enough.

In this way, they liberated about a dozen systems over the next month. Lucian realized that Syndic Laine had been right. Most of the Mid-Worlds were being blockaded by the Swarmers until a ground invasion force could arrive. Only in two cases did they find a world that had already been invaded.

Lucian explored the surface of one of these worlds, a planet called Adjurra, which was firmly a Border World. It was clear the planet had been abandoned for many months, while its cities were heaps of ruins. Lucian could hardly believe the

Swarmers had been so thorough at absorbing the population. True, the planet was mostly desert and not highly populated. That told Lucian the *Alkasen* were efficient at spreading the Bond. Anyone who attempted escape would only get shot down by the ships in orbit, lying in wait. The surface of the world felt empty, and not just of people. There was a strange sense that something horrible had happened. It was a premonition of the Manifold, like a fading scream.

It only inspired him to keep this from happening to other worlds.

Every world liberated from then on was a crushing victory for the Starsea Fleet. While they always absorbed more civilian ships into their fleet, along with willing sailors, they sometimes even requisitioned military ships. The Gradene System, for example, was home to a major League base whose commander had been wise enough to hide the League's capital ships in the asteroid belt. Lucian didn't condone the cowardice, but he had to admit it had worked out well for him; it added five more battleships to his fleet, which he desperately needed to combat the larger Swarmer carriers.

After a month, a large swathe of the Trailward Mid-Worlds had been liberated, and the Starsea Fleet's numbers had swelled to five thousand ships. There had been no resistance on the last few planets; it was as if the Swarmers recognized Starsea's threat and gave up their gains to regroup. Isis seemed to be the main mustering point, a system Lucian had no interest in since it had no population or resources. The enemy had long absorbed the League Base there.

The Starsea Fleet was in the middle of planning its next operation when Lucian felt a mental tug. Selene's face appeared in his mind, and he knew she was trying to contact him from Psyche.

Selene? Is everything okay?

Lucian, the Alkasen *are here.*

He felt himself go cold. *How many?*

Too many. We're logging at least ten carriers, plus other ships besides.

Ten carriers. It was far more than they had ever faced.

Do they have transports?

Yes. They know there are a lot of mages here. Imagine how many Preserved that would be if they reached the caves?

If the Swarmers were in the Cupid System, it was only a matter of time before they discovered Starsea's presence around Kandi, which they had so far kept hidden. If the Swarmers ever found the location of their secret base, they could attack it in force.

Hold on. We're on our way.

Lucian looked around at his command staff, the Mage Council, and the Transcends.

"Psyche's under attack. Ten carriers have been logged, plus many more ships and a planetary invasion force. Call up the entire war council. We're moving out within the hour."

38

OVER FIVE THOUSAND ships were lined up in the orbit of Kandi, ready to enter the portal for the defense of Psyche.

Opening the connection directly to Psyche itself would have been suicide. The Swarmers were sure to concentrate all their fire on it as soon as it appeared.

Fortunately, Lucian remembered Cupid itself from when they had escaped Psyche the first time on *Wayfinder* when the gas giant had only been the size of a small coin in the distance. Exiting there would place them about an hour from Psyche itself, which was far enough to set up before the battle began.

The fleet would take about two hours to pass through Lucian's single portal. It was almost faster to travel from Kandi, but the Swarmers would pick up their vector and know where to meet them. Not only that, but it would reveal the location of their base.

All Lucian had to do was create the portal, allowing each ship in the line to pass through.

Within seconds, the portal appeared, which Lucian branded so that he would not have to maintain an active stream. The first ships filtered through. Smaller vessels like corvettes and destroyers passed multiple at a time. Cruisers and battleships had to pass through alone. The Thermalists and Radiants would mask the fleet's presence on the other side.

After less than two hours, *Mekong* was the only ship left. It, too, went through the portal, and Lucian allowed it to close behind him.

The fleet was already waiting for Lucian on the other side, arrayed for battle. It was a glorious sight, but Lucian also knew they were up against a force that could field just as many or more ships. Ten Swarmer carriers could easily spew out five to ten thousand interceptors. Working in tandem, they could wreak havoc on any ship class. The key would be to bring down those carriers as quickly as possible. So far, the carriers had no adequate defense against a gravity point of sufficient strength. That was how Lucian planned to deal with them.

"Ahead full," Mira said.

The fleet kicked into action, going full speed toward Psyche. Lucian drew from the Orb of Psionics, creating a massive ward around the entire fleet, inspiring feelings of bravery and complete focus on the task at hand. Under the effects of the ward, every sailor would fight far beyond their natural abilities. The measure would save countless lives.

It didn't take long before they reached the scene of the battle. Thousands of ships, mostly interceptors, were lying in wait. At once, they engaged the Starsea ripsaws, corvettes, and destroyers.

"Focus all lances on the leftmost carrier," Mira said.

A moment later, the blue streaks of light fired upon the carrier. Its Binding shield broke immediately as the ship began busting apart at the seams.

But so numerous were the Swarmer interceptors that they were already breaking through the main lines, going straight for the battleships. Lucian stopped setting up this gravity point to throw up a massive shield to defend against the attack that would have left *Mekong* crippled.

Sensors Officer Karlsen's voice boomed through the chaos. "Logging Swarmer assault transports heading for the surface! Twelve total."

Lucian drew more ether, blasting a Gravitonic wave that rippled through space. A Swarmer attack group was torn asunder, but it was a drop in the bucket.

"Portal opening to starboard!" Helmsman Morales said.

Indeed, Lucian could see the new threat with his own eyes. A small portal had formed to the right of the battle, through which more *Alkasen* vessels were pouring.

"Admiral Yang, focus all your lances on that portal," Mira said. "Lucian, take care of those carriers."

Lucian was already working on that. He had to ignore the troop transports going down to Psyche. He saw the tactic as a ploy to force him to move his ships dangerously close to the carriers. For now, the front lines were holding, and the earlier break had been mended, thanks to Lucian's Psionic ward keeping his sailors calm.

However, holding the ward was a heavy investment of ether. Lucian began drawing more, knowing it would take much longer to get the required amount to achieve victory. The Psionic ward needed to stay up, or else the fleet would break before the Swarmer onslaught. All they had to do was hold for ten more minutes. That would give Lucian enough time to create the gravity point.

Lucian was completely blind to the battle's progress. He just had to hope everyone was doing their jobs properly.

At last, he felt he had enough ether. He formed the gravity point, the action second nature by now. He placed it right into the center of the carriers.

Almost as soon as the brand was active, the carriers were pulled toward it. Swarms of interceptors retracted to their home bases as if they were a single organism. It seemed the Swarmers recognized the danger and were attempting to retreat as the Starsea ships gave chase. While another portal opened, this one was meant for the Swarmers' withdrawal.

Even as Lucian kept the gravity point active, he barked an order, despite the concentration required. "Order the ships back here. Don't let them get too close!"

A moment later, the ships drew back. Thankfully, none had ventured close enough to the gravity point to be drawn past the point of no return.

But this was not the fate of the Swarmer vessels madly vying to retreat. They fell in droves to the pulsing gray orb, drawn into it only to be instantaneously crushed. Five carriers were included in that number. However, the rest could escape, slipping past the plane of the portal.

The increasing gravity was drawing the Starsea ships. Lucian cut off the stream, and the gravity point disappeared. No longer restrained, the crushed metal and rock exploded outward, breaking through the shields of several Starsea vessels that had gotten too close. The destroyers' auto-targeting cannons dispersed or shot down most of the remaining debris. The rest were eaten up by the shields or burned through Psyche's thick atmosphere. The few straggling Swarmer vessels were quickly hunted down.

Lucian let go of his Focus and dropped to one knee. The Psionic ward covering the fleet dissipated, and the confidence that had bolstered the fleet's spirits faded. Despite the victory, Lucian knew their losses would be grievous.

"Battle report," he managed.

There was a long silence before Karlsen gave the numbers.

"Eight hundred eighty-two vessels lost. Among those lost were two battleships and twelve cruisers."

Lucian closed his eyes. Almost twenty percent of the Starsea Fleet evaporated in under two hours.

"Impossible to say how many we killed," she went on cautiously. "Double that, at least, before the rest got away."

"And the surface? You reported *Alkasen* transports entering the atmosphere. We can't let any potential Preserved reach the Darkrift."

"I'm sending the ripsaws after them," Mira said. "Not one will make a landing."

"Regardless, have to keep the moon safe. We can't guard it around the clock, and the Swarmers know they can use it against me."

"What do you propose?" Mira asked.

Already, an idea was forming in Lucian's mind. "I need Carthen on the line."

It only took a moment for the action to be performed, and Carthen quickly answered. "Sorcerer-Ascendant. How might I be of service?"

"Is there any way to get the defense platforms working?"

"Yes, that can be done," he said. "Of course, they will need to be manned by my tachyon crews."

"Get them all on board," Lucian said. "Can you manage it?"

"Of course, Sorcerer-Ascendant. I assume the task is to guard Psyche when the fleet leaves?"

"That's right. I know it's not the perfect solution, but it's something."

"Yes, I see your meaning. Don't worry about it, Sorcerer-Ascendant. I can have my men heading to the platforms within the hour. They will also need support from Warden Prime, which is currently being manned by a skeleton crew."

"I want you to take all five thousand you originally had," Lucian said. "Those still with us, anyway. Have them watch for new portals. As soon as one is sighted, concentrate all fire on it."

"Understood," Carthen said. "I'll get to work right away."

"Good," Lucian said. "I want Grand Captain Warwick to work with you, too. You both know Psyche's defense network better than anyone. Our fleet has grown powerful enough that we won't miss a couple of hundred ships and five thousand men."

"I would be glad to be of service, Sorcerer-Ascendant, and I think I speak for the Grand Captain as well. I appreciate the trust you've placed in me."

Lucian was confident in the strength of his Psionic brands. Even if Carthen were to buck it, his troops were loyal to Lucian. They would never betray his confidence, especially now that they had seen the threat of the Swarmers.

"Good luck, Commander."

When Carthen dropped off the call, Lucian felt more at peace.

Lucian's attention turned to Mira, who was watching the central monitor. "Ripsaws have caught up to the transports. Scratched two so far."

"Good," Lucian said. Things seemed like they were coming back under control.

A hail request lit on the terminal from Selene. Lucian accepted it from his slate.

"Selene, everything all right down there?"

"Yes, we're fine. Everyone is safe, though we've heard a few ships go down."

Mira responded. "Some Swarmer transports got through the battle lines. We saw exactly how many and where they went. They'll be destroyed soon enough."

"Good to hear. I guess it's safe to say the Swarmers are taken care of?"

"Yes," Mira said. "We took some losses, but I don't think the Swarmers will bother Psyche soon. We're taking measure to ensure the moon stays safe."

"What measures?"

Lucian cleared his throat. "I have Carthen and Warwick staying behind, along with two hundred ships and five thousand men. All the platforms will be manned, pointing out into space. I've instructed them to keep watch for any new portals."

"Hopefully, that takes care of the issue," Selene said.

"Everything's under control," Lucian assured her.

Karlsen turned to Mira from her station. "Just received word that the last Swarmer transport was just destroyed."

"Excellent," Mira said.

"Another thing," Lucian said to Selene. "We have more transports available . . . enough to evacuate more people if need be. Thousands, if they want to come with us."

"I thank you for the offer. However, if we aren't safe here, we aren't safe anywhere. The Darkrift has been fortified against attack, and we have months of supplies left. We have the terrace farms in the rifts and the food the frays stashed away. There are more fish than we can catch. We're too low for the wyverns to be a threat, and no Swarmer ships can navigate these canyons. We'll be fine, Lucian. Just focus on what you need to do. It would take too long to evacuate people, anyway."

Lucian saw the wisdom of her words. "Is there anything else?"

"No. Thank you again for your speedy response. The people of Psyche—and I— thank you for it."

Lucian was relieved things were going so well. Whatever misgivings he'd had about leaving Selene in charge completely evaporated. "Take care, Selene. Keep up the good work. If you need anything, reach out to Carthen and Warwick."

"Will do."

Selene ended the call, and Lucian regarded the moon before him for a moment. It was time to pick up the pieces and head back to Kandi.

39

THE STARSEA FLEET spent the next week at Kandi to resupply and recuperate. Many ships were damaged in the fight, and there wasn't enough time to repair them fully. Thankfully, the people of Port Kandi were skilled shipwrights, as all pirates were; the fixes might not have been by the book, but they got the job done. Zheng's crew were also experts at fleet upkeep, and each vessel was swarmed by shipwrights diagnosing and making restorations.

After a week, the fleet was ready to set out again. Lucian couldn't afford to wait any longer. They had a detailed attack plan to liberate most of the Trailward Worlds. Most of the worlds had no Swarmer vessels defending them. As Lucian noted, they had given up defending against the Starsea Fleet. Even the Swarmer fleet at Isis had vanished.

So, over the next weeks, the fleet worked tirelessly to mop up the Trailward Worlds. If there were any Swarmer defenses, they were mopped up effortlessly. By now, the fleet was battle-hardened and took few losses even as its numbers swelled. After four weeks, the last Trailward world on their list was liberated, and what was left of the Swarmers was all concentrated in multiple systems bordering the First Worlds.

Lucian's scouting groups logged at least ten thousand vessels in each fleet, perhaps even more. Those numbers didn't even include the thousands of strike craft spread amongst the Swarmers' many carriers. There were even ships of human-make among the crystalline hulls of the Swarmer vessels. That told Lucian plenty of people had been turned by the Bond.

There were no more easy targets, but the Swarmers were no longer challenging the Starsea Fleet. They already knew they couldn't keep up with it or guess where it would strike next. Though the *Alkasen* had access to Space-Time Magic, none could break the power of the Sentinels' constant wards. And they still didn't know the location of Kandi, the only reason they hadn't been challenged directly.

All the *Alkasen* could do was gather in larger fleets, too large for Starsea to attack directly. It was obvious what the next stage of their plan was: the conquest of the Solar System and driving a dagger into the heart of human civilization.

———

ALL THE COMMAND staff were gathered on the bridge of *Mekong*, or present via holo-call. About fifty people were there to learn the next actions of the Starsea Fleet now that they had achieved their aim of saving every Trailward world that could be saved.

Even Lucian didn't know what came next. The answer seemed obvious: join with the League and defend Earth. But something told Lucian this was the wrong move. Sharo Khalin was still out there, possessed by the Ancient one, and he had yet to make his move.

"We have to decide what to do about Sharo Khalin," he said.

"He's just hanging out in the orbit of Nessus, waiting for God knows what."

"You don't know what he's waiting for?" Serah asked. All eyes went to her. "Sharo wants one thing. Your Orbs. That's his only game."

"He's not getting them," Lucian said.

"Maybe not," Serah said. "But that's not going to stop him from trying. We need to be doing everything we can to defend against that."

"Like what?" Fergus asked. "The Sentinels are warding us at all times. Our fleet outnumbers theirs. We have more mages than they do. *Way* more."

"He'll wait for the right opportunity," Serah said. "Count on it."

"Well, we have *two* enemies," Plato pointed out. "The Ancient One, *and* the Swarmers. It would be nice to use one to take out the other."

"That's not happening," Lucian said. "The Swarmers are only focused on Earth right now. Even now, thousands of ships are pouring in from Dark Space. We have to stop that."

Serah's eyes went wide as if having a sudden realization. "Rotting hell. Why has no one thought of this yet?"

"Thought of what yet?" Transcend White asked.

Again, she became the focus of attention. "Okay, this might sound like a crazy idea. But weren't the Gates created by the First Immortal using the Orbs? If he created them, then could they possibly be destroyed?"

Realization seemed to dawn on everyone simultaneously, and they watched Lucian for a reaction. If he could somehow use the Orbs to cut off the Gates, the Swarmers could no longer reinforce the Worlds as quickly. They could only do so using portals, which were extremely difficult to make.

"That would seriously limit their fighting capacity," Fergus admitted. "But already so many have entered League Space. And, of course, we don't know if it's even possible to destroy a Gate."

"I'm not sure if it's possible, either," Lucian said. "But assuming it *can* be done, it gives us a fighting chance. Cut off their reinforcements, and then all we'd have to deal with are the ones already here, plus the ones who can skip the Gates using a portal. We already know it takes many mages working together to make a portal. As Fergus said, it'll seriously impact their ability to reinforce. If they are truly gathering to end Earth, we need to win that battle and close off the Gates leading into League Space. That would give us a chance to win the war overall."

"Another thing, too," Transcend White said. "It's likely that most of their mages will be brought to bear for the attack on Earth. If not *all* of them. If we can somehow win that battle, they won't be able to make portals anymore. At least, not easily."

"How do we know they will throw all their mages at us?" Emma asked.

"Because they know *we* have a lot of mages. You need to overwhelm the other side to win a battle with magic. We'll cancel each other out if they bring an equal number of mages. But if they overwhelm us, they can nullify our magic while attacking with impunity. They will want every mage they have to stand against us, to crush us without mercy."

"If they're going to outnumber us so much," Fergus said, "then what are our options?"

Transcend White nodded toward Lucian. "The Chosen of the Manifold. With the Orbs, he may have enough to tip the balance. I stand with him and the Chief Gravitist on this plan to nullify or destroy the Gates. The Swarmers are not ready to strike Earth. Not yet. But every day that passes, more ships arrive in the League's borders. If we plan to try this, we had better move quickly."

"Well said," Mira said. "The only question now is, which Gate do we target first?"

Everyone looked at Lucian for the decision.

Lucian shrugged. "It might be best to target one in an isolated system. Less likely to be attacked."

"There are a fair number of Border Gates to choose from," Transcend White said. "I think the fair question is, does the mental map you created cover them all?"

Lucian projected a holographic map of the League of Worlds, highlighting the seven Gates that led out into Dark Space. "There are seven Border Gates. If we were to cut these Gates off entirely, it would isolate the League from the rest of Dark Space. No Swarmers could get in except by portal." He frowned in thought. "All this is hypothetical, of course. And unfortunately, I only have direct access to four Gates. I can portal pretty close to the other three, within a star system or two."

"That would make this entire process take months," Mira said. "We don't *have* months."

Lucian nodded. "I know. But we might at least shut off four of the seven and then focus our attention on Earth. Of course, if the Swarmers make their move before that, we'll have no choice. We'll need to drop everything and portal to Earth."

"So that leaves the question," Emma said. "Which system first?"

Lucian thought it over. The four systems he had memories of were Kasturi, Sani, Varda, and Terminus. Kasturi and Sani were well-populated worlds that the Swarmers had long conquered. Emma had provided him with a memory of Sani, while another of his Sentinels had provided him one of Kasturi. He had his own memory of Varda since he had passed through before. The memory of Terminus had come from the Sentinels' second-in-command, Mwangi, who had grown up there.

That left three systems Lucian couldn't easily access: Umber, Eroth, and Sulisto. He could get within two Gates of each one, making accessing those more difficult.

Still, if they could quickly cut off four Gates, that would severely limit the Swarmers' reinforcements.

He nodded, having decided. He zoomed in on the Terminus System. "This is where we start. Terminus is arguably the most distant star system in the League. It's our best option for testing this out."

Everyone was silent as they considered the suggestion.

Transcend White cleared her throat. "It risks a lot. Then again, we are reaching a point where there are no more easy gains. There is also the risk of being unable to reinforce Earth in time. While we're in Terminus, the Swarmers might make their move. The battle for Earth could be decided in a matter of hours."

Lucian thought that was a good point. "Yes, it's a risk. But it's also a risk to leave these Gates open." He thought for a moment. "Maybe the best move would be for me to go by myself."

"No way," Emma said. "As Captain of the Sentinels, I won't allow it. You'll need someone to watch your back."

Lucian almost suggested getting the old crew back together again, except he knew they were needed here to lead their respective brigades.

"I agree with Captain Almaty," Mira said. "It's too dangerous for you to go by yourself."

"I'll take four Sentinels with me, then."

"More like *twenty*-four," Emma said. "The rest can stay here under Lieutenant Mwangi and keep the ward going."

Mwangi nodded. "I think it's a good balance to strike."

"Twenty-four seems like a lot," Lucian said. "*Blood Wyvern* won't even fit that many."

"Yes, it will. We won't be gone for months on end. A few days, at most. You created the Sentinels to ward the fleet *and* protect you. We wouldn't be serving our purpose if you left us behind."

Lucian couldn't argue with that. "All right, then. Twenty-four Sentinels. Not a person more."

"I want to go," Serah said. "It was *my* idea."

Everyone watched what Lucian would say. He had originally wanted the Mage Council to stay behind to keep up with the Mage Division. They wanted to see if Serah would get an exception because of his feelings for her.

"This will just be the Sentinels and me," he said. "I understand it was your idea, but all the Chief Mages need to remain here. This shouldn't take long, anyway."

Serah looked as if she would argue for a moment, but something in Lucian's face told her she shouldn't. At last, she sighed.

"Be careful, then. I know it's Terminus, and nobody is out there. But the Swarmers might use that Gate to send more ships in."

Lucian nodded. "I know. We'll be careful."

"The only question," Emma said. "When do we start?"

"As soon as we can. Captain Almaty, make your selections. Meet me in *Blood Wyvern's* hangar one hour from now."

40

WITHIN AN HOUR, *Blood Wyvern* was out in space, piloted by a Sentinel named Ingmar. Ingmar was a broad-shouldered man with a happy, calm countenance. After joking with him for a bit, Lucian learned he had been a pilot since he was a young boy, and before his time with the Sentinels, he had piloted for the Irion Mages. With him, *Blood Wyvern* would be in expert hands.

"Creating the portal," Lucian said.

It took more ether than usual, owing to the distance. Terminus was several thousand light-years away. Lucian brought to mind a planet quite far in the system that Mwangi had shown him. Cyclops was a green gas giant best known for its single, massive eye that took up much of the planet, making it look like a floating eyeball. Along with the planet, three moons of ruddy gold formed in his mind's eye. Lucian held to the memory and streamed from the Orb of Space-Time, the picture becoming complete.

The portal opened before *Blood Wyvern*. Once the ship had

passed through, Lucian's image became a reality. Thousands of light-years had been bridged in mere seconds.

"Setting course for the Border Gate," Ingmar said.

"How much time?" Emma asked, standing behind him.

"Four hours. Stars, this ship is fast!"

It wouldn't be fast enough for Lucian. An idea came to him then, and he wondered why he hadn't thought of it before. Using Dynamism and Space-Time, he could create a warp bubble around the ship to speed things along as it went through space. He didn't know where the idea had come from, only that it was possible. He knew he shouldn't experiment, but Lucian was confident he was strong enough to pull it off.

"I want to try something," Lucian said. "It should get us there a lot faster."

"Try what?" Emma asked, somewhat nervously.

Without answering, he created an aura around the ship composed of Space-Time and Dynamistic Magic, to which he continually added ether. *Blood Wyvern's* instrument panel went haywire, the lights flashing on and off. The electromagnetic nature of the aura was messing with the ship's systems.

He was aware of shouting outside his awareness, but Lucian was confident in his abilities. He added more power, the reality of the Shadow Realm replaced by the ethereal energy of the Light Realm. Lines of ether infused into his body and were redirected into the warp aura.

Sometime later—how *much* later, Lucian couldn't say—he tapered down the stream. The Light Realm dropped from his awareness, and he returned to the ship's bridge. The instrument panel and readouts resumed their usual activity while the Sentinels gathered on the bridge to look at the system map in shock.

"We're here," Emma said in disbelief. "What the hell did you do, Lucian?"

"A warp bubble. At least, that's what I think it is. It compresses space along the ship's path, making it reach its destination much faster."

"Amazing," she said. "Slow down for arrival. We'll be there in a few more minutes."

———

BLOOD WYVERN SLOWED to a stationary orbit in sync with the Border Gate. The space all around them was empty. It was strange to think that more Swarmer reinforcements might slip through that Gate unannounced. He had to work quickly.

Lucian wanted as little distance as possible between himself and the Gate. "Get us in closer. Almost touching it."

Sentinel Ingmar complied. Over the next ten minutes, *Blood Wyvern* drew closer to the massive structure. Lucian realized he had never seen one up close; as a matter of course, when a ship passed through a Gate, it was going thousands of kilometers a second, all but invisible to the naked eye. At such speeds, it was impossible to see a Gate. Any human-based infrastructure, such as space stations or transmission relays, was set up within kilometers of the Gate's sides where they wouldn't threaten passing ships.

Out here, however, there was nothing but cold dark space extending for tens of millions of kilometers in all directions. Stars shone just as brightly as at the core, but somehow, just knowing there wasn't so much as a human-made radio signal for hundreds of light-years just added to the sense of isolation.

That Gate grew in Lucian's vision, a pair of ethereally glowing parentheses that shone with all the Aspects. Between the two sides stretched a dark plane studded with the stars of the bordering system. Even now, the *Alkasen* were on the other side and probably heading straight here. His only condolence was that if they passed through, it would take days to turn around to fight them. Not even a cursory guard was posted this far; the *Alkasen* would have never dreamed Lucian was about to attempt this.

Or so he hoped.

Part of him wanted to remove himself from the ship entirely, to touch the surface of the Gate itself. There would be no barrier, no loss of power from his stream.

In the end, however, the sight through the viewscreen would have to suffice.

"Lower the wards," Lucian said. "I don't want anything interfering with my stream."

Emma nodded to her soldiers. "It's all right."

Lucian felt the wards—Thermal, Radiant, and Space-Time—dissipate from around him. That made the ship vulnerable, but nothing could impede his stream. Though he hadn't even started the stream, he knew the power required would be beyond anything he had attempted so far.

He had to believe it was possible. He had to believe it was necessary. Humanity's survival depended on his success.

There was nothing more to wait for. Lucian opened himself to all the Orbs. Instantly, his consciousness ascended to the Light Realm and became a conduit of ether. Lines entered him from all directions. He reached for the Gate with his Focus. The brand creating the Space-Time Gate had held together for over ten million years, as strong as the day the First Immortal made it. It felt strangely familiar to Lucian, perhaps because he held a part of the First Immortal in the Orbs. Despite the brand's seemingly infinite complexity, he knew what steps to take to unravel it.

He didn't question where the knowledge came from; he could only assume it was the providence of the Orbs. Silumko said that within the Orbs, he held the intelligence of creation itself. Lucian saw this play out as he disassembled the mighty, eight-sealed brand that made up the Gate.

It would take a lot of time poking and prodding. And, of course, a lot of ether.

He worked tirelessly as time itself disappeared. There was only him and the work. It might have been an entire year that passed or just a few seconds.

And then, in a last burst of magic, the job was finished.

Lucian opened his eyes and nearly collapsed to his knees. No longer fueled by ether, sheer exhaustion hit him. His vision went dark for a moment. Someone caught him.

"Lucian!" Emma said, holding him steady. Ingmar was there next. With their help, Lucian could stay upright.

"Water," he said.

"Get it," Emma ordered.

The sound of footsteps exited the bridge.

"It's done," he said, his voice rasping. "How long did it take?"

"Over two standard days," Emma said. "You never stopped, not even for a bit."

The news didn't surprise him. He opened his eyes and looked at his handiwork. In between the Gate's two curved sides, no energy stretched. The plane was gone, and no one could bring it back. Not without all the Orbs, anyway.

Someone put water on his lips, and he took a few sips and then coughed.

"One down," Lucian said, "six more to go."

They were his last words before he collapsed onto the deck.

———

Lucian woke in the med pod to the alarms blaring. He reached for his Focus, using it to rouse himself to alertness.

The pod hissed open. The ship gave a sudden jolt, throwing him toward the wall. He reached for Space-Time and Radiance, phasing through the wall toward the bridge. He reformed on an empty spot next to Emma, surrounded by half a dozen Sentinels staring out the viewscreen. Such was their focus that they didn't even notice him.

Well over a thousand ships were arrayed before them, though none were firing.

"What the hell is going on?" Lucian asked.

Emma gave a jump from beside him. "Lucian! Where did you come from?"

Lucian ignored the question for now. "It's time to leave."

"We've been trying!" Emma said. "They're shielding Space-Time, and none of us can punch through."

Lucian quickly noted the ships. At first, he thought it was the *Alkasen*, but the ships were all League make. If it were the *Alkasen*, there probably would have been at least a few with crystalline hulls.

The League made them, but Lucian also knew it *wasn't* the League. Somehow, Sharo Khalin and the Believers had tracked them here.

Lucian had little time to wonder how this could be. He reached for the Orb of Space-Time. Though ether roared through his Focus, it was impossible to create a portal. The more he pushed against the Space-Time barrier around *Blood Wyvern*, the greater the resistance he met. Even if he had more power, the shield absorbed it effectively.

Whoever was behind this shield was strong, and Lucian didn't have to ask who the source was.

As if thinking of the Ancient One was a summons, Lucian

felt a Psionic pull at his mind. It wasn't an attack, but a request for conversation.

Lucian allowed the connection to form, but remained wary.

You are trapped, Chosen. There is only one road left to you now.

Lucian didn't bother responding. His eyes focused on *Holy Fire*, the Believer flagship. *Blood Wyvern* might be faster than every ship in this fleet, but it could never outfly a torpedo before they got out of range of the Space-Time ward.

"We need to dock on *Holy Fire*," Lucian said.

Emma looked at him as if he were insane. "What? You can't break through the ward?"

Lucian shook his head. "We'd have to get some distance first. No way we're doing that. The Ancient One wants me alive. If we ran, they'd shoot a stunning torpedo at us. One way or another, we're ending up on *Holy Fire*."

"How did they know we were here?" Ingmar asked, puzzled.

Lucian realized the truth. "Serah was right."

"About what?" Emma asked.

"The Ancient One was waiting for an opportunity. And he found us because he can sense when the Orbs are being used."

"What do you mean?" Emma asked.

"He's a part of them. And when they're gathered together like this, and I used the amount of ether I did, it's like a beacon. I was streaming for two days straight, plenty of time for him to home in on exactly where I was."

"We should have brought the entire fleet with us!" Ingmar said.

"We'll have to make do with what we have." Lucian looked at all of his Sentinels. By now, they were crowded on the bridge or outside the corridor. They hung on his every word.

"Look. All of this is happening faster than I would have liked. But we have to do the unthinkable. The Ancient One is on that ship. If we take him out, he'll no longer be a threat. It'll just be the Swarmers left to deal with. Maybe he thinks he's trapping us, locking us in a room, and throwing away the key." Lucian gave a grim smile. "There's no escape from us, either. We're not locked in here with him; it's the opposite."

"What do we do, then?" one Sentinel asked, a fair-skinned woman with red hair that Lucian remembered as Lora. Her face was steely and determined, as if ready to fight to the death. "Whatever is coming, we are with you, Sorcerer-Ascendant. Nothing will happen to you. Nothing."

The other Sentinels voiced their agreement. Lucian wondered if they truly knew what was at stake. *Holy Fire* would be filled with hundreds of Believer soldiers—and not only them, but their feared Holy Warriors, who had been specifically trained and equipped to combat mages. There would also be dozens upon dozens of Prophets, all intent on protecting their master.

And, of course, there would be Sharo Khalin himself, possessed by the Ancient One. Though he had no Orbs, he was not a foe to be underestimated, especially considering the strength of the Space-Time ward he and his Prophets had conjured.

Lucian faced out of the viewscreen. *Holy Fire* was edging closer, and the dash lit with a message that ordered them to dock in Hangar C.

Emma frowned in confusion. "What does he want? To talk? Why not just kill us?"

"There's only one reason I can think of," Lucian said. "If he destroyed *Blood Wyvern*, the Orbs would separate, blasting out in different directions. Separated like that, they would become impossible to retrieve. He can't detect them unless they're held by someone and being used."

"So he's going for a clean kill," Emma said.

Lucian nodded. "That's right. He doesn't want to talk.

Maybe he wants *us* to think that. But as soon as we're inside that hangar, all bets are off."

"We'll be with you every step of the way, Sorcerer-Ascendant," Ingmar said.

Already, Lucian felt each of them warding their primaries, with a designated few warding Space-Time. Emma was among that number since she was the strongest Space-Time mage among the Sentinels.

"Ingmar, head to *Holy Fire*."

"Let's rock and roll," Ingmar said confidently.

Blood Wyvern leaped forward through space, heading for whatever fate the Manifold had in store for it.

41

LUCIAN HALF-EXPECTED a hail of railguns and swarms of torpedoes to end their lives at any moment. But as they passed in utter silence toward the gargantuan battleship, Lucian realized his theory was correct. The Ancient One hoped to get a clean kill and get all the Orbs in a single stroke.

This was his gambit, his one chance to achieve his aims. Lucian had to ensure it never happened.

All the Sentinels stood in the central staging area, wards up and shockspears at the ready. Lucian held no wards, committing every part of his Focus to stream offensive magic. Lightspear shone brightly in his right hand, a single line of white-hot fire he knew was the key to driving the Shadow out of this reality. If Lucian could do so, the Ancient One would only abide in one place: his prison in the Light Realm.

The ship came to a stop, the auto-pilot sequence complete. No enemy fire fell upon *Blood Wyvern*. The Ancient One didn't even want to risk destroying the ship within *Holy Fire's* hangar. After all, stray fire could cause the vessel to explode, ending with the same result as if it were destroyed in space. Or, more likely, the Ancient One wanted to finish him personally.

Lucian reached out with Psionics, feeling a dark presence toward the back of the vessel. That surprised him; he had expected the Ancient One to be on the bridge. But it seemed they'd have to travel the entire length of the ship to reach him. A way to soften Lucian and the Sentinels up, perhaps.

"Just stay close to me," Lucian said. "I know where Khalin is. There are only twenty-six of us, and hundreds of them. But all of you are Sentinels, and each of you is worth a hundred of them."

At that moment, the deck rocked beneath them. Maybe it was the Believers' way of encouraging them to vacate the ship. The longer they waited, the longer the enemy had time to set up a defense.

The door opened, and Lucian strode out with Emma by his side. But before he could even exit, at least a dozen Sentinels rushed before him, spears alight with electricity, almost immediately coming under fire on the boarding ramp.

The first few pulse waves were deflected harmlessly off the Psionics' shields. The rest of the Sentinels poured out, followed by Lucian and Emma. Lucian faced out into the hangar, sighting several dozen power-armored marines, each bearing a heavy impact rifle while taking shelter behind metallic emplacements. The pulses streamed one after another, each calibrated to rip flesh and break bone.

Lucian quickly streamed a Psionic shield to add to the general defense. He sprinted forward, amplifying his speed with a gravity brand that pulled him ahead, right toward the first emplacements. He held out Lightspear, diving toward a squad of four marines. They extended the bayonets of their guns, attempting to stab Lucian. He tethered their weapons and threw them against the wall.

They responded by trying to tackle and crush him with their heavy armor, but Lucian was ready. He shot a fork of lightning from his spearpoint, the deadly electricity covering their armor. They went down writhing, the flesh of their faces melting behind their faceplates. Lucian put them out of their misery with four quick stabs. Lightspear passed through the thick armor of their helmets as if it didn't exist.

Now, Lucian was the sole focus of all the marines' impact pulses. He redoubled his Psionic shield, enduring the attack. The Sentinels fanned out, aiming for an isolated marine emplacement. Lucian focused his attention on his next targets, four marines taking shelter behind a stack of metallic crates.

Lucian streamed a powerful kinetic blast wave that toppled the crates, burying the soldiers on the other side. Lucian leaped high with a Gravitonic-assisted jump. Before the soldiers could even throw the containers off their power armor, Lucian tethered himself into the group, sweeping his spear and decapitating two marines as they emerged from the pile. The other two approached from behind, bayonets out. Lucian pushed them back with Psionics, then locked them into place with a Gravitonic disc. From there, it was simple to stab them through their chest plates.

The Sentinels mopped up the rest of the soldiers, with no losses on the Sentinels' side. Ingmar let out an exhilarated whoop.

That was when the double doors to the hangar bay slid open, revealing six more marines coming to reinforce. Lucian reached out with Psionics, creating six simultaneous possession brands. Each soldier came to a dead stop with violet-glowing eyes. Lucian floated toward them, pointing Lightspear back toward the main part of the ship.

"Clear the way for us."

The soldiers saluted and turned, intent on carrying out his orders to the death. Once out of the hangar, the whirring pulses of impact rifles could be discerned.

The Sentinels fell in around Lucian. He nodded toward the hangar doors.

"That leads to the central corridor. We need to go to the end. That's where the High Prophet is."

"This is going well," Ingmar said. "We might even get out alive!"

Lucian nodded. "Keep up the good work. The Prophets are still out there. Let's not get complacent."

"They're probably with the High Prophet," Emma said. "Keeping up the ward so we can't escape."

Lucian realized she was probably right. "Let's end this. Keep those wards strong."

He led the way into the main corridor, ensuring his Binding and Psionic shields were strong. As soon as the doors opened, they found the six soldiers he had possessed lying sprawled on the deck. Hundreds of soldiers waited beyond; power-armored marines, dozens of crimson-robed Holy Warriors bearing shockspears, each wearing a personal shield pack powered on. Added to these were three white-robed Prophets, surrounded by ethereal auras.

The next moments were chaos. Within the Ether, Lucian became a flurry of activity, hardly conscious of his actions. The Sentinels' wards made the Prophets' magic useless, while Lucian's shields nullified the marines' impact rifles. The Holy Warriors stalked forward, trained in melee combat from birth. This was their element.

But try as the Prophets might, Lucian's magic was too powerful to be resisted by their wards. He began by pushing three approaching Holy Warriors with a reverse tether, sending them rocketing back into another group and scattering them like pins. Several marines leaped down from the catwalks above, landing on the lower deck with deafening clangs. Lucian fried them with lightning.

The Sentinels had engaged the Holy Warriors in a deadly dance of death. Lucian focused his efforts on the Prophets. If he could take them down, the Sentinels would be free to use their magic.

Lucian leaped with a gravity-assisted jump, avoiding the three warriors converging on him. He crashed into one of the Prophets with Lightspear, his face a mask of fear when he realized his Binding shield wouldn't protect him. The other two Prophets closed in, each bearing shockspears. Before they could close the gap, Lucian threw Lightspear, guiding its course with a tether. The ethereal weapon pierced both like a lightning bolt before Lucian recalled it to his hand.

With the Prophets eliminated, the melee turned in the Sentinels' favor, but Lucian couldn't help but notice a few had gone down. The red-haired Lora was among the dead, blood splattered on her black robes. Emma fought beside her fallen body, her face calmly serene given the carnage, while Ingmar fought furiously at her side. Fireballs, lightning bolts, and tethers formed a lattice of offensive magic, taking down wave after wave of Holy Warriors and marines.

Lucian floated down to join the fight. Lightspear had a mind of its own, guiding his hand and cutting through flesh and armor.

A few minutes later, the butchery was over. The corridor was empty, with no signs of reinforcements.

"Let's keep moving," Lucian said, mindful of the goal.

"What about our dead?" Ingmar asked.

"We'll return when the Ancient One is taken care of."

None argued against him.

The rest of the trip went quickly. Lucian probed at the Space-Time ward, discovering it was as strong as ever. The Prophets were definitely working together to keep it going; only three had defended the passage to the stern. The Ancient One *really* wanted him not to escape.

They came to a pair of doors at the end of the corridor that slid open. The Sentinels went on ahead, shockspears glowing like torches in the dim hall beyond. Lucian's Radiance-enhanced vision could see that it was empty.

Their footsteps clomped on the metal deck. Lucian could feel the Ancient One's dark presence getting closer. Beyond the pair of doors at the end, they would find him and likely all the Prophets he had gathered.

The Sentinels paused, looking to Lucian for direction. He considered telling them to prepare themselves, but they were as ready as they ever would be. Their wards were strong, their purpose sure. There were only twenty of them now, plus him and Emma.

They needed to make it work. From the steely expressions on their faces, they were ready to fight to the death.

"Go for the Prophets," he said. "Sharo Khalin is mine."

They nodded their understanding.

"I'll go in first," Lucian said. "I'll create a seven-fold shield that'll buy enough time for you guys to set yourselves up."

"Do what you need to," Emma said. "We're with you every step of the way."

"For the Sorcerer-Ascendant!" Ingmar said.

"No," Lucian said. "For all of you. Let's honor those who fell. Maybe we'll be joining them soon. But until we're dead, we fight with everything we've got. We have a chance to end him for good. Let's not miss it."

He locked eyes with Emma, and there was no fear. She was ready to fight. He felt torn, knowing that this situation would place her in more danger than she had ever been in. But it was too late to go back, and it was her job to fight.

He took a deep breath, and before he could second guess himself, he blasted the metal doors open, revealing a scene of madness.

42

LUCIAN FIRST NOTED the bodies in the large space before him. White-robed, blood-stained Prophets lay scattered across the deck, their forms contorted in unnatural positions. Entire limbs would even be removed, and the cold air reeked of the coppery scent of blood. There were dozens of them, as many as a hundred. All were dead, and from the lone figure standing at the end of the hall, there was no doubt about their fate.

Sharo Khalin watched them with a sadistic smile, his entire body coated in an ethereal light. The rainbow of colors surrounding him signified a seven-fold shield that would protect him from every Aspect. He clasped a long, dark spear in his right hand, the counterpoint to Lucian's own.

With a start, Lucian realized that the source of the powerful Space-Time ward was Sharo Khalin. He had absorbed the Prophets' Focuses just as Xara had done with the mages on Psyche. If he truly had the power of all these dead Prophets at his disposal, he would be a terrifying opponent indeed. More powerful than even Xara Mallis, despite her two Orbs.

Each Sentinel took quick note of the dead bodies, seeming to come to the same conclusion.

Lucian considered all this in less than a second while strengthening his seven-fold shield to cover all the Sentinels filing in after him. Each Sentinel amplified their own ward into a shield, knowing the power of the threat before them. A rainbow light covered them as they took up their positions, shockspears out.

Lucian stood at their head, his grip tight on Lightspear. The ethereal weapon, the manifestation of the Light Realm itself, was the only chance against the Shadow Lord possessing Sharo Khalin.

"We meet again, Chosen," Sharo Khalin said.

His words were eerie and discordant, as if he weren't the only one speaking.

"This ends here, Ancient One. You will not leave this place alive."

Sharo's smile widened. "How little you know, Chosen. This is where it begins."

Lucian wondered why they were talking instead of fighting. The longer he waited, the more ether Sharo could draw. He was trying to stall them.

"Attack," Lucian said.

As a unit, Lucian and the Sentinels shot forward. Sharo's body was lit with ethereal brilliance, his seven-fold shield expanding and clashing with Lucian's own. The shields shattered, a great ripple undulating through the air. Half a dozen Sentinels were caught by the blast and were thrown above the deck, screaming. The rest continued the charge unabated.

As Lucian worked to reform his shield, the Sentinels moved to engage Sharo. The High Prophet raised a hand on high, ushering a massive streak of chain lightning that surged outward, taking down another four Sentinels. Their bodies lifted into the air as tortured screams ripped from their throats. Ingmar reached the High Prophet first, throwing his shockspear with all his might. Sharo phased forward, planting his spear of darkness in Ingmar's torso. Ingmar convulsed before a stream of ethereal light shot from his body and entered Sharo; another Focus absorbed. Similar ether streams were flowing from the dead Sentinels eviscerated by the lightning, powering Sharo even further.

All of this happened in fifteen seconds. Having reformed the seven-fold shield, Lucian rejoined the battle against Sharo. He surged forward using a tether, aiming for a quick kill. But Sharo responded with surprising speed, their spears clashing with a high, discordant shriek. The Sentinels harried Sharo's flanks like enraged badgers, but Sharo fought with godlike form, clearly possessed by the higher power of the Ancient One. Without the Sentinels, Lucian would not have stood a chance.

But the Sentinels were dropping until only half their original number remained. Any time they thought they had him cornered, Sharo would use Space-Time Magic to phase away.

Even as Lucian held his shield, he began a separate stream that he hoped would break through Sharo's defenses. Perhaps it would provide enough of an opening to drive Lightspear home. But Sharo phased into a new position, completely untouchable.

Emma was still alive, waiting in the wings for her chance to attack Sharo. Realizing that she could die at any moment gave Lucian a drive to win. He redirected some of the ether from his shield to create a magical attack that even Sharo couldn't counter.

Before Sharo could take advantage of the weakening of his defense, Lucian struck. A rainbow line, composed of the Seven Aspects, shot straight ahead into Sharo's shield, once again shattering it. Sentinels swarmed the High Prophet, but he phased to the other side of the mustering hall.

More streaks of lightning issued from the point of his dark spear, arcing their way across the space and hitting their marks. Now, only ten Sentinels stood, with Emma thankfully among them.

Lucian shot toward Sharo with a tether, but Sharo was ready, tethering himself to the ceiling to escape. The High Prophet circled above the deck, setting the air afire. Lucian reversed the flame with Thermalism, but not before a couple of Sentinels were incinerated to the bone.

The air was deprived of oxygen because of the fire; thankfully, enough Atomicists remained to flux some back. Lucian got close to Sharo again, stabbing with Lightspear a few times before getting pushed back Psionically. Lucian cushioned his fall with Psionics, rebounding and shooting straight for Sharo again with his spear extended.

Sharo phased at the last minute, and Lucian sensed him right behind. Lucian tethered away to avoid the stab, circling in midair to knock Sharo's spear aside again.

By now, the Sentinels were catching up, providing much-needed relief. Sharo phased to the other side of the hall, though he didn't shoot lightning this time. The Sentinels fanned out to attack once again. Though their expressions were brave, even defiant, Lucian could tell they were weakening. And to his surprise, he felt his Focus wavering, such was the effort of the battle.

There was a momentary lapse as Sharo smiled and gathered his ether in an attack that Lucian assumed was the coup de grâce. Lucian once again drew his ether, surging toward Sharo. Things after that seemed to go in slow motion; Lucian couldn't tell whether it was his perception or if Sharo was doing something to the flow of time itself.

Whatever the case, the High Prophet shot a shining blue line from his hands, which Lucian recognized as a shattering laser. Anything it touched would instantly disintegrate.

The laser roved along the line of Sentinels, obliterating them one by one even as Lucian continued to fly toward his goal, Lightspear out. Lucian knew what Sharo meant him to do; to counter the shattering laser to save them. But Lucian knew it meant diverting his ether from this attack, the one meant to end the Ancient One for good.

So, he did something against every instinct inside him. He allowed the Sentinels to die.

Everything slowed even further as the Sentinels made their last charge, like soldiers charging across a no man's land. Sentinel Elena became wrapped in bluish light and disintegrated into a cloud of fine dust. Sentinel Jacob was next, letting out the beginnings of a scream before he was snuffed. Lucian kept his attention on Sharo, whose demented eyes seemed to drink in the destruction with relish.

But Lucian was almost there, Lightspear extended and just meters away. Something in Sharo's eyes seemed to realize Lucian wasn't going to stop. He gave a sick smile before directing his magic at Emma.

A portal opened right next to her, revealing the vacuum of space. Emma was immediately sucked through with a shriek, quickly cut off by the airless space beyond.

Lucian felt the beginning of a scream come to his lips. That powerful stream to create the portal, Sharo's last gambit, had left him utterly defenseless. Lucian could finish the job, drive Lightspear right into his heart, and get rid of the Ancient One forever. But as soon as he did so, the portal would extinguish, and Emma would be lost.

Lucian knew what Emma would want him to do: finish the

job. He had let all his Sentinels die, after all.

But he knew he couldn't. Sharo smiled, realizing this. It was just him and Lucian now; everyone else had been lost in the few seconds it took Lucian to decide.

Lucian pulled himself toward the portal with a gravity point.

ONLY A FEW SECONDS had passed since Emma had slipped through the portal. Despite the darkness of space, Lucian could still see her in the distance. He had seconds to surround her with a Binding aura and create a breathable atmosphere.

Thankfully, his Focus still surged with fresh ether. He tethered her, pulling her close. Her eyes were closed, but that didn't mean she was dead.

Next, a Binding aura went up, and he opened a small portal within to the closest planet he knew of, which was Mako. Air slowly filled the bubble, ensuring the reintroduction of pressure wasn't sudden enough to shock her system.

Still, her eyes were closed, and she wasn't breathing. Lucian reached out with a Psionic link, finding a glimmer of consciousness. Her skin was bruised wherever it was visible. Noticing the stiffness of her body, he also created a Thermal aura designed to warm them both.

"Breathe," he said. "Come on!"

He streamed a small bit of electricity into her with the slightest touch. Her body gave a sudden jolt, her eyes opened, and she sucked in breath after deep breath. Her brown eyes found him, seeming to be lucid. Blood had frozen on her cheeks.

"What happened?" she rasped. "Is Sharo dead?"

Lucian chose not to answer for now. All that mattered was

that she was alive.

"It's time to go," he said. "I'll explain in a second."

Lucian looked around, finding no recognizable landmark. But the Believer fleet wasn't around, meaning Lucian would have no trouble warping them to a safe location.

He recalled the bridge of *Mekong*. As far as they were from the Starsea Fleet's flagship, it took a couple of minutes until he could draw enough ether. But as soon as he possessed the right amount, they appeared on the carrier's bridge.

43

LUCIAN AND EMMA spent the next day recovering in the medical bay. Emma's injuries during the battle with the Ancient One had been more serious than Lucian's, so he exited his pod first, which was overseen by almost all the medical staff on board the ship.

A tawny-haired doctor addressed him. "Not so fast, Sorcerer-Ascendant. How are you feeling?"

"Fine. How's Emma?"

"Captain Almaty is recovering well. Let's focus on you."

"I want the entire medical contingent dedicated to her case."

"Sorcerer-Ascendant, I assure you there is no danger to her life. The radiation burns have been cured, and the hypoxia and frostbite were not severe. Give her a few more hours, and she'll be good as new."

Only now did Lucian realize it wasn't just the doctors with him. Others were being allowed in. Serah ran up and threw himself at him, with his mother close behind.

Mira turned to the doctor. "Please see to Captain Almaty, as the Sorcerer-Ascendant ordered."

The doctor seemed to take her order more seriously. "You heard her. Clear out."

After a moment, it was just the three of them alone.

Serah drew back from their embrace. "Are you okay?"

"What happened, son?" Mira asked.

Just then, everything came flooding back. From the look on his face, they must have been able to guess the truth.

"Everyone's dead," he said. "Just Emma and I got out alive."

Serah's face paled. "That's what we were afraid of. What happened?"

Lucian explained everything to them, from disabling the Gate to the sudden ambush by the Believer Fleet. Three days had passed since they left. Lucian had spent most of the past twenty-four hours in the medical pod. Upon returning to *Mekong*, sheer exhaustion had caused both him and Emma to keel over.

He almost didn't want to tell them how it ended, seeing the Sentinels picked off one by one, even seeing their Focuses being absorbed. It just reminded him of his failure.

And all of that for what, a single Gate disabled? It was an accomplishment, to be sure, but not worth the death of the twenty-four Sentinels who had fought to defend him.

Ingmar. Lora. Elena. All dead.

"You're alive, and so is Emma," Serah said. "That's something. *More* than something."

"We also know without a doubt that the Ancient One can sense exactly where you are when you're streaming a lot of magic," Mira said. "Until you tried to take the Gate offline, you hadn't used enough to warrant attention. You said yourself you'd never used that much magic before."

Lucian nodded. "That's true."

"It means he'll know where you are every time you try to stop one of the Gates," Serah said. "We have to take *him* out first."

"It's my fault," Lucian said. "I told them to lower the ward. That allowed the Ancient One to attack."

"The ward had to be lowered for your magic to work," Serah said. "You couldn't have known what would happen."

"He took out half of the Sentinels. He used Emma against me, knowing I would save her. I'm glad I saved her. Of course I am." He shook his head. "And maybe that's the problem. He always said my friends were my weakness. Maybe he was right."

"You can't let yourself believe that," Serah said. "You can't do this alone. I thought you'd figured that out by now. Without the Sentinels, you wouldn't have even gotten *close* to the High Prophet."

"You're acting like they were cannon fodder."

"No, I'm not," Serah said. "They were people. People dedicated to fighting to the death."

"What Sentinel will want to follow me now after this?"

"They know what it means to be a Sentinel," Mira said. "Fighting, even dying for you, is an honor."

It was an honor of which Lucian didn't feel worthy. Twenty-four were dead because of him. Twenty-four Space-Time Mages couldn't exactly be replaced.

The metal door slid open, revealing Fergus. He said nothing, seeming to sense the dark mood. All Lucian could manage was a weak nod.

He faced Mira. "Did you get my message?"

She looked down at her slate, her expression paling. "Jesus."

"What?" Serah asked.

"The Swarmers are in the Solar System. The attack's beginning!"

———

WITHIN THE HOUR, all five thousand ships of the Starsea Fleet were ready to fight.

Emma had recovered more quickly than expected, and she stood beside Lucian. As the last of the ships fell into the portal line, she cleared her throat.

"Why did you do it?"

He had hoped she wouldn't figure out the truth on her own, that he had let the Ancient One live to save her.

"It's what I needed to do," he said.

She faced him, seeming to ask for more than that. "You let the others die. But not me."

Lucian remained silent.

"When you appointed me Sentinel Captain, I was ready to die. It meant you were willing to risk me. And yet when the opportunity comes to take the Ancient One from the Shadow Realm forever, you balked."

"Are you saying I should've let it happen?"

"Yes. I was ready to do my part."

"Your part is bigger than dying."

"How do you know that? Another one of your visions?"

He hesitated. "I just know."

He left it at that, even if he didn't know what he was talking about. He wanted to believe Emma's life had a bigger purpose since she thought her potential death held more meaning.

"You should've just let me die."

"You're alive for a reason, Emma. Try to find it."

"Bringing down the Ancient One *was* my reason. Keeping

you alive long enough to finish the job was my reason. You took that from me."

"What do you want? An apology? Because I'm not sorry. It was the right thing to do."

"What if that was our last chance? Would you still be happy about your decision?"

"Give me a break. I had a split second to decide. Do you think I had time to make a list and go over the pros and cons? I saved you because it felt right. That's all you need to know."

Serah came up to them. "Everything okay over here?"

Lucian was grateful for her presence. Maybe Emma would stop bugging him.

"I've got to see to the Sentinels," Emma said. "If you'll excuse me."

Serah watched as Emma stalked off. "She seems a bit . . . heated."

Lucian didn't want to get into it. Serah could probably guess what she was mad about, anyway. He focused on the fleet ahead of him, all in position. Though the battle was about to begin, it felt like he had already fought it. And lost.

"Stand by for portal," Lucian said.

He began gathering his ether. Though he knew they were likely traveling to their deaths, it didn't feel like it. Though it had happened hours ago, he still felt riled up from the fight with the Ancient One. All he could think of was Sharo's horrible smile, which said victory was ultimately his, no matter what.

Lucian drove the image from his mind. He had to focus on the task at hand.

He allowed the portal to form, and as soon as it appeared, the ships slipped through one by one. It was an hour before it was *Mekong's* turn.

When they emerged, it was to the sight of a grand fleet set

before the backdrop of Jupiter. There were no Swarmers here; it was merely the prearranged mustering point for all the fleets. Where the *Alkasen* ships were located was anyone's guess.

Within a few minutes, the last Starsea ships fell into line.

A hail request lit the dash, which Mira answered from her slate. Admiral Thorin's gruff voice exited the panels.

"Glad you could finally join us, Admiral Abrantes."

"I wouldn't be anywhere else, Admiral Thorin."

"Look at it. Isn't it a beautiful sight?"

Lucian looked out the wide viewscreen, seeing a fleet of twenty thousand ships arrayed before the whorled gas giant of Jupiter. There were tens of battleships and carriers. He couldn't believe that this large force was outnumbered so greatly. It was easily the largest human fleet ever assembled. Lucian had a surreal feeling, as if this were a dream. It was all happening so fast.

"How many Swarmer ships are in the system?" Lucian asked. "Where are they?"

Thorin gave a harsh laugh. "Too goddamn many. Wouldn't be surprised if we're outnumbered ten to one. If not more."

"That's over a hundred thousand ships, Admiral."

"You don't believe me?"

"On the contrary, I think that estimate is conservative. We may be up against as many as a quarter of a million."

For a moment, it seemed as if the Admiral were rendered speechless. He cleared his throat. "Let's pray not. If there's a hundred thousand, there is a chance of victory. We estimate the Swarmers are within eight hours of striking Earth. We can get there in half the time. Already, we have another fleet stationed in cislunar space; if one of these portals opens up around Earth, they'll stop it cold."

Lucian nodded. The weakness of portals was that only a few ships could come out at a time. They were good for flanking maneuvers and hurrying fleets across enormous distances as long as the target location was safe. If the Swarmers tried to portal the entirety of their fleet around Earth, the League forces would destroy them piecemeal.

"We'd better get into position," Lucian said.

"Agreed," Admiral Thorin said. "We can discuss battle plans in the interim."

———

DURING THE PASSAGE, Admiral Thorin laid out his strategy to all the senior staff of the League and Starsea Fleets, his hologram pacing the deck as if he were really there.

"We'll park the entire fleet between the moon and Earth," he began. "In the past six months, Earth has prepared many orbital defense platforms. Hundreds upon hundreds of them. The most deadly of these are the tachyon lances, much like what Psyche has. We will train the lances on the Swarmer capital ships. Of course, this will draw the attention of the smaller vessels." Admiral Thorin's hologram looked at Lucian. "This is where the Starsea Fleet comes in. You're to protect these platforms from being targeted, as they are the key to bringing down the Swarmer Fleet. You'll use your smaller vessels and mages to destroy anything that threatens the defense network."

A hologram of Earth and the moon was projected from Lucian's slate. The image zoomed in on the moon.

"We have thousands of missiles based on the moon," Thorin went on. "These will be fired constantly at the medium-sized Swarmer vessels. Maybe not all of them will hit, but they will be forced to deal with them. This is the genius of our strategy. The moon and the planet will shelter our fleet, allowing us to punch above our weight."

"And what if they realize this and *ignore* our fleet?" Mira asked. "They could easily park themselves on the opposite side of Earth, raining down destruction. That might kill hundreds of millions. More, if we allow it to go on. Many space habitats are under threat. Hundreds of them. Not all can shelter in the moon's shadow."

Admiral Thorin's face was grave. "Yes, that's true. Unfortunately, it will be impossible to protect every noncombatant. What's important is that our fleet lasts as long as possible. We can only do that by giving ourselves every advantage. If they do what you describe, ignoring the fleet while attacking Earth from the other side, I'm afraid there's little we can do. We must be patient and wait for the attack to come to *us*. Of course, they will outnumber us so much that I believe they won't even bother with trickery. Especially if they outnumber as much as the Sorcerer-Ascendant believes."

"We shouldn't underestimate them," Lucian said. "The Emissary won't be pulling any punches."

"Who now?"

Lucian shook his head. "Never mind. I think we've got the gist of the plan."

"The exact details will be forwarded to your slates," Admiral Thorin said. "Of course, the command falls to me, but unless I give a direct order, Admiral Mira Abrantes has free rein over her fleet."

Admiral Yang cut in. "We had better win. I was promised Archea for my participation."

To Admiral Thorin's credit, he didn't contradict her. "That will be up to the Hegemon. Let's try to survive the battle first." He cleared his throat. "If you need anything, I'm just a call away."

"Thank you, Admiral," Mira said. "And good luck."

44

THEY WERE STATIONED in orbit between the moon and Earth within four hours. Many habitats called this area home. It was hot real estate as far as where to locate orbitals. For the citizens' sake, Lucian hoped they had long been evacuated.

Below them, Earth's surface was cloaked in night. It felt strange to be back, given the circumstances. The land below showed India and Southeast Asia, city lights burning like yellow fire on the surface. The half-cloaked moon was similar on its night side, filled with yellow lights home to hundreds of thousands of citizens.

In just a few hours, millions were going to die. Such was the population of Earth, its moon, and the surrounding habitats that tens of millions of deaths were simply unavoidable.

But with luck, they could save most of them.

"Swarmer vessels inbound," Sensors Officer Karlsen said. "ETA is ten minutes."

Over the next few minutes, the sensor panels went haywire. The entire screen was dominated by lights representing thousands upon thousands of hostile ships. They approached from all sides, enclosing Earth like a fist crushing an egg. It seemed *impossible* that there could be so many. As the minutes ticked by, the hopelessness of the situation took hold.

Against such numbers, Lucian could only do so much. Using his magic to crush a ship here and there was inconsequential. Even attacking carriers would be pointless. There were bound to be *hundreds* of them, each with a payload of five hundred to a thousand Swarmer strike craft.

The only thing he could do was make the fleet fight better. With this in mind, he created a massive Psionic ward large enough to cover the entire human-led fleet. That ward would bolster morale, enhance focus, and make every person fight their best. Instantly, he noticed the mood shifted on the bridge from despair to intentionality and hope. A fire was in their bellies, and they were determined to win this battle, no matter how desperate and impossible the situation was.

"Here they come," Mira said.

Sure enough, the first Swarmer vessels slipped into view. First, there were a few, then dozens, and then hundreds of ovoid, crystalline shells of carriers. And they approached not just ahead of them but also behind. As soon as the ships were in range, lines of blue light streaked from the direction of the defense platforms orbiting the planet, concentrating on the carrier closest to Earth. Within seconds, the rocky hull exploded.

But there were hundreds more. And every one of those carriers unleashed deadly swarms of strike craft for which the *Alkasen* were so famed and feared.

"They're everywhere," Fergus said, his voice tight. "I've never seen so many ..."

"They're the Swarmers," Serah said. "They swarm."

Serah's obvious observation went unanswered because thousands upon thousands of Swarmer vessels fell on the combined fleets. Still holding his Psionic ward, Lucian streamed a gravity point in the distance, just as he had in the previous battles.

The only difference was he felt significant resistance to his stream. He knew there had to be hundreds of Preserved fighting to reverse his magic. He got it strong enough that a few carriers crashed together. The Orb of Gravitonics pulsed with energy, but it could only draw ether so quickly. There were enough mages on the other side to counteract the force. To overpower them, Lucian would have to draw far more ether.

Lucian let go of the stream, dispelling the rest of his ether in a kinetic wave that blasted apart a squad of *Alkasen* interceptors that slipped through the lines.

Lucian saw at least fifty carriers and their attendant ships heading toward Earth and its defense platforms.

"Head to port," Mira ordered. "Stop them from reaching the lances!"

As one, the Starsea Fleet responded, unleashing its fury on the numerically superior foe. Though the Starsea Fleet fought valiantly, there were just too many *Alkasen* vessels. And it wasn't just the ships with their lasers and torpedoes. The smaller corvettes were being crushed as if by an invisible fist.

Lucian reached Serah on his slate. "Serah, counter those Gravitonic streams!"

"We're trying! We're getting rotting overwhelmed here. They must have a thousand rotting Gravitists over there battering us down!"

Lucian added his Gravitonic defense with the full might of the Orb of Gravitonics. It seemed to help, and Starsea ships stopped going down left and right.

That was when a Starsea cruiser became molten red; it was far too late for Plato and the Thermalists to save. Serah was right. There were so many Preserved on the *Alkasen* side they could overwhelm the Starsea Mages.

A large part of the Swarmer armada peeled off from the main force, outnumbering the Starsea fleet at least two to one. They intended to cut the Starsea Fleet off before reaching the platforms.

Zheng's voice exited the speaker. "Mira, leave them to me."

"Admiral Yang, you're out of position. You could lose all your ships."

"Those platforms need to be saved. They're our only hope of victory. You need to get there."

"Zheng—"

"I won't take no for an answer. Just take care of yourself, okay? And . . . take care of Fergus."

Lucian didn't understand why she was making things weird. "Admiral Yang, pull back. I won't let you sacrifice yourself."

But it was already too late. The Golden Armada and *Stars' Blood* were pulling ahead of the rest of the fleet, intent on their course.

"Zheng!" Mira said. "Get back here!"

The Golden Armada entered the fray, putting up a fierce fight. The pieces on the board had been moved, and nothing could be done. Zheng's action meant the rest of the Starsea Fleet was in the clear to reach the platforms.

"Fire on all hostiles," Mira said, her voice tense.

The Starsea Fleet began shooting the Swarmers attacking the platforms. With Zheng guarding their backs, it was only a matter of minutes before the Swarmers were shot down.

"Morales, circle back around and get back to Zheng," Mira said. "It might not be too late."

Morales complied, and the light show of death continued outside the viewport. The Pirates were besieged on all sides, and the Swarmers were so thick that Lucian could hardly see the Pirates' vessels. And still *more* were streaming from the carriers, a never-ending flood. Thorin's forces attempted to plug the gap in their lines, but there were too many *Alkasen* ships.

That was when hundreds of Swarmers bombers broke through, raining destruction on *Stars' Blood*. The ship ripped apart end to end, a massive explosion disintegrating the mighty battleship before their very eyes.

All watched, hardly able to believe it.

"Admiral Abrantes," Karlsen said, "*Stars' Blood* has been lost."

Mira's face paled, ignoring the obvious statement. "Any escape pods?"

"Impossible to tell with all that debris."

"Five carriers, coming in hard to starboard!" Helmsman Morales said. "Advising alternative course."

"We have to protect the platforms," Mira said. "Be a punching bag long enough for them to punch back."

Despite Mira's words, the platforms went down one after the other. A new contingent of fighters and bombers were targeting them. One after another, dozens of explosions were lit by the endless stream of strike craft issuing from the carriers. There were so many that they almost blocked out the stars.

Lucian, this entire time, had been gathering his ether to stream a massive attack to punch through the Preserved wards. There was no other way for this battle to be won. His Orbs pulsed with power; he knew this amount of ether would only attract the Ancient One.

But perhaps that was a good thing. If the Ancient One came here with his fleet, it might prove enough of a distraction, giving him time to prepare the magical attack.

As he drew more and more ether, as the Starsea Fleet fought for its very existence, as the deck heaved beneath him, he looked out the viewport, watching for the Ancient One's arrival.

"Come on," he said. "Where are you?"

It was hopeless. The Starsea Fleet, in addition to the League Fleet, had lost well over half of their forces. His estimate of a quarter of a million Swarmer ships was closer to the mark than Admiral Thorin's. They didn't have the slightest chance of winning. Even as *Mekong* took repeated hits of laser fire, barely hanging on, Lucian continued to draw ether, sheer desperation his only fuel.

But the desire to save humanity wasn't enough. He thought of Serah. Of their future, which wouldn't happen if they lost the battle. She was his truth, what made life worth living.

He wanted that future with her. He didn't want this to end now.

The Orbs responded to that need, ready to perform the impossible. His body shone with pure white brilliance that was blinding to behold.

This had to work. The Ancient One *had* to come.

Just when it felt like he couldn't draw more ether, a portal opened in the middle of the battlefield. And from that portal poured Believer ships, who turned their weapons on the Swarmers rather than the League.

Lucian had no illusions. The Ancient One only wanted the Orbs, nothing more. This battle was his way of getting them. But for now, they had the same purpose. It wasn't going to get any better than this.

Within the pure white brilliance of the Light Realm, Lucian could perceive everything. Every ship, every friend and foe, every potential threat. The Believers were being hammered, losing their vessels as soon as they left the portal. Lucian expanded his Focus until it encompassed the entire battlefield.

The tension was palpable, like air sizzling before lightning struck.

Hundreds, then thousands, of Swarmer ships registered in his mind. Large and small, the number kept growing. His magic cut like a knife through the enemy's wards as he sensed the entire Swarmer fleet, all while drawing even more ether.

Nothing could stop him now.

With a scream, Lucian let loose. A massive white sphere, composed of all Eight Aspects, radiated just outside *Mekong's* viewscreen. That sphere released a single line that connected to a nearby Swarmer cruiser. The cruiser was instantly pulverized from existence.

But the destruction didn't end there. From the cruiser, three more lines branched out, finding new targets that were instantly destroyed. And from those, more lines were issued, seeking new ships to attack.

Lucian maintained hold of all the Swarmer ships in his mind, knowing that as long as he envisioned them, the lines of destruction would find their way. Every Swarmer vessel was marked for death as long as he could hold the stream.

The lines spread out, growing exponentially. Tens, then hundreds, started igniting. The contagion spread among the Swarmer fleet, building a lattice of destruction.

Only now did the enemy seem to recognize the threat. Every Swarmer ship turned on *Mekong*, firing everything they had. And they might have succeeded had it not been for the Believer fleet intercepting. It was enough time for the lattice to continue its deadly work.

After half a minute, hundreds of ships were being obliterated every second. A moment later, it was *thousands*. Debris exploded outward, raining on the ship's shields. The Binders could finally augment the Starsea Fleet with a massive shield, which was possible to stream because enough Preserved had died. It was the only thing keeping the fleet from being torn to shreds. Outside his awareness, Lucian heard his mother order the ships close together to shelter within the shield.

Now, it was the Swarmers that were fleeing. Portals were hastily being conjured, a few ships even slipping through. But the lattice found any not fortunate enough to be near a portal, the blinding white lines eradicating them from existence. The portals collapsed as the Preserved powering them died.

At last, the momentum seemed to slow, with fewer ships left to target. Mere thousands remained where once there had been tens of thousands. The remaining lattice found a few more targets until Lucian's stream petered out and died.

Lucian swayed and fell, unable to keep his eyes open. He heard voices, but they were quite distant. His mother was barking orders. Serah was trying to make him come to.

He receded into darkness for the second time in the last twenty-four hours.

45

LUCIAN SWAM through dreams for seemingly an eternity. It was as if he were playing his life all over again. Not just since he left Earth for the stars, but even before that. Dreaming of his old life was surreal, like watching another person. So vivid were these dreams that they felt entirely real.

It was impossible to know just how much time had passed. Sometimes, Lucian would hear voices. The voices were the only things that convinced him he wasn't dead, clinging on in some limbo between Shadow and Light.

But after an indeterminate amount of time, his senses sharpened, and he heard his mother speaking somewhere above him.

"—she was very clear about what would happen. We need to decide on the next steps. The Hegemon's charity only goes so far."

Lucian tried to move, to respond, but he was paralyzed.

"Lucian can rotting stay here as long as he wants." The voice made him want to smile, though he could not do so. He longed to see Serah's face, but his muscles wouldn't obey him.

"I wish it could be so, but the office says we have three days to find new arrangements. As long as he's out cold, she wants him gone. Now that all the press is gone, she's showing her true face. She sees Lucian as a threat to her hegemony. After all, he's why anyone on Earth is still alive."

"Maybe you shouldn't say that too loud."

"Whatever," Mira said. "Just know we're on the same side here, even if we disagree about what comes next."

"I want Lucian to come back home with me."

"This *is* his home. Earth. This is where he can get the best medical care. There are armies of doctors who all want to have a go at him." She laughed bitterly. "Who wouldn't want to be the one who revived the Chosen of the Manifold?"

Lucian coughed, and both women gasped.

"Lucian?" Serah asked desperately. "Lucian, is that you?"

He felt her warm hand on his, and that touch sent an electric charge throughout his entire arm, spreading life through his limbs. At least he could move now, albeit slowly.

"He's waking up!" Mira said.

Next, Lucian could move his mouth. When he spoke, his voice was cracked with disuse. "Where the rotting hell am I?"

"Lucian!" Serah hugged him closely, but as of now, he couldn't see her, though he could smell her familiar clean scent. It reminded him of the white mountain flowers he saw growing in the rifts of Psyche by the rushing streams that fell over the canyons' sides.

"Am I blind or something?" he asked. "I can't see a thing."

"Your vision should come back," Mira said, her voice thick. "They told us if you woke up, that might happen. Don't worry. Thank God you're awake!"

At last, he could make out hazy images. Two faces were above him, and it took a moment for the double vision to correct itself. His eyes hurt; it wasn't just his voice that needed a workout.

"I'm so happy," Serah said.

His vision was almost fully back now, and he could see them. They looked much the same; his mother wore gray service khakis that were more casual than the full uniform she had worn in the fleet. Serah was dressed in designer pants and a red blouse. Seeing her in modern civilian clothing was strange, but Lucian didn't ask where she got it. Her blonde hair framed her beautiful face, and her blue eyes radiated pure joy.

He glanced around to see that he was in a luxurious king-size bed with thick, soft sheets. Medical machinery and a couple of IVs were hooked up to his arm. The floor was marble, the walls richly decorated with paintings and statues, and large windows admitted generous amounts of sunlight. In the distance was a cityscape spread across hills with high mountains in the distance. The sky was a pure robin's egg blue.

Lucian unhooked the IVs. "All right, where am I? And can you get me some food?"

"Let me order something from the kitchen," Serah said.

She quickly ordered a meal and told them to leave it outside the door. She probably didn't want anyone to know Lucian was awake yet. Not until they'd gotten their chance to speak.

"You're in the Hegemon's Palace in Geneva," Mira answered. "You have been for the past month."

The past *month*? "Is this real? What happened to the Swarmers?"

"They're on the retreat, believe it or not. You knocked almost every one of their ships, and we're guessing most of their Preserved, too. The League Fleet is pushing back and regaining everything it lost."

Lucian could hardly believe the news. "What about the Border Gates? Aren't more coming in?"

"Yes, there's that. We can deal with that—once you've had your chance to rest."

At that moment, there was a knock. Serah retrieved the food, and Lucian tucked in—a large steak cooked to perfection, along with potatoes and vegetables. He'd never been so hungry. Though he'd been asleep most of the time, it was the first actual food he'd had in a month.

Lucian squeezed out more questions in between bites. "So, the Gates are still a threat. What happened to the Believers? *Holy Fire*? The Ancient One can't have just left me alone."

"That's the mystery," Mira said. "They just picked up and left the minute you started that huge attack. The one that brought down the entire Swarmer fleet."

"We figured he was probably scared you'd attack him next," Serah said. "He probably didn't like his chances after seeing what you did."

Lucian nodded. "He was trying to get to me. I'm surprised he didn't try something."

"As Serah said, there was so much going on that it would have been suicide for him," Mira said. "Either way, he retreated into the portal. No one knows where he is or what remains of his fleet."

That didn't sit well with Lucian, and it was enough to make him lose his appetite.

"The *Alkasen* are on the back foot," Lucian said. "It's good most of the fleet is gone, but we need to hurry and close those Gates."

"When you're healthy," Mira said. "It's still too early to be doing anything. We'll get to the Gates in time, but if news reports are to be believed, Swarmer reinforcements are slow to trickle in. It'll be months before they've gathered a force even *half* the size of what you destroyed. And even then, you can destroy them again. Right?"

Just the idea of it was repulsive. Usually, streaming magic felt good. But the amount of ether he had been controlling had been enough to knock him out for good. It was proof that even *he* had his limits. Or at least, his Focus did. What if next time he knocked himself out forever?

"There's another loose end," he said. "Not just the Ancient One."

"Silumko, right?" Mira said. "No one knows what happened to him, either. If he was in that battle, he's as good as dead."

"There's still the Preserved, though," Lucian said. "Did they attack anyone on Earth?"

"Very few transports made it to the ground, though they sent thousands. Most were torn to shreds because they didn't have fighter support. The Swarmers' goal was to take out the platforms first to clear the way for a ground invasion. Without air support, Earth's anti-space batteries and tactical missiles shot down all their ships. There wasn't enough time for them to gain a foothold."

"No Preserved spreading the Bond, then?"

Mira shook her head. "Not that we can see. It's been a month. The League has closely monitored the landing sites, but nothing has been found."

Lucian hoped so, but he supposed it was one of those things where they had to wait and see.

"So, long story short," Mira went on. "We did it. Earth is saved, and it's just a matter of time before we mop up the rest of the Swarmers. And now that you're awake, everything is perfect, and all is right in the Worlds. I'm sure the *Alkasen* still have a few Preserved left. Enough to make a few portals here and there, but if they could attack us, they definitely would have by now. And now that you're back, we'll have the Gates locked up, too. Give it a month or three. You'll see."

Lucian smiled, but only because his mother and Serah

were. To him, something seemed missing. It almost felt too easy.

"There's the Ancient One," he said. "We haven't won until we've killed him. And the Gates won't stop the Swarmers forever. If they can find enough Preserved, they can sneak another fleet in, especially if Silumko is still out there. Space is vast. They can hide somewhere and reform their fleet."

"Maybe," Mira said. "But there hasn't been a single whiff of a portal since the battle. They could lie low until they're ready like you said. But as long as we cut off the Gates, we can manage any who come into League space. There are already talks from the League Assembly of mapping out every square AU of space with detection buoys, so they have no place to hide. A massive project, to be sure, but a necessary one."

"Silumko is out there still," Lucian said, sure of his words. "I *know* he didn't die in the battle."

"How can you know that?" Serah asked. "Can you feel him out there or something?"

Lucian shook his head. "Nothing like that. Just doesn't seem like he would allow himself to go down like this."

Mira put a hand on his arm. "Son, allow yourself a victory. You saved Earth. You saved *humanity*. Billions of people owe their lives to you. Isn't that something to celebrate?"

"It is, but as long as the Ancient One is out there, and Silumko too, are we safe? What if there's some way he can attack that we don't know about yet?" He looked from one to the other, but neither seemed to have an answer. "If you'd seen how strong the Ancient One was, you'd know what I'm talking about. He was almost as strong as me."

Maybe even stronger, though he kept that thought to himself. Whatever magic allowed him to absorb the Focuses of other mages had the potential to strengthen him even further.

And worse, the Ancient One could warp wherever he wanted. There was the potential for a lot of damage to be done.

Irreversible damage, even.

"Yes, you have a point," Mira said. "But everyone is partying like the whole thing's over. It's hard not to get caught up in the fever. The rebuilding has already started. Of course, Hegemon Madi is taking credit for the whole thing, saying you and her planned it out beforehand."

Lucian wouldn't begrudge her that. It wasn't as if he wanted her job or anything.

He pushed his plate away and sat up in bed. "I'm finally convinced this is real and not just some crazy dream."

"Not so fast!" Mira said. "You need to take it easy. I'm your mom. Whatever I say, goes."

"She's right," Serah said, nodding sagely. "At least take a shower before trying to save the rotting universe again."

Mira checked her slate. "Something's come up. I don't know if it was the food delivery, but people seem to know you're awake now."

"Why would that be a big deal?"

Mira looked at him, amused. "Are you serious? You're probably the most famous person in the galaxy now. You saved it, after all."

Lucian laughed. "There you go again. It *hasn't* been saved. Did you not hear anything I said?"

Mira seemed to miss that. "I have to go now. There are a lot of things to prepare."

"Like what?"

"Well, your speech, for one. There's going to be a reward ceremony, too. You're to be awarded the League Sun of Valor."

"I hear it's the highest honor the League can give a soldier," Serah said. "Like, six people in all of history have gotten it.

Including Transcend White, funnily enough, during the Mage War."

"Really? Interesting . . ."

"That's not even the best part," Mira said, smiling. "It comes with a one hundred thousand credit stipend. Tax-free."

Lucian's eyes widened at that. "Seriously?"

"Seriously," she said. "I'm proud of you, son." She checked her slate again. "All right, you kids be good. Be back soon."

With that, Mira left them alone.

Almost immediately, Serah scooted into bed with him. Lucian was a little self-conscious since he hadn't showered in a month. But someone must have been giving him sponge baths, at least. Otherwise, he would have reeked more.

"How are you feeling?" Serah asked.

"Overwhelmed," he said. "Tired. But glad to be alive."

She wrapped her arms around him. "Me, too."

"How are the others doing? I didn't even ask."

"Everyone's alive, if that's what you mean. A miracle, of course. Zheng didn't make it. All hands were lost on *Stars' Blood*."

"That's too bad," Lucian said. "Without her, the battle would have turned out differently."

"I think it shocked all of us. Completely out of character to sacrifice herself like that. I don't even know where it came from."

"She said something strange about Fergus and my mom. I guess it's pretty obvious now that something's going on between them."

"Oh, yeah. Definitely. They think they're good at hiding it, but nah. I, for one, am happy for them. They make a strange match, but a good one. Fergus, as we all know, is the perfect gentleman. A bit of a stickler, but that jives with your mom's personality."

"Maybe," Lucian said, wanting to change the subject. "Anything else?"

She suddenly brightened. "Oh, guess what?"

"What?"

"With the world saved and all, the release for MFS8 went off without a hitch! I'm already level twenty-seven."

"MFS8? Oh. Medieval Farming Simulator. Right. Where do you find the time?"

"I would play in here right next to you. Don't worry. I had the game calibrated to end as soon as you moved a muscle. Maybe we could play together since we have some time." Her eyes suddenly grew mischievous as she moved her face closer. "Unless you had something else in mind?"

Lucian smiled. "Maybe I do. But it'll have to wait."

Lucian was glad he said that because that was when Mira reentered the room. Serah slunk out of bed as gracefully as she could, and thankfully, Mira pretended not to notice.

"Hey, looks like they're ready for you now. They're going to have some doctors look at you, and assuming you're squared away, it's all systems go."

Things were moving along quickly. "All right. Let's get this over with."

46

NOW THAT LUCIAN had woken up, Hegemon Madi could hardly kick him out of her palace without looking bad. So she pretended to be as happy as she and Lucian stood before a crowd of thousands. It was a sunny spring day with the perfect hint of coolness. The scene was tranquil, a morning that seemed to promise new beginnings.

He went through the motions, gave the required speeches, shook the right hands, and said all the proper words. Then, the Hegemon herself pinned a shiny new medal to his Sorcerer-Ascendant robes, giving a wide smile that almost convinced Lucian of her sincerity.

After a couple of weeks, the festivities wound down, and Lucian's time wasn't demanded as much. The media and people of Earth slowly lost interest as life returned to normal, and the rebuilding continued. Though Lucian had the power of a god, he supposed even gods weren't interesting once you got used to them.

Lucian eventually returned to the fleet with Mira, Serah, and all the rest, including the mages that wanted to remain

389

with him. They set out on a mission to lock all the Gates to prevent easy access to League Space. This was accomplished in about two weeks; Lucian's discovering of the warping bubble made the work go far more quickly. Not once did the Believer fleet get the jump on them, with the Mage Division and the full might of the Starsea Fleet backing him up.

Once that task was done, Lucian didn't know what to do with himself. He knew he should go after the Ancient One, but it was hard to know where to begin. There was no sign of the Believer fleet anywhere, though the League was scouring every planet and moon in League Space. Lucian wondered whether the Ancient One had created a portal to Dark Space until he realized that would make them the target of the *Alkasen.*

They were in League Space *somewhere.*

With the Gates locked down, and no sign of the Swarmers, Lucian had to decide what to do with all the power he had amassed. He had achieved his goal, stopping the Swarmers from destroying Earth. With the Eight Orbs, he had godlike powers, and the ability to do anything he wished.

So the first thing he did was take time off with Serah. The others went their separate ways, too, with the understanding they would get back together in a few weeks to reassess.

They traveled for a while and just spent time together. It took a long time for Lucian to unwind and fully relax, such was the incredible stress of the past few years. It was the happiest time of his life, lying on beaches, hiking up mountains, and exploring the League's various natural wonders. They were also the saddest times of his life because he realized how much normality he had missed out on. It was a dream, something that could never truly be his.

After a few weeks of traveling, they were staying in a luxurious treehouse on Mimir, in one of the planet's famous

Yggdrasil trees. Lucian couldn't get the dark thoughts out of his head.

"What's wrong?" Serah asked, putting down her game.

It took him a moment to respond. "Just thinking."

"About what?"

"Everything."

"It's hard to forget, isn't it?"

Lucian nodded, but didn't elaborate. He felt heavy. Unable to release the weight of his feelings.

"You've been through a lot," Serah said. "We all have. But you most of all."

All Lucian could manage was another nod. All he wanted was to relax, to forget about things. Seeing Serah's joy at all the sights they'd visited had been Lucian's joy.

And yet, the rest felt unearned because there were still loose ends. And in quiet moments like these, everything Lucian had gone through, the violence and the pain, kept him up at night. He had visions of killing, the blood on his hands, the hundreds he had killed. All people with lives and stories who ended up taking the wrong job, being in the wrong place at the wrong time, or being born on the wrong world.

That pain couldn't be erased with a vacation, and Lucian doubted any therapist could fix it.

"I still have these rotting Orbs," he said, unable to hold back his frustration. "It isn't supposed to be like this. We should be halfway to the First Gate by now. But these last few weeks with you have been the best of my life. They've reminded me what it feels like to be human again. Because when we get going again . . ."

Lucian didn't need to finish. After a moment, Serah responded.

"We'll get rid of them. You'll see."

"There's only one way to do that," Lucian said.

Serah was quiet for a moment. "Are you ready to keep going then?"

Lucian nodded. "I'm . . . sorry. I know you wanted to see more. To do more. But I can't be present in the way I'm supposed to be. The burden I feel is too much."

He couldn't look at her face because he couldn't bear to see her disappointment. But she surprised him by touching his face, forcing him to look her in the eyes.

"I know that, Lucian. And I agree."

He blinked. "You do?"

She nodded. "It was fun at first." She looked out the window at the kilometers-tall tree before her. "But when you've seen one rotting tree, you've seen them all."

Lucian laughed, but suddenly he remembered what the next step meant. There were two roads before him. He could try to keep the Orbs and fight to keep humanity safe from the Swarmers and to hell with all the Ascendants in the Light Realm. When the lights went out on reality because of the loss of ether—then that would be it.

But Lucian knew he couldn't go down that path. For one, it meant being immortal while everyone around him aged. Sure, he could reverse their aging with Space-Time Magic. He'd already done that once with Serah. Something in him knew, however, that he could never live a normal life, even if he discounted the whole immortality thing.

He would be forced to become the Third Immortal and take control of the League. To become someone he was not. The Orbs would move him down that path. The Ancient One still clung to them, and his influence over the Orbs would slowly dominate his mind.

Already, he was tempted by that path, if only because it would give him more time with Serah.

More and more, he thought about his conversation with

Silumko, about how the Emissary had told him all those things in the vain hope that he might make the right decision when the time came. He must return the Orbs, even if it meant his death and the end of magic itself.

That meant no future with Serah. No marriage and kids unless he could find another way out, one unforeseen. He wasn't sure how much to hope for that. Now, close to the end, it felt like there was only one path before them.

Lucian stood. "I have to bring them back to the Heart of Creation. It's the only way to end the Starsea Cycle. The only way to make things go back to normal." He looked at Serah. "Magic *isn't* normal. We think it is because we've lived with it our whole lives, but in all of human history, it's only existed for a century and a half. Things need to go back to the way they were before as much as they *can* go back. And there's still all that stuff Silumko talked about, how existence itself will unravel . . ."

"A very bad thing," Serah said.

Lucian nodded. "I have everything in me to finish the job. I can follow the Seven-fold path. It would mean leaving the League forever."

"What about the Ancient One?" Serah asked. "He's here somewhere. Can we leave the League while he's still at large?"

It was a good point, but Lucian realized something. "You said it yourself. Remember?"

"He only wants one thing," she said, also realizing. "He doesn't give a crap about the League. He'll come after *you*."

Lucian nodded. "That's what I'm thinking, too."

"All right," Serah said. "When do we start?"

"Tomorrow," Lucian said. "We'll get the whole crew back together. I won't force anyone to come who doesn't want to, of course. But I will need help. That much is for sure."

"Well, you've got me. I'm not letting you go through the First Gate by yourself."

Lucian was about to protest until he realized that was what they *all* would have to do. Assuming he successfully returned the Orbs, the Gates would not function. It was a death mission, no matter who went.

Lucian couldn't ask anyone to put their lives on the line like that. Not when they had the choice to live a normal life. Serah was one thing. She was the love of his life, and she wouldn't take "no" for an answer.

"We could go together," Lucian said. "Just the two of us."

Serah smiled but shook her head. "I've already talked to the others. Every single one of them wants to come."

"What do you mean?"

"Just that. Emma, Fergus, Jagar, Linus, Plato, your mom. Even Khairu. They've told me to let them know when we're heading out. Everyone wants to come except Selene, anyway. I think she's enjoying bossing people around on Psyche."

It was more than Lucian could have hoped for, but he couldn't help but feel a sense of loss. They, too, would perish at the end of the road if they joined him.

But Lucian knew he couldn't stop them. The hard truth was he needed them. The journey would take a long time, even with what Lucian discovered with the warping bubble in the Terminus System. Maybe not the years he thought previously, but still many months.

"I'm speechless," he said.

"We're all here for you, Lucian. This is our fight just as much as it's yours. Now, let's enjoy ourselves while we still can. We can leave as soon as you're ready."

Lucian nodded. "I don't think I'll ever truly be ready."

"Well, we have one more night here. We can sleep on it."

They settled down to bed, lulled to sleep by the swaying of the trees.

————

WHEN THEY WERE BACK on the spaceship, Lucian noted a missed message from Fergus on the ship's communications panel that had been sitting there for about a week. He hit play.

"Lucian. Big news. The League's found the Believer Fleet. Or at least, what's left of it."

He leaned forward in his seat as Fergus continued.

"It's in the Mako System. Who knows why it's there, but from what they've discovered, all the ships are destroyed. The damage goes far beyond the battle. They're guessing Sharo himself did them in."

"Why would he do that?" Serah asked.

Lucian shook his head. "I don't know."

"Anyway, I know you've tried to unplug yourself from everything, but I thought this was worth passing along. The main crew is all meeting at the Grand Dome on Nessus, with the idea that you would be there, too. The Grand Dome is the big one; we've booked a suite to share so we can all catch up and plan things. If you're wondering about the venue, Nessus is the central meeting point for where everyone is right now. We should all be there in about a couple of weeks. I've tracked down just about everybody who's asked about continuing. I'm sure they'll be on their way when you receive this message.

"I've forwarded all the pertinent details. Looks like things are about to get real again. Anyway, take some time to enjoy yourselves longer. Stars know you've earned it. So, on July 23rd, try to be there. See you soon."

The message ended.

"July 23rd," Serah said. "That's a week away!"

"If I knew where everyone was, I could gather them faster," Lucian said. He looked at Serah, then smiled. "But why would I do that when we can have another week for ourselves?"

"Another week, huh?" Serah asked. "We can do *a lot* in a week."

"Where to, then?" Lucian asked, taking up the controls. Piloting a starship wasn't too difficult. As long as you weren't getting into battles constantly, the autopilot was more than capable of handling itself.

"I've always wanted to see Eroth. There are cute alien whales under the glaciers. I've also heard they're pink."

"I *love* alien whales," Lucian said. "Especially the pink ones."

She blinked. "We can go then?"

"Of course we can. We could go to an asteroid mine if that's what you wanted."

"Oh, can we?"

"That was a joke."

"Lucian, I know. Anyway, let's get going!"

Lucian smiled. One more week for themselves.

He could more than live with that.

EPILOGUE

THE HIGH PROPHET entered the cave, a Thermal ward active to defray the oppressive heat of Mako's lower reaches. He walked as if he were a reanimated corpse. The Focuses of over a hundred mages were contained within him, so he no longer was truly himself. He was merely an avatar controlled by the Ancient One. An avatar far past its expiration date. The Ancient One needed a new body.

Only he wouldn't find that body here.

The Ancient One drove the High Prophet deep into the cave, into the darkness. No monster disturbed him, perhaps sensing the Shadow's dark presence. Sharo floated past the inner lake like a ghost and shuffled down the long corridor toward the deep cliff from which light emanated over the edge.

He fell over the side, breaking his fall with a gravity stream. The source's brilliance bathed his cadaverous face, this place where he first absorbed the Shadow. It was here the Ancient One had bidden him to return.

He had failed to obtain the Orbs. Sure, he could attempt to assassinate the Chosen, but he couldn't find him as long as he wasn't using his Orbs. And it seemed the Chosen was content to rest on his laurels. All the better for the Ancient One's plans.

Another fight with the Chosen was inadvisable. His puppet was beaten down terribly. Absorbing those mages' Focuses had wreaked havoc on Sharo's body and mind, and the Ancient One couldn't risk facing the Chosen in open battle.

He had to become stronger, and the source was the path forward.

The Ancient One forced Sharo closer to the source of power. He could feel his avatar's mounting fear, buried as it was. The Ancient One drove him mercilessly on. All those promises of power he'd made in this cave over five decades ago were lies to gain access to a tool.

As he was bathed in the source's power, he felt its raw warmth. His Focus shivered in delight. This was how things were meant to be.

Undoubtedly, the League would drive the Swarmers back after that display above Earth. But they were far from defeated. The Bond of Unity couldn't be destroyed as long as the Emissary lived. The Chosen closing the Gates would buy humanity time, but it wouldn't be enough.

Sharo's emaciated form smiled as the ether entered him, channeling itself through the Focuses of every mage he had so far absorbed.

It would be a long while before he accomplished his aim. Weeks, and perhaps even longer. The ether would sustain his puppet for that time.

He forced Sharo to the ground. The Ancient One bathed in the ether, forming it with his Focus to create a stream not seen since the time of the First Starsea. Long ago, the First Immortal attempted to create a second Manifoldic Gate to the Light Realm here. That attempt had failed, as it was defended by the Ascendant Beings, who were wary of further incursions into their domain. But they couldn't stop the ether from bleeding out like a wound.

The Ancient One drank greedily. The ether would allow him to do something as unimaginable as it would be unreversible.

It was time to begin the Starsea Cycle anew, to set everything into motion.

But first, he needed the Orbs. Not here, in this time, but in a distant past where the Chosen could not find him. And if the Chosen *did* find him, the Ancient One could stop him.

The Ancient One streamed silently, slowly but surely forming the Time Gate.

———

THE END OF BOOK EIGHT

THE STARSEA CYCLE CONTINUES IN BOOK NINE:

THE GATES OF TIME

THE WORLDS ARE SAVED—BUT not for long.

Lucian Abrantes and the Starsea Fleet have driven back the *Alkasen*. While the Worlds rebuild and recover from the brutal war, the Ancient One threatens to undo the uneasy peace.

On the world of Mako, the Ancient One has done the unthinkable. Marshaling the ether of the Source of Power, he has escaped through a Time Gate, an action that threatens to unravel Lucian's heroism and even reality itself.

Lucian has no choice but to follow him. But time travel has terrifying consequences that require him to go down a dark path. What price will Lucian pay to protect his reality and loved ones from complete destruction?

ABOUT THE AUTHOR

Kyle West is the author of multiple science-fantasy series, including The Starsea Cycle, The Wasteland Chronicles, and The Xenoworld Saga. While his fiction is set on strange and alien worlds, he strives to write characters that are human and relatable.

He enjoys the outdoors, hiking, and all things sci-fi and fantasy. He's lived all over the southern United States, but can currently be found in the Atlanta area with his family.

Please visit kylewestbooks.com to learn about his books and stay in the loop with future releases.

facebook.com/kylewestwriter

twitter.com/kylewestwriter

bookbub.com/authors/kyle-west

ACKNOWLEDGMENTS

Special thanks to the Beta Team for their hard work hunting typos: Cindy, Jeremy, Dina, Barbara, Becky, Krzysztof, and Mark. You guys are the real MVP's!

If you've found a typo in this text, please email kylewest@kylewestbooks.com.

READING ORDER

You can find the complete reading order of Kyle's series here. It lists every book and every series he's written, and is updated regularly with new releases.

www.ingramcontent.com/pod-product-compliance
Lightning Source LLC
Chambersburg PA
CBHW011927190726
48284CB00015B/2809